UNDERCURRENTS

UNDERCURRENTS

FRANCES FYFIELD

ALFRED A. KNOPF CANADA

PUBLISHED BY ALFRED A. KNOPF CANADA

Copyright © 2000 by Frances Fyfield

Canadian Cataloguing in Publication Data

Fyfield, Frances
Undercurrents

ISBN 0-676-97338-8

I. Title.

PR6056.Y47U52 2000   823'.914   C00-931381-8

First Canadian Edition

Visit Random House of Canada Limited's Web site: www.randomhouse.ca

Typeset in Plantin by M Rules

Printed and bound in the United States of America

RRD   10 9 8 7 6 5 4 3 2 1

To Jill and Robin Stockwell,
with love from your Fyfield cousin

ACKNOWLEDGEMENTS

Thanks to Dr Ben Lloyd for information generously given on the subject of hemiplegia. All mistakes or inaccuracies are my own. Thanks also to John Granville of the Prison Service for answering questions so fully, and to Stephen Marriott, George Woolford and Senta, for being there. And finally, thanks to Joyce, for the song.

Happy the man whom the truth instructs not through passing words and figures but in its own self, just as it is. Our opinions are often mistaken and our vision dim. What is the point of much hair splitting about the recondite and the obscure, our ignorance of which will not even be mentioned in the judgement?

Thomas à Kempis

PROLOGUE

SPLISH, SPLASH I can hear the sound of quiet waves. The water heaving gently and the mewling of seagulls. A HOT summer on the beach.

Someone took the shawl and someone gave it back. There are strange courtesies in this place and more tolerance than I could ever have believed, just as there are features of my own behaviour I could never have believed either. Although I do have a certain status, I have had to give up any illusion of being in control, and I have to limit talking, making this a substitute. It is my chance to rationalize. At least I'm alone in my own room.

My father taught me a command of words but being articulate can be treacherous. There is always the point when one might say too much. If I told them everything, they would hear a noise of words, but they would not listen. I see their point entirely; I can't even find it in myself to resent it. Why should anyone listen when guilt makes us produce such a tissue of lies? Whatever we say in here is far more likely to be lies than truth. We are bound to lie; it is almost a duty, to avoid the tyranny of conscience. But we rarely steal. Someone brought back my shawl and I felt absurdly blessed. When I talk, I talk about nothing as if I were at a party, minding my manners.

I miss the sea most of all, which is a terrible reflection when I think about it. I should miss the children most. I should have been far more exclusive in my affections in order to be a better mother. There are no excuses; only guilt, but I do, I do . . .

Miss the sea, most of all . . .

Francesca Margaret Chisholm

CHAPTER ONE

SOMEONE should have advised him against a February arrival. He knew what winter was like at home; cold and sharp and dry, manageable even in eight degrees below, but somehow he had not associated an English coastline with any notion of a serious chill. *She* had never described it like that. There had been mention of bonfires and brisk walks; of a breeze stinging the eyes when admiring the sea from the battlements of a castle, descriptions augmented by a memory of Dickens and picture postcards suggesting a modest covering of snow or a comfortable blanket of fog outside, all cleverly orchestrated for no other purpose than to make the fireside welcoming and the hot toast delicious. The sort of kindly cold which was a home designer's asset, purely to act as a contrast to a comfortable room.

Outside the station, the wind tore at his coat like a mauling dog. The rain skittered in the eddies of wind to scratch at his face and hat. His suitcase was ballast, lifting from his shoulder and leading him in a sideways sloping sprint across the carpark. It defied the mild sense of triumph he had felt in alighting from the train at all, beating the challenge of the antiquated door as the carriage lurched to a halt in front of a sign so obscure he could scarcely read it. WARBLING, a name like a dowdy bird. Doctor Henry Evans, poetry-loving scientist, with impeccable transatlantic credientials and comfortable North American lifestyle, felt himself unfairly fooled by the weather and did not enjoy the sensation of being outwitted. He congratulated himself briefly at the same time for that level of preparation which was his own hallmark. He had purchased a map; he had listened carefully to telephone instructions and he knew precisely where he was going.

Rain, spitting at him with renewed vigour. You can't miss it, squire. Straight down the road by the station until you reach the sea; turn left. Big hotel, squire. Nelson stayed there long before they built the pier. Henry had enjoyed the train, dirty though it was. At least he could open the window and breathe. He hated to be inside those capsules of transport where he had no control.

And he craved his first sight of the sea. His was a land-locked heart, in love with gentle ocean sounds. He could see it in his mind's eye, calm and dark, moody with moonlight and full of inspiration. The shops on his route were small and, in the shuttered darkness, less than quaint. He noticed a deserted cinema with posters of films he thought he might have seen a decade since, a forlorn wine bar with single occupant, the closed premises of a post office apparently doubling as a pharmacy and a florist's without flowers, but apart from a couple of illuminated signs, the only significant lights were the Belisha beacons where the road dipped into a pedestrian crossing before rising towards the sea. The yellow globes winked at a lone woman who waited as if needing some extra sign which would give her licence to cross an empty road. She was followed at a distance by a big, black dog, which did not seem to belong. Henry nodded and said hi. There was no response, reminding him of another feature about the natives he had encountered so far. They were not so much rude as preoccupied at any given time. They would not ignore the outstretched hand if you waved it right in front of their faces, but any gesture not initiated by themselves required repetition before gaining acknowledgement. They were not unfriendly, he decided bravely, simply undemonstrative and destined to lead him into a deliberate and useful heartiness through the means of their natural reserve. *You have to learn to come out of your shell, Henry. No one else is going to winkle you out.* He was trying to remember what *a winkle* was.

The road which had dipped by the crossing rose to meet the seafront and its attendant sounds. He had forgotten the mad gust of the station carpark on his way thus far, relatively sheltered from the wind and the rain which struck him now with a series of staggering punches so hard and mean he yelled and grabbed at a railing. The shout was shoved down his throat in a lungful of icy air; the wind struck at his arm; the railing was sticky wet to the touch. As he staggered back into a doorway, his nose collided with the glass and he was suddenly eye to eye with another poster on the far side, depicting ice cream piled high in a fluted glass, topped with a cherry and set against a summer blue background. The wind howled round his head; he was glad of the hat and while on another kind of day he might have laughed at the ice-cream poster for its sheer incongruity, the wind was pummelling his back. The sea was an insane chorus of animal roars, followed by the vicious hiss of angry water clawing at stones, clattering and snarling in frustration; then the next crash, boom, hiss, a battle of sibilant fury, counterpoised by the deep bass of echo.

Henry pulled down the hat, levered himself out of the doorway remembering the directions. Turn left; he had done that. Cross the road; he would do that now. He saw the dog again, maybe a different dog, trotting along the opposite pavement. You can't miss it, squire, only building this side of the road. Nelson stayed here. He remembered his own *frisson* of excitement at the mere idea of staying in a place where Nelson had stayed with Lady Hamilton, no less. He could visualize a hip bath in the middle of the room, a screen with strewn clothing, the lady *déshabillé*, the hero reclining on a chaise-longue with his glass of port, replete with conquests. Thick curtains, blocking the moon . . . The wind had a fit of kindness and propelled him across the road, unscathed. The sky was luminous; spray hit his face. The bulk of the hotel loomed before him, unlit and forbidding and as he drew nearer, other sounds began to compete. Voices shouting, machinery humming.

There was candlelight in the reception area, lulling him into a sense of welcome. He sighed with relief; then the alien nature of the noise and the intensity of the draught chilled him again. A massive desk was the only furniture, old and solid above a rich red carpet which squelched beneath his feet like a claret-coloured bog. He stepped forward carefully, the weight of his case suddenly unbearable. There was a bar down those stairs, described in the brochure as a select venue with views of the English Channel, currently occupied by persons wearing rubber boots, sloshing through inches of water. One man detached himself from the rest, waded towards the narrow passage where Henry stood and proffered the pile of cushions he carried. It seemed an odd kind of offering.

'Get out of the way, will you? What do you want?'

'I have a reservation . . .'

'You want a *room*? In here? Oh, that's rich, you know, really it is. There's someone wants a *room*!' he shouted back down the stairs, to the sound of answering laughter.

'The Nelson suite, in fact,' Henry said apologetically. The sound of breaking glass came from beyond the stairs and the din of the sea seemed closer still. The man's laugh choked on itself. There was a whiff of whisky on his breath, but nothing else about his face to show he was anything other than distressingly sober.

'Haven't you ever seen a fucking flood? Come back next week.'

'My suitcase . . . my room . . .'

'Next week.'

'But where should I go?'

As he spoke, Henry felt he was reciting the most regular and plaintive line of his life. Jet lag was no excuse. He knew he had uttered these words many times before and he sounded, to his own ears, demanding and childish. He should be doing *something* – rolling up his sleeves, responding to the situation, making himself if not useful, at least acceptable – but he was suddenly overcome with exhaustion, rocked with a cataclysmic disappointment. For twenty years he had postponed a visit to romantic England and he did not want disillusion now. He wanted his own optimism, weakened in the long reaches of the night, tested in that damn train with its vandalized toilets, further damaged by a town which was *shut* at eight in the evening, for Chrissakes, deafened by the racket of that poisonous-looking sea. And wet feet and a suitcase with a life of its own, getting heavier by the minute but unputdownable on this filthy damp floor . . . how could he help? This was the end of the line and it was he who needed help.

'Where *could* I go?'

'Oh, for God's sake, anywhere but here.' The man brushed him forward. Henry could not move. He was weighted by feet which seemed to have grown larger and heavier and he knew he was wearing his mulish face. The man pushed past him and squelched his way to the desk.

'Here, hold the bloody torch, will you?'

'The what?'

'The *torch*, you cretin.'

'Oh, you mean the flashlight. Sure.'

A torch was something which carried flame. It illuminated a barbecue on summer evenings and was an emblem of peace in the Olympics. He held the flashlight while the man leafed through an address book, his movements radiating irritation.

'Probably all full. Too late, you were the last. Ah yes, of course. Wait a minute . . .' There was a gleam of malice in the eyes, caught in the flash. Henry felt himself intensely disliked and bridled at the unfairness of it. The man was eyeing his coat. He should have smiled himself, commiserated, done something, cracked a joke. A clever, diplomatic person would do that.

'There's only one place for you. And that hat,' the man added, snapping the book shut and shoving Henry towards the door. 'The House of Enchantment. Lovely place,' he added in a voice rich with irony.

'The what?'

'The House of Enchantment. That's what they call it. Look, you aren't prejudiced, are you? Homophobic or worried about ghosts or anything like that? It'll do fine.' This time, he was pushing Henry, hard. 'Go right. Follow the seafront for about a hundred yards. No 196 and a half. Keep left and keep counting. You can't miss it, squire. Princess Di might have stayed there. All we ever had was fucking Nelson.'

Henry and his suitcase were back on the road. He pulled up the collar of his jacket. It was a special jacket, soft grey leather with plenty of pockets, lined with fur, an understated piece of casual luxury and he was glad of its warmth. He turned left and walked on the seaward side. On his right, the sea growled and crawled and boomed. On the other side of the road, he could make out the irregular contours of houses, some dark, some illuminated, all impervious to the weather and the carnage inside the hotel. The patent indifference of those lit windows was oddly comforting. The suitcase, weighed less by clothes than the vitamins, minerals and therapies he found so vital to his health, felt like an ungainly rock bouncing sharply against his back. His hat (deerstalker with flaps, Sherlock Holmes style, purchased in a hunting store and sartorially ridiculous anywhere else) suddenly left his head like a bird in flight and he watched by a streetlight as it flung itself into the waves and danced for a split second in the foam. There was nothing he could do about the hat. The beach was steep, the waves high and he was cold to his bones. It was only a hat; he could not even keep a hat and the hat seemed an emblem of his own ineptitude. He was lost.

The contours of a huge wall loomed on one side. There were no houses along here. He passed the wall and the houses resumed. *She* would have called them *higgledy-piggledy*. He counted slowly, eighty-one, eighty-two, eighty-three, before the numbers reverted to fifty. He attempted to whistle to forestall the ignominy of tears, tasting salt on his lips. He had come all this way to find a woman and that made him five times the fool.

The House of Enchantment stood on a corner at the highest point of the road facing the sea. The room was elegantly, if heavily furnished. The only touch of modernity was the TV screen, which showed a series of silent, summer images. Peter Piper sat in an armchair inside the bay window of the first floor sitting room, holding the dog in his lap and pointing out features of the seascape, namely the crests of the retreating waves and lights in the distance. 'Now look there, Senta, that one's probably some kind of tanker. It isn't the lightship. Love the way it's all lit up, like a Christmas tree, don't you? Static, ain't it? My, oh my, they must be pleased to see land. Might make them think they could swim for shore. I bet they're wishing they were right here, with us, instead of out there, with them. Do you think we'll *ever* get anything to eat? Tim's being a horribly long time with it. A man could die before he gets any food round here.' He fondled the soft fur of the dog's ears. 'One more, dearest, only one more.'

He took a walnut from a dish and Senta took the nut from his fingers, daintily. She held it between her paws, cracked the shell with her teeth, delicately, and consumed the fragments of kernel with a precision which amazed him. 'One of these days,' Peter said, fondly, 'you'll be able to sweep up the pieces, too. We used to get Harry to do that, didn't we? Make him exercise his hands, poor darling Harry.' He got up to stoke the fire with a log and several chunks of old wooden flooring. It seemed wasteful to put such good wood on a fire, but it was free from the skip and anything they could gather or garnish for nothing was used. Scavenging was an art form, a challenge, an integral part of the way they lived. The fire spluttered. There was always that crucial point in the tending of a fire: the making of the decision to refuel it, lower the temperature, heft the fuel. Part of the discipline. 'By ritual, so shall you live,' Peter murmured to the dog, handing her another walnut.

'I'm so glad you're alive. I'm so glad there's no one else here but ourselves. Who cares about money?'

He went downstairs. The dog followed. Condensation dripped from the landing window; he pulled his cardigan across his chest. Rooms were warm enough; stairwells and corridors were freezing; contrast was good for health. He must remember to put hot bricks in the beds. House bricks hidden inside envelopes of fur, constructed from an ancient coat of his mother's, were an invention of which he was particularly proud. They were also perfectly true to the spirit of the age in which they wished to live, and unlike the conventional hot water bottle, did not leak.

There was a long, rather grand flight of stairs from the first floor to the ground. The dining room was to the left of it, lit with a fire. From the kitchen beyond, traversed by another chilly corridor, there drifted the smell of curry. The table was set with a white linen cloth; three places laid this evening, he noticed. Sometimes Timothy went mad and laid it up with crystal and silver for five or six, and Peter knew they would be eating the excess of the meal in another form the following day, but tonight his deference to either ghosts or other guests was limited to one, placed to the left of an artful arrangement of twigs and leaves in front of the seat nearest the fire. They always ate in style: Tim insisted. Food, he said, was far too important to treat with disrespect. There had been a tricky spell when Tim had been determined to raise a pig and a few chickens in the back garden. Considerations of neighbourly relations had prevailed, but he still nurtured hopes of raising an ostrich. At least a month's supply of low-fat meat. If we had livestock, we would have to hide them, Peter had murmured, and I do so hate deceit, don't you? It might be feasible to keep an ostrich indoors in a house of four floors, to say nothing of the cellar. A house which was ideal either for hiding people or leaving them in perfect peace, and that included the paying guests. Once they were up in the attics and the second floor, no one would know they were there, but Peter said an ostrich would make a noise on the stairs.

Or interfere with privacy. Timothy adored the guests, but he did tend to go over the top in his concern for their comfort. He believed that anyone who came to the door arrived by divine intervention. Peter never liked to mention it, but he had the strange feeling that some of them thought they were not so much being made at home as seduced, and that would create entirely the wrong impression. They were there because they were needed.

Tim's evening apparel varied according to whim and whichever of his motley collection of charity shop clothes was clean at the moment. It was part of the rituals governing their lives that clothes were changed before dinner, although this did not mean that evening dress as such was *de rigueur*. It simply had to be something that had not been worn all day and it could never be shorts or a swimsuit, even if they intended to bathe after dining in the height of summer in the sorts of temperatures currently difficult to imagine. Peter had donned the tweed suit which almost fitted over his ample chest, with an unbuttoned shirt beneath, revealing the least colourful of his tattoos, the ensemble complete with pristine white socks and training shoes. Timothy, in celebration of a vaguely Eastern style of meal, wore a heavy cotton jellaba which swept around his ankles and to save himself from tripping over its voluminous length, the folds were hitched in at the waist with braided yellow furnishing cord, bright against the scarlet of the cloth. With his slender height and hooked nose, he looked like a misplaced cardinal. Homemade bread and salad was placed on the table; spinach leaves, Peter noticed with salivating approval, in sufficient quantity for a small army. Then the doorbell rang.

Clanged, to be more precise. It was an old school bell attached to a spring, activated by a prominent, salt-rusted handle pulled from the outside. The oldest devices were the best. Peter eyed the empty place setting at the table, beamed approval to Timothy, who tutted in response and consulted the watch hanging round his neck.

'He's cutting it a bit fine, isn't he? It's eight-thirty already and I'm starved. Supposing he wants a bath first?'

'Well, he can't have one, can he? The food won't wait.'

The House of Enchantment was the one Henry could see, standing out from the others as he walked towards it, prominent because it had pointed turrets on the roof, like something out of a fairy tale. The details were obscured in darkness, which was some kind of mercy, because he was already thinking, trying as best he could to distract himself from heavy feet, a foreboding, the ever present sense of being a fool after all, and a mounting depression which boomed inside his skull to the same tune as the waves. He was struggling for composure and counting the numbers of the houses, gazing at the front doors as he passed and imagining what something with such a name would look like. He knew as soon as the turrets loomed into view that he didn't want it to be *that* one. He wanted something more homely, looking as if it were made of gingerbread, big enough to accommodate a landlady who might serve hot soup, as a minimal compensation for being frustrated in an attempt to dwell in a suite where Nelson might have dallied with Lady Hamilton. A little bit of conventional kindness would go a long way. He could feel tears gathering behind his eyes again, decided it did not matter if he cried. The rain had pasted his hair to his head; he was showered with spray. Julius Caesar was supposed to have landed somewhere near here. He could not think for the life of him why an Italian would bother.

What a house. Painted black, as far as he could tell, with a studded door two steps up from the street. Another fear assailed him as he yanked at a handle marked BELL. Supposing there was no room here, either? Don't think of it. Go back to that station, back on to that slow, slow train. Dover was next. Go to France. Go. He had always maintained an option to retreat. There was the sound of a bell clanging, followed by furious barking.

The door heaved open with a creak. A vision stood before him, head to toe in scarlet, smiling but slightly impatient, like someone interrupted at an important task and too polite to mention it.

'Oh, come in, come in, come in. Foul out there, but better presently, oh yes. Come in.'

The door closed behind him with a thud. He was propelled to the newel post of steep stairs leading upwards for ever and ever in a rising tide of polished mahogany, the hallway extending way back to foreign regions, tapestries on the walls and gas lamps in sconces, flickering, and an appetizing set of smells. The priestly vision was helping him off with his coat, tutting at the rain on it, admiring the texture; the suitcase was lifted from his shoulder. Before he had uttered a word, he was handed a towel for his hair, his tears, whatever it was that soaked him last and he felt suddenly weightless.

'We have to eat *now*, or it spoils. I mean *now*. Have the seat by the fire and take your shoes off, I would. This way. Timothy, pour the wine.'

More gas lamps in here, a fire warming his back. The wine was purple, glinting through heavy crystal. He remembered to raise to each companion in turn before swallowing. Christ, that was good. The bread passed on to his sideplate was nutty and warm; the salad stung the palate with an aftertaste of pepper; the plate was whisked away. There were two elegant tureens in the centre of the tablecloth; he gazed at the rising steam, drunk on the smells. Tweed suit and cardinal helped him to food as if he was a baby unable to help himself, murmuring encouragement.

'*Plain* rice, I'm afraid. *Always* better with hot food, we find. Have *plenty*.' He did. After a second helping, interrupted by minimal conversation, 'Have you come far? America. Oh yes, that far. Is it warmer there? No. Don't mind if Senta sniffs round your ankles, do you?'

'No. I have a dog at home.'

That last remark, slurred through a mouthful, was a lie dictated by politeness. He did not have a dog; he did not have anything he would like to have except sufficient money, but he had always wanted a dog and did not want to cause offence. The lie was a way to be accepted. He had noticed the dog in passing, a sweet little puppyish brindled sheepdog which was given the same food at the same time but led off to eat in a separate corner out of a separate bowl, for which mercies he was grateful. Plates, dishes, tureens disappeared as miraculously as they were presented. Henry could not remember if names had been exchanged. Yes. Timothy. Peter. Henry. Weird. No last names, no mention of payment. Tomorrow would do.

'So why are you here, Henry?'

'Oh . . . Me? I'm a pharmacist. Work, but that's not really why I'm here. I like castles, I guess. I don't know why I'm here. Been all over the world, but never to England. My father died, I needed a change of scene and . . .' Those tears were back, pressing against the back of his eyeballs, just when he was almost dry all over. He tried to get his toasted feet back into his shoes; he felt for his handkerchief and could not find it.

'You need sleep, Henry. Loads of it. You can't talk now. Come along.'

He was bemused, unnaturally obedient. He could have been led upstairs to a masochistic brothel for all he cared, although such a thought did not enter his mind. Henry did not have that kind of imagination. There seemed to be a mountain of stairs. A swish of the cardinal's cloak, an attic room, reached only when he was out of breath. One of them was carrying his suitcase, the other his shoes and the leather jacket bought for the journey, both men chattering explanations like soft-voiced starlings.

'. . . Afraid the only bath is at the back of the kitchen . . . we'll leave the lights on . . . Water hot again, soon.'

'. . . the loo's on the landing . . . your loo, that is . . . Peter, you forgot the bedside light ah, there it is . . .'

'Towels are here . . . you switch off the electric fire over there. We'll make you a proper one tomorrow.'

The fire defied his own notion of antiquity. Two electric bars glowing like parallel fireflies, creating a patch of warmth extending towards the bed but not quite reaching it. And such a bed. Not large, not even a queen size, but high off the ground; if he fell out of that in the night, he could break a leg. Henry's tired eyes noticed the series of bedspreads which were strewn over it, greens and blues with the shimmer of silk, giving the bare room its only opulence. His companions fussed a little more and then retreated. It was as if the whole of the world retreated with them and the silence they left behind was quite complete.

You can't talk now. The words held an echo. When would he ever be able to talk? He had been unable to talk freely for more years than he could remember, or not the kind of talking which was communicating. He never quite knew what to say, except to his father. All these years of saying little, as if he had some kind of impediment that made him incapable of expressing what his brain was telling him to say. A kind of scold's bridle, the curse of the shy man. He liked the easily opened window; he liked the bedspreads, stroked them, and despite the chill of the room, he was suddenly intensely grateful to be in it. It occurred to him that he had been churlish to these two bizarre men; that he had failed to express or even to *feel* gratitude for the fact that they had so obviously responded in double quick time to a call from the flooded hotel, and that he ought to feel grateful also to the man who had made the call enabling his hosts to be so charmingly ready to receive him. And then, as he peeled off his clothes and tried to remember where on the way up the stairs was the bathroom, deciding everything could wait until daylight, *everything*, including judgement, he realized the man from the hotel would never have phoned, would have forgotten his existence as soon as he was out the door . . . Nothing mattered.

Dressed in his underwear and his now dry socks, shivering, but only a little, he moved to the window. The moon shone on the water in a calm, silver pathway. The sea looked as if it was trying to efface itself, nibbling at the pebbles of the beach with discreet, foamy bites which teased the shore, eating at it with the quiet determination of the dog with her separate bowl of food. The whole of it had a poetic tranquillity, a normality he found reassuring and enough to suppress the conclusion that none of this was normal, or anything like. He looked at the door of the room, suddenly and irrationally afraid that he had been locked in. He did not know why he should begin to imagine such a thing and experimenting with the quiet latch showed him he was wrong. An eccentric household was all. Nothing here to worry a stout heart. He took off his socks, got into the bed, relishing cool linen sheets and heavyweight blankets. He wanted to be pressed into sleep, ironed into unconsciousness, but just as he stretched to feel the parameters of the high bed, his feet touched warm fur, and he screamed. There was an animal in here.

Henry flung back the covers and roared towards the door. There was silence from the landings below; he looked down the open stairwell and saw light. Foolish to scream at some cat. What was he, a child? He held the bedside lamp aloft like a weapon, and examined what it was his feet had found. 'Get outta here,' he ordered. The thing did not move. He touched it tentatively, then grabbed it angrily. He *needed* this bed. The fur was hot; a sick animal. Then he felt the contours of a brick, picked it up, turned it over. A brick in a pocket of fur. Ingenious. He got back into bed and twiddled his toes against it. Began to doze.

Woke with the moonlight in his eyes and his armpits sticky, convinced yet again that the fur at his feet was alive. Hearing *her* laugh at him and tell him there was nothing to be afraid of. Wide awake now, with a sudden urge to take a shower, trying to remember what either the cardinal or the tweed suit and tattoos had said about showers. There wasn't one; there was a bath, next the kitchen. He was hot; his passion for hygiene had been subsumed by exhaustion and now he felt dirty. He put the socks back on, took a towel and set off to explore.

Down, down down . . . Looking towards the gaslight in the hall, he stopped on the third landing, arrested by sound. There was the lightest possible patter of feet, coming from a room he had not seen. The figure, tall but slight with a mass of pale hair, stood on the landing below, indecisive for a matter of seconds, paused as if the last flight was just too much, then slid down the final banisters in a flurry of white gown. There was an almost imperceptible *thump* in the landing. The figure blew on both her hands, flexed her fingers briefly and disappeared.

Henry's warm feet had taken root in the spot. He seemed to have stood where he was for an hour, while the feet grew cold again, before he continued down the stairs, clutching his towel, rubbing his eyes with it, trying to dispel the illusion of what he had thought he had seen.

There was a fine Indian shawl draped over the newel post. It was incredibly soft to the touch, as soft as the fur in his bed. It could have been Francesca's shawl; the one he had given her. Or the one at the bottom of his suitcase he had bought as a gift. From the depths of the house, he could hear the sound of running water and singing. Feeling awkward, Henry Evans went back to bed.

The fur was still warm. He moved it level with his heart.

Don't talk now.

It is always warm in here. As warm as a hospital, or a baby's bedroom. I always loved children, which seems a trite thing for a teacher to say. Before he died, my father discouraged teaching as a choice of career because he said it would wreck my perception of childish innocence and stop me from being able to play. I was preparing to follow his advice (I usually did and he was usually right) when he died. I've been yearning for his advice ever since. It seems so short a step from being the one who was given the wise advice to being the one who is relied upon to provide it.

I wonder what he would think of me now, and I think I know. We all hark back to childhood here; it is consistently and often accurately blamed for everything. Not in my case, except insofar as it gave me the burning ambition to provide for other children the same sort of security that was given to me.

We would sit by the window, my cousin and I, attempting to learn verse. There are things worse than learning verse, my father said. Harry might not have been able to do that; he liked the sea and he wanted to learn to fish. I tried to teach him nursery rhymes, the old-fashioned, meaningless kind, because I love things which do not change, like the sea.

There was an old woman who swallowed a spider
That wriggled and wriggled and wriggled inside her;
She swallowed the spider to catch the fly,
I don't know why she swallowed the fly.
Perhaps she'll die.

Nursery rhymes make me think of birthday teas and I must not. I've been warned that anniversaries are dangerous; they loosen the tongue with grief. And this is supposed to be a record of my thoughts, to prove that I can still think of other things. I must NOT venture into facts.

FMC

CHAPTER TWO

He first deceased; she for a little tried
To live without him, liked it not and died.

HENRY woke with these words being muttered to him from a far distance of memory. A very compact poem, but one which moved him unbearably. He tried to see if it would work the other way round; *she* first deceased, etc., but it did not. The sounds which confused him, along with the words he could have sworn he heard whispered in his ear, were those of a cacophony of seagulls and the irregular heartbeat of the sea, echoing through his room, dragging on the shingle in a series of sighs, drawing him towards the window.

The window stood out from the roof in a small bay made for one, angled against the slope of a turret, so that when he stood inside the frame of it, he felt part of the sky. The gulls wheeled round his head, quarrelling and screaming so close that he ducked automatically, convinced it was he who angered them. There was a streak of guano on the glass, blurring the sight of the watery sun. It was paler than pale egg yolk, opaque, almost no colour at all. He lived with such artificial colours, the bright primaries of packaging and pills, colours made for noticing and remembering. Not like this. Cloud moved across the egg yolk sun. The sea itself was too vast to contemplate; the horizon melted into mist. Henry looked down towards the ground. It was not nearly as far away as he felt it was.

There was greater comfort in looking down than looking up. The vastness of sea and sky made him feel small, while the activity on the ground made him feel human. There was a jogger in a red fleece, varying the muscles deployed in his exercise by jogging backwards on the broad pavement opposite the House of Enchantment, flanking the sea. The jogger stopped moving, breathed deeply, hands on hips for a second while he surveyed the sea before stretching his legs, placing them one at a time on the low wall of the parapet and bending his torso towards his thigh. Good boy, Henry applauded. A woman with a posse of chattering children and a baby in a pram passed by the jogger, oblivious to anything but her own amiable instructions. She slowed the pram to avoid a couple with two yapping dogs, one small and piebald, one large and tan, overexcited, pulling at the lead, dancing in tail-thrashing frenzy. The jogger continued his stretches. Another runner appeared from stage right. A child sat, waiting for a bus, hugging herself into her coat. A black dog was at the edge of the water, recovering a brown, crumpled object and worrying at it. Henry had the fleeting thought that the object might actually be his hat and hoped he was wrong. He felt a brief and inexplicable moment of happiness. There were people here, after all. A backwards-running jogger, guys keeping fit, that was normal. The dog owners chided their animals.

The dogs made him sentimental. He should not have lied about owning a dog, just to ingratiate himself. The black dog, tail blurred in movement, yapped and growled at the water's edge, big, bold and secretly scared. Henry scratched his chest and smiled encouragement. When a big wave came in, the dog retreated, barking defiance. Know how you feel, buddy. We all have to bark, whether we mean it or not.

Then, from stage left, came a strange figure, walking so fast he could compete with the jogger. He was tall and thin and nothing seemed to fit, a suit and coat hanging from his frame like a series of scarves. Business attire, if you happened to be a funeral director, Henry thought; a rabbi on a bad day, some distraught unorthodox, orthodox Jew, smoking, talking to himself, looking at nothing but the inside of his own skull, forgetting in between furious drags on the cigarette that it was lit at all. How could anyone smoke in that breeze? His hair stood on end, black, like his clothing, the skin of his hands alabaster white. He strode past Henry's line of vision, arms waving, cigarette unsteady, engaged in a debate with an invisible adversary, a client, a confessor, maybe mouthing words of admonition and advice, so earnest he was laughable. Henry smiled again, engrossed in the view; then sensed the presence of breath other than his own, misting the window. Someone standing level, closer than the seagulls.

'One tends to spend *a lot* of time staring out of the window,' Timothy was saying with a sigh, pointing at the figure below. 'He's barking mad, that man, but frightfully clever, you know. Where do you want me to put this?'

He was carrying a delicate tray of fragrant smells: coffee, sweet scented toast, a hint of silver pots under a large, stiff linen napkin. Henry had the irrelevant thought, hung over from a similar one of the night before, of how odd it was for a house to possess such fine crystal and silver, such elegant china cups and not have central heating. Speaking for himself, he might have sold it all and turned the proceeds into warmth. Timothy was dressed in heavy cords, boots, shirt, sweater and cardigan, relatively normal and a comforting contrast to the outfit of the night before, despite the yellow cap which was squashed on his head at a rakish angle. Behind him strolled Senta the dog, carrying a newspaper in her mouth which she dropped at Henry's feet.

'Oh, I didn't expect breakfast. That's nice of you. Should have been up sooner, I guess.' He forced a laugh, suddenly full of the shyness from which exhaustion had preserved him the evening before.

'It isn't *breakfast,* it's simply toast. *Breakfast* is another matter altogether, has to be ordered. Actually, it suits us quite well if the guest stays put until Peter's sorted us out downstairs and done the fires, at least. Such a mess. We though we might go shopping after that. Would you like to come with us? We could, you know, sort of help you get your bearings.'

'Is there a shower?' Henry asked.

'No, we told you, didn't we? Only the bathroom behind the kitchen. Free at the minute and plenty of hot water. Eat the toast while it's warm, won't you?'

For a moment, Henry thought Tim would stand over him until he had eaten the toast and drunk the coffee, in the way of an anxious parent with a picky child. Or leave the dog to ensure cooperation, but Tim merely adjusted his cap and departed, holding the door for the dog to lead the way. Henry could hear him whistling until he reached the second landing, and then the sound died away.

He steeled himself for the journey down. Slightly breathless from the long climb back, Henry was reflecting that the room where he had just taken a shallow and hurried wash was probably the most archaic bathroom he had ever seen. A bath the size of a family coffin, taps equally grand, a washbasin of similarly vast proportions, plumbing which sounded like thunder, and an outside temperature reminiscent of the Arctic. He was left clean but hardly refreshed by the effort of buttoning his shirt with numb fingers. The action of choosing items from his suitcase (neatly folded cashmere sweaters, scientifically packed: Henry was meticulous about clothes) worried him. Did he really want to walk into town with these guys?

He sat on the high bed, buttoned his cuffs and thought about it. Told himself he wasn't a homophobe, had nothing against gay guys, not really. He just didn't happen to know any; they didn't move in his kind of circles, or if they did, they didn't shout about it and stuck to their own clubs. He did not quite know the code. All he knew was that he didn't want to be counted as one; didn't want to walk into this funny little town in the company of a pair of oddly dressed men and have people think he was of the same persuasion. Henry looked out of the window again. The road by the sea stretched into the distance, culminating in a crazy pier. He did not know which way was shops, could not remember his rehearsal of the map, or which way he had walked in the disorientating rain. He took a handful of pills from his enormous washbag, swallowed with a shudder.

Yes, he needed a guide. He was not in a state to be fussy, or to preserve an element of his own kind of snobbery; he needed to be led. Is that what it is, Henry? *You are a snob, you know.* He closed his eyes for the sound of her voice. Francesca Chisholm, with the cut glass British accent, talking about living in a castle and calling *him* a snob.

'He first deceased; she for a little tried | To live without him, liked it not, and died,' Maggie Chisholm recited.

That was *not* the way it was supposed to be, especially if the *he* in question was not actually *dead. She,* being an emancipated creature of the twenty-first century, might have pined for a bit, but then she would think of the compensations, such as freedom, and then she would *get on with it. She* would realize, after a while, that life was more than an emotional vacuum; that is what she would do. There would come a point when she stopped sitting in her rented room late at night writing him recriminatory letters which were always addressed to herself. *She* would never seek to rely on men and she would sink herself in her work. Only that, at the moment, was difficult.

This office where Maggie sat was remarkably free of comforts, which in the normal course of events she would not notice since comfort was not a priority, but in the cold lack of light of a February morning, a lumpy seat was no aid to concentration already impeded by just that tiny touch of hangover and the presence of a number of cardboard files which felt damp to the touch. In another era, she would have insisted on changing things, shouted or murmured disapproval, assumed an air of authority, whichever seemed appropriate to seek an improvement in her lot or the state of her chair, but this was not the place, or the time. She signed a letter with a flourish, wincing at the sight of the typing with the faint letters and the occasional misspelling, corrected by her own fair hand in the same blue as her signature. Margaret F. Hooper, her married name, used professionally, the signature sloping over the page towards the bottom left corner, as if it too, was on the run. That would do for now. Nobody would notice her absence for an hour. Part-time jobs were not important. She was killing time; she did not want to do anything that carried weight. What she really wanted at this point in her life was a lifelong contemplation of the sea, doing absolutely nothing.

Maggie lit a cigarette and watched the smoke rise and descend in an unequal battle with the cold air of the room. *Bugger you, Philip; why did you leave me? Why, oh why, oh why?*

He could have been a help, but now she had no choice. She would go to the pier. The sinking pier was good for the soul, because it was rotting. From start to end, it was the same length as the *Titanic*. She would shiver and chill and postpone awkward things, eat breakfast at the caff, back within the hour. She bolted from the back room to the front door, pulled it behind her with full force. It was a large door and the *slam* reverberated through the building, making her departure less than circumspect. She paused to wipe the brass plaque with the sleeve of her coat; the thing was a disgrace, but then, so was a door to a solicitor's office which was so difficult to open and close in winter that it required the firm application of a boot or shoulder to deal with the warp. Not the kind of behaviour to be encouraged amongst the ranks of those in desperate search of legal advice, precisely the category she wished to avoid. Ten in the morning, the place far too populous for her liking; too many familiar faces in this street. She was born and raised in this town, escaped it, came back ignominiously and did not, at the moment, want to be acknowledged. By anyone.

★

The slam of the door caught his attention, briefly. Henry was delighted with the High Street. A butcher, a baker, a candlestick maker, Timothy was pointing out to him, a fishmonger, plus all those other things so *useful* to mankind, or perceived to be so, such as Dixons for televisions, a *delicious* shop for linens and a greengrocer with yellow milk and white, free-range eggs. In absolute pride of place in Tim's eyes were the thrift shops, four or five of them, each described enthusiastically to Henry's mystification, as if they were more important than anything else. Supermarkets? he muttered, not really familiar with the idea of anything else, and already, by the time it took to draw level with the slamming door, both charmed on the one hand by the row of disparate shops, puzzled by the thrift shops in particular and irritated with the time it took to get around them all. By the time they reached this point, Henry was giddy with gossip and information. The slow passage, with long commentary on the buildings, each fulsomely described down to the last occupant, was accompanied by bewildering pauses, when all he wanted to know was *Does this street run parallel to the sea? Where is the castle where she lived? Where am I? How can I get back?* He patted the map in the top pocket of his immaculate jacket. The map was difficult to detect but he needed to know it was there, reassure himself. He had, after all, come here to find *himself*, and even in his slightly disorientated state, suddenly wanted to be *by himself*. Again, he felt ill mannered. It was a cheerful, bustling street, a complete and reassuring contrast to the desolation of his limited view of the place the night before, and it was not raining, but still he was impatient.

'And there's the church,' Timothy was saying, grabbing his arm and pointing out the obvious structure further down the road with an urgency which suggested it was about to fly away. 'Well, *one* of the churches. There are rather a lot . . .' They had drawn parallel with a narrow building on Henry's right, dwarfed by its oversized front door and a tarnished brass plaque fixed to one side.

CHISHOLM, LAWTON AND COOPER, Commissioners for Oaths. It was the name *CHISHOLM* which caught his eye and held him transfixed, a reminder, as if he needed one, of his real purpose. Not the real purpose, he told himself angrily; not the real purpose at all; he was here to earn his living, to see a part of the world he only knew by proxy, to be a *tourist*, but all the same, the hidden agenda which had underpinned it all came up and slapped him when he saw the name.

'What's one of these?' Henry said, stabbing a finger at the sign. 'Commissioner for *what*?'

'What? Oh, lawyers, to you, I suppose.'

Henry cleared his throat, which was suddenly constricted. 'Are there a lot of people called Chisholm around here? I mean, is that a common kind of name?' He was trying to sound as if the question was not urgent. Peter shook his head, in mid-flow.

'A few of that name,' he said cautiously.

'I think I'll just go in here.'

'Why?'

Henry shrugged. Peter was offended, but his offence was minimal. He rallied and smiled brightly, 'Well, don't forget to take a walk on the pier, before you come home.'

Home? Did they think he was going to stay there? With *that* bathroom?

Peter and Timothy linked arms unselfconsciously and waved him on. Henry hesitated before he applied force to the handle on the door and went in. A pencilled sign, pinned to a wall, told him to bear left. He stood, uncertainly, wondering why he had done as he did, wishing he had rehearsed something to say, feeling a touch defensive. But lawyers were lawyers: there was no task a lawyer would not accept, however frivolous. They were the ones with the local and long distance knowledge, and as far as the lawyers Henry knew were concerned, the customer was always right. The client did not exist who was turned away, unless he had no money. Henry's disorientation, which was becoming habitual, like that of someone wandering around with a mild dose of flu, increased as he stood there trying to decipher the source of a *clack, clack, clack* noise, interrupted by the *ttring!* of a bell.

He turned into a room lit by the window, the light penetrating on to the two tables, where two large females sat, hammering away on stand-up-and-beg ancient typewriters big enough to dwarf the size of their formidable bosoms. He had a dim memory of his father typing on one of these infernal machines when he was a child, putting into it the kind of manual effort which would be useful for mending a road. He looked on in amazement. The nearest woman, with a bleached frizz of hair and a comfortable face, stopped work and whipped off her spectacles.

'Yessir. What can I do for you?'

It was a ratatat command, in tune with her neighbour's continued typing, accompanied by a smile which informed him at once how she could strong-arm him out the door, or welcome him in, depending upon his own manners.

'Could I speak to Mr Chisholm?'

'Dead these fifty years, but if you'd like to see the current partner, I'll see if I can raise him. Not from the dead himself, if you see what I mean. I'm sure he's somewhere in the building. Maybe. Can I ask what it was about? Only Mr Chisholm's substitute might not be the right man at all.'

'I'd rather not say. It's . . . kinda personal.'

She nodded, understandingly. The word *divorce* was mirrored in her eyes as she moved into the foyer and yelled into the cavern of the stairs. 'Mr Burns!' There was an answering, indeterminate echo. She nodded. 'Have a seat in the waiting room. He'll be out in a minute.' She made it sound as if Mr Burns was unfortunately stuck on the toilet, and the length of time a client might wait before receiving the privilege of the great man's attention was uncertain. All the same, Henry was grateful.

The room into which he was ushered seemed, in the harsh light of a central bulb scarcely concealed behind a paper shade, to consist more of metal than anything else. One side was occupied by three massive safes, balanced against each other, the one in the middle acting as prop to the two, slightly smaller versions of its iron-clad self, like ancient cousins in three-way conversation. They smelt metallic; they looked icy cold to the touch; they were two metres high, leaving a stretch of yellow wall between their heads and the yellower ceiling. The touch of green on the metal suggested the presence of something perishable inside. Henry turned away and looked for a chair.

Twelve chairs, he counted, ranged round the sides of the room not occupied by the volume of the safes, each of a different style, a couple made of plastic alone, two more which his untutored eye could see in a museum taking pride of place with their frayed, Georgian beauty, three of lesser, but refined Victorian vintage, despite the rotting forepaw of a leg here and there. The wooden floor dipped dramatically, nothing particularly clean or polished; his hand encountered a piece of extra-cold chewing gum on the underside of the seat he had chosen. He waited. The outside door slammed with the same shuddering reverberation which had drawn him towards it in the first place. The *clack, clack clack* of the typewriters went on, interrupted by a telephone and a burst of irritated speech. He waited. A head appeared round the doorway.

'Do come up, Mr . . .'

'Evans. Henry.'

'Good morning. Cold, isn't it?'

The black legs in front of him took the stairs two at a time, and then they were in a bigger room overlooking the street, where it was light and mercifully warm. Not warm enough for Henry to want to fling off his coat, but tolerable.

'American, Mr Evans?'

'Oh . . . how can you tell?'

'Clothes, dear boy. Can always tell by the clothes. Also by the way people shake their heads. Your first visit?'

'Why, yes. Always meant to, never did . . .'

His head had been nodding, Henry realized and steadied it, immediately. His jaw had dropped, too. He was trying to pull himself together. Mr Burns, with the white skin, appalling haircut and ill-fitting clothes, was the man he had seen hurrying by in his ungainly way earlier in the morning. His hair still stood up in tufts and his shirt, on closer glance, was frayed at the collar. The cuffs were invisible since the sleeves of his jacket were long enough to cover his knuckles, giving the impression of long, thin fingers attempting to escape over the desk. The desk itself, partner sized, had once been magnificent, not an epithet Henry could have applied to the man, but the leather top was worn from red to dusty pink and looked as if Burns, or a pet of his, devoted some of each day to chewing it. There were two coasters, strategically positioned for the placing of cups, a precaution against further wear and tear which was redundant since the surface was already pitted with circular scars and the evidence of spills.

Henry made sure his mouth was shut and tried to look Burns in the eye, man to man, but his gaze was distracted to above his head, where a large, stuffed fish was posed inside a glass tank, petrified against a background of alarmingly green weed. Burns caught Henry's eye.

'I didn't catch it, oh dear me, no. The original Mr Chisholm probably did. One of my predecessors anyway, probably about 1910. It's lasted fairly well. They existed for that kind of sport, the lawyers, just as many of my contemporaries seem to exist for golf. Very good golf round here. I suppose you've come to work at Fergusons?'

'Why, yes. That was another good guess, Mr Burns.'

'Simple deduction, dear boy. You see an American in Warbling, and he's either working for Fergusons or being a tourist, and we don't get too many of those in winter, unless they're insane. I suppose you're looking for a house.'

Henry's chair wobbled dangerously. He remembered to lean forward rather than back. There was something delightfully disingenuous about Mr Burns. There would have to be, for him to let himself out into the world, looking like that.

'No, sir. I'm not looking for a house, not yet anyway. I don't have to start at Fergusons for a week or two yet and I don't know how long I'll be staying, but—'

'Pioneering another drug, are you? New, improved Viagra?'

Burns laughed. People always sniggered at the mention of the most famous drug Fergusons distributed, Henry thought with irritation; it was like kids discovering rude words. He waited for a few seconds, anticipating the next question so frequently asked – *Have you got any spare?* – but then decided Mr Burns was not vulgar enough for that. Henry was struggling to equate this gargoyle with attorneys of his own strata, beautifully suited, booted and spurred with power hair. He leaned further forward. The chair creaked again. The room reeked of cigarette smoke.

'Mr Burns, I'm not buying anything. Truth is, I'm looking for someone. A woman. She was born and raised in this area and I knew her, what . . .' he coughed, embarrassed, '. . . oh, about twenty years ago. We were both kids, met backpacking in India. We were pretty good friends for a coupla months, lost contact, you know how it goes. But I know she came back here. She said she'd never live anywhere else.' He coughed again awkwardly and directed his gaze at the fish. 'I got the impression that her family were in the upper bracket, A-grade sort of people, called Chisholm, like your firm. Francesca Chisholm. Does that ring any bells with you? Or if it doesn't, could you find out for me? I just thought, being an attorney in a town this size, you're all set to know who lives where.'

His voice trailed away. There was a sudden image of Francesca in her shawl, passing by him in that ramshackle bus, missing him by minutes. He had dithered, said his stiff goodbyes, made for the station and the train as planned because Henry could never change a plan, and then he found the courage to do just that, run back, intercept her before she got on that damn bus, and say to her, either you go with me or I go with you, right? Makes no difference, as long as we go together. You mustn't go by yourself, you're not fit; I love you. I'll take you home. Too late. He had been running up the hill like a madman in the heat as the bus stormed down. She had not seen him, but he had seen her face at the window, crying into the shawl round her neck. Abandoned by him, haunting him ever since.

'I didn't go back for her, Mr Burns,' he found himself saying. 'I didn't go back for her soon enough. I should have. She had to come back here because her father had died. I didn't understand. We had such plans. I tried to change my mind, but not soon enough. Should have turned back.'

There was a silence, interrupted by the drumming of fingers on the ruined surface of the desk.

'Twenty years ago, Mr Evans? Twenty years? It's a bloody life-time.' Burns' peculiarly black, tufted eyebrows were arched to meet the mess of his hair. Henry's eyes wandered back to the fish in the glass case and he encouraged himself to wonder if beasts that size were swimming in the English Channel, like monsters of the deep. *Your mind hops about like a frog, Henry*, Francesca had told him once. *It hops in a straight line more or less, via a series of sideways jumps. You can't sit on the fence, Henry; you'd never concentrate long enough.* As well as thinking about the likely origins of the monster fish in order to distract himself from his own embarrassment, Henry was also wondering if everything Francesca had ever said to him was pertinent and observant, or whether it was the romantic deception of memory which made it seem so. They had laughed, much of the time; he had never since met a woman who made him laugh so much, but she had always seemed so much older than he. She seemed, in retrospect, to have emerged from her adolescence a fully formed woman, whereas he had been a boy.

Burns lit a cigarette with all the furtive clumsiness of a boy; the smell of it brought Henry back to the present, made him aware he was in an old office space which was either entirely decrepit or deliberately eccentric, and a place where smoking was not only a health hazard but also a fire risk. Burns looked for an ashtray in the chaos of the desk top, failed after a desultory attempt and absent-mindedly tapped the ash on the floor. Downstairs, the door banged; the building trembled and settled back to a kind of somnolence.

'What a *shame* you aren't looking for a house, Mr Evans,' the lawyer resumed, chattily. 'Then I'd really be able to help. Wills, estates and the transfer of houses, that's basically what we exist to do, especially houses. There's one section of the better-off population do nothing but move house, move house, until finally they die and the fun really starts. Bit of crime, of course. We've got three dozen public houses in this town, plenty of stimulants and unemployment, bound to cause trouble from time to time. If only they'd all go home and take your Viagra, ha ha! Less bloody trouble all round . . .'

'I don't want a house, and I don't want to make a will,' Henry said.

The cigarette flew out of Burns' hand, and landed, smouldering on the carpet. A few dozen others must have gone the same way, judging from the marks on the wood to the side of the desk. Henry winced, watching as Burns retrieved the cigarette with surprising grace, swooping upon it like a bird of prey, taking a quick, desperate puff and throwing the remnant into the fireplace behind him. Henry craned to see where it had gone, calmer for the pantomime and privately delighted to see the man move. He seemed to consist of overlong legs and arms, with a narrow torso. Burns leaned back in his chair, something Henry did not dare to do, and laced his long fingers together. They disappeared inside the cuffs of the funereally black, suspiciously dusty jacket. The voice was suddenly precise and dry.

'Of *course* I know of Francesca Chisholm. I wouldn't need to be a lawyer to know. I'd just have to read the newspapers. But because I *am* a lawyer, Mr Evans, and Miss Chisholm is a client, there's not a single thing I have to tell you, and I may add, I'm distinctly suspicious of your motives. If what you say is true – which if it is makes you just another menopausal man in search of an old romance – then I couldn't possibly take your money to tell you what you could find out for free in our excellent reference library. I'm not a detective and I'm not for hire. *If* what you say is true, the only advice I can offer you is to regard her as DEAD.' He was lighting another cigarette, shrugging his thin shoulders, either seriously cross or faking it. 'This place does not exist to make money, Mr Evans. It exists to keep the confidences of others, as far as possible. Come back if you need that house or that will.'

Henry felt obscurely ashamed and furious at the same time. 'I didn't mean to bother you,' was all he could say. 'I'm not asking much, Mr Burns.'

He was rewarded with a radiant smile. 'In which case, you have nothing in common with the rest of my clients. Do you know the way out?'

Downstairs, where the temperature dropped with each step. A sudden panic when he could not open the door and thought he would have to ask, braced himself as he pulled on the handle, slammed it shut. Out on the busy street, remembering nothing else than the fact that all the roads led to the sea. And Francesca Chisholm might as well be dead.

Maybe he shouldn't have stared at the fish. Maybe he should have put money on the table, but he'd got the general idea that that wouldn't have made an ounce of difference.

But I think I've seen her, Mr Burns. Of course she's alive. She left her shawl on the banisters.

Maggie sidled into the room, carrying two mugs of coffee which she placed on the worn leather of the desk. She tutted under her breath and searched under a pile of paperwork to unearth the ashtray, which she placed closest to him, plucked the cigarette from his nerveless fingers, took a quick drag, and stubbed it out.

'You could have charged him a walk-in fee, Edward, you could at least have done that.'

'Why?'

'I dunno. Silly suggestion, really. What was it all about?'

'Nothing.'

'OK, I dare say you'll tell me in a minute. I just heard you sounding a bit, well, you know, clipped. Not like you, Edward, I mean not normally.'

She picked up the newspaper which littered a corner, sat back in the chair recently occupied by the client and read it nonchalantly. The day before yesterday's news was good enough. Edward Burns gulped his coffee and scalded his tongue, patently upset.

'Mrs Forbes says he looked a nice man,' she said. 'He's staying at the House of Enchantment, because the Nelson wasn't up to hospitality, I heard. Smith sent him there as his own little revenge on the world for the fact the bar was flooded again. "The man was wearing a silly hat and was an anally retentive little prick." I quote verbatim.'

Edward nodded. 'I know. I was in there this morning, looking at the damage. He's quite unfit to manage that hotel, even with us – you, rather – checking his books and the register twice a week. He simply cannot cope in a crisis and he takes instant, completely unfounded dislikes to strangers. Hardly a qualification.'

'Is this American good looking?' Maggie asked, casually. She seemed more than usually restless, moving round in her seat like a cat making a nest, failing to catch his eye.

'*Frightfully* well dressed. Otherwise unremarkable. You'd miss him in a crowd. I don't know. I never notice things like that.'

'No, Ed, you don't.'

'He *seems* nice enough. Going to work for Fergusons. But what could I say to him? He wants to find Francesca. Says he's a long-lost friend. Met her in India. Before my time.'

'Ah, yes. That was ages ago. Before life began or started to end, whichever way you look at it. He might be genuine. Nothing to suggest he's a journalist in disguise, was there? After all, Francesca's hardly news any more. We're all trying to forget her. As if we could. Although we should. I can't.'

'*You* defended her,' he said flatly.

'Yes. To be the best of my ability, darling, to coin a phrase. Don't frown so. *Yes*, you are entirely right in your estimation of me, Edward. I may have qualified as a lawyer but I am profoundly frivolous and likely to remain so, but it doesn't follow that I'm incompetent. I'm just absolutely determined to avoid responsibility. I've done the career bit and the married bit and I don't give a shit. No roof over my head: do I want responsibility? Like hell I do. Sixteen hours a week is what I do for you . . . Quite enough. The crime around here is so *boring*. Get drunk, get sick, hit each other, was it the left fist or the right . . .'

'With the exception of Francesca Chisholm. Your cousin. Whose ancestor founded this firm.'

She sipped at the coffee, decorously. Her normally pale face was pink from the cold.

'Francesca didn't *care* who defended her. Anyone would have done. And *two* hours a week was plenty enough to organize the defence of a woman who insisted she was guilty. No debate about it and none allowed. Are you sure, I'd say? Are you absolutely sure? and she'd say, Course I'm sure, I was there wasn't I, I should know. It cost twenty pence to fish on the pier, she'd say, as if that was the whole thing about it which surprised her. And it's the same length as the *Titanic*. Don't waste money, someone else needs it. Just get it over with for me and tell them I'm sorry. I mean, all I did was get a man to translate that to court as kindly as he might. I check up on her protégé and her friend, small thanks for it. I bring her reports from her own, lost world. She delegated rather a lot of tasks and I do them.'

'Do you think you might have done a more thorough job if you hadn't been in the midst of divorce?'

'Get *stuffed*, Edward. *You* were supervising. We took instructions; we obeyed them to the letter. That's all we could do. And I suppose you refused to tell that American anything about it? Sent him away without a word? Client confidentiality? She needs friends, even if she hasn't got them, and he might just be one. So what if he's a fool?'

'She doesn't deserve friends.'

'*Deserve* them? What's that got to do with anything? She always says, *I can't talk now,* as if she ever will. Do you know, she's been there almost a year? I hate anniversaries. So will she. Where's he gone, that man?'

Edward considered carefully. 'He's gone for a walk on the pier. Listen Maggie, *officially* we shouldn't tell him anything.'

'Officially,' she said, picking up the coffee mugs and looking out of the window. Edward sighed again, and fumbled for the cigarettes.

'He isn't good looking, you know, Maggie. There's no real reason to bother.'

'He's just another man who fell for Francesca,' Maggie said. 'And left her. Like they all did. Like they all do. You're a bunch of shits, really.'

'Not all of us,' Edward said.

I treasure the shawl because it was a gift, not for itself, however useful it is. But I suppose I disapprove of sentiment, or sentimental gestures. They get in the way of genuine emotion and disguise it thoroughly. I was trying to make an inventory yesterday, of all the people I've LIKED in my life. I don't mean loved, or adored; I mean LIKED. There was a man a long time ago whom I adored because he had no idea of how singular he was. I should have kept in touch with him, but I didn't.

Those were the days when people were expendable. One always assumed there would be someone else of equal calibre. Wrong. Would you shoot tigers with him? my father would have asked. Yes, but I went on to prefer the deliberately extrovert and sociable type of male. Then there are the people I adopted because it was so unfair that no one else would. I cannot bear to see loneliness when I can do something about it, but empathy with people who need you is not quite the same thing as liking. I think that LIKING is a cousin to respect, but respect is more important. Angela was often difficult to like, but she deserved enormous respect. I like Maggie; she does not know how generous she is and I must not take advantage of her. I have a phonecard. I could speak to her but I don't, it isn't fair. I shall dribble on to paper instead, avoiding facts and dates.

Father once took us to the house of a military friend of his, very old school. He had stuffed animal heads on the walls. Maggie and I must have been about two feet each, gazing at them in horror. It was Maggie who said that the rest of the tiger was behind the wall, ready to come crashing through as soon as we left.

And I believed her.

FMC

CHAPTER THREE

HENRY walked down the length of the High Street, took the next left and made for the sea. A stiff breeze raised the hair on his head and made him vow to buy a new hat on the way back. He had noticed a shop that seemed to specialize in what other men seemed to wear, a strange species of cap which did not seem to protect the ears, but he also noticed that the men who wore hats seemed to spend most of their time bareheaded. Into a shop they would go, and off came the hat; if they met a woman, off came the hat, a constant doffing of the thing, as if it was an embarrassment. There was something else he noticed too, in the bustle of the narrow pavements, and that was the way that whenever they bumped into each other, both parties said 'sorry', regardless of fault. The word was a kind of password, a prefix to whatever came next, 'Sorry, could you hold the door for me . . . Sorry, I haven't got change today . . . Sorry you bumped into me.' It seemed mandatory to apologize for taking up space.

All in all, his encounter with the lawyer was one Henry decided he had found oddly exhilarating, despite the accompanying humiliation, and he was trying to work out why as he walked up towards the sea through a series of narrow streets, remembering to say 'sorry' to whoever crossed his path. He felt he had got something off his chest by at least admitting to someone, even someone as alien as Edward Burns, that what he really wanted to do, above all else, was find Francesca Chisholm. And he had *done* it; he had actually made the admission to a complete stranger; he had taken a *spontaneous* risk and he had not felt quite such a fool as he'd thought he might feel. That was number one reflection. The next was a sense of release that the lawyer had not said Francesca who? Or murmured, my dear man, of course Francesca Chisholm is alive and well, but how on earth could you imagine she would want to renew an acquaintance with a lousy little bore like you? And thirdly, a sense of mild triumph which was the most difficult to explain. Francesca Chisholm was patently alive and not in the graveyard, as a few of his contemporaries already were as the result of rash experiments with drugs, ambition and fast cars. He could not see Francesca as self-destructive, but he could see her crashing a car with the greatest of ease. She would be impulsive with her enthusiasms; she would never be scientific enough to know how an engine worked. She would press the pedals and tell it to go.

How do you know that? he asked himself. You don't know anything. You didn't really know her; it was she who seemed to know you. What pleased him most about the lawyer with the dead fish in his office was what he had revealed about Francesca, rather than what he had withheld. The woman was not only alive, but she had made the news, done something that made her attorney bridle so defensively. She might be a notoriety of some kind, raising Cain, running protest movements, leading a wild life, behaving scandalously, or at least oddly, shocking the natives one way or another, and he was distinctly proud of her for that. The sense of vicarious achievement grew with each step. You are *known*, Francesca; people *know* who you are; they talk about you. You're a *somebody*; you didn't become a nonentity with a dry career like me; you stayed that bright light you were.

So bright, she could shine in the darkness, it had seemed to him, twenty years ago. Had her beauty been so spectacular, or was it another kind of singularity which made her so haunting, even against the dramatic scenery of the Indian subcontinent? Brilliant blue skies, the almost surreal colours of vegetation and the peacock shades of clothing against the dull browns of dried palm fronds which cooled the village houses . . . the vivid cerise of split water-melon; the yellow of the daily pineapple . . . He could struggle to remember the debilitating intoxication of the constant, visual feast it had been, and yet remember her, dressed in dull khaki trousers and her long hair in a twist. He could recall, with difficulty, the impact of the Indian women, the poor in the country, the rich in the hotels, universally exquisite but achingly untouchable. They were removed by their eyes, dress, language, decorum and, surely, indifference to a large, hulking young man who went pink in the sun and could not digest their food. The one who watched them covertly, aware of his clumsiness and their fragility. He should have remembered them; he should have remembered the magnificence of the scenery, captured painstakingly on his camera, but all he remembered was her, the one he was never allowed to photograph.

Henry walked slowly through the streets, seeing nothing. He had been fragile when they had met, his stomach recovered to the extent that he could eat selectively and drink litres of bottled water a day. The water supplies weighed down his rucksack more than anything else and he was too weak to sling it over his shoulder. And he was starved for conversation, too, after the deliberate iso-lation of his travels. He had been determined to avoid the wandering tribes of travellers with their incessant boasts of cheaper accommodation, cheaper dope, better bargains. He had wanted to climb hills and see unknown views, and had almost done it; he was sick of it, and sicker of his own indolence. Wherever he went, everyone else was working. They worked with incessant, labour-intensive industry while all he had done for three months was to follow an elaborate, carefully prepared itinerary and watch them about the business of their sweated labour. He was humbled by generosity, infuriated by incurable poverty; he was lonely and nervous and sick of responding to Hallo, how are you? with the single response possible, *I'm good, thank you,* in the hourly recitation of a daily lie. Coming into the sanctuary of a shaded guest house to find her sitting on the veranda, telling stories to children, her instant appeal to him was not unique, but simply inevitable. Perhaps because she liked poetry and thought it entirely natural to carry around a volume of verse when a packet of nuts would have been more useful. It was a cool evening; she wore a cheap shawl to cover her thin shoulders. He had thought, from behind, that she was an elderly woman.

Henry had reached the view of the pier without noticing any building he had passed, lost in memory of another time and place, and he swore under his breath. This was the most regular habit of his lifetime, making journeys to foreign destinations, covering every inch on foot and then somehow not seeing a thing, walking around with his eyes on the ground, privately occupying another space. That was why, years since, thinking of Francesca even then, he had stopped carrying a camera, because when he looked at the pictures when he got home he recognized nothing, as if he had turned a blind eye to the lens, like Nelson to his telescope. He did not feel he had ever *been* there, and here he was now, just the same.

You don't really look, Henry, do you? You take an inventory and pass it on.

Francesca had not been critical when she said that. She had simply been curious, as she was about everything. It was an essential part of her charm.

He had seen the pier from the window of the House of Enchantment that morning, made himself notice what a strange and ugly structure it was, made of colourless concrete with stiff, spindly, jointless legs which seemed to bow as they met the water. *The pier's legs have no ankles and no knees,* the words of her description coming back to haunt, as if they had been as important at the time as the quality of laughter in her voice. There were four shelters on the pier, built into the concrete for the benefit of fishermen, and a series of utilitarian street lamps leading towards the low-slung building at the end, which housed a caff and lavatories, flanked by semicircular platforms at a lower level nearer the sea. The caff looked like some miniature manufacturing plant, squatting on its own industry, while the whole of the pier looked like a benign mistake, simply a road which was intended to go further across the sea, ending where it did, the half-hearted beginning to a pedestrian bridge, because someone, somewhere, has simply decided to stop. Henry walked towards it, determined to keep his eyes off the ground and not to think about the cold around his ears.

There was no need to seek information: it was all there, written on two blackboards carefully placed to waylay the unwary at the porticoed entrance. Selective information, Henry guessed, since the blackboards allowed the pier's caretaker to deliver different facts every day, changing them with a swipe of cloth and new, laborious lettering, according to whim. *This pier is exactly 882 feet, nine inches long and was opened in 1957. It replaces another pier which got hit by a ship in World War Two. Entrance is free, unless you wish to fish, in which case, 20p. The wind force today is 1–2 and the sea temperature is nil centigrade.*

Low. Henry huddled into his jacket, reminded himself of the errand to buy a hat, and then reminded himself not to keep on thinking of what he was going to do next, but think of what he was doing *now*. Walking the concrete deck of a crazy structure unadorned with anything except the black umbrellas of fishermen, wooden benches fixed to the side walls, other walkers. It was relatively quiet; no loud music, no obvious sounds of fun, but the sound of human chatter against the sea. He loved the openness of it and he was hungry; memories of India made him so; memories of never being ravenous, but never feeling fed, causing his stomach to growl ferociously. He blamed the sea air. From a ventilation shaft next to the door of the structure at the end, there wafted the forbidden, mouthwatering smell of frying bacon.

Henry forgot the view. The warmth inside was fuggy and

humid and he found himself passing a hand over his stomach beneath his jacket, comforting it with a circular stroke, then measuring the extra flesh. He had been very fat, he had been *gross* for five years, and in those seven years since, he had craved the unnatural thinness which had been his in the rucksack-carrying year. Without that weight, he might have tried to find her sooner. He had carried his luggage of vitamins, minerals, trace elements, supplements over several continents, leaving this until last. They weighed more than his baggage of water, twenty years ago. He scanned the menu for the vegetarian meal. There had been a sign affixed to the entry door, announcing opening and closing times. *Sometimes early and sometimes late*, it said.

'Can I have the vegetarian option?'

'No call for it, squire, not really.'

There was no contempt, only patience. The tea was the colour of rust. Henry closed his eyes, drank it with sugar and went back to the counter and asked for more. Then he ate bacon and egg with soft, white toast, agonizing over each mouthful. His father would have liked this. There was never a day when he did not think about his father.

Henry watched the calm skyline and thought about his father. Dead these last three months and, along with Francesca Chisholm, occupying at least one half of his waking thoughts as well as many of his dreams. It was only when he thought of his father, and what he might have inherited by way of personal worth, that Henry Evans allowed himself to think he might be a decent enough man himself. He looked down at the fishing platform and noticed missing planks, the water churning beneath. The sense of fatigue came back.

The child looked angelic in sleep. Looking at her in this state made Angela wince with sheer pleasure, amazed that she should be such a graceful and placid sleeper, no tossing and turning, no signs of distress in her unconsciousness. She lay flat on her stomach, her perfect hands pressed into the pillow above her head, face on one side, displaying on the white of the linen the dark, rich curls of her hair. A proper auburn, Angela admired; the colour of horse chestnuts startlingly combined not with the pale skin and blue eyes of the traditional redhead, but a sallower complexion which always looked kissed by the sun. And remarkable brown eyes, above a delicate nose which was sweeter than ever in profile like this, breathing in and out with the minimal sound of a contented baby animal. The lips were slightly parted; the fingertips were lightly curled; there were no nightmares and she was a piece of perfection who deserved to be the centre of the universe; she deserved any sacrifice which could be made and she would sleep for hours. Angela turned from her, feeling satisfied. The child slept the sleep of healthy exhaustion, fresh air, exercise, stimulation and plenty of food. She was a wiry little thing. Not so little, and incredibly strong. She might make an athlete; she shone at school sports and showed a capacity to excel if only she was not so *bored* with it all. Difficult to get the hang of the rules. Why not outrun everyone else and shove the ball in the net, using the quickest route, even if it did mean going out of the ground and pushing people over? Why obey the whistle if you were ahead? Why not use skull, feet and fists and anything else which was useful, even if you were only supposed to use your hands or a stick? She was learning, though; she learned fast. Angela smiled fondly, touched the pillow in benediction, then touched her own hair, hidden beneath a rustling shower cap. Time to rinse. Twenty minutes maximum, or her hair would look like a bonfire in full flame once it was dry. There would only be a slight resemblance to the rich auburn of her daughter. Tanya had said that a girl at school had said, why hasn't your mummy got hair like yours? The fond and logical explanation that only half the mothers who collected at the school gates had a colour of hair resembling that of their children, or even their own, had failed to reassure. There were gaps in Tanya's logic, as well as her sensitivities, and if she wanted Mummy to have the same hair colour as herself, well then, Mummy would fix it. Angela glanced in the mirror and wondered if Uncle Joe would

notice the difference when she visited next; she'd take a bet on it.
Henna was such messy stuff and the application was roughly the
equivalent of shoving her head in a cow pat of warm dung, with a
not dissimilar smell and texture. It stained where it touched the
porcelain; she had spent half the waiting time scrubbing at it, and
the towel round her neck would never be the same again. It would
be relegated to towels to be used for swimming in summer. If they
ever did that again. Of course they would. By the end of the
summer before, Tanya could float like a cork and swim like an eel,
although eels had better understanding of the tides.

Angela set about the task of getting the muck out of her hair
with the aid of the shower attachment, cricking her neck at an
uncomfortable angle over the sink. All finished, and she felt a
huge impatience to get it dry and see the result. Tanya might not
like it and she might have to do it all over again, but if the little
brute said she wanted a blonde mummy next time, that was what
she would have.

No. Not blonde. That was Francesca's colour. It might remind
her.

Coffee; too early for a drink as long as it was daylight. She
looked into the refrigerator, anxiously, checking supplies. A piece
of cold chicken, a bottle of cheap Bulgarian wine, a dozen kinds of
the yoghurt that Tanya loved, enough for a meal, later. Gone were
the days of finer foods, all ending, as they had begun, with
Francesca. When the doorbell rang, she made a quick, furious
check of the tea and coffee supply, and hoped to heaven it was no
one she owed the politeness of hospitality. As if there was anyone
to who she owed nothing, or any time when she could refuse to
answer the door, or fail to explain why it was her daughter was
asleep in the afternoon. Because we get up so early, see? On her
way across the carpet (worn, but subject to rigorous cleaning;
must not let anyone imagine standards were slipping) she flipped
the switch to the radio, filling the flat with the calm music of
Classic FM. Made her look as if she was in control; relaxed; in
command, not someone wating for inspection.

Maggie, looking bloody brilliant, in the way she did. A ripe, well proportioned figure in just the right kind of warm, lightweight coat, slimline trousers, neat little boots which combined practicality with a touch of elegance, and a somewhat breathless Hello! *Just wondered if everything was all right* . . . Bitch. Hate her. Coming round for a sympathy fix, the sort which was given but never solicited, making Angela feel deficient. It was hard accepting solicitude from someone who never seemed to need it. Angela knew what she was going to say before she said it; the words were already assembled like something wrapped for the post. *Hello! Maggie, nice to see you, come on in, won't you?* the smile on the face ready glued like the stamp on the parcel, hoping she really was just passing.

'I was just passing,' Maggie said: the way you did when you lodged in the other direction. The *just passing* stuff was nosy neighbour code and it was bad manners to be seen to doubt it. 'On my way out,' Maggie continued. 'And I'm late already. I just thought I'd bring you these . . .' Now this was better already; an immediate announcement of no intention to stay. Angela liked that kind of visitor and she smiled with extra special warmth as she accepted the flowers. Winter blooms, on closer inspection, snow-drops wrapped in brown paper, not long picked and artfully bound. Angela never knew what to do with flowers. These were tasteful, without being edible.

'I was thinking of sending some to Francesca,' Maggie was saying. 'Only then I remembered they wouldn't let her have them. Don't know why. Infectious or something, some new rule.'

'Bastards,' Angela said with real feeling. 'Bastards.' She squared her shoulders, put the proffered flowers on the chair by the door with a nod of thanks she did not feel. 'I've got to dry my hair. Why don't you go and look at Tanya? She's fast asleep, poor love.'

It was important that she make this child accessible to anyone who wanted to see her. She must always answer the door and behave politely, make it clear there was absolutely nothing to hide. Maggie crossed the floor of the living room into the bedroom with long-legged speed. Angela heard the muted *ahhh* of appreciation as she stood by the bed, and almost liked her for that. No one could be all that bad if they loved the child. She liked Maggie all the more when she was back within the minute, adjusting her scarf, ready for the off without a single suggestion of lingering longer. She had a ski hat with darling little tassels bursting from the crown, poking out of her bag. It matched her brown boots, would look perfect over her voluminous, well dressed hair. There was a pale scarf at her neck, too; she would never get cold. Sheer, naked dislike returned. They stood by the door. Maggie had opened it, stood elegantly with her hand on the jamb.

'Has Neil been round recently?'

'Yeah. Took her out, Saturday. It's great she likes the castle so much.' As if she didn't know. As if she didn't check on Neil, too.

'Oh, by the way. There's this bloke in town, got here yesterday. He, hmm, says he knew Francesca years ago, wants to get in touch. I . . . hmm, well, any idea what I should say? I mean, I'm her cousin, but you were her closest friend and you, you sort of hmm, know her best. What do you think she would want me to say?' She spoke as if she were tossing away a careless and purposeless question, but she was hesitant and slightly flustered, the way she never was. It made Angela more suspicious than ever. She shrugged, thought of the sleeping child, and crossed her arms, defensively, careful not to let irritation show.

'I dunno what you say. Truth's best, isn't it? Tell him where to write to her, I would. I expect she likes letters. She used to write enough of them. Always writing something.'

Maggie nodded, smiled and was gone. Angela picked up the artfully wrapped snowdrops, and after three seconds' contemplation of stamping them underfoot, unwrapped them carefully and found a cup to put them in, with water, so that they should not die. They must be prominently displayed until they decayed. They had the fresh look of half-budded winter blooms which would last in a cool room for days. She would take them to Uncle Joe. The child began to stir in her sleep and cry. Sudden sounds like that made Angela anxious. When this child had come to her, she had newly mended bones and scars the healing of which she could never quite believe.

It was nonsense for anyone to believe that a woman could not love an adopted child as much as if it were her own flesh and blood. Impossible to love anyone more than this. But real mothers, real, neglectful, selfish mothers, did not have to open the door to every knock. *They* could ruin their kids and no one would know.

The cry of the seagulls woke Henry from his doze on the pier. He was aware of a vague sensation of being watched. A long doze which left him consulting the time to find the day waning. The last bench had been sheltered and caught the sun; it had invited him to sit on it, but not for so long. Tired again. He blamed the influx of cholesterol having the same effect on his arteries as all those militants blocking negotiations somewhere in the countries of Europe beyond the horizon. He had dozed with the readiness of an old, old man, and the afternoon had struck him unawares. His eyes were rimmed with a brittle crust of salt. He rose stiffly, peered over the rails to the fishing platform, and saw again the broken boards and the sea, swelling gently beneath. He remembered the things he needed to do – buy a new hat, find another place to stay – and felt indecisive, fuddled by sleep and ashamed of it. He started to walk back the length of the *Titanic* towards the town, slowly.

The shoreline met the sea in a curve. He felt, as he stopped, that he was approaching the rim of the world, a newcomer to it. To the far left he could see the suggestion of a cliff, at odds with the flatness of the coast, as if marking the beginning of new, alien territory a mile away. In the nearer distance there was the squat outline of one of the castles he had come to see, and for a moment, recognizing it from illustrations, he was disappointed. It seemed mean looking and close to the ground, squatting like a toad, instead of rising high against the sky into misty battlements like the castles of fairy tales, and it seemed sadly dwarfed by the redbrick block of flats next to it.

Henry did not want to register disappointment, so he let his eyes wander, away from the dun castle walls, across a fine parade of white buildings to the junction and then to the houses which stretched out to the right. All of them seemed to be different heights and colours, pinks and blues and whites, red, pantiled roofs, slate roofs and a riot of chimneys. They looked as if they had been randomly built, each to its own idea, and then huddled together for warmth and company, the better to face the sea. Smoke idled from crooked chimneypots. By the time he was halfway down the length of the pier, Henry could imagine the houses shuffling together to fill the gaps; he could see greater detail; a variety of windows and widths of frontages, brave windowboxes sporting ragged bursts of greenery. He noticed with a curious pride that he could see the House of Enchantment in the distance, larger than its neighbours, with its distinctive turret worn like a hat making it markedly different from any of the others, although nothing was uniform. He imagined the streets they had walked that morning wriggling away behind this frontage into a warren of picturesque dwellings, each with a chimney stack for Santa Claus. The houses, from further back, looked as if they should have been inhabited by pixies; closer in, they had an utterly human and humane scale. Henry found himself grinning. The splendours of the big hotel, which simply disturbed the line of his vision with its obtrusive presence near the end of the pier, seemed suddenly inappropriate. Why would he want to stay there? He felt invigorated with a peculiar sense of homecoming.

There was a bulbous sculpture at the pier entrance he had not noticed before. Men and boats and fish, all of rounded shapes, were intertwined in the design. It was metal, but weathered like stone. Henry patted it in approval.

The breeze, which had died and, in its dying, lulled him into sleep, sprang back into life, and he missed the hat. He plunged downhill again, confident of his route back to the shops and the house which he decided to call home, for a day or two more at least, even with that bathroom. He wanted to be back there, watching the sky grow pink, looking at the view in reverse from his high, casement window long before dark. He noticed the details of buildings he had missed on the earlier route . . . ah, there was the library, but tomorrow would do for that. And then, turning into his path from a narrow road at the side, he saw a tall, slender woman, walking briskly away, her head and neck wrapped in a white scarf which trailed down the back of her long, dark coat. He could hear the click of heels on the pavement, louder than any other sound, but all he noticed was the luminous whiteness of the scarf. Some fine woollen cloth which drifted in the draught of her movement. A peculiar stride; it could be her. He hesitated, embarrassed and indecisive; her stride seemed to lengthen as if she was determined to increase the distance, and then Henry broke into a run. What did it matter if he touched her on the shoulder? No one could arrest him for that.

He was stiff from sitting still; the body which he forced to run at home, for the good of its health, was reluctant to cooperate. The exercise regime had slipped since his father had died; everything had, and he was wearing too many clothes for comfort. The soft leather jacket was cumbersome. The whiteness of the scarf tantalized; Henry felt he could reach it, at least draw level and glance at the face before he committed himself to a greeting. He could say *I'm sorry, but* . . . , that would make it OK; then he tripped, stumbled and fell with agonizing slowness, breaking his fall against a wall with a jarring pain in his wrist that made him yell. He landed heavily on one side, lay there, winded and blind. There would be lump on his forehead. His heart was pounding.

The sidestreet had been virtually empty, he seemed to recall, but now there was a crowd.

'Eh! That was a tumble! What's your hurry? Are you all right?'

'Oh, you've given yourself a knock. Up you come. Steady does it . . . There we are!'

It seemed as if a dozen hands were hauling him to his feet. His face was level with the wrinkled, weather-worn face of a grandmother and her arm steadied him protectively. He smiled, automatically. 'I'm sorry . . .' he began.

She grinned back. 'I should take more water with it, son, if I were you,' she said, and the other three people laughed, too, in relief. Henry felt ashamed, as if he had been drunk, falling down in the street like a bum, to be rescued by a woman a good thirty years his senior and, at the moment, twice his strength. Perhaps if he *had* stunk of booze, she would have dropped him back.

'I should get home and bathe that scratch if I were you,' she was saying authoritatively. 'Where do you live?'

'Down the shore. The rooming house with the towers. That way.' He jabbed a finger.

'I'll walk with you.' Not an invitation, a command.

And that was how Henry Evans came to be walking home, to a place he had never meant to stay, not in the company of a woman who had haunted his dreams, but with an old lady who might have been his mother.

He found himself burbling to her about Francesca Chisholm. Probably concussed; ridiculously loquacious; something to be ashamed of later. Maybe that was why he had come away, to burble to strangers in a way he could not to friends. What friends? Which of them had ever understood his overwhelming grief at losing his equally shy father? Take a week off, Henry, it'll pass. It did not pass; it was a subdued madness of grief. Go to a counsellor, Henry. No. No. No. If I have to pay somebody to listen and straighten me out, I'd rather die crooked; I don't want to be straightened out. I want to talk to *her. Because hers died, too.* And I didn't know what it could be like.

'Why's that?' Granny was holding on to his arm. He forgot what it was he was saying. They were walking on the inside pavement, with the sea, choppy but docile, safely on the other side of the road, a presence rather than a threat. If only he could concentrate on where he was. He could see the turrets of the House of Enchantment coming into focus in the distance. The Holy Grail.

'Because she'd know what I was talking about. You know what you talk about when you're twenty-two, twenty-three? Your damned parents. I criticized mine, but she was proud of hers. Loved him like mad. He wouldn't have been so different from the age I am now, I guess, Francesca's father.'

'So?' They were walking steadily but slowly. Her grip on his arm had become his grip upon hers, so he slowed even further because he did not want to stop talking. It felt like a turned-on faucet, no, he was steeped enough in English literature to know he meant a *tap*.

'She could make me talk. And I only know *now* how much I let her down. Because she knew me and loved me and then when she got the news that her father had died, I really didn't know exactly what to do. Like she was leaving me, you know? And I had a plan, so I just went ahead with it. Left her to go home alone. No idea what she felt. No idea what she was losing, where she was at. Now I do. I guess I just wanted to apologize. Tell her I tried to turn round.'

'Of course you do.' Granny stopped for breath. He looked at her for the second time. It was a fine old face, he noticed, encouraging him by attentive silence.

'She'll have kids by now. Grown-up kids, even. She had a way with them, you know?'

They had reached the door. For the last few steps he had been dragging her along and in the course of his last recitation, she had been actively trying to detach herself gently, turning away with the cautious consideration of a person about to sneeze.

'Are you all right?' he asked.

'Me? Oh yes, of course. You're home now. The boys will look after you.' She took a handkerchief out of her pocket and blew her nose. It had been quite a distance they had walked; Henry wanted to ask her in, offer tea and a ride home. But it was not his house and he did not have a car. She might live miles away. His manners were all adrift; he had talked nineteen to the dozen; he did not know if there was something he ought to do, like offer money or something; he could not even tell if he were dealing with rich, poor or middling. Confused, he was failing to notice the hardening of her tone. She was standing with her hands thrust firmly into her pockets, with something to say.

'Francesca Chisholm let that son of hers be looked after by *poofters*. Poor little sod. What are men like that doing looking after a child?' The last word was almost spat. Then Granny controlled herself. She patted his arm and attempted a smile.

'Eh, don't listen to me. You seem a nice enough man. You take care, now. No more falling over, eh? Not unless you're really pissed. No need otherwise, is there?'

'You've been very helpful . . .'

She pulled on the doorbell and hurried out of sight before it was answered. He watched her go.

The hallway was richly warm and colourful as he stepped inside; the brindled dog yapped a welcome and sniffed at his trouser leg. Tim was dressed in the voluminous jellaba, this time held at the waist by a bulky sash of green silk. There were spectacles pushed back into his hair and he was waving a ladle.

'Oh Senta, do stop. He knows you're pleased to see him. Aren't we all? Come in, Henry, come in. We were worried about you; thought you'd got lost. No sightings of you for hours. Did you enjoy the bacon and eggs? Oh dear, what have you *done*?'

Henry was a medium-sized man (Henry Evans, Mr Normal, he had once heard himself described) while Tim was tall, staring down at the lump on his forehead with great concern. 'Not *fighting*, I hope?' Tim questioned. 'Not so soon? Peter!' he yelled in a voice surprisingly deep and loud. 'Come and take over!'

The pair of them stood and surveyed him in the gaslight of the hall. Dirt on his trousers, lump on head, slight grazes on hands. They seemed to come to an unspoken conclusion, sealed by simultaneous nodding. 'Hot bath, don't you think, Tim, while you get on with supper and I deal with his clothes?' Another nod. Henry was frog-marched down the corridor, through the kitchen, into the bathroom he had loathed this morning, but which was now comfortingly warm. Tim turned on taps with a greater skill than Henry had managed when he'd secured this morning's trickle. Water gushed into the bath with the force and noise of an angry fountain; steam rose.

'Put your jacket and keks outside the door when you're ready,' Peter said. 'I'll press them. And when you're lying in the bath, try and keep this pressed against that swelling. It'll bring it down.' He handed Henry a wad of damp white muslin, smelling sweetly of lavender.

Henry did as he was told. This had become more than habitual. Handed clothes through a chink in the door, somewhat shyly, felt them plucked from his grasp and the door closed. Sank into a deep bath and held the muslin wad to his forehead. The room was clouded with steam; it was like bathing in a mist, floating free into profound warmth. From the kitchen, he could hear the radio sounding the hour . . . *beep, beep, beep* . . . followed by the echo of big Ben: *This is Radio Four news*, overlaid with conversation.

It occurred to him that he had never in his life been administered to by men, with the exception of his father when he had been a very small child, before they both grew into their gruffer courtesies, and that this sensation of being looked after, fussed over in a fashion bearing on the intimate should make him feel uncomfortable, and for a moment it did. The door opened a crack; he saw the steam rush towards it, watched as his trousers and jacket, neatly assembled on a hanger, were left on the knob and the door shut again. He told himself he should be deeply suspicious; men were not kind to men, especially strangers. It was odd, possibly sinister, but in the end, he could not be bothered to think about it.

There was too much else. Such as why – when his falling in the street, just when he was so close, had made enough noise to attract those passers-by – why had *she*, whoever she was, failed to stop? Francesca would have stopped. Even if she had thought she was being chased by an enemy, she would have stopped out of sheer curiosity.

The radio news droned on, made more important by the perfect English voice reciting it. That must have been where she learned to speak. From a glance at the back window as he rose in the steam and dried himself on a thick, rough towel, Henry could see that it was already dark. He was beginning to like this house. It had a pervasive influence of calm. It was free from all the claustrophobia he feared in strange places.

I suppose we are profoundly influenced by the surroundings in which we have lived. I sometimes think that buildings are a bigger influence on life than anything else, including people. Not that anyone here could exist without being completely indifferent to the surroundings. There are no views; only faces.

I must not think of the sea and yet, I do . . . miss it most of all. Even the sea smothered in weather with nothing but the sound of it.

I am learning new skills. It's called occupational therapy. There is even a choice, so I've opted for the entirely non-intellectual as opposed to the library, which was far too obvious. I spend my days in the kitchen where the company is not curious and there is plenty of noise to block out the sea which I cannot hear and I have worked out who to avoid. I have a friend in the kitchen; I like the smells.

Oh what drivel I write. Is this the best I can do? No, but I'm afraid to do better, I must simply do more. Steel myself for the anniversary of the day I arrived (anonymously, thank God) at this grand hotel, and all the goodbyes I shall have to say again.

Better to write about nothing much. Think of the castle and the town, but not about who lived there. Including me.

FMC

CHAPTER FOUR

'IT'S very good of you to help, Maggie,' Neil said, as he always said.

'Not at all. A pleasure.'

'I counted them in and counted them out,' he went on. 'Just like the vicar in church. Do you know, he keeps a running tally of his congregation, written down in a notebook, so that he can work out "seasonal differences"? Odd man. I would have thought it was perfectly obvious, like it is here. The colder it is, the fewer go out of doors. Doesn't matter whether they want culture, history or religious solace. Or even an excuse to wear a hat. Here we go.'

They walked through the entrance which led from the castle's shop out on to the yard beyond, the metal of his steel-capped shoes ringing on the stones. They climbed the steps to the first battlement, following the route of the tourists, past the cannons, then down the steps and round the circular wall of the inner keep. Neil picked up a couple of sweet wrappers which lay on the ground, grumbling as he did so. 'When I think of what people put in their pockets,' he muttered, 'I'm amazed they should think that a bit more litter would make any difference. Why not take it home with you? Who do they think cleans it?'

The complaining was a standard accompaniment to the last trek round the castle before Neil closed the doors for the night. Not the whole castle; that would take half a day; simply the visitors' castle, a fraction of the whole and floodlit after darkness as they entered the gloom of the third bastion, past the display and down the long tunnel to the kitchen. There were deep, black bread ovens set in a wall, a vast fireplace for open roasting in an otherwise unfurnished chamber the size of a small church, surrounded by smaller rooms with apertures in the walls for cannons and holes in the ceiling for the escape of fumes. Then down the stairs to the lower level. They were in one segment of the castle's flowered shape, five semicircular outer bastions looking out on to an empty moat, five inner for the guarding of the central keep. King Henry's fear of French invasion had persuaded him to build an impregnable fortress of cunning design. From above, it looked like an open rose built in stone, while below, any soldier who got beyond the outer walls had to face the next and then the next, and no invader had ever made it. No foreigner had ever breached the safety of the central keep, although now they came in gentle hordes to pay their money and look.

For Maggie, there was something indescribably touching about being inside a place which had once housed an aggressive village of hungry fighting men and now housed nothing other than a few of their souvenirs. It was as if the walls could only live and breathe with the help of occupants to warm it, and at night closed itself down in an enormous sulk. She knew why Neil appreciated company on the last round of the evening whenever he could get it, especially when they descended into the base of the third bastion. He might detest the tourists and love the place by day, but after dark he was afraid. Neil knew there were ghosts waiting for those prepared to recognize them, and he saw himself as cursed with that propensity. He saw ghosts everywhere; it made him an excellent storyteller, prone to wonderful embellishments for tourists, but each time he told stories about ghosts, he invented another and as soon as the creature was created in his mind, it remained in real existence. By now the place was teeming with them, especially in the runs.

The 'runs' were the corridors at the very bottom of the bastions, below sea level, leading from the centre in a curve round the base of the structure to rejoin it at the other end. *You will pass fifty-three small windows before you reach the next tunnel . . . count as you go.* Maggie could hear the words of the tourist audiotape, imagine shuffling footsteps. The lights illuminated white damp on the walls, a lump of something vaguely fungoid she would not have wanted to touch. He warned her to sidestep a puddle of water as she followed him round the narrow passage. He walked ahead, confidently, with deliberately noisy footsteps, shoulders braced, and she knew if he had been alone he would be whistling as loud as he could to warm *them*, whoever they were, to get out of the way. He was a good-looking man, from behind. It was a pity he and Angela had divorced. A terrible waste. The shoulders of him almost touched the walls on either side in the runs. Medieval man was so much smaller. She could see miniature soldiers, shorter than her own five feet four inches, running around here on the double, each ready to shove the musket through his own window, and fire. Fifty-three to each bastion, two hundred and sixty-five men with muskets, and on the level above, the cannons. Under siege, they would surely have died of noise alone; now there were only footsteps.

There were no more sweet papers, no signs of vandalism, no missing persons. They walked up the exit tunnel to the outer door, Neil obviously relieved, closing the door with a satisfied *clang*. She wondered what he would do if the smoke or burglar alarms went off at night and he was the only keyholder when the warden was away. He would hardly relish a nocturnal visit all by himself and she supposed if he were paged, he would call the police to go with him. They might not be enthusiastic either; it seemed to be men who were afraid of ghosts.

Neil gave the door an extra shove, to make sure. It was studded and bound with enough iron to keep out an army of foreign barbarians, but spirits and ghosts did not recognize such flimsy restrictions, and no door would keep them inside. She was always slightly surprised at the inconsistency of his superstitions. It seemed unreasonable to believe in the ghosts while refusing to concede that their supernatural nature meant they could not be confined. If they liked his company, or simply wished to torment him, they were surely at liberty to follow him home if they chose, but then maybe he thought that ghosts, like burglars, tended to stick to their own territory. They would be uncomfortable in Neil's tiny terraced house near the leisure centre. Like the distance across the dry moat for a soldier facing the inner keep, it would seem like a long way.

What were they like, these ghosts? she had asked. Small and pale from living in the dark, he had told her. And angry. They think everyone is an enemy. Maybe they were prisoners here. A castle has many uses. But then Neil was a mixed man. *He's not a man at all*, Angela had said in her divorce petition. *Not his fault, with diabetes and all, poor sod. He just can't get it up. Or only once in a blue moon.*

They ascended the steps back to the battlements on the far side and paused to look at the view.

The lampposts on the pier were lit, ten pairs of them like benign sentinels, delineating the length of it. There was a slight mist, blurring the lights and making the glow from the caff blur at the edges. Saturday night was party night. Out to sea, Maggie watched the hazier, moving lights of a ferry on the horizon, passing far beyond the lightship. The effect was jaunty.

'Doing something nice tonight, Neil?'

He hesitated. Sometimes he was overwhelmingly talkative, a real confessor, but not consistently. On one day he had told her all about the ghosts in great detail, and then never mentioned them again. Or, he would talk about Angela and himself, sometimes with a fury of indignation which made her wonder about his uncertain temper. *She only bloody well stayed with me so we could look like a pair and adopt . . .* or, *Poor cow, can't blame her, can I? Anyway, she helps me out here sometimes, and Tanya loves coming here. Knows it as well as I do. Can't complain, can I?* The frankness with which he revealed anything depended upon drink consumed, the place he was in, the weather conditions, the state of his incipient depression, not necessarily in that order. He could reveal more on a crowded street corner than in a closed room with the lights off, she would take a bet on that. The battlements were ideal; he felt free up here and it usually loosened his tongue.

'Well, it could be a terrific evening. Could be a disaster.'

'A woman, then,' Maggie stated.

'How did you guess? You psychic or something?'

'*Me?* Get on with you. Obvious, isn't it? Nothing is the recipe for triumph or disaster except an evening out or an evening in, for that matter, with a woman.' She shrugged. 'Or a man, in my case. Same difference, same—'

'*No.* It isn't the same. It never is the same for a man like me. You don't know what it's like. I can fancy a woman rotten; I can sense she fancies *me,* but I never know if I'm going to be able to do anything about it. Variable response, you know. Chaotic, unpredictable response, if you must know. Deeply unreliable and embarrassing, made worse by emotion, if you must know. The more I want, the less I can do. Erectile dysfunction, caused by diabetes. Try telling a woman about that the first time you kiss her.'

'Difficult.'

'Bloody impossible.'

They stared out to sea in silence. The ferry twinkled out of sight. The lightship was turning, slowly.

'Only I've been to the doctor,' Neil continued without prompting. She knew better than to prompt. 'Not for the first time, I can tell you. You've gotta go a dozen times to a dozen bloody quacks before you can find one who doesn't laugh. And then tell you to do something which doesn't hurt or make you sick. Thank God for a gay doctor. No sniggering.'

'So what's he given you?'

'Viagra. Only enough to experiment. What did you think?'

'I was asking, not thinking. This girl, does she know?'

'Know what?' Neil was defensive.

'Know what she might be in for . . .'

He shrugged. 'Not any more than I do, really. She told me the other day how she really likes the fact I'm such a gent, so sensitive and all that, but wasn't it time . . .? I'm hoping she's in for a roll in the hay with a normal bloke. That's all. And that,' he added, banging his fist against the wall so hard that he made himself wince, 'would be absolutely fucking terrific.'

She smiled at him and took a small, unobtrusive step back. There were things she wanted to know and things she didn't, but any invitation to confidence meant an invitation to the whole thing, didn't it? She couldn't select what she heard and wanted to hear, and he was a decent man, for all that. A fairly conscientious father to a child who was not his own, persisting even when Angela tried to shut him out, which she did when the going was good, calling him into play only when she and Tanya needed him.

'Well bloody good luck, read the instructions on the packet and don't take an overdose. What more can I say?' she said lightly.

They were back in the castle vestibule, facing the bridge over the moat, him switching off lights, fixing the lock. The sound of the sea, so prevalent at height, was subject here to the intermittent noise of cars on the road. She wanted to ask him about his dog but that was another sore point.

'What about you? *Saturday Night Fever* again?'

'I've got my own telly, Neil. I'll watch it on that.'

She had her own key and her own mobile phone in this phoneless house and her entry was virtually noiseless. The only dead give-away would be the smell of the wrapped fish and chips she carried or the chance encounter on the way to the far back regions of the first floor, above the kitchen and removed from everything else. She delayed on the way home, glass of wine in a pub, just to show she was alive and well. People in pubs never asked questions provided you asked them first – they were far too busy answering – but if she were to keep up this habit of social evasion, she had better get a dog. She could hide behind a dog; a dog would signal that she was not alone. Dogs deflected questions quicker than bubonic plague. Dogs in this place could become the most abiding topic of conversation. If she got a dog, she could hide out with other dog owners and talk of nothing else.

'Shhhhh,' she said to Senta, once inside the door. She paused on the landing, arrested by the voices from the dining room. The vicar, the baker, the candlestick maker, but particularly the American saying something in his shy accent which made them laugh and her flee to the shelter of her own room where she closed the door, firmly. Corkscrew, salt, pepper, TV, all there. The rest of the world, the English Channel included, could live entirely as it wished, provided, until morning, it left her alone. In the morning, she would be braver.

But the televison programmes were inane; they could not begin to hold her attention. She refilled the wine glass and began to write the letter, all over again.

Dear Philip,
    I hope all's well with you and the love affair has lasted. I just wanted you to know there never were any hard feelings, whatever I might have said at the time. I really just want you to be happy . . .

She took a large slug of the wine. *No, I DON'T want you to be happy. I want you to be non-existent. If I weren't so full of funerals, I'd dream of yours, but it wouldn't be the same, would it, standing round as the EX partner, while some other bitch is allowed the lion's share of the grief.*

She continued: So, if you're happy, I'm happy for you . . . best of luck darling . . .

You bastard, you cold-hearted stinker. You never knew me; you never wanted to know Me. What about Me? You DISTRACTED me, when I should have been paying attention to someone far more important than you. You never helped. I needed someone who would HELP.

She blew her nose. Scribbled through the lines, then began writing again.

*Over the mountains and over the waves, Under the fountains
    and under the graves,
Under floods that are deepest, which Neptune obeys;
Over rocks that are steepest, Love will find out the way.*

And then with her hand scribbling faster, fresh wine in her glass,

*I'm jilted forsaken, outwitted, Yet think not I'll whimper or
brawl – The lass is alone to be pitied, Who ne'er has been courted
at all . . .*

That was much better. And there were other things to think about. Such as what to do next. How to handle the next stage. Thinking of Philip was merely filling a gap. Trying to stuff the holes in the heart.

'What an extraordinary man you are, Henry! A scientist with an interest in the arts, a knowledge of English poetry, you said, and a burning desire to explore English castles! What a pleasure to have you among us! How long is your contract with Fergusons?'

'Well, that's a question of how long is a piece of string. I have to suck it and see,' Henry said earnestly. 'I mean I have to see if I like it; they have to see if they need me . . .'

'Developing a new drug?'

'Well, maybe improving an old one . . .'

'He's probably doing highly *secret* research into how to make Viagra work for women, or other pedigree animals otherwise reluctant to breed,' Peter said mildly. 'Or genetically engineering vegetables,' he added, offering more potatoes and then wagging a finger at the vicar. The vicar, Henry noticed, was just as an English vicar should be; he could have stepped from the pages of an Agatha Christie novel with his high voice, precise gestures, half-moon spectacles and domed forehead which would require the protection of a panama hat in high summer. He also had an aversion to sherry and a huge appetite for wine shared by the rest of the guests which, along with the mobile phone in the shirt pocket, made him differ a little from stereotype.

Also attending the elegant dining table of the House of Enchantment was a haughty woman who reminded Henry of some ruined actress or other; someone whose face had seen better days and whose thin figure was swathed in layers of gauze. The widow of a locally eminent artist, Tim had whispered on the way down-stairs from inveigling Henry out of his top room. You must meet her. Don't say I told you, but whenever she's hard up, she fakes a couple of his paintings and says she found them in the attic. Then there was a beautiful young man who had remained silent, eating and drinking steadily, impervious to the constant buzz around him. There were no pockets of conversation; no one person of the six spoke exclusively to another without interruption, and mostly they all talked at once. The effect was slightly dizzying and Henry was enjoying himself immensely. His second night in a new town, and already he was in the middle of a party. Must be his charm.

'Wife and family at home, Henry? Will they be joining you?'

'No. *No.*' That came out a little sharper than he intended. There was a second's silence.

'I always think there's an ulterior motive for travelling,' the vicar went on smoothly. 'Some inner journey of the soul which becomes imperative. Some *need* which nothing else can satisfy. Or why

would we ever leave the comfort of our own homes and the benediction of the familiar?'

'Oh, fiddlesticks,' said the artist's widow. 'People travel because
it's fun. Or for very simple reasons. My husband travelled to
foreign parts because he said the light was better. Really, it was
because he was so loathed at home. Frightful man. Me, I travel to
get away from my children. Otherwise I might kill them.'

There was general laughter at that. The widow spoke with a
fetching drawl.

'Pity Francesca Chisholm didn't do the same,' the vicar said
solemnly. He seemed determined to add a little gravitas to the
occasion. 'Poor woman.'

'Poor woman!' the widow yelled. 'Poor woman, be damned!
She had a tough time, drew a short straw with that child of hers,
but who doesn't? Every child's a monster. Doesn't seem sufficient
excuse to *murder* it. If it was that bad, she could have got someone
else to look after it.'

The silent young man looked up from the action of clearing his
plate and gave an exaggerated shudder. 'I really don't think *murder*
is a suitable subject to raise at a dinner party,' he remarked in a
melodious voice. 'Especially in front of our welcome stranger. Mr
Evans will think it happens all the time, but it doesn't, you know.
Hardly ever. Once in a blue moon, here. Not like New York.' He
smiled beatifically, inviting a defence.

'New York's safer than London,' Peter volunteered helpfully,
covering Henry's silence. Henry was looking peculiar, stretching
his face into a reciprocal smile, unable to speak. His throat was suddenly swollen; he was about to choke. He nodded, speechlessly.

'How can that possibly be, with all those guns?' the widow
demanded belligerently.

Henry was feeling cold and slightly less welcome than he had
been half an hour earlier, discussing seventeenth-century verse
and castles with the vicar. The room was warmed by a roaring fire;
his face was flushed and his feet were chilled. The bruise on his
forehead throbbed.

'What difference do weapons make?' the young man asked, suddenly communicative, as if he had been unable up until now to eat and talk at the same time. 'It's the attitude to life which counts. I mean, if you want to kill someone, you'll do it, won't you? All Francesca Chisholm had to do was throw her baby off the pier—'

'It wasn't a *baby*,' Peter interrupted. His face had a purple tinge and he was angry. 'It was a five-year-old, much-loved *child*.'

This time the silence stretched for longer. 'Sorry,' the young man mumbled. 'Sorry, I forgot. You used to babysit, didn't you?'

'Yes.' Tim, this time, sounding terse.

'Well, a prayer for the dear deceased, I think,' the vicar intoned diplomatically, crossing himself and bowing his head. 'And talk of happier things.'

'Such as pudding,' Tim said brightly. 'Will you all hand your plates this way, please?'

There was a clatter of compliance, murmurs of *delicious*, a piling of forks and knives, all travelling from hand to hand towards Tim's end of the table. Senta the dog, banished to the hall, yapped from beyond the door in anticipation of scraps, and in the activity and resumption of chatter, Henry leaned forward to the young man, swallowed rapidly and spoke in a whisper.

'This . . . Francesca . . . Was this a long time ago? Where does she live now?'

'Oh not very far away.' He plucked a grape from the fruitbowl centrepiece. 'Cookham prison since last year, actually. Good Lord, almost a year to the day. She'll be there for life, I expect. Where else could she be except in prison?'

'And she really killed her child? Not an accident or anything?'

The young man picked another grape, chewed carefully, obviously approving the taste.

'Oh no. It was all quite deliberate. She stuffed him through a broken floorboard of the fishing platform on the pier. Have you seen our pier yet? You must, you know. It is quite bizarrely 1950ish. And it's sinking.'

Henry felt sick. He waited for the pudding to arrive, and then excused himself politely.

The wine did it. Bad breakfast food, rich supper food, *fucking foreigners*. French wine, purchased on the other side of the Channel, bargain prices, better value. They had all talked about bargains; everyone, everywhere talked about bargains. But not in the same breath as talking about Francesca. Not *his* Francesca. Of course it was wine. His chronic weak stomach should never be treated with wine, although it did make him sleepy. His stomach liked bourbon and vitamins, precious little else. He might have told *her* that, given the chance. Hey, Frannie, remember how I always got sick in India and you found the Ayurvedic doctor who fixed me up? You sure were good at fixing things . . . you used all your money to pay for those kids to go, too. That was when I got you the shawl, because you'd given yours away. Ideal for a backpack, a ring shawl, because it folds away to nothing. See? You can drag all two metres of it though a wedding ring; it floats softer than silk, but it keeps you warmer than . . . toast, you said. And it's far too expensive, you said. Especially since I bought two for you, one to use and one to keep for best.

Henry lurched towards the tiny toilet which served the remoteness of the top two floors, inconveniently situated between the two on a half-landing, just so everybody had to travel up or down a flight. *Travel broadens the mind. Fuck travel.* And you know what, Francesca, you know what I did when my father died? I went out and bought another shawl, not for me, just a kind of talisman to remind me I'd once been generous. Bought it here to give you, and yes you are right about the expense. In Boston, they cost a small fortune.

He retched and delivered the roast lamb of a dinner almost whole and entire into the bowl of the toilet. *Lav, lavatory, ladies, gents, netty, the heads, the loo, the bog, but NEVER the rest room. Why do you call it that?* Ancient questions on an Indian patio. *We call it the rest room because you can take a rest in it. What? In a loo? Nobody rests in a loo.*

Henry rested. Flushed the bowl, wrapped his gown around him

and let his head rest against the ice-cold wall of the narrow room. This was wine and travelling and getting bummed out everywhere and it had nothing whatever to do with grief. He wasn't having anything to do with grief. *Grief as in mourning?* Grief. He had a poor stomach, was all, and yet he was here, sobbing like a crazy boy coming down from drugs, sobbing maybe because he needed more, sobbing for his father and the words of a poem she had sung him on an evening full of fireflies. *When there is no place, For the glow worm to hide, Where there is no space for receipt of a fly; Where the midge dare not enter, Lest herself fast she lay, If Love come he will enter, And soon find out his way.*

Sentiment, bloody sentiment. He knew the sobbing was loud and uncontrolled; he would have fled upstairs if there had been any prospect of an embarrassed eavesdropper, even the damn dog. Henry had manners, even *in extremis*, which was more than he felt he had witnessed in the English he had admired from afar for so long. Finally he moved, stiff with cold, made sure the place was left clean in his wake, another automatic response, and clambered into his high bed. The fire they had lit in his room had died, leaving a faint, residual warmth. The fur hot water bottle comforted his feet. He had a dim memory of looking down that stairwell and seeing the same shawl draped over the bottom post. He took the shawl he had bought out of his bag and draped it over the covers. It seemed pale and insignificant beside the silk.

It was the wine did it. Just that one glass too many. Enough to wake her, make her restless, prowling round her rented room, dreaming without regret of the house she had once had and then looking at her handwriting, looped sloppily over the page, filling it with self-pitying rubbish and a memory of poetry learned in school and related to cousin Francesca in the holidays. Always seeking approval; anything to please. Always listening to Francesca, the fountain of wisdom, even when Francesca said, stay with your husband, Maggie; he'll get over his infatuation and men need forgiveness. They may need it, she remembered shouting, but they don't necessarily deserve it, do they? Yours left, didn't he? He left because he couldn't stand the image of himself in his horribly flawed child, so what qualifies you to give advice?

Maggie did not want to think about Francesca. She did not want to think of Francesca's crossing the road to punch the boy who had thrown a firework at her, or Francesca lending the right clothes for the occasion and saying she looked marvellous even when she didn't. Or Francesca encouraging her to take the exams, or Francesca leading out the kids from the primary school where she taught. Nor could she bear to think of Francesca's devotion to neurotic Angela Hulme and her adopted daughter, or of all the mess and the shame and the obligations Francesca had left behind. Maggie wanted to dwell on her own fractured life and reach a point where she could start to mend it, without creating a whole new set of complications as she was doing now. She also needed to sleep a whole night from start to finish and not wake up in the middle with a raging thirst and an unaccountable desire for a bath.

Or to find she could not get into the loo because the man was locked inside it sobbing. Maggie listened for a long time, troubled and disturbed by his misery, wanting to knock on the door, but waiting until the sound became controlled before she returned quietly to her own room, draped the shawl over her nightdress, grabbed a towel and went the long flights downstairs.

Timothy was sitting at the kitchen table, smoking a cigarette, staring into space. Clean plates were marshalled next to him. Maggie had watched the laborious, washing by hand process; she had even helped, and she marvelled at the industry this impoverished pair put into the creation of an elegant and eccentric lifestyle. It was comfortable to live here but humbling to contemplate the effort it took, she thought a trifly sourly, surprised to see him there at all, especially with a cigarette. Tim didn't usually allow himself such luxuries: all luxuries were saved for others or the dog.

'Any hot water?'

'A bit, maybe. I used most of it for the dishes.'

'Damn.'

He waved the cigarette. 'Vicar left them.' She sat down.

'Good party?'

'Oh yes. Until someone started talking about Francesca. Seemed to upset the paying guest. And Peter and me, too.'

'Damn. Ah well. He had to know. Jumping the gun a bit, but at least the discovery looks accidental. Is it very wrong to use him like this?'

'No. Yes. No. I don't know what you have in mind, you haven't said, so I doubt if you know.'

DAMN Francesca. If only people would stop talking about her. Francesca and Harry, her boy, the ghosts at every feast. She made unwilling conspirators of them all.

'It's like cookery,' Tim said. 'All experiments are fine. As long as they work. But you shouldn't use people for ingredients.'

'No,' she said, slowly. 'Not unless they volunteer.'

The light woke him. A unique kind of light he had never seen before, but had somehow imagined as peculiar to the sea and part of the reason why he had craved to live close to the ocean. It made nothing of the fear of being enclosed. A lake was not the same. He could always see to the other side and that limited it in his imagination. Lakes and rivers were for respectable traffic from bank to bank, not for the risk of being lost without bearings, without sight of land, drifting with the current. It was only the sea which was suitable for high endeavour and escape.

The sky which glowed outside was luminously white. It pressed against the windows and the glass seemed to bulge inwards in meek resistance. It forced his eyes open; it was like white smoke, thick, dense, unyielding, almost brighter than sunlight. For the second morning in succession, Henry got out of bed and went to look.

Nothing. A vast expanse of nothing, the intensity of the light hurting his eyes. He looked at his watch: 0700 hours. Not early by the standards of a hard-working commuter, but all life, all movement, was dead. Until he heard the rumble of the sea and the more specific sound of an engine. Discernible in the mist, a rubbish cart was at work in the road below, *thump, crump,* the engine revving, ready to move, a *clang* of metal. Henry could make out the squat machine and take a guess at the colour. Some kind of municipal green. It moved on, stopping a few doors down. Henry looked ahead and then right, turning his head deliberately to make sure there was nothing he missed. There was nothing to see. A dense fog of sky, descending all the way to earth, no contours, no landmarks, no visible life, no nothing. He squinted and peered to see if the pier would appear out of the heavenly white murk, but there was no sign of it. The scene invited him to walk into a pleasant and mysterious oblivion. There was a little excitement as he put on his clothes and searched for the hat before he remembered it was lost and he had not replaced it. Forgot to take the daily dose of vitamins and minerals, or think how he might get back in if no one else was awake, tiptoed downstairs and out the front door before the dog could bark, determined to know what it was like to be out in *this,* with no one else alive.

The air filtered into his throat like a prickly thistle, so raw and sharp it made him gasp. From upstairs, the white mist looked warm. The cold was intense until he started to walk, and then it was damp rather than freezing. He knew exactly where he was going, but he was not sure why, which seemed the way it was in this town. This was a different world, everything about it surreal.

He walked briskly. Gradually, the outlines of the seafront houses became less obscure; he could recognize the occasional front door and dripping leaves in windowboxes muted into pale shades by the mist. He crossed the road without looking left or right. No need; no sound, but he could see the beginnings of the pier. Even the noise of the wallowing sea was muted by the weight of the mist. Henry liked that. He loved to be without barriers or walls; no sense of distances, nothing to close him in. The monument of the fisherman, melded gloriously with his fish and his boat, looked like a guardian of the gate. Henry walked on. It was suitable weather to be on an edifice like the deck of a ship. Eyes adjusted to anything, to extremes of light as well as dark, and the more he looked and the less the damp air raked his throat, the more he could see. Sinister things, like the signs attached to the stubby little lamp-posts, black with white lettering. RISK OF DEATH. NO JUMPING. NO DIVING. There were less prominent signs on the bins attached below. *Litter, please place here.* Before you jump. A green umbrella and a picnic box lay abandoned on one of the benches.

He needed to see those fishing platforms which flanked the caff at the end. Needed to, needed to, needed . . . He remembered them from yesterday, thinking how much Dad would have liked all that, how he would have chatted to those ageless anglers who grinned and got out of the way, careful to look before they cast. He needed to see what it was really like. See if the mist made soft.

Looking over the locked gate which led to the platform on the left of the caff, he could see that the tide was far higher than when he had been here last. The slurry sea looked as if it was oiled beyond the breaking of a wave, smooth on the surface but churning and boiling beneath like some giant, artificially quiet, industrial-strength washing machine doing serious business and resenting interference. The whole edifice was closer to the water than he remembered: the legs seemed shorter, the sea so close it splashed up through the broken boards. He was close enough to see the dimensions and the mist was beginning to break up and swirl like spun sugar. The missing boards, visible by the gaps they made, like missing teeth in a mouth, were obvious in their absence, but none of the boards were uniform in size, any more than a canine to an incisor. As the mist cleared in a teasing way, and then rolled back in gorgeous wisps, wreathed around the iron rail he clutched for support, he could see that the floor of the platform was a patchwork of wooden boards, metal boards of different age and size and colour, replaced and repaired only as time and weather dictated. There was a sign: KEEP OUT.

How would an *average* five-year-old boy manage to *slip* through one of these gaps? The five-year-old boy he had once been himself could not have slipped through these gaps with any degree of ease; his skinny shoulders would get in the way even if his hips and fat tummy could make it. He would have to breathe and wriggle to go willingly, which was possible in the course of a game. You would do anything in the course of a game or a dare when you did not want to look a fool. Even so, it looked a struggle to wriggle like that, with the sea almost tickling the ankles and wood splinters but yes, a boy could do it. A boy was like an eel, with a skin immune to the feeling of a graze.

Especially a boy who came out here to play on a morning like this, only when it was warm, not cold like now. Prancing out from a nearby house, running down the length of the *Titanic*, saying, *I dare you!*, on a summer's day. *Yeah!* You go first, you older boy, then I *must*. The presence of an iron railing would be no barrier at all. Henry had done that, grabbed the swinging rope off the forbidden oak tree in someone else's back yard, swung into terrifying space without a single scream. Got his bruises, all right. Would have been an awful father himself, because he would have mollycoddled his own son from doing any such damn thing, just like his dad didn't, and for all that, he was still timid.

He could see it. Clutched the iron rail, forced himself to look down. The distance was small, but the sea was immense. The abiding fears of his life ranged from awe when faced with open spaces and the far more acute, claustrophic fear of being enclosed. Claustrophobia was the bane of his life, the devil which sat on his shoulder, trained into submission only most of the time. He could tolerate lifts and aeroplanes through the application of logic and keeping his eyes on a page; he could sit in small rooms jammed with people and keep his eyes on their faces, telling himself it was temporary; he could enter a long tunnel provided he could see the other end; could kid himself the devil had died, and then there would be a panic so blind he could not even scream. He breathed deeply; the air no longer tore at his throat. He felt calm. There was an explanation. He breathed deep. It did not hurt. Nothing could hurt here. A child had fallen, tragically. The mist would bandage wounds.

It muffled noise. He thought he had seen that same black dog trotting ahead and disappearing, but apart from that illusion, had not seen a single living soul in the fifteen minutes which had got him so far, and he did not hear her, either. He was in the frame of mind where he could tell himself he was the only soul on a small planet, looking at a place where a child had *slipped*, until the last second when he sensed her approach. Turned and saw her coming towards him out of the mist. A long-limbed, swift walking person with a pale shawl round her head, striding towards him with a determined step. He looked around, wildly, like a cornered rat in search of a shelter. The footsteps, and the shape, came on.

Her to the life, with the baggy khaki trousers and the slouching coat and the air of authority. Francesca. *You've got to go home, Henry. How can you get satisfaction from being a novelty? If you want to know what you are, Henry, you have to go home.*

The very soul of aristocratic womanhood was striding towards him, almost breaking into a gallop, the sort of woman who had always intimidated him until he met Francesca. Taller than he remembered. He wanted to run, but on this little road out to the sea there was nowhere to go. He also wanted to laugh at the reversal of tactic: the day before he had been chasing *her* and now she was advancing on him like a ghostly witch. He had a sudden impression that she was going to walk straight through him and hover above the platform. And then the spectre was beside him, standing too close for comfort, staring at him. She had Francesca's colouring, at close quarters, a lopsided version of her features, nose, eyes, mouth, younger than he would have imagined, older than he dreamed, and a voice which bore slight resemblance. She had highlighted, curly hair with nothing sleek about it; she was statuesque and groomed, her coat matched her shoes, she was completely different. Francesca resisted the camera; it made the last image of her all the more memorable. He was frightened of this appalling facsimile, but when she spoke, she only sounded anxious, flustered and shy.

'Oh God, Mr Evans. You had me worried there. What the hell are you doing out here?'

'Who are you?'

'I'm Maggie. You sounded so upset last night, all that sobbing . . . I thought . . . well I thought you might be going to jump. You're not, are you?'

'Of course not.'

The resemblance to Francesca was passing and fading into nonsense. This face was pale, hers had been as brown as a nut. The voice was so harshly different. His recall of the face might be flawed, but this woman was bigger and surely taller. He could never forget standing next to Francesca and the top of her head being level with his cheek. It was only the stride and drifting shawl. The hair, brownish gold, tinted, grew from a different and bigger head.

'What *are* you doing, then?' she demanded, stridently.

He felt faintly hysterical, reminded of his own long suppressed sense of the ridiculous. This long-limbed woman was seeming to suggest that anyone on the pier without company must be contemplating suicide. As if there was nothing else to do, such as fish, take pictures of the mist, wait for the caff to open, contemplate. He was about to bark back a wisecracking response about this being a free country, until he remembered that his motives for being here were dubious by anyone's standards, including his own.

'I came to see where that child slipped through the boards and drowned.'

She gazed at him hard, hesitated, and then nodded, resolved on something. Her shoulders seemed to slump in relief and a brief look of annoyance crossed her face. Then she shrugged. The slightest movement made her hair move. She had plenty of hair.

'This side. They mend each platform, every other year.'

She led the few steps across the concrete width of the pier until they leaned over the black painted railings on the other side. The boards twenty feet below were smooth and wet, solid, pale and complete. The sleeve of her coat touched his.

'There were holes in the boards last year. The boy got out of the house by himself, must have annoyed her. And he didn't slip. Post-mortem results showed he was pushed. Oh, he may have slipped initially, but then he was shoved the rest of the way. Really shoved, no messing about. His shoulders were dislocated and his ribs cracked. Someone pushed him through the hole. He was alive and bleeding by the time he hit the water. Then he drowned, but not right away. He bled a lot. The fishing boat picked him up, even though no one had raised the alarm. It was this time of the morning. She lived in the flats near the castle. Quite a change from the castle where she used to live. Francesca must have gone straight home, after she'd done it.'

'No,' he said. 'That is *crap*. Complete and utter *crap*.' He was looking at the churning water, listening to the sound of it, imagining the ice cold of its embrace. Hitting the water, hurt and terrified. The woman was leaning closer, speaking loudly into his ear, enunciating clearly and slowly.

'*Yes*. Francesca was quite adamant about what had happened. She *confessed*, Mr Evans. She insisted. The boy had cerebral palsy, spastic hemiplegia to be exact. He was hell to take care of, she couldn't stand it any more. She told them how she did it. She pleaded guilty to his murder. She *insisted*.'

She paused. Henry could see white fists, protruding from her coat sleeves, gripping the black rail.

'Francesca pushes the kid through a gap too narrow for his body,' he said, surprisingly calm as if he were voicing a question of merely scientific interest. 'She *shoves* him. The kid's five years old. They're strong. Damn strong.'

He could sense, rather than see, how she shook her head, the curls almost touching his face.

'Not this one. Not very. He had paralysis down the right side, malfunctioning right arm and leg. She said she stamped on the weak side and down he went. Gentle encouragement.'

Henry moved away from her abruptly and vomited. His stomach was empty; the involuntary effort produced nothing but bile.

'I did what I could for her at trial.' Maggie's unfamiliar voice continued crisply. 'At least I got them to leave out *some* of the more gruesome facts. Not that it makes any difference in a guilty plea to murder. Life imprisonment, regardless of the age of the deceased. At least we don't hang people any more.'

He wanted to disbelieve her and he wanted to get away from her. Henry began to walk back towards the seafront. He folded his arms and clutched at the comforting leather of his jacket. He watched his own polished shoes putting one step in front of another and made himself concentrate on keeping his feet marching at a regular pace and in a straight line, realizing as he concentrated that he was moving faster and faster and any moment now he might break into a run and hit something, unless he slowed down and looked up. Heard the sound of a car on the road, and found she had kept level with him all along. He felt furiously inclined to take a swing at her, simply bat her away and listen to her fall, but then there was a dim memory of violence, so recently described, which made him ashamed of that impulse, too. Not that he believed a word of it. Henry had come in search of a good woman, or at least an *interesting* sinner, not a bitch who killed children.

He let her take hold of his coat. She was smiling at him and all he wanted to do was spit.

'You don't have to believe me, Henry,' she was saying. 'You can check it all out in the library. You never have to believe what you *see*. And then you can go home, if you want.'

He was leaning against a lamppost, the pier behind him. There was a stone in his shoe.

'You will go home, won't you?'

It sounded like a plea, but he could not guess what it was she was hoping he might do. Henry could see his suitcase in the hall, today or tomorrow, but soon. He hesitated.

'I can't believe a woman like Francesca was could ever be so barbaric.'

'We've all had difficulties with that, Mr Evans. Which has nothing to do with anything, does it? *She* believes it.'

'But I *knew* her,' Henry said. 'I *loved* her.'

'Loving someone,' Maggie said bitterly, 'has never been a guarantee of their virtue. Not even if they behave like a child.'

You should not be promiscuous with love. Or even with liking. You should not try to help everyone because you end up letting half of them down. You shouldn't be good; you should only be loyal and build on that, brick by brick.

Did I leave any clues as to the depravity of my existence? No. I parcelled it all up and sent it to people who would not look at it, everything. Those were the days when I was in control.

It is something of a relief not to be NEEDED. To be superfluous. I was always so managerial. But the sense of loss of any real role at all makes me so agitated that tranquillizers are advised. They should stop me pacing at this time of night rather than writing. I should have had them in my other life, suppressed some of that bossy energy, but if they make me stay still, perhaps I'll write more. About anything except Harry and T.

It is so HOT in here. I long to be cold.

FMC

CHAPTER FIVE

THERE was no one walking, other than those accompanied by dogs. Henry formed the impression of a series of dogs leading their subservient owners on well worn routes. The dogs seemed alert, the owners on autopilot. Henry concentrated on the dogs to suppress the bile which kept gathering at the back of his throat.

It was the dogs that got the owners out of the houses. Henry was realizing that he knew very little of how other people lived. He would have to maintain a twenty-four-hour surveillance, repeated at intervals during all four seasons of the year, to get a single idea of how they behaved, and even then all he would have observed was public habit, peculiar enough in its own right but not particularly revealing. You learned so little by simply watching. You could learn how to rob a place, but not what was in it. All he could see at the moment was the fact that the few stalwart elderly and early-rising occupants of Warbling, *en route* to the newspaper shop, were roughly the same shades of grey as their dogs, and all of them needed grooming. He felt angry and sick.

'Coffee?' Maggie was saying briskly, clutching his arm again, as if she belonged, or as if he himself was a wilful pet. 'Awful coffee, but warm?'

'Who did you say you were?'

'I told you. I'm Maggie.' She was standing with her hands on her hips, impatient, but not unsympathetic. That look of annoyance again, as if she was disappointed in him. 'By definition, a very part time lawyer of this parish, colleague of Edward Burns. Status: recently divorced and deliberately homeless. A fellow lodger of yours, in case you hadn't noticed. But I'm much more famous for being Francesca Chisholm's cousin. Do you want this filthy coffee or not? Or are you just going to stand there looking pale and interesting?'

He nodded.

There was one establishment open, although 'functioning' was how Henry might have described it in a more lucid moment, but only just. A burger bar with steaming windows, facing the road, and next to the newspaper shop which was attracting the dogs. There were three occupants, with faces variously hidden behind the *Mail*, the *Times* and the *Express*. Beneath a sign which announced NO DOGS, he and she stepped over the large, unleashed specimen which lay draped over the step, eyes glaring mournfully through the glass. When Henry sat, he could feel the sad eyes of the dog scrutinizing him. Maggie came back with a tray. As she sat opposite, he was wondering how it was he could ever have confused her with Francesca.

'Where did you get that shawl?' was all he could ask, sipping coffee which was even worse than she had hinted, weak but bitter at the same time. She fingered the fine, creamy wool round her neck, with the hint of embroidery hidden in the folds, and looked at him in surprise, temporarily lost for words.

'Francesca gave it to me,' she said hurriedly. 'She had several of them. They were part of her hallmark, really. When Harry was a baby, she would wrap him in one—'

'*Harry?* He was called *Harry?* Why the hell would she call him Harry?'

'I've no idea,' Maggie said. 'But I doubt it was a tribute to a long-lost friend. He was born in the shadow of the castle, and she once lived in the castle and a King Henry built the castle, I suppose. And we have a Prince Harry . . .'

'Oh.' He felt foolish, even imagining there could have been the slightest association between this dead child and himself, some half-assed, sentimental memory of his existence influencing her choice. Silly thought, stemming only from Maggie's remarks about shawls. Something he'd done right, then, giving Francesca those shawls. She had obviously liked them, made them into a lifelong habit, might have appreciated the one he had brought with him. She had wrapped her baby in a shawl, killed it . . .

Henry's hand trembled round the rim of his mug. Anger. He was incredibly angry with her for besmirching her own memory; remembered what that other lawyer had advised him for free: *better regard her as dead*. He sipped the coffee and absorbed a smell of burning toast. There was a king size loaf of saggy white bread on the counter; Henry shuddered. The food he had eaten at the House of Enchantment was the best; he had interspersed it with the worst. It was not only his mind that was being poisoned.

'I can take you to the castle if you like,' Maggie was saying, over-brightly. 'It's interesting if you like that kind of thing. I presume you do, or you wouldn't be here. I mean, you didn't come all this way to find Francesca, did you? There must be *something* else about us, I mean about this place, which captured your imagination.'

She was speaking so quickly, accelerating as she went, that he had difficulty following, but the voice was so clipped and effort-lessly patrician he wanted to mimic it, the way he had once tried to mimic Francesca's, and she his, although he had never been able to master her ability to produce sentences as if they were fully formed. She never said, it's *kinda* like this, if you know what I mean . . . She never said *I dunno*, or *I just need to think about this*. She had spoken her statements and her observations as if she had thought about them first, even if she retracted them later. It had seemed archaic to him then, her articulate and entirely certain manner of speech, but all it had been was fluent.

'Can I ask you something?'

'Certainly.'

'She told me, I mean, Francesca told me, that when they sat around as kids, having meals and all, her dad would correct them if they didn't get their grammar right. I mean, when they were three or four he started doing that. And he made them learn poetry by heart. Do you know if he did? Sounds like some kind of tyrant to me.'

She shook her head. A stray hair floated across his vision and landed on the Formica table top. He stared at it, trying in his mind to describe the colour, attempting at the same time to recall some of Francesca's anecdotes about her father which had coloured his opinions of the man, made it so inexplicable that she should be so distraught at the late-arriving news of his death. Then he remembered how he had spent so much of his time slagging off his own parent for being a reactionary jerk who liked fishing and understood *nothing*. It was only time which had altered his perceptions and allowed admiration to intrude.

'Did he do that?' he repeated.

She shrugged. 'Yes. I wasn't his daughter and I was a few years younger than her. All I know is that if he corrected his wife and daughter and yes, he was a stickler for all kinds of protocol, even at the breakfast table, he married it with a quite uncanny charm. He insisted on good manners and *clear* speech, no mumbling. Strict about that. Talk in phrases, child, that's what they are for, you must make yourself *understood*. That aside, he taught me how to cheat at cards and play a tune on the recorder in an afternoon. He was a rather charismatic man, I recall, a feature certainly inherited by his daughter. There was nothing tyrannical about him. He was a born teacher, like her. Could've taught pigs to fly. Probably did.'

Henry spooned sugar into his coffee. An improvement to the taste which he could feel, furring a tube somewhere.

'I could tell you all sorts of things about the locality,' Maggie went on. 'And all Francesca's people if you want to know. They're all over the place. Over there –' she pointed to where a dark-haired man sat with his newspaper. 'That's Neil. He was married to

Angela, who was Francesca's best friend.' She waved at him; he waved back, dismissively. 'Not very sociable this morning, he'll be thinking of his fishing. And then there's – oh, I'm sorry, you're upset.' She drank her coffee with gusto. 'Forgive me for eavesdropping on your conversation with Edward Burns yesterday, but eavesdropping is a necessary habit.'

'Yes. I can tell.'

'You've so much to see before you leave, Henry, may I call you that? You should start at once. The castle opens at nine; Angela does Sunday mornings, so they'll let us in early, and anyway, you've just consumed enough sugar to energize a horse. Shall we go?'

'Why not?' She was bossy, but he did not want to be alone. Anything was preferable to that. Alone he would slump; accompanied, he could listen, recover his wits.

The mist had cleared into a haze and the sun persisted in adding a benign and gentle glow. Inside the steaming burger bar, there was an illusion of warmth, dispelled as soon as they hit the air. The February sun cheered without heat, nothing but a teasing foretaste of spring.

'We can walk, or drive,' Maggie said. 'I've brought my car, but normally I walk everywhere.'

'Like most people, I guess.'

'Isn't that strange for you?'

'No. Yes. No stranger than anything else. I mean it *is* strange, but it doesn't feel strange,' Henry said, thinking of the daily routine he had abandoned at home. Into the car in the morning, back home in the car in the evening and he remembered his fear of the traffic jams. He had not been behind the wheel of a car in days and liked not having to think about it. He felt incapable of hurrying, just as on the day before he had felt incapable of running. He looked at Maggie, walking on his left on the outside of the pavement as if she was protecting him, slowing her steps to match his own. In the normal run of events, it would have been he who was brisk and precise; now he felt weighted down with dismal knowledge.

'The best way to approach the castle is from the sea,' she was saying. He followed her down steps on to the beach. The beach banked steeply; the sea was close and calm. The walking was slower still: Henry could see this heavy-footed treading over loose stones as a punishing exercise. The shingle yielded at each step with a crunching sound which reminded him of someone eating breakfast cereal. It was a satisfying noise, marking slow progress which could not be hurried. He stopped, picked up a pebble and lobbed it into the water. She followed suit: hers went further. Henry selected a larger, more aerodynamic stone, flung it. This time it outdistanced hers and disappeared with an audible plop, encouraging him to follow with another and another. So did she. Then they threw simultaneously and the stones entered the water at almost the same spot and same second.

'A draw,' she said, slightly breathless, turning up the slope they had slithered down.

'Quits,' he said. *Crunch, crunch, crunch.* I'll do that whenever I'm tired, Henry thought. Come down to the ocean and toss pebbles into it. Such a pointless, therapeutic activity, they should make a drug to match it.

'No one could make an exactly quiet approach to this castle, could they?' he volunteered through the noise of their steps. 'How could anyone get close enough to take them by surprise? They'd be heard right away.'

'And seen.'

'If I were the enemy,' Henry said, 'I'd ignore the damn castle, get my men ashore further down the coast and come around the back way.'

'You'd still have to get into the castle.'

'That's what bribes are for.'

'You know what, Henry? You talk like a woman.'

They were walking the circumference of a massive wall, low enough for them to stare over the fifty feet of wintry grass which separated it from the main body of the castle. The whole edifice began far below them, lower than sea level, and looked as if it had been excavated from beneath the ground, discovered complete and fully formed, exactly as it was. Henry paused to remove a stone from his shoe and when he looked up again, the grey-green walls of the bastion seemed higher and darker than before. The muzzle of a black cannon peeped at him over a plain parapet, the mouth of it filled with red. It looked like a toy placed carefully on a model, ready for someone to play with. The wooden drawbridge was quaint and the great iron-studded oak doors were almost beautiful below an arched ceiling of figured red brick. Maggie pointed out the holes in the mellow stone above.

'Those are for the boiling oil on your head if you got this far. Did she tell you she lived here?'

'Yes, she did.'

'Well, it was true.'

And she turned into a murderess, Henry thought, trying not to think about it. Maggie kicked the door as if she owned the place, and as if in tribute to her command the right side moved outwards, slowly, pushed from behind. It was not fully opened, but enough for a child to step through. The most beautiful girl child he had ever seen, her face so purely medieval that in this setting, it shocked him. The skin was white with lips so red they could have been painted; she had enormous, unblinking eyes which regarded him with hostility, and a mass of chestnut curls sprang from her neat skull. She was dressed entirely in black: black trainers, leggings, black bomber jacket, all one, chic piece which made her seem more like a miniature adult, although the voice and the pout were entirely that of a ten-year-old.

'Hi, there Tanny. What are you doing here?' Maggie's voice was full of warmth.

'I'm opening the door,' the girl said, matter of factly. 'I'm on duty with Mummy. Only till Neil gets in, but I might stay all day, 'cos Mummy goes to see Uncle Joe . . .'

'Can we come in?'

'Yeah.'

Another forbidding door, then a comfortable shop area, illuminated by yellow sunlight from a window set deep in the wall, where a woman, also with auburn curls, was tending a kettle steaming behind a counter, looking up without smiling.

'Aw, come on, Maggie . . . What the f— are you doing here?'

The expletive was choked back. Not in front of the children, although Tanya looked as if she had heard it all before and was grinning appreciation. Henry was easily charmed by children and he found her enchanting. The girl twitched with suppressed energy, every inch the child despite the design-consciousness of her clothing, eyeing each of them in turn as if to judge which would supply the most attention.

'I'm just here with an early bird of a tourist,' Maggie was saying, talking too fast again. 'Angela, this is Henry Evans, our visiting American I was telling you about yesterday. Henry, this is Angela Hulme, and this is her daughter, Tanya.'

'Hallo.' The greeting from Angela was perfunctory. She did not present to Henry as a happy person.

'I want to go out, I want to go *out*,' Tanya was chanting, hopping from one foot to the other.

'Look, I haven't organized the tapes or turned on the lights yet. It's too damned early for a proper tour round. What the hell do you think you're doing, Maggie? I suppose bloody Neil lets you do as you please.'

'I should apologise,' Henry said, spreading his hands. 'I guess this is my fault.'

'Perhaps Tanya can show Henry the cannons,' Maggie interrupted smoothly. 'And Mummy can make her tea.'

'Yeah,' Tanya yelled. 'Yeah, yeah, yeah!'

Angela gave Maggie a venomous look. Her hair glowed titian in the shaft of light, making her strong features seem harder. Henry wanted out of there. He liked kids although he felt so unskilled in their company that he never sought it, but anything was better than seeing women suppressing a quarrel. It made the walls of the room close in and inspired him to do something. He doffed an imaginary hat, and bowed low to the girl, with a flourish.

'Would Mademoiselle lead on?' She laughed, responded with a

full curtsy, daintily lifting an imaginary skirt as she put left foot behind right and sank in a parody of a courtly lady.

'I learned that for the fucking school play. Come on, then. I can jump over the guns.'

'*Don't* swear. And don't *let* her—' But they were out and into the courtyard beyond. The girl ran ahead of him, scampering up steps to the heights while he followed with greater care, breathing slowly in his relief. The steps were green and moist; she was as sure-footed as he was not. '*C'mon,*' she shrieked, 'Come *on!*' Then they were out on the apron of the south-east bastion with a view of the sea. The area was encircled by a shoulder-high wall. Henry put his toe in a gap and hauled himself up, leaning over the top to see what he could see. The top of the wall was so wide his arm could not extend to the other side across the paving which covered the surface, sloping away from him at a slight downward angle, slippery damp to the touch. The sky and the sea filled his vision, but when he looked down, the bottom of the moat was a very long way down indeed. Henry stepped back, hastily.

The child, her name already mislaid, even though he was fascinated by her face, was clearly not going to act as a guide and seemed to have forgotten his existence except as a spectator and that suited him, too. There was a cannon, mounted high on a block, standing in the next bastion. She ran towards it, scrambled up and crawled over the mechanism to the neck. She slithered round until her arms and her legs clutched the barrel, and moved, hand over hand, towards the muzzle. She dropped her legs and hung by her arms, the slender body stretched and her toes a couple of feet from the ground. Then she dropped, ran back round the cannon and began again. It was like watching an agile monkey on a horizontal climb, but this time, when she reached the muzzle she kept her legs locked round it, let go with her arms and swung head down, with her hair streaming and her hands stretched towards the floor. She looked deceptively helpless until she curled her torso upwards, re-embraced the metal, released her legs and dropped, elegantly, as before. Henry was moving towards her, a shade anxious, but clapping his applause. 'That's great, young lady, but that's enough, OK?'

He was about to touch her shoulder, maybe calm her down a little, but she sprang away and ran. He watched as she climbed the wall. She stood on the sloping surface, held out both hands for balance and then began to skip along. *Christ.* Henry wanted to run towards her, grab her ankles and hold on tight, but he could only watch. She skipped daintily, oblivious to height and danger, the movements growing faster. He thought of the small, lithe body crashing to earth on the other side, remembered the obscenities he had just heard about the boy called Harry, imagined her scream on the way down, closed his eyes for a whole second. When he opened them, she had disappeared.

He staggered forward blindly, the bile back at the root of his throat, hand over his lips to stop himself gagging. Felt himself shouting, *Where are you?* with no idea of whether the words were coming out. He wanted to shout, *Daddy, help me!*, in some half-remembered scream of his own boyhood. He broke into a run, past the two other black cannons which stood like silent sentinels, pointed towards nothing. His shoe scrabbled for purchase on the wall as he tried to heave himself up to look; the surface of the slabs grazed his fingers and he fell back, twice. He could feel the beginning of sobbing, thought he could hear a whimpering, but knew it was his own, turned back from the wall, despairing. What use was this? *Help. HELP.* The cannon caught the corner of his eye, a flash of movement behind it. He turned back to the wall. Then there was a flurry of soft footsteps from behind him and the child was clutching at his waist, laughing. 'Fooled you!' she cried. 'I fucking did, didn't I?'

Henry detached her hands, twisted towards her and hugged her tight. She struggled for a few seconds, resisting the closeness, unaware that he held her thus out of a mixture of relief and fear that if his hands were free, he might slap her out of sheer fury, so he hung on while she twisted like an eel. Until she stopped. Her arms crept round his neck; her clean-smelling hair tickled his face and she sighed softly into his shoulder. Half kneeling to accommodate her height, Henry locked his arms behind her back. He was not going to let go of her jacket either until he got her back to her mother and as the thudding of his heart lessened, he loved the hug and the fact that this little imp pressed her cold cheek against his own and crooned into his ear as if he was everything that ever mattered. As if he could render her world safe while she did everything to make it perilous. They stayed like that for a little while. She hummed a tuneless song he could not recognize.

'We'll get cold up here,' he murmured, finally. 'And you know, baby, you shouldn't get up on that wall. Long way down.'

She pushed him back, her hands on his shoulders, the better to see him. Her smile was outrageous. He felt it like a blessing; it made him want to cry.

'Why not? Neil lets me do it.'

'Who's Neil?' Ah, *that* Neil.

'He's my sort of daddy. He lets me play.'

He must want you dead, Henry thought. They were walking hand in hand by now, nice and quiet. He felt absurdly protective and in an odd kind of way, privileged.

'. . . And Francesca used to let me, when I was much smaller, you know' – a wise tone had crept into her voice, like that of an old woman talking about another age entirely – 'but only if I had a piece of rope round my middle and she held the other end and watched all the time. 'Cesca was my sort of Mummy, but she's gone away for a long time. Neil says she'll leave me all her money, one day. I couldn't give a shit, could you?'

He could feel the blood pressure begin to rise again. He squeezed her hand, stopped the perambulation and looked at her seriously. She began to dust down her clothes with exaggerated care, checking for marks, wiping them away with her sleeve. 'So why did she bother with the rope round the middle?' he enquired, nonchalantly. 'Way you are with that cannon, sweetie, you could run round these walls without falling off. Couldn't you?'

Tanya wrinkled her nose and shrugged without letting go of his hand. Her own felt small, trusting and cool. He was trying to think when it was that youngsters started to sweat. Not yet. He was listening.

'*She* said that only an *idiot* would fall off a wall and into a moat. *She* said I could break my arms and legs any way I liked, 'cept through stupidity. Being brave is fine, *she* said, but being stupid isn't.'

He could hear the phrases and that authoritative voice. Tanya's vowel sounds lengthened to copy the intonation. The battlements were colder; they were walking slower. He tucked her hand into his pocket.

'So why do you skip round the walls?' She was ferreting in his pocket, striking gold. Chocolate. He had no idea how it got there, could not remember the existence of it at all. She held it up, assumed it was hers, transferred it to her own pocket and then, to his relief, put her hand back against his.

'So pleased you found that,' he said, conversationally. 'Clearly yours, because you're so clever, aren't you? But I was asking you why you like to run around these walls, scaring me like that. I mean, why?'

'Because I *can*. That's why. She could, too, when she was little.'

'OK.'

''Cesca said "OK" was a lazy way with words,' she added. 'I don't say it any more.'

'OK,' he repeated. 'That's her opinion. You don't have to follow it. OK with me.'

'You're OK,' she said and Henry felt nicely flattered.

They had walked the full circle of the battlements and he had not really noticed a thing, except that after passing a few more of the cannons on the seaward side, there was not a lot going on by way of different furniture or scenery, and they were almost back to where they started, only higher. His companion had had enough of this and that, chatted beyond her normal length, led him back towards the glazed door marked SHOP/EXIT. From beyond it, he could hear the intense sound of voices, talking fast and furious without shouting. It was a sound which could penetrate walls. With extreme reluctance, he let go of Tanya's hand, forgave her the fright. She was a beautiful child. He would have jumped in the moat and let her land on him if that would have helped.

They entered the shop area with the sudden change of temperature to which he was beginning to become accustomed. By some odd, common accord, they had both begun coughing as they descended the steps. Silence had fallen. Maggie and Angela were smiling at them both, solicitously. Henry was reminded of the people he had seen on the beach, awaiting the return of their animals so they could put them back on a leash.

'Hallo,' Maggie said. 'Had fun? We had tea. Finished now. Sadly.'

Angela bent under the counter, looking for something. Tanya, who had relinquished her hold on Henry's hand, seemed confused. Henry turned towards Maggie.

'Guess I just got a taste of parenthood,' he said. 'Not sure I like it. Must be like one long heart attack.' Maggie smiled, weakly. His eyes turned to the shelves of the shop, pretending interest. Spotted bars of chocolate, cylindrically shaped and wrapped in white, like a tube of coins. He remembered the feel of it in his pocket, transferred into that of the child, but he could not remember buying it. Poor kid; she pinched it and he felt huge admiration for her sleight of hand. He felt in his pocket for change. 'Guess I owe you . . .'

'Mummy!' Tanya shrilled. 'Mummy! *He* hugged me and called me baby, an' called me sweetie an' gave me chocolate, an' he's coming back soon, isn't he, Mummy?'

There was complete silence.

Angela emerged from behind the counter. Her face was white. 'He did *what?*'

Maggie tugged at Henry's sleeve. Her other hand plucked at the batch of tourist leaflets for other attractions which she was stuffing inside her top pocket even as she spoke.

'Think we'll go now, Henry, don't you?'

'Mr Evans can come back another time,' Angela said tightly. 'There's lots of other things for him to see. Like the old town jail. Maybe he'll go and live in it.'

★

The sun had won over the haze. The traffic had increased. Henry could hear the sound of church bells. He and Maggie walked back to the beach in silence. He wanted to feel the shingle beneath his feet. They sat on a bench and looked at it.

'You have any children, Henry?'

'Nope. Never quite got round to staying long enough with the right woman. Or asking the right questions. you?'

'No. And I'm never quite sure what to do with them. Especially that one.'

'She's quite a kid. I can see why her mom's protective.'

Maggie unfurled the shawl from round her neck and folded it neatly. The morning was warmer, the hint of spring less deceptive. She pointed towards the horizon. 'Look,' she said, 'you can see France. That means it's going to rain.' Her voice was sad, with a touch of resignation.

He waited. Henry was good at waiting for information. He had waited in lecture halls, waited on academics, businessmen and confused pupils; he was a patient disseminator of information and a listener.

'Tanya was Francesca's protégé,' Maggie was explaining, smoothing the shawl between her hands. 'She was adopted by Neil and Angela. Francesca knew them, encouraged them, and finally they got the child that no one else would take. Not a baby, a five-year-old with freakish colouring and a history of terrible abuse. Very vulnerable. Angela and Neil parted soon after. Francesca took a lot of responsibility, even though Harry was just a baby when Tanya arrived. I suppose she and Angela bonded even more after Francesca's husband buggered off.'

'Why did he go?'

'Who knows? It was a tricky pregnancy and there was no time for him, I suppose. Francesca always had all the time in the world for everyone. He wasn't the only one to resent the intrusion.'

'Bastard,' Henry said feelingly.

'Aren't they all?'

Maggie found a packet of cigarettes, proffered them: Henry

took one absentmindedly and accepted a light. Another bit of poison, taken to ease conversation, did not seem to matter. He had forgotten his vitamins this morning; the nicotine made him dizzy, but even with his social skills muddled by this new environment, he knew that the accepting of the cigarette was important.

'So. Francesca's in her late thirties. She's got a job and a sickly child and she shares a vulnerable one like Tanya, too? She must have been a sucker for punishment.'

'Francesca had great energy and greater spirit. Her father had been warden of the keep. She *did* once live in a castle; she was *designed* to take charge and hide feelings. She *seemed* amazingly competent, tough. But she wasn't, you see. She simply wasn't. She was coming apart at the seams.'

'Then she should have come clean and admitted she couldn't hack it,' Henry stated angrily, stamping the cigarette with the heel of his shoe, grinding it to shreds. Thinking of something else. *She should have ASKED me to stay with her and not to leave. Relied on the fact I was older. She should have said she was afraid. She should not have said, you must do what you need to do, Henry. She should have said, I need you.*

'Yes, she should,' Maggie said.

A dog paused to sniff at the bench. The owner stopped, too. The chain of command was obvious; one led, one followed.

'I could ask Francesca if she'd like to see you.'

'No.'

She rose and hoisted her bag, fished out tourist information leaflets from the inside of her jacket and thrust them at him. 'Then you'd better go on with the sightseeing, hadn't you? Try the jail, like Angela said. Then you'll know what barbarous people we are. Harry's hemiplegia was severe. In another age, he might have been thrown off the walls. Maybe she had some excuses.'

Henry walked. He walked first on the shingle, away from the town, until, assisted by the returning haze, the outline of the castle was faded when he turned to look. He walked and watched his feet slurring through the pebbles with a satisfying sound, until his thighs felt as if they were on fire and his shoes no longer insulated his feet. The pebbles became larger, the beach steeper, so that at times he was hidden in a stone valley, with no view either of the sea or the land. It suited his mood. He had passed an untidy collection of fishing boats which looked unfit to sail with their heavy hulls and ungainly lines; he had paused to watch a team of men winch one out of the water and heard it groan like a half-dead whale. Then he passed a children's playground, listened from the beach to the sound of high shrieking on the swings and hurried on. He supposed a mother could tell the difference between a howl of excitement and one of pain. And then he was beyond the reach of the road on beach so steep that the prospect of clambering back was awesome and he could imagine he was finally, completely alone.

The coastal path above the shore took him through flat scrubland, littered with small shrubs, flattened by the wind. Outside of the conurbation it was a bleak enough place; there was nothing verdant or comforting about it. A mile further on, the flat land rose into a cliff, skirting a cove, looming above it. The path ran out. The bay reverberated with the ghostly sound of a hovercraft crossing from England to France, a strange, diffused, booming sound he had heard in the distance the morning before. The sound filled the sky. He wished he were on the damn boat, hovering or not. He wished he had never seen this stretch of coast or invested it with the romance she had conjured in her descriptions. *You can see for miles and miles; you can see another country.* Yeah. Only if you live in a castle designed to kill any poor bastard who tries to get in. Henry turned for home. That damn black mongrel had been following him again. He shouted at it and when it went, he was sorry.

Home. Had to stop saying that. He rang the bell, grunted a greeting and went up to the room in search of privacy. Flung the suitcase on the bed and did an inventory: passport, travel cheques, tickets, the name of the Fergusons contact, diary. Don't any of these people know how important I am? The light began to leak out of his room; all the documents strewn on the gorgeous silk coverlet looked like an unconvincing statement of identity and purpose. They were so small. He was drawn to look at the sea, so hazy, so absolutely endless, it repelled him. Besides, the sun had moved round, away from it. It shone through the window on the other side of his open door. The sash window opened easily. He put his elbows on the sill and looked down.

There were twisted red roofs of a dozen different contours, chimneypots, large and small trailed with smoke; nothing he could see contained any uniformity. He could see the worn red tiles, warped with age, glinting windows, a medley of warm colours and a thousand entry points for Mary Poppins. He could see the white painted walls, the rounded gable of the opposite house and the little alley in between. Then he looked down into the garden of the House of Enchantment, drawn by the sound of tinkling water.

Tropical down there. A mass of foliage in green, some damn thing with flowers, a great bursting bush with tiny white blooms. A small pond against the side, catching the sun, water gushing out of a terracotta mouth into a clear pool. A floor of old brick curving away in a circular design, greenery between the stones, mature, evergreen shrubs hiding the beds from which they sprung, brilliant gentian blue in a rockery of alpine plants in the corner away from the pool. A curving path, leading to a pergola covered with greenery, sheltering a small, wooden love seat which looked as if it, too, had grown where it stood. From this height, it was a piece of perfection with a single flaw. Tim in a boiler suit, bent double with his bottom sticking out of a Wendy house settled square in the middle of it all. The house was plastic, built in lemon yellow with pink shutters, lime roof and royal blue door. It sat, as offensive and disparate as a wart on a beautifully manicured finger, defying all standards of taste. Tim was on hands and knees, dusting it. Henry forgot everything else, ran down the stairs, through the kitchen and out the back door. He passed Peter, marshalling coal into buckets for the fires.

From below, the garden was even more impressive. The comparative ugliness of a large utilitarian shed and a compost container were hidden beyond the pergola. The place was larger than it had seemed from on high, extending further than he could see, and even in the doldrums of winter there was colour.

'This is just *great*.' Henry was passionate about gardens, read about them, viewed them and dreamed of creating something different from his own dull lawn.

'All our own work,' Tim said. 'Everything begged or recycled, you know. We got the bricks from a demolished wall, backbreaking it was; we've raised most of the plants, and we built the pond from scratch. We're extremely grateful for what other people throw away.'

'But what about *that*?' Henry pointed with trembling finger at the obtrusive Wendy house with its hideously artificial pink and blue. Tim's dusting and cleaning operations were complete; he was looking at his work with satisfaction. The plastic was conspicuously dirt free and had none of the sadness of summer items left out in the cold. It looked prepared for imminent occupation. 'Oh, I get it,' he said, relieved as the dog approached and sniffed at the door of the house. 'It's Senta's kennel, right?'

'Good Lord, no. She's only allowed inside by special permission.' The two men were looking at each other, as if deliberating on a proper explanation that would not offend him. Peter took charge, with Tim's tacit agreement.

'Well, I hope you don't mind, but we do know that you had a little chat with Maggie this morning. About knowing Francesca, and everything, so we may as well tell you. This is Harry's little house. He used to play in it, you see, when Fran left him with us, and we keep it nice for him, for whenever he wants it. He lives in this garden, you see. Not all the time, just sometimes when it's sunny.'

Tim nodded confirmation of this unquestionable fact. Peter was pointing through the open shutters of the Wendy house. 'He has his little sleeping bag, which he was ever so fond of, and his little shawl, which he used to chew, and his teddy, which he used to abuse dreadfully. Always throwing it away and then yelling to get it back. Love-hate, you might say. Of course, we take the bedding indoors at night. He'd be frightened outside in the dark.'

'The kid's been dead for more than a year,' Henry said, brutally. 'Drowned, buried, cremated. Dead.'

'Yee-ees,' Tim said, considering this. 'Yee-es, you could put it like that.'

'So his ghost comes back to play? Slips down a damn moonbeam?'

'We knew you'd understand, Henry,' Tim beamed. 'You seem such an understanding man. We had such a *terrible* time after he was killed. We really weren't allowed to grieve, you see. There were plenty of people thought Francesca was completely bonkers to give him to us three or four afternoons a week, but he *loved* it here. We *know* how to nurse people, especially little people, and we adored him.'

'You see, Henry,' Peter continued the narrative, 'there are so many people who still think that being *queer* means paedophile. As well as *rampant*, always *at* it, like rabbits. Instead of being an old married couple like us who would guard a child from harm like a pair of anxious grannies. When Harry disappeared, I tell you, the police were round here like a shot. They would have dug up the garden if he hadn't been found so soon and Francesca confessed. I suppose we should be grateful to her for that.'

'And for plenty of other things,' Tim murmured. 'Such as letting us get to know him in the first place. He was a sweet, sweet child.'

In the day's emotional turmoil, and in his grief the night before, Henry had not had time to contemplate the identity of the dead child and did not want to dwell on it. All that had mattered was the impact of his awful demise. He got the picture: this 'murder' had messed up plenty of lives, not least that of the murderess; fallout still coming down. No one so far had spoken of the child with love. Tim was weeping openly, and Peter was patting his shoulder. 'Oh, come inside, dears, we all need some tea,' he said. 'And besides, in case Henry here starts seeing spirits, we'd better show him what Harry looked like. In case he gets the wrong idea.'

Henry wanted no such thing; the conversation horrified him, but he could not see how to evade it. It was he, after all, who had invited himself into the garden, he who had failed to keep his distance, and now he was trapped. A comfortable trap in the warm kitchen, with the world outside clouding over and his elbows resting on a scrubbed table and a tame dog dozing at his feet. Tea poured from a huge, brown pot which looked too heavy to lift but yielded sweet scented Earl Grey, flavoured with a slice of lemon in the cup. It cut through the clog of the day's snack diet, refreshed him, even as the warmth of the Rayburn fortified him for this exercise in politeness. Peter was coming into the room carrying the TV.

'We've got a video, although I like photos better. See what I mean? He was an *angel*.'

'Was there ever a suggestion of any other culprit for the killing?' Henry asked desperately.

'Well, no. Someone had been fishing on the pier earlier on. Left his stuff and didn't come back. And lots of people resented Francesca. And we do have *bad* people here. Oh, look!'

Henry saw the head of Francesca, face completely obscured by falling hair as she knelt behind the child and supported him with her hands beneath his armpits, fingers waving at the camera. She was keeping him upright; he seemed in the act of lurching forward. And then he ran, right arm flexed like a piston, right wrist bent. The angle of the arm increased as he moved. He ran like a slow drunk preserving the arm for the next drink, a look of painful determination on his face, mucus round his nose and a bruise on his forehead.

'That's him at two, when we met,' Henry said fondly. 'He was even more beautiful later. When he learned to fall over properly.'

Henry made himself swallow the tea which threatened to close his throat, pity at war with something like revulsion. The child whose face he examined was ugly. It could have been an old, old man. The face was pinched and wizened and the smile was twisted. Desperately unappealing, at best. Something to smother beneath blankets and hurry through streets. A child physically cursed, begging to be shunned. Ugly as sin. He struggled for an appropriate response. An image of Tanya's perfection floated across his mind, along with the remembered feeling of holding her close in his arms. The child in the picture looked ready to bite and consumed with rage.

'Poor little mite,' said Tim, his voice tremulous. 'And looking at him, Henry, you have to agree, it's very important to find out who killed him. Otherwise, he'll just keep on coming back to his own little house. Don't worry, though, he won't haunt *you*. Why should he? He only haunts *us* because we don't want to let him go.'

'His mother killed him.'

'Well, sadly and officially, yes. But *he* thinks there's a question mark, he's *told* us so. Unfortunately, he was never very articulate, speech difficulties, you see, so he doesn't seem able to advance an explanation. But he's perfectly right to express reservations. After all, he must have known his mother better than anyone else.'

Henry put his hands over his ears to blot out the words. He wanted to thump the table and rattle the teacups. He took his hands away from his ears and laid them flat on the table in front of him, willing them to behave. Tim patted his wrist, consolingly.

'Which is why it's so nice you're here, Henry. We've been expecting you for ages. Someone has to find out, and it can't be us, so it has to be you. Isn't that right, Peter?'

They were beaming at him, as if he were a prodigal son returned and all was forgiven and the fatted calf was in the oven.

Henry shook his head and left them. Walked up all the stairs to his room. The fire they had lit mid-afternoon, without knowing when he would return, glowed softly. The shirts he had flung into a corner had been washed and pressed. He continued his inventory, repacked the suitcase, left it open on the floor. He wished his battery of vitamins included a tranquillizer.

Opened his laptop, wrote himself a note.

GET OUT OF HERE, HENRY.

NOBODY NEEDS YOU.

YOU HAVE NOTHING TO OFFER AT ALL.

Easier today. Easier to breathe and easier to write. I like these little pills.

I could no more tell my friend in the kitchen that I was brought up in a castle than I could fly over the moon. She would think I was taking the piss, although if I explained that my father was merely the caretaker, and I the caretaker's daughter, she would find it less offensive. Initially, she disliked the way I speak. I can't amend my accent and although I have the family talent for mimicry, which children love, I can't sustain it. She has forgotten about the voice, now, which is just as well, because it's easy to make an enemy here and she's bigger than I, as well as more socially powerful. I think I'm forgiven the voice and the habit of sentences because I like her, I really do and she doesn't know quite what to do about that.

I DID grow up in a castle, although it was only the small part in the middle, and when I was a child it didn't feel unique. There was certainly no sneaking in or out of it or possessing my own key. Nor was the space we occupied either huge or luxurious, simply sufficient for the standards of an ex-military man who put efficiency far ahead of comfort, and a wife who found she had married a late-blooming eccentric and gave up making decisions. We would re-enact the Normandy landings and she would knit. She couldn't sit and knit as well as look at the view, because the windows were too high, so she would stand. The keep was utilitarian and meant for soldiers. It was a terrific place for parties and family gatherings (I can't remember when Uncle Joe was excluded), a complete playground, but for a houseproud wife, it was no wonder she preferred her bungalow.

Privileged? Of course it was, if I had thought about it at the time. I loved those battlements; I loved hoisting the flag and I loved standing level with the sea. We didn't repel invaders; we invited them in, especially Maggie, but we locked the doors once they had gone. We ruled the world, my father said, and he was absolutely right. He didn't mean the English ruled the world; he meant we, ourselves. The psychiatrist who saw me in the early stages asked if that gave me a certain attitude to life. (He was very keen on the isolation of environment and class.)

I'm becoming wordy. I must stop.

It made me thrifty, capable, good at cooking, washing, sewing and careless about appearances, because we did everything and owned nothing. We were caretakers for the next generation. I told him there were times it made me want to live in a treehouse inside someone else's garden.

I inherited an outrageous sense of duty, but I did not tell the psychiatrist that: nor did I tell him that, above all, it made me extraordinarily humble.

As well as arrogant and talented in manipulation. With a craving for status in the wider community, couldn't stand the failures of ordinary life and parenthood. A tendency to take over and give orders. Raised around cannons and the veneration of war; therefore capable of violence and aggression.

I'm glad I remembered that part. He found it entirely convincing.

FMC

CHAPTER SIX

IN the late afternoon, just as it began to rain, Angela Hulme drove to see Uncle Joe. He lived in a senior citizens' home, appropriately situated next to the golf course where he had spent as much of his life as possible. When giving her the task of visiting this stranger, Francesca had assured Angela that she would know exactly which one he was. The idlest survivor of three brothers, the only one left of that generation and their wives. A reprobate, and after all those years golfing and drinking gin, the one with the face like red sandpaper. Angela had promised Francesca and although she now owned Francesca's car, it was a promise she often resented, because it was another obligation. *My father's surviving brother is the only thing I have left of my father; please do this, Angela.* It was Francesca who should have been the lawyer, the way she could persuade without it sounding quite like an order, although perhaps being a teacher had the same effect.

The suggestion was that she should take Tanya with her, but Angela reneged on that part. They had tried it; Tanya liked Uncle Joe but she talked too much, exhausted him. It was Francesca's opinion that it was good for the very young to have contact with the very old, but Tanya did not belong with these relics, although they loved to see a child. Angela did not agree with the need to mingle with the older generation: they had a general tendency to carp and criticize although this hardly applied to Uncle Joe. He was all sweetness and light, another reason for leaving Tanya behind with Neil, because Angela secretly enjoyed seeing him privately. There was a dearth of adult company in her life; there was nothing he did not understand and he was completely uncensorious.

She drove in the Ramsgate direction, past another town and into the flat hinterland. The road took her through the vast Fergusons plant. She could have a job here; everyone else did. The area of the operation was vast, spreading over the fields like a rash, and even on a Sunday the carpark was full of bright, new motors. It must take thousands of sick people to make and distribute drugs; so much everyone knew. Maggie had told her in the castle that Henry Evans, the tourist, was going to work there; no wonder she hadn't liked him, even before he started making eyes at her beautiful child. What kind of idiot thought Tanya could be bribed with chocolate? An idiot like that. She might just tell Uncle Joe all about it. Maybe Henry Evans knew of a drug which could make her daughter forget everything unpleasant that had ever happened to her, and remember only the good things, such as being born at all. Make her completely dissociate herself from the child whose drug-sodden parents had burned the inside of her thighs with a cigarette, left her with a rash on her face from lying in vomit. They should find a cure for that, these fucking scientists, instead of finding drugs to make men worse than they already were.

She passed the featureless buildings and began to relax a little. She did not, in all honesty, have any doubts about leaving Tanya with Neil. Although he was an unpredictable man with the sexual ability of a slug, he was a good enough part-time father to a beautiful girl child who needed unbiased attention with the minimum of attachment. At least Neil suspended his irritation and was alert enough to notice danger. Although Angela thought that Tanya could have done without the swearing and the ghost stories, that was fine too, because she didn't believe a word of them, which made for a good combination, really, what with her trusting Neil, and yet all the time thinking he was a bit silly. That way, he undermined nothing, which probably suited them all.

She pulled up on the Ramsgate cliff, a desolate place in winter, fit for nothing but sheep and this house, which was as grand as a seabitten house in need of maintenance could be: frayed at the edges and cancerous round the windows at this time of year, the white paint a shade grey and flaky and the whole thing less than ancestral. The new golf clubhouse stood a few acres distant over rolling greens saturated with rain. This house, which she approached from the carpark at a running crouch through the rain, had once been the golfers' bar. No wonder Uncle Joe loved it. Reaching the entrance, sheltered from the wet in the age it took anyone to answer, she remembered her resentment, standing here with her arms crossed, obeying orders a year ago. What business had she, coming to see Francesca's uncle on another rainy day, only to get that bovine nurse from an agency who said, Mister Who? I'm sorry, I don't know the names. Oh yes there he was, the one sitting over there, with the red face and the fine white hair. The one in his favourite armchair, reading a paper, just as Francesca described. The accuracy of the description and the awkwardness of the introduction started off the little game they still played now.

'*Are* you Uncle Joe?' she greeted him, shedding her coat.

'Who wants him?' he replied, just like the first time. He sat alone in the close warmth of the foyer, looking out through the double-glazed doors whenever the paper dropped into his lap. She liked the fact that he simply presented his papery cheek for a peck from her lips. She gave him Maggie's snowdrops this time, aware that he might have preferred sherry or chocolate, but that was what she had and he always protested about the gifts.

'My dear, you *shouldn't* have . . . But how lovely to see you. Pretty as a picture. I do like the new hair.'

Uncle Joe always observed things, looked at her with such keen approval it made her preen a little. She found herself wearing a skirt for Uncle Joe, putting on earrings or a bracelet to see if he would notice, and he never failed. 'I love that, where did you get it?' It was part of a regular if not invariable Sunday ritual, this slight dressing up for him, the way other people might do for church. If she missed a week, he never reproached her, something else she appreciated. He said he quite understood what life was like with children. Overall, it was one of those social tasks she did not relish, but all the same enjoyed.

Because he wanted to listen. He preferred that to talking, relishing stories from the outside world, delivered for his mild commentary, especially if the anecdotes featured Tanya. Francesca was never mentioned after the first time, when Angela had explained how she had come as a replacement because Fran was otherwise engaged. He had accepted the substitution with alacrity as well as grace – 'How *lucky* I am to have you instead . . .' – and if he had read about his homicidal niece in the local newspaper, he did not say, but then Uncle Joe despised the local paper and only went for quality broadsheets. When she ventured to explain what had happened, he had merely shaken his head sadly, as if nothing in the world surprised him any more. 'How awful for *you*,' was his primary comment, 'but never mind. Very sad, but probably all for the best'; and while Angela knew this laconic response was hardly appropriate, she secretly and guiltily agreed. In numerous ways, life without Francesca's assiduous and generous assistance was harder, but infinitely easier in other respects. At least she was no longer there, with her tireless energy, swallowing Tanya's affection and attention, influencing her the way she did, and in a while, perhaps Tanya would stop talking about her. Forget about her, as she was managing to forget so much else.

They were left to themselves in the foyer, although if she timed it right, one of the agency staff who took over at weekends wandered along with a tray of tea and a plate of the sort of tasteless dry biscuits Tanya would have rejected. Angela wondered if the biscuits were the choice of the staff or of the patients, who might have been raised to regard rich tea or gingernuts as a treat.

'Why do you sit out here, by yourself, instead of in the living room with the nice fire?'

'I like it here. Get away from the others.' Today he twinkled at her.

'So cold out there. Splendidly kind of you to come out in this. So lucky.' He settled himself. He had tremor in the hands and virtually no use of his legs, but he could dress himself. The clothes were endearingly old and good and he was pinkly clean. 'How is the gorgeous child?'

'Well, she's acting up, but what's new? I dyed my hair to please her and she has the nerve to say she doesn't like it . . .'

'Tut, tut,' delivered indulgently, smiling.

'And she still talks about Francesca. At school, I gather. At home, even to strangers. She was doing that this morning . . .'

'Give it time, give it time, my dear.'

'. . . to an American, I ask you, up at the castle. A tourist Maggie brought in. I think Tanya was flirting with him a bit, but more to the point, he was certainly flirting with her . . .'

'Really!'

'I don't want to get it wrong. I want her to be easy with strangers, but I don't want her being familiar. You never know with people, do you?'

'No. You never know.'

'Anyway, she's safe with Neil. I'll try and bring her again, one of these days.'

'Oh yes, one of these days.' Not *you should* or *you must*.

'Well, I don't know. She might be doing somersaults in the rain. She hates sitting still. Neil manages to make her, sometimes. Me, I have to make her run and jump until she's worn out, but I don't always like to do that, because she gets so fractious when she's tired. We set up a series of hurdles on the beach the other day, after school. She needed wearing out. She can run along the shingle, like it was a running track. Amazing. Sometimes I feel as if I'm exercising a great big dog.'

'A dog!'

'Yes. Just like exercising a dog. Relentless. Needs taking out twice a day and then feeding. She'd like to have a dog, she says, but never mind the money they cost, I'm not sure. To be honest,' she lowered her voice confidentially, even though there was no one to overhear, 'I'm not sure she has the patience. Not sure I would, either. What do you think?'

'Dogs, yes . . . dogs are good.'

'Yes, but think – if I let her out with a dog by herself, everyone would stop and talk to her. Unless I got a horrid dog that nobody liked. One that snapped at everyone else but us . . .'

'Yes!'

'That would keep people away, wouldn't it? Sort of guard dog, yes it's quite a good idea when I think of it. But not that bloody dog Neil wanted us to have. Do you know, this morning he was so cheerful? He's not usually like that. He's usually tense and miserable, he always was. He annoyed me, though. I told him about the American making eyes at Tanya and he just shrugged. I said there was something creepy about him . . .'

'*Creepy* American?'

'Yes. Creepy. Men like that want locking up.'

Uncle Joe adjusted himself in his chair and smiled widely at the nurse who brought tea. She smiled back. The progress of the cup towards his mouth was tortuous. It clattered back into the saucer. He leaned towards Angela and tapped his nose, wisely.

'This American . . . You should lock him up. With a dog!' He laughed loudly and Angela joined in. He always made her feel better; they often ended up giggling like kids. She could tell him anything. He wasn't really a chore, after all. He pushed the snowdrops to the side of the tray, not really caring for them either and knowing she wouldn't mind, because, really, they thought the same way about irrelevant things. She did not come here because Maggie would ask if she was fulfilling the promise; she came because he liked her and agreed with her when it seemed nobody else did. It was lonely out there, being watched all the time, to see if you got it wrong.

'We *are* better without Francesca and Harry, aren't we?' she asked anxiously, taking two of the biscuits. Lunch had been scanty.

'Better? Much better.'

'I'm not a bad person, am I, Uncle Joe? I'm a good mother, aren't I?' He patted her hand and gazed at her fondly.

'No. You're *very* good. Like dogs.'

He always said what she wanted to hear and remembered nothing.

The rain came down in sheets, altering the landscape again to a leaden grey before the black of evening and the violence outside provided Henry with a comfortable excuse for lying still, listening to music and doing nothing. Then, with the rain beating out a steady, unrhythmic lullaby, he slept the sleep of the dead. Woke once to a sound and the red glow of the dying fire, saw the shawl where he had laid it on the bed, and then slept again.

He would get Maggie to give Francesca the shawl. That would be the end of it.

The morning sky made him consider the pleasures of living in a house like this where he would never need to draw the shades and could stretch, naked, in front of a window. Henry felt the small ridge of fat which was forming round his middle, pinched it ruefully and thought, to hell with it. Better be fat than believe in ghosts; better be a porker than a nut.

He said a prayer for his father; not a prayer to any known deity, simply an address to whoever might be able to interpret it and pass the message on. *I hope you're OK, Dad. You might like it here, especially the fishing, but I'm not sure I do . . .* It was simply a continuation of a daily conversation, keeping his father up to speed, seeking his opinion, not really expecting a reply, but encouraging himself to see things with his father's broad perspective. They had talked by phone so regularly, it had proved a habit difficult to relinquish and Henry had sat at his desk on many an afternoon with his hand ready to dial before he realized what he was doing. Waiting to chat to Dad, nothing much, just an exchange of words, sometimes a discussion. Dad loved nothing better than a debate.

It seemed to Henry in this single moment that his intellect had gone to sleep since his father died, submerged in grief, loss, self-recrimination and, floating among it, this murky sediment of sheer sentimentality which had driven him over the Atlantic. He was appalled to remember himself reading poetry and crying like some juvenile, throwing himself back into sorrow and all of it reminding him of *her* and how hellish she must have felt. Making himself weep, if only to exhaust the supply of emotion and attempt to extract that hairball which seemed constantly lodged in his own throat. Any woman with half a brain would have left him; any child would have despised such unreliable thrashing about of the type which affected him even now. Dad would surely not like it. Henry sat up in bed with his arms clasped round his knees. *That* was what he was trying to remember during the night, the lost intellect and his own dedication to scientific *fact. Don't simply accept so-called facts; go to the source before you have the arrogance to believe.* He hit his forehead with the heel of his palm. Come on, Henry. All he had absorbed in the last couple of days was people telling him so-called facts, chilling facts or maybe fantasies, and why should he believe any of them? Sure, he was going to go home, but surely not on the basis of a lot of happy drunk dinner guests, a crazy Francesca cousin with a possible angle to her legends . . . Hearsay is *not* fact, any more than dreams; fact has no motive or axe to grind. Fact is in libraries and it did not become a man to forget the disciplines so essential to his own nature.

In a new mood of virtue, Henry took his elaborate mix of vitamins and minerals which weighed a ton in the bulk he had carried, a waste of space for a short journey. He was planning the day, and that felt like his old self before all this *stuff* intervened. No more alcohol; no more fatty food; he was going to damn well sightsee, and not let all this *stuff* sour him, and he knew the way to the library. Henry felt like a drunk experiencing what it was like not to have a hangover, but all the same, he crept from the premises rather than roared. There was an envelope with his name on it, containing a key, left for him with the coffee. *Just so you don't have to ring the bell.* It touched him.

Library. Old newspaper reports. The reference was computerized, but the source was the newspapers themselves, not yet old enough to be yellow. They were delivered by a face he had seen in the street.

> A small boy was recovered by men on a Ramsgate fishing boat, yesterday morning. He had suffered considerable injury. A member of crew reported seeing him floating on the tidal current and thought at first he was attempting to swim. Enquiries reveal that the dead boy was Henry Chisholm, son of Francesca Chisholm and her estranged husband, Jonathan Saunders, who resides abroad. The child had been reported missing by his distraught mother shortly before he was recovered. Ms Chisholm, who lives in a prestigious, two-bed flat on Warbling seafront, told police she had left open the door to their apartment 'to get some air' and did not realize the boy had gone. The boy was partially disabled, but extremely mobile. The mother is being treated for shock. The exact cause of death is unknown. Police would like to contact the fisherman who left his equipment on the pier.

OK. FACT. He could feel fact in the pit of his stomach. They were right. The child was dead. That ugly little brute had passed into another zone. *Mrs Saunders has identified the body of her son . . . Asked if she had any explanation of his injuries, she said she did not know.* And an editorial, LET THIS BE A LESSON TO US ALL!!! *Children must be attended at all times . . .*

He read on, into the next day, a small piece detailing the

continuation of enquiries, and adding a moral tone, to the effect that nationwide, the death or neglect of children was not confined to the lower classes, but occurred in the best and richest of families, single parenthood was a classless disease, etc. There was a description of Francesca's flat, in the block next to the castle, with *spacious living accommodation and fine sea views*, as if this had somehow contributed to the tragedy. Henry could not recall the block, as viewed from the pier, as anything other than dull and ordinary, but all the same there was, in the article, a hint of loose-living privilege. Had Francesca been rich? Surely not. Not rich enough to pay for regular help, it seemed. *She let her boy be looked after by poofters.* She was a primary school teacher from an upper-class family, and Henry had learned already that in English terms, class and cash do not necessarily coincide. Then the day after. *A woman has been arrested in connection with . . . and will appear at Dover Court tomorrow.* It was the photograph for the day following which caught his eye, along with a brief description. *Mother remanded in custody for her own safety,* and there she was, with a blanket over her head, being pushed into the back of a police car while cops with stern faces kept back a small but vociferous crowd of screaming women apparently intent on tearing her to pieces. *Bitch, bitch, bitch.* Henry closed his eyes, imagining.

The date of the trial surprised him. Just short of a year ago, so near and yet so far, made it seem all the closer. The guilty plea had not been unexpected, although there was another, moralistic addendum about Francesca's slight virtue by refusing to deny this terrible offence and thus saving public money. Friends and relatives had been adamant in their refusal to speak to journalists. Less circumspect neighbours, mostly old and retired, said the defendant was *generally very nice.* No photographs of the boy. He had been cremated, service for family and friends only, no pictures of that, either. There was a brief discussion of his hemiplegia which Henry read carefully. Then he went back to the photograph of Francesca being pushed inside the car outside the court. He found it unbearably moving. Without thinking very much about it, apart from being surprised at his own vandalism, Henry tore it out carefully, folded it and put it in his pocket.

Then he moved to the poetry shelves, not much patronized on a Monday morning. Looked up one he remembered.

> *A sweet disorder in the dress*
> *Kindles in clothes a wantonness . . .*
> *A careless shoe-string, in whose tie*
> *I see a wild civility;*
> *Do more bewitch me, than when Art*
> *Is too precise in every part.*

A blanket over the head could never be elegant. It was not the same as a shawl. Why hadn't they let her have her shawl? Why not let her comfort her own misery?

Henry felt exceedingly old and not a little foolish to be lurking by these shelves. It seemed to him that poetry was the province of the very young, forced to learn it as part of their heritage, or the very old, who had come to understand that nothing else lasted as long. It was only the slight *failures* in life who had recourse to the stuff in adulthood and carried a volume to India in a backpack, to aid the romance of the journey. Or girls like Francesca Chisholm, whose father had made her learn so much of it by heart to give her an unselfconscious love of verse. Not always solemn verse; silly verse, too. *The thunder God went for a ride, Upon his favourite filly. I'm THOR! he cried. The horse replied, You forgot your thaddle, thilly.* Henry found himself smiling. He put back the book in his hand, feeling conspicuous for lurking although he was not alone. There were others drifting round shelves, looking vaguely shifty. Henry patted the pocket with the torn newspaper piece. He would throw it away, later.

He wandered out into the street and followed a sign to the OLD GAOL. It was atmosphere he wanted, to help digest facts, and besides, with the help of these facts, he might be going home even sooner. He would have to have something to report, as well as something to mitigate the memory of these other *facts*. He could not just turn round and go with *nothing* to remember but an old friend on the equivalent of death row. He was a tourist, not a maudlin fool, and the seeing of sights and absorbing of history had always been on the agenda. He had made a plan before he got here: he wanted to look at castles and things he could not see anywhere else; he was damn well going to *do* it.

In terms of tourist attractions, the Old Town Gaol was unpretentious and he was the only visitor. There was an antiquated courtroom, full of life-sized models, eerily lit, so that the details of their dusty waistcoats and wigs could be seen in full splendour. This, Henry read in his leaflet, was the place for the trial of local thieves in Victorian times. A mob had torn it apart to rescue smugglers incarcerated in the cells. The stench of humanity would be overpowering enough to make the magistrate retch when the hatch was opened and the prison below was full.

Henry went down steps to the cells, intrigued without being fascinated, feeling that in some way he was simply doing his duty. Sightseeing often felt like that. He reached the barred door to the first cell and touched the cold, rusting metal as he looked through into a tiny room of spartan quality. Cold stone walls, an iron bedstead, a shelf and a wax figure reclining listlessly on a thin mattress, clutching a bible. Henry could feel the chill of the floor rise up through the stones; there was room to stand, but not to walk; the width of the cell was merely the hand span of a small man. He moved down a row with cells either side, each with its own model of a skeletal prisoner. Touched his forehead and felt it sweat. NO.

There was the time with Francesca, when they had gone to see the caves and she had led him out, gibbering and fainting with indefinable fear, times when he had forced himself out of the railway carriage, careless of who he shoved, because he had known without shadow of doubt that he would die if he did not escape. The same feeling now, the hot grip of claustrophobia swelling his throat. There was something, someone small, stroking his thigh.

He stumbled forward, past more of the cells, searching for the exit sign, scrambling up stone steps, bursting out past a startled girl at the entry desk, and into the street. He walked with a ludicrous jerky, fast walk until he was in sight of the sea, and once that was in range, leaned against the wall and breathed deeply. He balled his hands into fists to stop them shaking. The seagulls whirled and screamed in derision; Henry looked at them until the feeling subsided, leaving him weak. He scrambled down to the edge of the water and waited until the world came back in focus.

No breakfast; low blood sugar. A cup of coffee somewhere in between the library and the gaol to send it soaring, and then the lights and the fusty warmth, the dust and gloom, all factors contributing to the lack of control he recognized; all of them part of an explanation, but not a *reason* and never an excuse. He had felt the dead boy's hand brush at his leg, pulling him back, but knew there was nothing but a vision of Francesca, wearing her shawl, sitting in a cell for ever and ever, unable to move, opening her mouth to whisper, I can't talk now; I *can't* talk *now*. And he *had* known her.

She would never have risked a fate like that unless she had been entirely mad. If she had been caught, she would have lied and lied and lied.

'I don't owe you anything,' he shouted. '*Nothing!* Leave me alone, why don't you leave me alone?'

I'm not asking you for anything, Henry. I never did.

'If you were to remove the glass case from that bloody stuffed fish, Eddie,' Maggie was saying to him, 'I could throw darts at it. I don't know how you live with it.'

'Because I never look at it. Always have my back to the wall. What's wrong with it, anyway?'

'It looks quite incredibly smug. And it isn't a suitable adornment for the office of a fine legal brain. It speaks of savagery, hunting and fishing, to say nothing of poor taste and laziness.'

'Laziness?'

'Exactly. It looks as if you're too lazy even to get up and knock it off the wall. As well as insensitive. You obviously don't care if the clients loathe it.'

The cigarette smoke rose from the ashtray on his side of the frayed desk. Edward looked pained, an expression which twisted his face into a strange contortion. Any minute now, she feared he might clean the wax from his overlarge ears, but instead he busied himself threading paperclips into a chain then stopped, stubbed out the cigarette and lit another.

'Clients don't give a flying fuck about the décor. They're here because they need to be here. I don't care about it either, but I do like a sense of continuity. Why on earth should a place change the way it looks every decade? Or even every century, for that matter. I think it does them good to be in a place which makes their own miserable living rooms look positively palatial. Anyway, we can't afford change.'

'No,' she sighed. 'Probably not. Where were we?'

He knotted the motheaten scarf round his neck, suddenly businesslike. His black, half-fingered mittens lay on the desk, tribute to the fact that although the room was not yet warm, it was getting warmer.

'Jonathan Saunders has not paid the maintenance for his wife since six months ago. It was all agreed when the boy was two, you remember? A separate sum for him, capable of variation, depending upon need, but a fixed sum for her for ten years, beginning then. Not a generous sum, but an *agreed* sum, written in stone. I told her to go for a capital settlement, but she wouldn't. First, she said he wouldn't wear it; he had income but small capital, second she said she didn't need a lump sum just now; she'd rather accumulate an extra, emergency fund for the boy and that was the only way to persuade him to do it. She banked half the maintenance and shared the rest. I thought she could just go on banking it for the next seven years, and then there'd be a teeny nest egg when she comes out and needs a deposit for something. Only our sweet Jonathan – what did she ever see in the slimy shit? – now writes a sanctimonious letter from Bahrain or somewhere saying he doesn't see why he should pay money for the wife who murdered his son and how do we think we're going to make him anyway?'

The long speech exhausted Edward. He was the nearest he came to fury. 'And what that fucking maintenance could also do is pay us for continuing to look after her interests. Supposing she changes her mind about anything.'

Maggie was silent for a minute.

'Have you *always* wished she would change her mind, Edward, or are you newly converted?'

'It's grown on me,' Edward said simply. 'But you can't appeal a conviction on a guilty plea unless the client asks you to do it. Especially if she's pleaded guilty and given a graphic description to the police. You can't. *We* can't. Especially *me*. Place runs like a fucking charity as it is. Fat cat lawyers, ha ha ha. Still,' he added, visibly brightening as if the last drag of the cigarette was markedly better than the rest, 'there's always Uncle Joe.'

'My distant Uncle Joe, too,' Maggie said. 'Who was supposed to be dangerous to little girls. Angela visits, not me, I never knew him.'

Edward was back at the paperclip daisy chain, pausing only to wipe his spectacles with the tail of the red scarf.

'Visiting where? Who?'

Henry Evans entered the room without knocking. He sat in a crooked chair, smiled at them both. The open door brought in a chill and the distant sound of typewriters. There was a moment's silence.

'Hallo, Henry,' Maggie yelled with a manic cheerfulness which made Edward jump. 'What are you doing here?'

Henry seemed to consider. 'I tore the lining of my jacket,' he said. 'It was flapping down the back and I thought it was someone . . .'

His voice ceased on a sigh. His glasses were misted. He took them off and squinted, then gazed fixedly at one point in the room after another, as if he were checking the contents, his eyes resting on the fish longer than on any other feature, his expression registering mild distaste. His hair was windblown, adding to the slightly ridiculous appearance of a man entirely uncertain if he were actually present, but apparently quite at home.

'Do sit down,' Edward said, sarcastically. 'We have absolutely nothing better to do.'

Henry addressed himself to Maggie. She was blushing scarlet. His hands appeared to be locked into some kind of debate with the coins in his pocket. Maybe he was unhinged.

'I went out on the pier again,' he told her. 'I guess I really like that place. Or I did. I suppose a pier is something you build when you don't have any cliffs or high places, so, if you can't look down, you can at least look across.'

Maggie was nodding understandingly. They waited. Henry seemed to be daydreaming, relying on their polite indulgence.

It was hopeless trying to explain things; it always was. Henry squeezed his eyes shut and pinched the bridge of his nose. Edward was suddenly quite content for the man to find the necessary words while he himself contemplated his appearance thinking that at last, in the realms of clownish eccentricity, he had found someone with whom to compete. The man had stopped looking so fucking well dressed. The thought was comforting. In the lost, intervening two minutes, Henry was back on the pier, looking at the beach and the fishing men with their black umbrellas as he realized that the ghost stroking the back of his leg was the lining from his jacket and no ghost was about to strike him down. Thinking of how all his life he had been wisely running away from events and objects as well as people. The headlong dash from the confined spaces, the slipping away from his love affairs and relationships by mutual consent. Thinking of all the times he had avoided confrontations, how his nickname had once been Tortoise, how someone had once said he actually resembled a terrapin when he swam, and how his mildness was not really the same thing as tolerance, nor his calmness anything more than the fear of chaos and a cousin to cowardice. He was always the one who left, to preserve his dignity. Henry Evans would be the wise man who walked away to sleep through another winter. Even if he did have the sneaking feeling that whatever had become of her, whatever she had done, Francesca Chisholm, who had once led him out of the caves, would not have done the same.

'I'm not going to do it.'

'Do what, Henry?' Maggie prompted, her voice coming at him from a long distance, like his father's gentle voice calling him into eat from the door of the house, across the long back yard.

Garden, she would have said; you mean garden.

'I mean I'm not going home,' Henry explained patiently, as if his meaning had been perfectly obvious. 'I mean, no, I don't buy this shit about Francesca being a murderer. I don't even buy this shit about anyone alive being capable of doing it, either. I sure as hell couldn't, I'd walk away first.'

There was the *click, click* of Edward's lighter, a *clunk* as it landed where he threw it, then the scrape of a match.

'. . . So I just want to know how she was living. You know, who she knew, who she didn't. And if she killed the kid, I want to know why. I want to know what was wrong. I want there to be a reason. Maggie here could help me. I'll pay for your trouble. Looks like you could use it.'

'*She* is absolutely none of your business,' Edward said. Henry shrugged.

'Well I've walked away a few too many times,' he said, 'when I should have been turning back.'

Turn back? If only one could. Run away: I would.

Ah, the anniversary gets closer, casting a shadow, eclipsing every-thing, making me loquacious.

They tell me that the anniversary of the day you first come inside prison is the worst day of your life.

We didn't notice anything wrong with Harry at first. Perhaps because there was so much wrong with us. Having a child was my idea; it was my imperative; I was a late starter and full of hormonal madness. I wanted everyone to have lots of children, so that I could know them and make a sort of football team one day. The fact that my spouse was so dead against it was something I dismissed as a simple case of nerves. He would fall in love with the result, especially a girl. I should have accepted what he was instead of assuming he would change, but this was what I was going to do and I did it. And of course, when you are pregnant, the baby is more important than the husband. He didn't like that; he hated the terminal stages when everything went wrong. It wasn't a joyful birth and Harry was not a pretty child. He'd been in such distress before he was born, I could hardly expect him to come out smiling.

The unutterably cruel thing about this kind of cerebral palsy is that wonderful halcyon period before anyone notices anything wrong. Harry was nothing more or less than a lovely, placid baby. It was when he started to move. He couldn't sit without falling, always towards one side, and I would notice how he made himself fall in one direction. In retrospect, there is something so pathetic about that, trying to fall in the direction where he could protect himself. Then there was this odd pref-erence for one hand over another; I thought he was going to be left-handed and wondered where that had come from. Then when he began to crawl, he would haul himself forward with his left arm, drag the other, which looked funny and sweet until it didn't stop.

There was that moment when I looked at him and knew something was terribly wrong. It isn't a moment I can really describe. Even then

I was terrified of what might become of him. I wanted to put him back in the womb and tell him to stay where it was safe.

I had several books on cerebral palsy and I knew all about it. I did clear out all the books, didn't I? And the diaries I kept of his progress? Yes, I did, I'm sure I did.

We had lovely times, Angela and Tanya and I, playing with Harry. He was tough and determined, features I love in a boy. Oddly enough, with two damaged and utterly demanding children, there were too many crises to notice the departure of a husband. It was as if they had never existed. Mine must have known I would not mourn him. Poor man, he was right to go.

And he didn't abandon us, whatever it looked like. He came back sometimes and he sent enough money to help us. He did love me in his own way; it was I who rejected him.

It took me a while to realize how much he hated Harry. Angela, too, although hate's the wrong word for it, indifference tinged with irritation is closer to the mark. It was another of those heart-stopping revelations, more sad than bitter. I adored her child and, kind though she was, she simply could not love mine.

And nor did other people. I was no longer the universal friend, the person with time for everything and everybody. Harry and I, we were the ones in need.

Who killed Cock Robin?
I said the sparrow, with my bow and arrow
I killed Cock Robin . . .

Stoppit, stoppit . . . There is no one to blame but you.

FMC

CHAPTER SEVEN

THE rhyme and the tune of it ran through Maggie's head.

> *Some think to lose him,*
> *By having him confined,*
> *And some do suppose him*
> *(Poor thing!) to be blind.*
> *But if ne'er so close you wall him,*
> *Do the best that you may;*
> *Blind love (if so you call him)*
> *Will find out his way.*

'The answer,' Henry said, 'is always in the facts.'

'No, it isn't, Henry. It's in the emotions. Trust me, I'm a lawyer.'

'Maggie, why do I think you're playing games with me?'

'Because you're a North American, Henry. You don't understand flippancy.'

She remembered this conversation from her supine position on Laura Bains' very old sunbed, which was an integral part of the Bain beauty clinic (I'll be the bane of your life, ha, ha) situated halfway up Thistle Road, on the left. Can't miss it. She was remembering Henry, sitting in his upstairs room surrounded by papers, as he had been for the last four days except when he was out of doors making a tit of himself by his awful habit of direct and literal speech and his equally unfortunate inability to lie. When the lights went out on the sunbed and the rattle of the machine stopped with a judder, she pushed on the canopy. It creaked like the door of a tomb.

'Are you done? Get yourself over here.'

A short distance, the route between the window bay of a small, dark living room and the back wall, separated down the middle by a ceiling-height curtain of flowered plastic. Pulling on clothes as she went, Maggie slouched from the hard couch of the sunbed to the slightly softer and higher one of the massage couch.

'You must have bought that sunbed before we left school, Linda.'

'So you thought you'd got used to better, eh? Something in a fancy gym in London where the top bit went up by itself? I don't know, why do we bother?'

Cleansing lotion was applied to her face with deft hands. Maggie looked up to a ceiling of Artex swimming in whorls. On the radio a crisis was discussed in a phone-in. Cottonwool pads skimmed the surface of her skin.

'Thought I'd bugger off, once,' Linda was saying. 'Like you lot. Got pregnant and here I am. Was him buggered off. All comes out the same, dunnit? No place like home. You can burn the girl's bra for her and she'll ask for it back. And her corsets. No good playing high and mighty here, petal.'

'I never did.' The hands paused for a moment. There were the sounds of a vigorous washing movement out of sight.

'No. You never. Nor your cousin, to be fair.' A cool astringent was applied to Maggie's chin and swept upwards towards her forehead. 'You were such a romantic, weren't you? Always pretending to be the princess and spouting poetry. I never knew who you were going to be from one day to the next. You were bloody good fun, Maggie Chisholm. You still are, even if you did change your name and marry the wrong one. Didn't we all?'

'He wasn't the wrong one at the time.'

'No, they never are at the time. Never thought it would happen to you though, not after a dozen or more years. And it isn't enough reason to skulk around the way you do, as if you were the only one in that boat. You want to come out with me and the girls. Keep your eyes shut.' Linda used a new pad of cotton wool to ease off the last of the mascara from Maggie's left eye. "Stead of which, you can't settle, you. Can't buy a house with your money. Live with the poofters and now you're walking out with this American. At least I know you still look after your face. What does he want, this fella? Is he rich?' A further dollop of exfoliating lotion was applied, a little roughly. Maggie could feel a small callus on Linda's middle finger and wondered, inconsequentially, how it had arrived. She had a memory of a massage, somewhere in the past, given with rough hands, concentrated on the callus and kept her voice calm. She did not like people discussing Henry unless they did so with a bit of respect.

'I told you,' she said. 'He wants to find out more about Harry's death. He was in love with Francesca once and he can't believe she did it.'

'Hmmpph. So where was he when he was needed, then? Bit late, isn't he? I know what he's doing, I heard. I hear most things in here in the end, more than you do in that office, I can tell you. And there's plenty would tell him to let sleeping dogs alone, the silly oaf. Not that I didn't hear a lot of theories about it at the time. About how Franny's husband wanted her back, made a flying visit, thought to get the poor little boy out of the way, took the chance when he saw him out by himself. And then someone said it was Neil. Or Angela Hulme . . .'

'Ah, c'mon, Linda . . .'

'Well, Franny had much more time for her cute little kiddie before Harry got round to running and mumbling, didn't she? All right when he was little, not when he grew. Someone else reckoned it was the poofters, but he never stopped there overnight and it was early on a Sunday morning, wasn't it? But I thought it was some drugged-up weirdo – we've got a few of them, haven't we? – until she said it was her. And then it all made sense. So I should stop the daft bastard asking questions before someone punches him on the nose, or worse. Stop clenching your fists, will you? You're supposed to relax.'

Small grains of a fine, sandy substance applied to her cheeks eased the remnants of grime from her pores. The effect was soporific. The room was blissfully warm and the world outside distinctly uninviting. Maggie unclenched her fists obediently.

'I can't stop him asking questions,' Maggie said. 'He's a scientist.'

'That's no excuse. Bugger that doorbell. She's early.'

Murmuring in the hall. Laughter. Linda returned. Maggie rubbed her eyes. The sunbed whirred into life and there was the sound of disrobing behind the curtain. The facial continued in silence.

You were such fun, Maggie. Once upon a time. Soon, no one will talk to you at all. She counted on her fingers as Linda massaged her neck and shoulders and she made small, appreciative noises. A van rumbled up the narrow street.

Get Henry the keys to her flat . . . Done it.

Get Neil to cooperate and talk to him . . . Reluctant, but I'm working on it.

Get Angela to talk to Henry . . . Impossible. She absolutely refuses. He'll have to try and waylay her himself.

Tell him he can use the internet in the library . . . He knows that already, sniffed it out like a dog.

'He's a bit like a dog,' she murmured to Linda as the hydrating mask began to harden round her nose.

'Who? The American?'

'Yes, a lovely big dog with a thick coat and big, soft eyes.'

'Well, I don't know, Maggie, I really don't. You never could pick them. You always picked the dope. What's he doing now, then, while you're not watching?'

'God only knows.'

She saw her coat hanging on the hook behind the door, with one sleeve sticking out, as if making a salute.

It never snows here, or not for long, Maggie had told him. He had opened the window of his room and caught a collection of snowflakes on the sleeve of his black jacket, displayed them to her and said, what do you call this? It had snowed for two hours, which did not make Maggie a reliable informant. She was a comfortable fixture in his room, admiring the tidiness with which he had arranged it, bringing up his breakfast and hers, examining the snowflakes as if they were a rare kind of insect, perching herself on the edge of his silk-clad bed from which all the case papers in *R v. Chisholm* had been neatly removed.

The world beyond the house was a dismal contrast, entered reluctantly after prevaricating on the way downstairs and going back twice for gloves. The snow lay, sludgy and unconvincing on the pavements, a nuisance so near the shore, but enough, he heard, to block the roads beyond. Long before his damp footsteps had traversed the quarter-mile between the house and the church, Henry wanted to return, but the inside of the building was moderately warm, to his enormous relief. It looked, from the outside, as if it should be cold. Peter was already there.

'Francesca came here regularly,' he explained, admiring Henry's leather boots, while wishing he had the sense to accept the offer of a pair of Wellingtons.

'Not as a believer, you understand,' the vicar interrupted in his fluting voice, which fitted better inside a warm and empty church than it did round a dinner table. The voice belonged in here; it invited an echo and the enunciation of prayers. The exaggeration of his precise syllables seemed to have a purpose in this space. 'More as a person, quite candidly in search of an insurance policy. Not for herself, although she did like the ambience, she told me, but for the children. She bought Tanya Hulme here when she was first adopted and not so long after, Harry as a babe in arms. She was perfectly honest about her motives; she always was.'

'Motives?' Henry queried. He eyed the ornate carving of the pulpit and visualized the priest enjoying his robes.

'Oh come now, Mr Evans, all who seek religious observance have a motive. Membership of a club perhaps, the opportunity to wear a hat, perhaps, peace and quiet perhaps; the chance to observe one another and be observed. The chance to spend an hour in a pretty place. And we do try with the flowers, don't we, Peter?'

Peter was arranging stems of winter foliage in a tall vase, standing back to gauge the effect, nodding. The church was Victorian antiquity, heavy rather than refined, but the pews were polished and the kneelers lovingly sewn. 'I'm quite sure if we didn't she might have gone to the Methodists for the sake of better hymns, but she wanted the children to get used to the idea. To gain the blessing of God in case there was one, she told me. Let them reject it later if they wanted, she said, but not on the basis of ignorance. I quite understood. If I insisted on believers, I'd never have a congregation at all.'

'So now I know what she did on Sunday morning . . .'

'What *we* did,' Peter interrupted.

'But it doesn't help me much with her problems,' Henry continued, earnestly. 'I mean if you were her priest, in whatever form, and Harry was a parishioner, why didn't she come to you for help? You didn't do much, did you?'

The priest and Peter exchanged a glance of resignation. Two persons, noticing in unison how Henry was not diplomatic in the posing of questions.

'I did help. I put her in touch with people who cared deeply. She'd no family left, you see; when you're conceived by relatively elderly parents as she was, you tend to lose them. I found her these two –' he nodded in Peter's direction – 'to help with Harry, but there was nothing I could do about the darker reaches of the night. Nothing. I couldn't make her invoke the aid of a

God in whom she didn't believe. In any event, *help* wasn't the problem.'

He sat heavily on one of the highly polished pews, curled one hand round the carved pommel and stroked it. His hand was dry and chapped, grazed with rough work, which Henry found endearing. Peter and Timothy had hands like that; so, he imagined, did Christ's disciples. It gave the vicar credibility, removed him further from the alternative image of the dilettante, dinner party guest with a fistful of wine. Henry waited. The priest continued to stroke the wood, as if it were a magic lamp, able to produce words.

'The problem was that she was such a good person. *Is*, or was, I don't know, but *good*. By which I mean blessed with a natural virtue which requires no outside nourishment. She wasn't *good* out of fear of the consequences; she was simply good. She had a quick tongue, all right, but she was incapable of harbouring malice. She could complain, but she couldn't retain a mean thought or harbour resentment, not to save her life. She had a unique capacity for nurturing others. Loving them, you might say. And if it weren't heretical, I'd say she could teach a Christian God a thing or two about forgiveness and generosity. She didn't need to pray for them.'

Peter coughed, embarrassed by the oratory. Henry winced. 'So what's the problem with that?'

The vicar heaved himself upright and clasped his hands in the lap of his cassock. It was not a dapper garment, and slightly grubby.

'A person blessed with a singular and natural goodness and great sensitivity, especially if matched with a handsome face and physical agility, is a draw for the weak and the lame. For the wicked and the afflicted, as well as the needy. They become indispensable. But they also repel, Mr Evans. Virtue is difficult to endure. People resent the bright spotlight of pure goodness. It makes them feel deficient. Which is why,' he added, 'I myself make a good vicar.' He grinned and Henry warmed to him again. 'My flaws and my boredom level are all too apparent. I lack the charisma of goodness, you see. The blessing and the curse of it. Nobody gets angry with me when I haven't got the time. They did with Francesca.'

Peter stepped down off the small ladder he had mounted to reach the vase behind the pulpit. His movements were noisy, his sighs gusty.

'This arrangement doesn't work,' he said. 'Won't last in this awful heat.' It was an over-ambitious arrangement of holly and laurel, wobbling. Henry adjusted his spectacles and nodded.

'Yeah, it's crap,' he said. He turned back to the priest.

'So it was *goodness* that made her spend so much time and energy on Tanya Hulme and her mother. They were a pretty inseparable foursome, I gather. Was that goodness? And who was it *good* for?'

'Ah, that. That, I think, was simply love. She fell in love with the child. And it was good for a highly strung, beautiful little girl who needed a bottomless pit of unreserved love to make up for the damage done to her. If you'd seen that terrified little savage, your heart would have gone out to her, too.'

'Does she come to church now?'

'Oh dear me, no. I don't think her mother wants any influence on the child other than her own. She may be right: consistency's the thing.'

Peter's arrangement overbalanced with a crash. Henry moved to help him pick up the pieces.

'I think these should have stayed on the tree,' Peter said ruefully.

'Yeah, perhaps.' Henry patted him on the shoulder, realizing as he did so that it was the first time he had touched him. Peter grinned broadly.

'There you are,' he said. 'We don't bite. Are you going to be in for supper? Only we're having a musical evening.'

'Perhaps not,' Henry said. 'But thanks.'

No one had ever mastered the challenge of heating the castle. It was entirely natural that no one should; it was not designed to be heated, or even to be pristine clean, Neil remembered as he retrieved a flying polythene bag from the legs of a cannon and hurried back inside. The billets of the common soldiers would never have been clean; the kitchens might well have stunk. Where the desire for comfort had intruded into the quarters occupied by the officers of the military, there would have been tapestries and hangings to forestall the draughts. There remained a couple of fine wood-panelled rooms, superior ranks for the use of. The painted panels bore portraits or photographs of heavily bewhiskered wardens of the keep from 1800 until the last was made redundant. Chisholm's was not only the last face, but the only one without facial hair and with the temerity to smile. Bad idea to banish living accommodation from the central keep, Neil thought, although he could see it was ridiculously expensive to maintain, but the lack of a family living at the heart of a fortress garrison encouraged the proliferation of ghosts, who could wander round these sombre rooms and make obscene gestures at portraits of the masters. Up yours, wardens of the keep; we rule now.

The castle was officially closed for the day; he was here, checking stock for the next, sorting the postcards and guidebooks, making it neat in preparation for his own day off and, although he was absorbed in the tasks, he was anxious. There were better things to do beyond these heavy walls. 'Get laid,' he said to himself. *For ever.* The weekend had been brilliant; she was gorgeous and the future worried him extremely. Viagra. The doctor said he was only allowed enough for three or four experiments; after that, the cost was private and amounted to a small fortune. Would his stupid, uncooperative prick decide after a while that his body had cracked the code and behave all by itself? Would he have to increase the amount? Would he even have enough for a week? Where would he find a supply now his life was unimaginable without it? Would he lose his girl like he lost his wife?

He collected three packets of peanuts, dismissing the slight guilt at failing to check downstairs and risk being late; why should he? Mustn't be late for Tanya. Angela would kill him. He hurried over the drawbridge, pulling the hood of his anorak over his head. There was a posse of people, huddled by the notice at the entrance.

'Excuse me, are you open?'

Neil put his face close and breathed salty breath.

'No, mate. Closed for *exorcism*.'

He had enough Viagra pills for tomorrow, maybe a couple more times and that was all.

Maggie faced her shiny clean face away from the sea and walked towards the back of the town. Slush melting on pavements and the sky leaden. She loved it. She wished she had no purpose other than to walk. She reached the humpbacked bridge which traversed the railway line. The train rumbling from the distance looked like the Toytown Express and she paused on the high point to feel it pass beneath her feet, the bridge trembling slightly as the engine slowed. There was a view from the bridge of the park and the town, peacefully calm and pacified by snow. The restlessness in her died. She did not want to be on the train out of here. There was really nowhere else to go and no one would know her when she got there. Life was remarkably consistent.

Snow had settled in the park next to the gym club. Indoor activities had been abandoned in favour of the novelty and kids were outside. Snow had settled on the grass; it layered the bushes on the borders. A snowman had grown in the middle of the space, rapidly built into a round trunk of a body and the semblance of a head too small in proportion. Someone had provided a carrot to make a nose on an otherwise featureless face; there were gloves on the hands folded over the fat torso, but no ears or eyes to give the head expression. The omissions were under loud debate, while Tanya Hulme, lissom and chestnut haired, hung back from the surrounding crowd. Skinny legs poked out of an overpuffed jacket and led to enormous, black trainer-clad feet which kicked the snow. The best-dressed kid in town and no one wanted to know her.

Maggie waded across the snow in her direction, soaking the cuffs of her trousers.

'What's up, Tanya?' Maggie remembered not to use any diminutive of her name. If you did not know about children, you did not know what they liked, except their own dignity, perhaps. Tanya kicked the snow until she found the grass beneath, went on kicking. The laces of her trainers were undone. 'Someone else found the carrot,' she whispered, pointing. 'And I wish it was me. I tried to get it off her, so they told me to sod off.'

'Hmm, I see black stones, perfect for eyes,' Maggie said, stooping to the pathway. 'And then we can have leaves for ears, plenty of leaves. You can have my hat for his head.'

'Why?' There were furious tears in her eyes.

'Because when you give him a face, he'll smile at you.'

The child stared suspiciously, grabbed the stones, backed off, guarding them, turned swiftly and ran into the crowd, offering eyes for the face. Then she was back alongside, like a puppy, *What about them fucking ears?* Laurel bushes framed the pathway: Maggie shook them free of snow and plucked leaves which frayed at the tip, brown at the ends, curling inwards. They looked earlike; Tanya grabbed them as if they were salvation and ran towards her tribe. The ears appeared on the head. She cantered back to Maggie, still full of urgency.

'Your hat! I *need* your hat. *Pleeeeease.*' Maggie bent her head.

'Tan, stoppit.'

Tanya paused for a second to look at Neil who had slouched to a halt beside them, sprang away with the hat in her hand, screaming back to the group, waving it. The hat next appeared on the lopsided head of the snowman and there was the sound of ragged applause.

'Sorry about that,' Neil said. 'I'll get it back for you in a minute.'

'Doesn't matter,' Maggie said. 'I don't like hats. Shawls are better.'

They watched the children. By common decision, the class had decided that the clumsy creation of their hands was now a suitable target for destruction. They were forming snow into solid lumps and flinging them. Maggie's hat was the target and Tanya was the only one to hit it. The hat was replaced at a rakish angle and the onslaught recommenced to the high, shrill sound of shrieking.

'It helps to be mad,' Neil said.

'I don't think I regret not having children,' Maggie said.

'The American you phoned about,' Neil said diffidently. 'Going to work for Fergusons. If I talk to him, do you think he'd get me some Viagra?'

'It works then, does it?'

'And how.'

'Be careful, won't you, Neil? You've got to be careful with any drug.'

'Oh, God, you sound just like Francesca, endlessly caring. But could he . . .?'

She flushed pink with sheer annoyance. 'Oh, I'm sure he could. He's got a suitcase full of pills in his room. Guards it carefully.'

'Probably peddling them to poofters. In his room? Like that, is it, Maggie? In his room often, are you?'

'No, Neil, it isn't like that. And I don't know how Henry Evans might help. Tell you how to get it, perhaps. All you've got to do is talk to him.'

'Me? I haven't got anything to say. I didn't know what was going on, did I? I was always excluded. Oh, not by Francesca; she did try and get us back together, but by Angela. She didn't want a man near that child.' His feet scuffed the grass where Tanya's had cleared the snow. 'I'd no idea about Fran's life. Only knew that Angela resented her a bit. Harry took up time she'd given to Tan, not that she always liked that either. Difficult to please, Ange.'

'Well, let our Henry buy you a drink. Persuade Angela to have a chat with him.'

'You must be bloody joking. Tell you what, school's closed tomorrow and she's doing my duty at the castle with Tan. Send him there, I would.' Neil closed his eyes and thought of the plans made for his day off. A trip to France, a meal to be cooked in the evening and . . . He waved towards Tanya. 'She gets better all the time, though. She makes me laugh.'

The children were losing momentum; slower shots, chapped hands beginning to bite, mothers on the sidelines beginning to fuss until the girl alone went on with unabated enthusiasm. The snowman withstood the onslaught with shapeless stoicism. Maggie's hat had disappeared.

'I have to admit that little Harry fair gave me the creeps,' Neil went on, frankly. 'He was like this sponge, absorbing energy without giving very much back, as far as I could see. But then, I wasn't his dad, so I'm not qualified. Never could understand how he got to the end of the pier on his own, though.'

Tanya was tiring, stopping to blow on her fingers and warm them. Neil turned to Maggie. 'Whatever Francesca did for us, she took it all back. She cancelled it all out. She made herself indispensable and then, *boom* . . . and then she has the nerve . . . Oh look, she's finished . . . Better get her home. I want to go fishing.'

Tanya raced towards them, waving Maggie's hat and to her pleasant embarrassment, she curtsied and presented it. Then she hugged her. Maggie was taken by surprise. 'Swing me,' she demanded of Neil. She was just the right size and weight to swing in a circle, legs flailing, screaming as if she was tickled. He put her down, breathlessly. '*Again, again!*' she shouted. 'Enough,' he said, and she moved ahead, obediently.

'She wouldn't have done that a year ago,' Neil muttered.

'What? Hug someone?'

'No, bring back the hat.'

She left them, then, unable to bear it. She could see it all, now. Neil, careful and responsible with a child he could never have fathered. And herself, going between them all, occasionally witnessed, like a ghost. Francesca's engineer, the bit part player who never engaged, the sort of understudy who learned the lines someone else would always say and stayed around at the end to pick up the pieces. Helping Henry rake over ashes, looking for some unidentifiable bone and knowing she had no choice.

They needed him. They needed a stranger.

Number 40 in the block, where Francesca had lived, was reached by anonymous stairs. '*Took lease here after husband left. Friend and daughter live other side of same building.*' A prudent and convenient arrangement to live close to friend, etc., but no one wanted to live in it now. Can't flog it, rent it or any damn thing, Edward Burns said. Desirable residence, ha, ha, ha. Bloody white elephant, even with sea views. The lock was awkward; there was the noise of a television, muffled by walls as Henry fiddled with the key and felt like a burglar. The interior was an enormous disappointment, but then the House of Enchantment had spoiled him. Warm in temperature, anonymous in style; a big, sea-facing living room with the remnants of indifferent, fitted furniture of the kind she might have bought from the previous occupant, nothing new or distinctive and all of it worn. Shelves full of books, cupboards beneath with chipped doors and a carpet which looked as if it had been used as a playing field with the central area stained and worn to the thread. A swivel chair by the window with a coffee table alongside and a shawl folded over the arm. Henry picked up the shawl and held it to his face. Inferior quality, faintly musty, and he tried to remember if Francesca had ever had a scent peculiar to herself. Perhaps, but he had not known it; he had no olfactory memories. She had a style, though; a definite style; a knack even with travelling clothes and a way of pinning her hair in a dozen different ways.

He looked at the bookshelves, found a few novels, a shelf full of nursery rhyme books, nothing more to indicate who had lived here, except the marks and the scuffs and the tracks made by feet. Where were the volumes of verse he had expected? Where were the poets? Henry sat in the chair and looked at the grey sky. The splendour of the sea was invisible; the level of the window was all wrong, set too high from the floor for anyone seated in a chair to get the best view. The sound of the television continued, an irritating buzz, like a fly in the room. To be deprived of a view of the sea seemed to be the ultimate insult for anyone who deliberately lived on the edge of it, a feature which would drive him mad.

He stood, therefore, and paced. A sizeable kitchen with table for eating, efficiently equipped by transatlantic standards with cooking and chilling facilities all of which looked beaten if not into submission at least into overfamiliarity. A bathroom which was simply rudimentary, and Henry was beginning to learn that the Brits did not seem to set much store on power showers and such. There were no ornaments anywhere. *Useful* objects – TV, phones, microwaves – had been removed, leaving signs of their presence such as a mark on the wall, an empty stand and small table with directories beneath. The apartment had been subject to controlled and authorized scavenging.

Think, Henry. Just damn well THINK. His father's voice, the reminder of intellectual rigour, resisted. Hey Dad, I'm thinking I don't like her much. The woman I knew would never have lived in a place like this. If she lived in it, you'd know she'd been there and there's not a single sign; I think I'll go now. It's all too *ORDINARY. No, you damn well don't. THINK.* Measure it out; do not do anything by halves. *Look at the shelves. Yeah, and a letter will fall out of a book. Happens all the time. THINK.* The shawl was the only personal object left and he wondered why. It looked deliberately placed; at odds with the lack of personality. Henry had moved house more often than he could count, always looking for the one with a greater sense of space. He had seen rooms left equipped with enough furnishings to make them appear habitable and give them some sense of scale, but never one so completely neutralized. Only an owner could take everything away; no one else could be as ruthless.

He sat in the window chair, but the line of the sill across his eyes and the view of nothing but ominous clouds irritated him, so he stood up, hands on hips, prowling like a prospective tenant. Maggie said Francesca had done it in the intervening days between Harry's death and her own arrest; her apartment had reached this state by the time she was taken in the third time for questioning. She had not expected to come back. The car and the etceteras went later, on her instructions, to specific destinations, but the correspondence, the mementoes, the family snaps, the Christmas cards, even the birth certificates and household bills were long gone, as well as most of her clothes and all of Harry's.

Not the systematic actions commonly associated with someone rendered unsystematic by guilt . . . or grief. Henry could feel dislike of her creeping all over his skin like a mild sweat.

Maggie said all she wanted in prison were books and reams of paper. Perhaps that's what she did in there: rewrote her own life. If you had felt the arms of a child wrapped round your neck in hopeless trust, how could you harm it? He did not know; he simply did not know. He felt unqualified to know: it was not a desperation or a temptation he wished to share.

The sound of the television had ceased, leaving a vacuum of silence. Outside sounds were muffled by the double-glazed windows. In the House of Enchantment, there were none of these; Henry had come to enjoy the intrusion of sound. He looked down from the living room window, preferring his own view. Second floor, less than ideal for a child; stairs to traverse on the way out. He could see the castle squatting to the left and the dark sea ahead of him.

Remembered his laptop. The scruffy library with internet access. *Cerebral palsy . . . no typical profile for a child of five . . . depends upon severity . . . epileptic fits?*

He could see a child crawling across the floor, with one arm tucked beneath, hauling himself along with the other. He had retreated to the front door with his back to it, feeling in his pocket for the key, his shoulder touching the painted wood. The timid knock on the other side seemed to touch his spine. Henry stood upright, shook himself. He had every right to be here. He was a prospective tenant. Must have been a dozen or three over the year. One of them left a cigarette end in the trash can; he'd seen it.

Francesca had smoked. Mild Indian cigarettes which were a password to conversation. That had been her smell. Henry opened the door.

'Oh. You.'

Standing on the threshold was the granny from the High Street who picked him out of the gutter and told him she lived round the corner from the house. Three-quarters of a mile from here, level walking, but still a distance. She had a lit cigarette she hid behind her back.

'Thought it might be you,' she said, matter of factly. She walked straight through to the kitchen and stubbed out her cigarette in the sink. 'I live downstairs,' she said, as if that explained everything. 'Heard you. You've never been falling over again, have you?'

'No. It isn't a habit.'

'One of these days, maybe. Lovely flats, these. Do you want to buy it?'

'No.'

She moved to the window and tapped the sill. The clouds outside and the fading light seemed to meet with her approval. 'It wasn't like this, you know. You can't keep a place nice with a kid in it and she knew not to try. But she had a ladder with cushions on it by this window. That's where she'd sit. Reading, when she got the chance.'

'What did she read?'

'Books, of course. She gave most of them to me. She was forever giving things away.'

He felt a faint fluttering of the heart.

'She said they'd look nice in my living room and she was right about that. I never thought she wouldn't come back. Nor him, neither, poor little chap. Not that I've got much use for books. My eyes are bad now.' She stared at him and looked away. 'I got the books and the poofs got the video. I could have done with the video. I could have done without those two kids over my head, yelling fit to bust, and all I get's a few useless books. I miss her to death. She did everything the wrong way round and she was smashing. Do you want these books, or not, since you're a friend of hers?'

He was nonplussed and nodding. She was on her feet, leading him out, telling him to lock up. She was a single-handed explanation of why the place could not be sold. He followed her downstairs.

'She should have let me look after him instead of them poofters,' she said over her shoulder. 'But I didn't really have the strength. I can't manage that dog, either. It keeps getting out. Harry was strong, you see, and wilful. But I tell you one thing. He wouldn't have gone all the way downstairs and out on the pier by himself on a morning like that. If there was anything Harry hated, he hated the cold. Are you going to come in?'

An hour later, walking home with the sea on his right, Henry swung his arms and let his fingers grow nicely numb with the cold. The chill was almost pleasant. Granny's double-glazed flat was hotter than Florida, with a breathless, hermetically sealed, humid heat. She was mortally afraid of the cold. The jungle temperature of her premises made him relish it now. Her phrase echoed.

He hated the cold, that boy. Henry knew why Harry hated the cold. Henry was walking home with the lining of his good jacket still torn, but his shoes clean. Thinking of facts and why a person would abandon their books. Thinking of all the thumbnail sketches Maggie had given him and what little he had learned.

There it was again, that damn black dog, coming out of a turning, wagging a tail at him and running off. It fitted his mood, as elusive as fact.

Saw the chaplain today. Distracted me from the facts I was on the brink of writing.

I always had a belief that Creation could not be random and merely the forces of nature, although if you looked long enough at the sea, you would doubt there was a human logic to it. The sea might feed us, but is alien, because its primary purpose is to feed itself and all the creatures who live in it. A brutal regime is imposed from time to time; there are mandatory culls of the predators and passengers. Man is endured, allowed to harvest as well as to cross, but if it all gets too much, the ocean shrugs him off and eats him. As dictated by a committee of Neptunes.

I tend to believe there are several gods; it is quite impossible to believe in one. There's a sort of parliament of Gods with ministries, definitely not democratically elected and all undermining one another. There's too much for one God to do; he had to delegate after the first failures, break the whole thing down into dukedoms and fiefdoms and they all formed rivalries. I can see it. Somebody shouts I WANT TO BE MINISTER FOR THE SEA, but he can't. His job this session is to be Minister for Weather.

> *The thunder God went for a ride (I told the chaplain),*
> *Upon his favourite filly,*
> *I'm THOR! he cried.*
> *The horse replied,*
> *You forgot your thaddle, thilly.*

That was one of Maggie's. Yes, a cabinet ministry of gods and their delegates with thor thaddles.

I digress. I MUST digress.

I had to say that the door was open and he took himself off. It was what I said first and I had to stick with it. No one else in the world knew the extent of his condition as well as I did, or his temperament.

They might have done if they had read all the books and the papers I read, searching for a prognosis. That was why I got rid of the books. I told them I went to find him, already cross with him, and when I saw him, naughty as ever, I decided enough was enough. I told them I had thought of it often. When I saw his limbs swell, when I read what he might become and he knew he was not one of the mild cases. When I saw that even at his most engaging, he was friendless.

But he did have friends, they said, and so did you. Ah yes, but not the ones I needed and he craved. He adored the ones who were at best indifferent. He adored Uncle Joe, who, harmless as he was by then, only had eyes for little girls. So much for family. So much for knowing anyone. It takes such a long time and the choice is such a gamble. I befriended Uncle Joe when he was old because it seemed to me that to be isolated from your tribe, and in particular from children, is a fate worse than any death. To be old, without visitors; to have lost your reputation, what kind of suffering is that? How prophetic. I wanted him to avoid the fate I have made myself.

The chaplain finds me frivolous. He says I must face facts.

FMC

CHAPTER EIGHT

CRUNCH, *crunch, crunch.* Their footsteps along the gravel of the beach echoed loud enough to waken the dead. She seemed sure-footed; he slithered and she took his arm.

'Steps up that way, Henry.'

'Thank you.'

Maggie liked the way he consented to be led. No macho non-sense. The sea was unnaturally calm and kind, kissing the stones like a flirt at a party, he said. It was a strange description for him to use.

'This won't be *haute cuisine*,' she warned.

'I'm into depravity. Carbohydrates and cigarettes are fine.'

Seven in the evening, blacker than a road. He did not care what he ate. They stumbled up steps from the darkness of the beach in a state of merciful quiet, walked down an alley he had never noticed, round several corners he had never noticed either and into the bowels of a building. He was not in an observant state this evening, and she was duly grateful. *She* could criticize Warbling's restaurant fare because she lived here; if *he* did it, she would be defensive.

'All there was was medical books,' he said flatly as they sat. 'And the old lady confuses books with magazines, same thing to her. Books on paediatric illness, psychology, abuse, and two dozen pamphlets on cerebral palsy. No poetry. No letters. What happened to her soul?'

House wine arrived on a checked cloth. He raised his glass to her. She waited for him to wince at the taste, but he was entirely indifferent to the quality and she sighed with relief, annoyed at the same time that she should actually mind if he liked it or not.

'Children were her job, Henry, as well as her passion. There's nothing odd about a collection of books like that, even without Harry. She was thorough. She would have known more about Harry's hemiplegia than anyone else.'

'More than the prosecutor. And the so-called *defensse*, it seems,' he said quietly.

'We spell it with a "c", Henry. As in fence. And an English lawyer, Henry, is not a writer of fiction. We do not create a *defensse*, any more than we can write a story. *If* we have a client who is responsible, intelligent and articulate, and that's a big *if*, our humble role is only that of translator.' She rearranged her knife and fork, aligning them with the edge of the table. 'The point of the role is to clarify the facts and the mitigating circumstances, make all of them understandable and sympathetic to the most unresponsive of tribunals. There is only one sentence for premeditated murder, Henry. Life imprisonment. As a translator of facts, *one* does not have a great deal of scope to influence the outcome. Especially with a client as stubborn as that. Someone who had decided that the sentence was necessary for her own redemption. The choice here, by the way, is pizza or pizza.'

'A truly universal dish.' His face creased with a smile and seen like that, it was an extremely pleasant face, made memorable by dimples and almost mischievous. In repose, the same face was perfectly inscrutable. One did not know, Timothy had observed to her, whether it was content, curious, angry or on the verge of tears. One simply hoped for the best. The smile was infectious and she smiled back. For people who had spent hours in conversation, the formality of dinner alone at his suggestion was making them oddly stilted with one another.

'What's so funny, Henry?'

'You,' he said. 'You get so didactic. You give me lectures. I can see you laying down the law. Only it doesn't go with anything else.'

'Such as?'

'The dress. The hair. The eyes.'

She crossed her eyes and pulled a face.

'You can leave the eyes out of it. They're simply genetic inheritance. The hair is tinted every six weeks. And colourful clothes are allowed, even for part-time lawyers. It's a nice red, isn't it? Like old bricks. I call this ensemble my battered English rose look.'

He eyed the dress. Modestly scooped neck, simple knitted thing with long sleeves. A row of pearls at the neck, cheeks pink from the walk and hair blown wilder. He looked beyond her to the door, always checking the exit, especially in basements, like a spy, and after that he felt relaxed, even though the day had been depressing. There was always tomorrow and he could not remember when he had last sat opposite a woman as oddly glamorous as this and it was fun, even if his attitude towards her was tempered with profound suspicion. He really should know her better; well enough to tease her at any rate.

'Listen, Maggie. If we'd met through, oh, say a dating agency or a mutual friend . . .'

'We did.'

'Just say we were having our first evening alone . . .'

'We are.'

'You just aren't cooperating, Maggie. I'm asking you to use your imagination. *If* we were on a prearranged, let's get to know each other date, without the agenda we already have and all the encrypted information you dole out, what would you want me to know about you? I mean, what would you be telling me?'

'OK, I'll play if you'll play.'

He nodded. 'You go first.'

She clasped her hands beneath her chin, hiding long fingers, fluttered her eyelashes theatrically.

'I'd give you a slightly self deprecating account of my life to date, the description carefully tailored to suit the occasion and leaving out the worst bits. I'd probably omit the childhood, because you wouldn't want to know. I'd tell you I left the small town for the sake of a career, but I probably wouldn't tell you that I went to find a better class of husband, who abandoned me for a . . . no.' She paused. 'No, I wouldn't say that. I'd say I was amicably divorced, in case you should think I was a contentious bitch who liked fighting. I'd mention somewhere along the line that I used to like designing rooms and cooking. Emphasis on home comforts. By the end of my little recitation you'd know that I was brave, modest, capable, bittersweet and available. Definitely available. I'd stress that as much as cooking. And I wouldn't be wearing this dress.'

He was laughing. She teased her hair with her fingers and looked at him soulfully, fluttering her eyelashes again in a parody of shy hesitation.

'I wouldn't, on considering, tell you that on my second date with my husband, I tried to impress him with steak for dinner in my weeny garden flat, only the dog got it and was trying to bury it in a flowerbed. I rescued it, quietly, dusted it down and served it up. He ate it like a lamb and persuaded me to give away the dog. That should have told me everything I needed to know.'

The order for food was written down laboriously. Henry had an idea it might take some time to arrive. Three other diners between himself and the exit had the look of starved resignation. Maggie nibbled a breadstick.

'I'd lie quite a lot, Henry. The quotient of lies to truth would depend on how much I liked you. Your turn.' Her face had reverted to normal: that of an intelligent listener without an ounce of the coquette.

'Well . . .' He coughed and cleared his throat.

'No hesitations.'

'I guess I'd start with my full name and qualifications. Tell you my status. Let you know I earned money, had no debts, travelled a lot. Was smart. Didn't go round with my flies undone. No sexual problems, but not a womanizer, like them too much. Failed relationships not the result of infidelity or malice. And it would all be true. In a way.'

He played with the paper napkin, forming it deftly into the shape of a hat while she watched intently.

'I'd say I wasn't so good at talking about myself and I was kind of shy on account of always opening my mouth to say the wrong thing. Also true. I don't like to lie. Low on social skills. But I guess I might leave out the stuff about being afraid of the dark, scared to death of being locked in, running away from confrontations and commitments so fast I'm out of sight. I'd probably pretend that I wasn't *quite* available, some little piece of unfinished business somewhere. I'd confess to being complex.'

'And are you?'

'Nope. Not as far as I know. I'm just a fully paid up coward.'

There was an uncomplicated silence, punctuated by the sound of her teeth with the breadstick and the murmur of conversation from behind.

'I wonder if we'd want to see one another again.'

Henry shrugged and grinned as the pizza arrived, thumped on the table in a loud challenge to digestion.

'Probably not. Such a paragon of a woman would destroy my confidence. If she said she liked gardening, it might be a different matter.'

'And I,' she said, 'would be worried by your haircut and all that bloody mystique.'

They began to eat, slowly. Henry struggled with a blunt knife, looked at the problem logically and opted to cut the pizza into four slices, which was easier decided than done. A portion of neo-Neapolitan cheese'n'tomato scooted from his plate across the narrow table and on to her lap. She flicked it to the floor, delicately.

'Shit, I'm so sorry. Didn't I mention the clumsiness?'

'If this was a date, Henry, you'd have blown it.'

He struggled silently, elbows flexed, then picked up a slice and chewed it carefully. It was only another pizza, which would go on and on being a pizza, the way they did. He was deciding that if he was ever going to have any preference for food, it was going to be for a lot of different little things on a big plate, eaten to the tune of impersonal conversation.

'I think Francesca gave away her medical books for a reason,' he said. 'Such as not wanting anyone to know how bad Harry was. Or how relevant his condition was to the manner of his death.'

'There's a medical report on the file, Henry,' she said patiently, resigned to his resumption of the topic. 'There was nothing to hide. The prognosis wasn't good. She was desperate for him to be able to go to a normal school and it didn't look as if he could.'

'There's nothing there about the daily details. Exactly what he could and couldn't do. What he *would*, or wouldn't do. Didn't you know?'

She shook her head again. The hair danced. 'I came back about a month before it happened, got a job with Edward. Saw them a couple of times, but I was so full of self-pity I didn't notice anything much. Except how cold it was. I was waiting for spring.'

'Did you love her?' he asked, hesitantly, then waited for her to finish a mouthful. The blunt knives did not seem to affect her efficient dissection of the food; there must be a knack to it. The silence went on for so long, he was afraid he had been impertinent, or worse, sentimental, but it was only her manners and the length of time she needed to demolish a mouthful.

'Oh yes. Better than anyone alive. But I was jealous of her, too.'

'Why?'

'Because she seemed to have an unerring sense of right and wrong. Because she was loyal and good and because everyone loved her.'

When he looked down, his own plate was bare, hers half empty. It was another thing he noticed about the Brits, that they ate so slowly and everything took so long. As well as what they said not making sense.

In the House of Enchantment, the boys had left the door on the latch, expecting a late arriving guest. A figure crept up the stairs. The dining room and the hall reverberated with Timothy's furious playing of the piano and Peter's voice, rising in wavering unison.

> *Say, gentle ladies, if love you know.*
> *Is love this fever troubling me so?*
> *Ees love this fe-evah troubling me so?*

The figure paused on the landing, pushed open doors, softly, a single, swift look inside enough to establish the negative. The room on the second floor was too feminine, the rooms below so obviously the domain of the resident. Another flight, panting as he reached the top. Hardly any need for a light, with the sky outside and the moon and the fire. The floorboards creaked; he tiptoed. Checked the clothes neatly hung in the wardrobe above an empty suitcase, looked around for inspiration, tiptoed back to the case by the desk. Emptied the contents on the bed, switched on the light and hurriedly rifled through them. *Ginseng; acidopholus, milk, thistle, vitamin E, iron supplement* . . . Dun-coloured wrappings and jars for worthy, indescribable goods. No familiar blue Viagra colour; nothing to cause a flutter of excitement. There was a rattle as everything was scooped back and the case dumped where it was found with a mutter of frustration.

The figure prowled round the room, looked beneath the pillow, swearing, felt beneath the blankets for some hiding place. His fingers encountered warm fur, withdrew quickly, stifling a scream. Stepped away, breathing hard, fingers in mouth. Nothing.

Then he noticed the shawl draped over the bottom of the bed, stroked it with the other hand, thought it felt pretty. He snatched it and went down the stairs slowly, stuffing it inside his jacket, froze on the first landing as the dining room door opened to a gaggle of greetings. Then it closed again and the music resumed.

Cold first attacks me . . . Then ardour burns . . . Then in a trice, my misery returns.

As he ran for the door, the dog inside the dining room began to bark; the barking turned into a wail of protest as the singing grew louder and turned into laughter. He was through the door and out in the cold, sweat cooling on his face, relief making him giddy. The last bit was the worst. He might have been forced to kick the dog. Instead, such was his fury as he walked away, Neil Hulme kicked his own pet, then went back to the beach to kick the shingle. He still had enough for the week, but enough was never enough.

They walked back along the shore avoiding the shingle. The quiet was impressive and the sky was vast with stars. Henry did not know whether he wanted to peer into windows or watch the steady calm movement of the sea and she decided for him. Inside one small house, dwarfed by a grander neighbour, a woman sat wearing a hat and painting at an easel with the television creating a bluish light in the opposite corner. In another room, only slightly obscured by net curtains, a man was sewing and talking; in a third, the final stages of a crowded supper were being served. By common accord, with arms linked, Maggie and Henry crossed the road to the seaward side. He craved an invitation into those rooms, to sit and belong without being asked to do anything. She noticed the details.

'They've changed the curtains,' she said. 'And they've got a new chair . . .'

On the seaward side he could see the glow of three small pools of firelight, punctuating the slope of the beach.

'What's *that*?'

'Night fishing.'

'They must be crazy.'

'Why? It isn't so cold.'

Mild, even. She was right: the temperature had changed again into a comfortable cold. They crossed back. From outside the front door of the House of Enchantment, they could hear the sound of the piano and a ragged chorus of voices, to the additional accompaniment of Senta's barking. Where they had linked arms, he was not sure, only aware now, as she shed her coat in the hallway, that there was a prominent greasy mark at the thigh level of her dress. Inside the hall the musical row was louder, voices in competition with instrument. He shied from it, but Maggie was already humming.

'G'night, Henry. Unless you want to sing?' she asked, but it was not an invitation, more of a dismissal, as if she had had enough of him.

'G'night.'

He tramped up the stairs into his room where the fire was lit, and he wondered again at their endless solicitude. The perfect room for a man of his disposition; a controllable space which seemed to be built out of the sky. All it required was a cocktail cabinet; he would buy sherry. From the window he looked for the small, firefly glowings he had seen on the beach. They were more romantic from here in the safety of his own warmth. Dad would have been out with them, rain or shine.

A sole man sat on the shingle with a lamp and a campfire directly opposite the house. As Henry watched, he stood and cast a luminescent line into the water, the thread of it extending against the fire and moonlight, entering the water beyond the gentle waves. Henry was sleepy, but he still felt a curious desire to go back out, hunker down by the fisherman and ask him how he did it, and why, keep him company through the small hours. But the man was totally absorbed: he would resent a stranger. Perhaps I'll learn to fish, Henry thought. The perfect activity for an introverted man, and on the cusp of that, another thought. *The boy didn't like to go out in the cold,* Granny said. *Could not grasp with the right hand, but he was desperate to learn to fish.* He was suddenly so shaken with pity, he could not move.

The answers lay in the facts. Henry turned on the laptop and looked at the notes he had made before dinner. *The hemiplegic limbs are commonly smaller than the normal ones, the dwarfing more marked in the hand. Vasomotor changes are also common in the affected limbs, which are colder than normal . . . The motor disability of the hand in some patients may be much increased in cold weather . . .* Cold weather, then, was not good for learning to fish. Poor little boy. Henry's concentration was gone. The answers probably lay on the internet.

Yawning, sad, not wanting any emotional reflection to intrude upon his chronic desire for sleep, looking for the damned sweatshirt he wore at night, Henry noticed that the shawl was missing from the end of the bed. Noticed without resentment or any particular curiosity. It was missing, that was all, and he was more concerned with the question of his own reluctance to go back outside, speak to one of the fishermen and ask what it took to learn to fish. They would know about tides, things he could never discover otherwise, and here he was, afraid of rejection and the sound of his own feet on the shingle. Perhaps Maggie had borrowed the shawl and he needed to tell her she was welcome.

He moved down a landing. Silence in this impervious house. One more floor down to the door of her room, identified, never explored, although she had become a familiar presence in his. A messy room, a third the size of his own, strewn with clothes and shoes and a dying plant. Papers and magazines and realtors' sheets in shabby heaps; a small bookshelf with a bunch of dying snowdrops in a vase and a score of slim volumes of verse. A shawl, not his own, over a bedside chair.

He drew the door closed behind him. Looked down the stairwell for the sight of her. The sound of the piano pulsed from the ground floor; he could hear her singing. Such a woman, determined not to feel. Decidedly frivolous.

In the morning, Edward Burns gazed at the fish on the office wall and waited impatiently for Maggie. The daily correspondence for the practice, remarkably thin at this time of year, lay on his desk and he had begun opening it as best he could while still wearing gloves and waiting for the electric fire to bring some warmth into the room. He opened the post at random, whether addressed to himself, his self-effaced, nondescript partner on the top floor, or his part-time assistant, Maggie. Edward took this to be a supervisory duty as well as an *aide-mémoire*, because if he did not read the correspondence, he would never remember what was going on. Once read, it was placed in neat heaps for personal delivery to the relevant quarters, apart from letters of complaint about delay, which he kept back for discussion. Delay was the commonest complaint, treated with courtesy and ultimately, complete indifference. Things took time and for those who complained, longer.

Edward had perfected the art of handling a cigarette between gloved fingers, but considered it did nothing for the flavour. There were two letters which gave him cause, if not for alarm, a sensation he discouraged, then at least consternation. Alarm was something he saved for his son's school reports. One letter was for Maggie, marked private and confidential, an instruction he invariably ignored. It was a letter from her husband, stating in abject terms that although they were now divorced, he found himself deeply unhappy and it occurred to him that he might have made a terrible mistake. He did not like the musical tastes and sartorial habits of his youthful partner. She made a noise; she was insatiable, she jeered at the onset of his baldness, probably. Edward read most of this between the lines since the ex-husband was a great deal more circumspect and articulate than that, but Edward had seen the aftermath of many a separation and felt he could decode the specifics of the regret, however subtly it was phrased. What he could not do was predict Maggie's response; he hoped it would be fury, but he was unsure enough to feel a huge reluctance to pass on the missive at all. Maggie might deem herself irresponsible, was a lousy timekeeper, had none of the gravitas of dedication, but if left to her own devices, she was undeniably efficient, and he liked her. A lot. And besides, there was this unfinished business with Francesca Chisholm, which disturbed him and for which the

American was paying at a modest, but useful, rate. Which led him on to the second letter.

Under the watchful, single eye of the fish Edward read it again, this time without gloves. A letter from that senior persons' residential home on the cliffs at Ramsgate, stating that Joseph Chisholm's condition had deteriorated to such an extent that his removal from there to a nursing home was imminent. The Director of the home wrote a neat letter entirely without recrimination. Uncle Joe was one of several in her establishment whose only link with the outside world was via a solicitor, to whom application was made for extra expenses not covered by his pension. He was effectively her responsibility; there was no one else to make the decision, so he would be moved to a sister home in the same group where nursing care was available, twenty-four hours. *'After several months of almost speechless incapacity improvement is not expected and distress, we hope, unlikely.'*

Edward Burns acted as trustee to several old buffers without relatives, or relatives so distant and geographically removed they were meaningless. He was as sceptical about the loyalties of blood as he was about those of marriage and did not see why, for instance, Maggie should pay any attention to an uncle she had been preserved from in childhood and never saw since. Blood was not thicker than water; you either liked your relatives or you bloody well didn't and it was only affection which created a bond, after all. And there was the other fact that Angela Hulme was deputed to visit dear old Uncle Joe, just as Francesca had done. What the hell did she say to a bedridden old man?

He left the Director's letter prominently displayed on the front of the strewn desk, and put the letter from Maggie's ex in his pocket. They were not lucky with husbands, these Chisholms. Edward himself valued and adored his own placid wife, who kept his house as tidy as his office was not, and never bothered about odd socks.

The downstairs door crashed and the building shook. Maggie came up the stairs, singing, horribly ebullient early in the morning. Just as she slammed into his office with two cups of coffee, he made the resolution that he would give her the letter in his pocket at the *end* of the day, *after* she had done some work, not before. There were two new clients for her to see in the course of the morning: petty criminals with drink problems, requiring to rehearse their mitigation for the Dover magistrates next week. Edward regarded the poverty of his office surroundings and his practice in general, wondered if he should have been a bank robber instead, but there was a slight problem with temperament. He found the pursuit of riches perfectly pointless. Catching a real fish on the end of a line was far more of a priority and he resented the fact that it was such a good morning for fishing with a lousy forecast for the weekend.

'Lovely day,' she said, making it worse. He pointed to the Uncle Joe letter. She read it swiftly.

'Did Angela mention to you that he was bedridden?'

'No. She said he ate a lot of biscuits, read the newspapers and was rather jolly.'

'I wonder,' Edward said, with the other letter burning a hole in his jacket, 'who the hell it is she's been going to see?'

'I don't know. Does it matter?'

'It might.'

'C'mon, Tanya. C'mon. Isn't it nice you aren't going to school today? C'mon. Eat up.'

Getting her to eat what she didn't want to eat, every mother's problem. Angela shared it with the married mums and the ones who never had to go to parenting sessions to prove they were fit for it. *Do not use bribery or blackmail.* Crap. A long walk on the beach this milder morning, Tanya chatting to the fishing people and then gauging the distance between the breakwaters to run out and back, again and again. They never went on the pier any more; Tan preferred the challenge of the steep slope of the beach. Pink skinned, she allowed her hair to be forced into plaits. Wisps of stiff hair curled from the braid. She would never have smooth hair, but it would always be magnificent.

'Finish the porridge. Then you can have chocolate later. If you're good.'

'Any kind?' The spoon was poised.

'Any kind.' Angela sighed and patted her head as the eating resumed and the braiding was completed. So peaceful like this.

'But I *like* going to school, Mum. I *like* it. Why can't I go today?'

'Do you, darling? Since when, eh?' The child's remark delighted her and the reaction was controlled. She had noticed the difference, of course, but it was not quite the same as hearing her beloved daughter admitting to a change of heart which coincided with the end of almost daily tantrums and a skull-rending clash of wills right up to the school gates.

'I still get into trouble, but there's loads of girls much worser than me.'

'Bet there are. Got your coat and your books and stuff? Time to do drawing today. Shouldn't be busy.'

'We could stay at home for that.'

'No, darling, we can't.'

Angela did not say, we need the money. We need the money from my little jobs and Neil's little handouts, even if we've got Francesca's car and other things she left.

'Mummy, when's Francesca coming back?'

The heart stopped for the second time. Whoever said that having kids shortened your bloody life? The question hadn't been asked for three whole months and it dropped like a stone. Something must have reminded her: an overheard phone conversation, perhaps, when she was on the blower to bloody Maggie, losing her temper and raising her voice. The bloody American, why the hell should she talk to him? Angela remembered to keep calm.

'Don't know, darling. Perhaps in the summer.'

It was difficult to envisage the summer as they walked over the bridge to the castle entrance, Tanya trailing, more or less pleased with the plaits and keeping hold of one of them with her spare hand. The other held her satchel, a labelled thing for street cred, envied by her peers and guarded like gold. The castle was a favourite place. In the normal course of events she reacted to the sheer sombreness of it, and inside the warm and cosy ambience of the shop, became a docile creature. It was Francesca who had taught her to climb but that, too, was in the summer. Damn you, Francesca.

In the kitchen of the House of Enchantment, Henry watched the video, with a different attitude now that he knew more. The boy on the screen ran with his elbow flexed, his right hand turned in towards his body and his right shoulder held higher than his left. He had scabby knees; the right foot tapped at the ground as if afraid of the contact; it made Henry think of the lopsided gait of a three-legged dog although he did not approve of himself for making the comparison. As the boy drew nearer the camera, Henry could see that his face was not as ugly as he had assumed on his first sight of it, but merely contorted into a ferocious frown of effort. When he came to a halt in close-up, a slender arm reached across his face and wiped the mucus from under his nose with a handkerchief.

'There were certain things he could not do,' Timothy was explaining. 'Things nobody can do if their right hand refuses to work. Such as blow one's nose and brush one's teeth. Or make the best of falling over. He was always a grubby little boy.'

'And he wanted to learn to fish.'

'Would have done, too. We'd have taught him, though it might have taken a long time. We were working on the creation of a new kind of rod. You see,' Timothy stated, pouring more coffee, 'he wanted something he could do *by himself*, although Fran always wanted him to be with other children. *Pushed* him to be with other children, so they could bring him on. But he was frustrating for other children. He wanted them, he *adored* them, but he knew they got a bit fed up with him.'

'Which is natural,' Peter said. 'Children are cruel.'

'They're rehearsing to be adults,' Timothy said sarcastically. 'How could it be otherwise?'

'Have either of you seen a shawl I left lying around in my room?' Henry asked inconsequentially.

'On the end of your bed, isn't it?' Tim said. 'Unless, of course, Harry's been in and borrowed it. He's awfully fond of a nice Indian shawl.'

Henry could see the damn thing now, tricking out that damned Wendy house.

Ghosts, bah, humbug. Rubbish. FACTS. He detested whimsy, and sat in the library to read facts about castles until the afternoon was advanced and there was less chance of visitors. This particular castle, he decided on the basis of his new-found knowledge and his own estimation of the place, was simply a miniature model for a king to play with, pretty in this light. Inside the main entrance, framed on a wall, was the text of a letter, dated 1842.

> To the Queen's most excellent Majesty . . . Most gracious Sovereign, we, your Majesty's dutiful and loyal subjects, the Mayor, Authorities and other inhabitants, beg leave to approach your Majesty with feelings of the most devoted loyalty and affectionate attachment. We hail your Majesty's arrival and fervently hope that your Majesty will experience every degree of satisfaction and pleasure and will graciously condescend to bear your Majesty's sojourn here in kind remembrance. Distinguished as this vicinity has been from the earliest ages by the visits of eminent personages, never did it attain to honour equal to the present . . . That the Supreme Being may, in His infinite goodness, continue to shower on your Majesty his choicest blessings is our sincere and earnest prayer . . .

Oh my, oh my, did they take their monarch seriously. Surely someone wrote that stuff tongue in cheek? Or did they have the committee round the table in an orgy of sycophancy? Then Henry thought of a citizen addressing a Senator in his own democracy, and the sedulousness of the letter was less surprising. Hell, he had watched people kiss the feet of the head of the Corporation. He went into the shop.

'Excuse me, do you have a copy of that letter? Oh, hello – Mrs Hulme, isn't it?'

She was seated behind the counter as he had seen her before, neat and hard as plastic with a look of fatigue round her eyes. The beautiful child sat next to her, using the counter top to construct a cardboard model of the building, sold in boxed form, price £5, and looking complicated. Tanya gazed at him and smiled her heart-stopping smile, then turned her gaze towards three teenagers who selected postcards and murmured over the choice. They were dressed almost identically in state of the art trainers, with unnecessary sunglasses pushed into their tawny hair; she was lost in admiration of their clothes. Angela Hulme took their money and they moved through the entrance to the keep, adjusting headphones.

'Entrance is £4.50,' she said. 'You got in free last time. And you didn't pay for the chocolate.'

'I'm really sorry,' Henry murmured, taken aback by the steely aggression in her voice. He found it difficult to understand. Maggie said she was a tricky lady, but then she had been unwittingly involved in a tragedy, brought up a child alone, and trickiness was surely her right; still, he did not think he had done anything to offend. Yet.

'Great place,' he said unconvincingly, placing money on the counter. Pound coins reminded him of a certain kind of gold-wrapped candy he had eaten as a child. He hesitated. Small talk was not going to work. 'I need to talk to you, Mrs Hulme, if that's possible.'

'No. What about?'

As if taking a cue, Tanya slipped the moorings of the counter and followed the teenagers. Anglea did not stop her. There was a stool on the customer side of the counter and Henry occupied it.

'I need to know about Francesca, Mrs Hulme. I was a friend,

oh, a long time ago, and I came here to find her and talk about old times. Wish I'd come sooner. I might have helped. Not that I'm much of a help—'

'There's nothing to tell,' she interrupted. 'Why don't you mind your own business? Going round, asking questions, stirring things up. You bastard. If any of this gets back to *my* daughter, I'll kill you. Bet you don't think of her, Mr bloody scientist snooper. What about *her* if she hears people talking about poor little Harry, her best friend, just when they've finally *stopped* talking about him? They played together all the time . . . she looked after him . . . what do you think it was like for her when he died? Kids shouldn't have to put up with that kind of thing, especially not a kid like her. She was just turning a corner.' Her voice was rising. Henry spread his hands, helplessly.

'Please, please, leave us alone.' There were tears in her eyes.

'OK, OK, I'm sorry. Don't tell me about him, tell me about her. You were friends for a long time, I know. Great friends.'

'Why the hell should that matter to you? What right have you got to ask?'

'No rights, Mrs Hulme. None whatsoever.'

She seemed to calm down, a false calm, he guessed and just as likely the prelude to a storm. The tears were rubbed out of her eyes with the red knuckle of her right hand. She had no time for tears. 'Yes, we were. Like sisters. I helped at her school.' She laughed, bitterly. 'Couldn't stay away from kids, me. Just liked to be close. I was trying to give up the idea of one of my own: couldn't. She steered me – us – through the adoption stuff. It's easier if you'll take a child rather than a baby. I suppose one of the reasons we were accepted was because they knew she'd give support. And she did. And then she had *him*. And then her bloke buggered off. Yeah, we had a lot in common and Tanya loved the baby. Now piss off.'

'Please . . . I can't do that, not yet. You see . . .'

'You don't even know what you want to know, do you? You don't even know what you want to find out. You don't care who you might hurt. Even *her*. You're just like one of those seagulls, picking at carrion and shitting all over. Here's your ticket, and if you see my daughter on the way round, don't you dare say a word except to tell her to come back here. We close soon.'

It was the *please* which unhinged him, and the tears. She was right about one thing, Henry thought uncomfortably as he followed the tourist path into the courtyard. He did not know what it was he wanted to know and her scornful observation troubled him as he skirted the wall. OK, Henry, take the tour; accept the reprimand; you have no right to make anyone unhappy. Not unless you have a worthwhile, morally viable objective in mind, such as healing the sick, bringing the dead back to life, alleviating suffering, feeding the hungry, consoling the wounded, and none of these ambitions, dear to his heart in the idealistic days of trailing round India, applied to his current enterprise. What *did* he want to know? The satisfaction of a personal curiosity seemed a puerile excuse for causing outrage and yet he felt he already knew more than anyone else.

India: the jewel in Queen Victoria's crown; no wonder the Mayor and the town councillors wrote her letters like that.

He could hear voices from the cannons and walked in the other direction round the walls. He turned on the audiotape and turned it off again, leaned, and watched the pennant fly. Then he followed the direction sign into the fat body of the castle itself. *Please*, she had said. Leave us alone.

The central area he entered seemed to be a series of huge, cavelike rooms with domed ceilings, dry, floodlit, dusty and surprisingly warm. He stood in awe in front of a huge fireplace of mellow pink brick, the brick beautifully designed into an arch supporting a lintel of wood so old and pale it looked ready to crumble at the touch. He touched: it felt as solid as iron. He tried to imagine the dimensions of the fire which required so massive a hearth and wondered how anyone would get close. Where did they sit the Queen? He wandered up a flight of steps and found a panelled room with portraits and framed photographs, the only furniture of any kind in the whole place, dawdled for while, wondering why none of these men wore eyeglasses at their age and wondering where it was in this crazy edifice that the Chisholm family had kept their quarters. The atmosphere slowed him down; the quiet made him careful and he made himself cough for the sake of sound. It was a very peaceful place of war.

Back in the kitchen area, he consulted the map which came with his ticket and realized it was getting dark. He had not encountered the others except for the sound of their voices in the distance. Not such a miniature castle after all; it had space without grace. He must repeat such a neat phrase to Maggie who thought he was so dull, and quite apart from any other consideration, the tour was incomplete. Without the aid of the audiotape, recited by a man whose cut glass accent reminded him of nothing more than a peerless Hollywood villain, Henry steeled himself for a swift sprint round the lower floors: where they had planned to fire muskets on the enemy from all those little holes in the walls he could see from the outside at the bottom of what he thought should have been a moat. It would be darker down there. There was floodlight in these cavernous rooms, sconces on walls creating a warm glow on stone which varied in colour from ochre to grey granite. For a full, poignant, hesitant minute, Henry wished his father was here, raising his eyeglasses from his hooked nose and saying, *Will you look at that, son, they dug up every damn quarry they could find to make this mongrel.* Even with that, Henry knew he did not want to go down. He would read the guidebook and pretend he had. He knew his limitations.

He turned from the larger room, marked at one angle with yet another sign WAY OUT, a description which was, for an American of his generation, deeply deceptive for an exit sign, looking more like a sixties description of approval: way out, man. At the top of the slope, and the place was fuller of slopes than stairs, as if stairs were scarcely invented, he had noticed a great brute of a big black door. Toiling towards it, he could see a welcome patch of puffy, grey sky and a light outside. One of those security lights which reacted to the onset of darkness by becoming at first luminous and then timidly brighter as evening encroached, the kind of device his father would have examined, too. *Such a cute thing*, he might have said, stroking it, always amazed at how the simplest of things worked. Halfway up the slope, the door closed. Then the spotlights went out.

He stumbled uphill to the door and thumped on it, not alarmed, simply annoyed in the same way he always was by the inefficiency of others. He thumped again, creating a small, ineffectual sound against the wood and hurting the heel of his hand on a metal stud. Henry did not shout; it was not something he did in response to simple mistakes; anger was something he controlled. He just wanted out. The solidity of the door muffled noise, but he could hear scrabbling on the other side. He knocked again, yelling this time *EXCUSE ME! EXCUSE ME!* His voice came back inside his ears, sounding foreign and false. Once he stopped, he could detect an increase in the scuffling beyond, then the child screaming, half hysterical: '*Nooo, Mummy, no. He's in there. If he stays in there, he'll get so cold. You mustn't lock it. Henry hates the cold. NO. No, no no, stoppit, stoppit, stoppit. LET HIM OUT.*' And after that, with his head pressed against the wood, Henry heard murmurs of brisk consolation: 'Aren't you a little silly one, aren't you just? It isn't a *person*, silly. That nice man went home. I told him *please* go. He's deaf. That thing in there is only one of Neil's silly ghosts.'

There was a further protest, Angela's voice shriller. 'What do you want, silly? Do you want me to be sent away too? Is that what you want? Come on, darling. Time for tea.'

I don't really understand the purpose of imprisonment (except as a form of revenge) and I don't really think I ever did. It alters nothing. A sentence like mine is only a warning, not an education. I am not imprisoned because I would otherwise take to the streets, killing children at random. No one suggests that my criminality is bound to become a habit. The only child who was ever vulnerable to me was my own son. No one is in danger from me, except me. Or from my friend in the kitchen. She killed her husband and she makes everyone think that's what I did, too.

I think I imagined, in a daft kind of way, that having sentenced me and sent out all the necessary messages about justice and condemnation, someone might say, What really is the point of keeping a useful woman locked away, doing nothing? They would think, what a waste of money and quietly let me out the back way. Maggie says that's basically what they will do, although not for fifteen years. It is the years that weigh on me, not the present. The only way to deal with incarceration is to take it one day at a time. Not a whole day, even: an hour, a minute. And the only way I can accept it is to remind myself constantly that it does have a purpose even if it isn't obvious to anyone but me. Without that, I'm sure I should go mad.

Not everything I've ever done has had a purpose. One's aimless so much of the time, which is just as well because it's when I've been my most determined that I've been my most mistaken. Poor Harry. You deserved better.

I asked for more of the pills. Otherwise I shall scream and cry.

Forget my stiff upper lip.

FMC

CHAPTER NINE

UNCLE Joe, Tom Cobbley and all could wait. '*Life without you is not the same . . .*' Maggie read in the letter. She put it down on the threadbare carpet of the office and stamped on the envelope, as a substitute for the immediate desire to tear it up. It was an odd aspect of legal training which made it impossible for her to destroy a letter because of its evidential value, but she could abuse it. The paper was creased from a working day's contact with Edward's pocket, improving the fulsome prose. '*I do not know what madness possessed me,*' he wrote, '*to imagine I could have a better existence with someone who is so much your inferior in every way . . .*'

'Life without you is not the same,' she mimicked to Edward, flourishing the letter at him. 'What did he bloody well expect? He didn't *want* it to be the same. And what *possessed* him was perfectly obvious. A *bitch* with big boobs, sixteen years younger than me. He's a cliché. A ten-foot transvestite, at least I'd have a topic for conversation.'

'What do you think of its style?' Edward murmured.

'He hasn't got any *style!*' she yelled.

'I meant the letter.'

She looked at the sentences, perfectly punctuated and nicely turned. He had taken his time to construct his thoughts and give his plea for a meeting the right degree of pathos and dignity. *'I can't get you out of my mind and I'm full of sorrow . . .'*

'Rather contrived, I thought,' Edward said. 'You shouldn't have married another lawyer. We're all pompous farts. What are you going to do?'

She looked at him and the fish behind the desk, all hazed in cigarette smoke.

'Drink,' she said.

Henry focused on the words. *Time for tea.* Quaint. He was trembling with fury and willing it to cease as his eyes adjusted to the gloom. A couple of dim security lights high on the walls blinked into life within minutes and for these he was profoundly grateful. He had space to move; there was a mean ration of light, sufficient for reading the large print of the direction signs, he was not cold, and in a minute she would come back and open the damn door. He felt in his trouser pocket for his packet of cigarettes, lit one and began to pace the floor, counting his steps, one, two, three. He shrugged inside the warmth of his leather jacket and soft sweater. He would circumnavigate the central keep, beginning here, fifteen times, and by the time that was done she would have come back. Or someone would come back; there would be a nightwatchman; someone.

On the seventh round of the bare rooms, kitchen with bread ovens, mess room with fire, interconnecting rooms off, he began to wonder if such a thing as a nightwatchman was necessary. There was nothing to steal except the fabric of the building, which was undoubtedly solid enough to resist larceny. The wretched woman would come back after she had given the child her *tea.* What a strange way of describing what must be dinner, and the thought reminded him that he was hungry. He lost count of his circumnavigations and repetition did not improve the view. He sat down by the fireplace and dozed for a while. When he came round, stiff and chilled, a dull anger began to settle into a kind of mental indigestion, combined with boredom and a sense of being completely ineffectual, a person who was simply a suitable candidate for a practical joke.

The worst that could happen was a hungry night alone and a touch of hypothermia. He could go upstairs and deface the portraits, or form them into a shelter in the middle of the room and play at camping. Pity he could not borrow their garments. It was beginning to become colder. Then he considered the prospect, not of the night, but the morning, when the door would creak open and he would be seen, abject and stupid. She might gather a crowd to jeer at a tourist who could not tell the time; she might send a posse of name callers to bait him like a dancing bear in a medieval illustration. The poor, captive bear who did not even try to bite or release himself from his chains. Who did not consider the affectionate solicitude of his hosts in this town enough to be concerned about them and their possible anxieties. The dummy who just *sat* there, and found a corner to urinate, and in the middle of that friendly crowd there would be Maggie with her metal hair and sweet, sardonic smile and it was Maggie's opinion which mattered most.

Time had moved on. Henry tried to recall what he had read about the castle in the relative comfort of the library and what he had learned from the map which he could no longer read. None of it helped, but it stood to reason that a place designed to house so many men must have a dozen exits, even if they were also designed to repel those who wanted to enter. Go down to the level of the moat area, Henry, where you saw all those little windows. You aren't too fat to squeeze through, find a door, get out, and once out, holler. Better the contempt of a single passer-by who might throw him a rope than that of the Mayor and the other inhabitants next morning. They would not beg leave to approach him with feelings of devoted loyalty and affectionate attachment.

Besides, he was sick of the sight of these particular walls. Any other set of walls would be an improvement. He took the downward slope from the fireplace room, marked THE RUNS, with enough of his sense of humour intact to notice how uninviting this description was. What a crass lot they are, he reflected, *Way out via The Runs.* The slope was shallow, and then became steeper, suddenly, so that he stumbled to a halt in front of glass in a wall and a painted arrow telling him GO LEFT. What was this? A political instruction? He was feeling slightly hysterical and followed the sign.

Henry entered a narrow passageway which curved away to his right. There were narrow windows recessed into the deep walls and, out of habit, he began to count. *One, two . . . five, six, twelve, thirteen.* Some of the windows were framed in crusty metal; he had stopped to touch, recoiling from the cold and the dampness of the condensation. The last security light had faded into memory. Now he touched each window; some stood open, level with his chin, but most of them were closed. The fifteenth window had no glass at all and cold air breezed over his forehead. He wanted to go back, but surely he would be round the other side in a minute. His right foot hit shallow water. In this lack of light, he did not know if was encountering a flood or a puddle, and in the pause, as he began to step carefully rather than hurry, he heard the rustling ahead.

Loud. A furious, fluttering sound which arrested and then accelerated the motion of his heart and made the blood it pumped turn into boiling water. Then a noise of furious knocking, *tap, tap tap, TAP TAP, tap tap tat, tap tap tap TAT.* He looked behind him and could not see from where he had come around the curving wall, looked ahead and saw the promise of another security light. The tapping ceased; the rustling, like the frantic shuffling of a hundred garments moving towards him, increased. Became still, for a moment.

Henry could not see the ceiling and he could feel the walls squeezing him. It was less of the fear of what lay ahead than the fact that he no longer knew where he was and did not know the way back out. *Fool, fool.* There were all the symptoms: the desire to smack his head against the bricks so that at least pain could distract; the impulse to run, moan, lie down, the sensation of some massive blow to the solar plexus, the acute lack of breath and the madness. The overpowering imperative to fight, kick, beat his way out, the inability to breathe or even to shriek. If the window had been wide enough and the drop a thousand feet, he would have jumped; if there had been knife, he would use it to mutilate himself, anything to stop it. *Anything.* And it would not go; he knew it could not go. Claustrophobic agony, each time a little taste of death so full of excruciating panic, he would cut off his hand to avoid it. Then he screamed and screamed and screamed, tried to stumble back in the direction he had already walked, tried to be logical, but he could not move; panic forbade. He braced himself against the narrow walls to get his breath, bashed his hand against the window, stuck his fingers inside his mouth and bit so hard he tasted blood. Crouched in a heap in the puddle of water, he struggled for breath and began, manically, to chew his fingernails. The sounds were irrelevant. He could hear nothing. Whatever he could see, was doubled. There was fungus on the wall; it reached out and touched. Henry fainted.

A second. Maybe an hour. Came round, deafened by his own breathing, *UHUH, UHUH, uhuh, uhuh, UHUH,* and the scream coming, unable to emerge. Apart from the thunder of his own breath, the silence was total, a background only to *UHUH, UHUH,* and the horrifying wheeze creeping out of his mouth in a desperate, gulping sound, like his father, close to death, *ownuff, ownhuff, ownfuff,* with the whole body of him involved in the effort. Henry fixed his eyes to the patch of indigo sky visible from the high slit of window above his head only because it was different from the black of the wall. Forced himself not to blink until his eyes watered from the strain. The cold of the water seeping through his jeans began to have some remote meaning. He was lying in cold water and he *must* get up. He managed that, but the panic did not subside. He could get himself upright and know he was cold, was all. Then the fluttering sound began again, came towards him and retreated. He took two steps forward. *One of Neil's silly ghosts, Harry is here to see you, kill you.* He took one more step. The only way forward was towards the next light. The bird struck his outstretched arm, flew away and began battering, pecking, fluttering at the next barred window.

A bird; a captive bird in a futile dance.

He could not quite tell what type of bird. A starling perhaps; a tiny creature in relation to the noise it made. He moved towards it, unsteadily. The bird sensed him and moved to flutter madly at the next window, and the next. His presence terrified; the loud movement of the wings grew more frenetic. When Henry stopped, it stopped; when he moved, the bird moved. Once more, it forgot and flew towards him, encountered his forehead, flew back to batter at the next window. Gradually fascinated, Henry made himself stay still. His breath slowed down. He watched the outline of it, a confused, demented bullet of being.

There were open windows; he remembered them, back there. Remembering the glassless windows made him remember, too, that all he had to do, keeping his eyes shut if he needed, was to turn round and go back, one step after another and finally, even if he crawled, he would be in the larger spaces where he could breathe. The bird was an idiotic bird which could not go back, only forward, instead of seeking the route which had brought it inside and using the same route to get out. Hammering again, at a narrow slit of metal-framed glass it would never open. How exhausted it must be, poor, desperate thing. More exhausted than himself. And if he had not appeared, it might have rested. Henry could not bear the thought that the bird might break its wings because of his presence, or that it would kill itself out of panic, die before morning. He was furious with pity for it. 'Hush,' he said softly, 'hush.'

If he approached, the noise of his boots would set it off. He would be freakishly lucky if he were able to catch it in his hands. He would have to catch it with something else; something to throw over it. Henry stood as still as the walls, thinking out the problem. It was the only problem. The only thing that mattered was to catch the starling and set it free.

Take these chains from my heart and set me free . . . She did not like his choice of music and it had not been a successful day, or not in the way Neil had hoped. Perhaps he simply was not used to the prolonged company of a female and a whole day together was a strain. Angela and himself had never been big on outings, even when their relationship was new; ah shit, he must not think of Angela. In the days when she had loved him, she had reassured him again and again that sex really did not matter and anyway, would improve in time if only his temper would do the same. There was the occasional, almost successful coupling, and he knew how to please her but it was not the orgasm she wanted as much as the child which should result. He could have been a king, a millionaire mogul, an artist, an international athlete and still be nothing but a controlled diabetic with a low sperm count and *erectile dysfunction*. Perhaps the strain of a whole day with the new girl lay in the fact that he could not tell her about all that; could not yet entrust her with the worst aspect of his history, and somehow she knew he was hiding something. Women never did like that, but she would like it less if she knew. One coupling achieved only made it worse; it was the second that counted.

It had made him a thief, and not even a successful thief. A day trip to France, slightly marred by his anxious hopes for the evening, and his feeling of shame for the evening before. She sat across the table from him in his own house, smiling at him and admiring his cooking and drinking the wine they had bought. Or at least she drank, to please him, because he pressed it on her in the hope of relaxing the tension which seemed to have developed, while he himself drank sparingly, afraid it might interfere with the little blue pill he was going to take, soon. *Try 50mg*, the doctor said. *100mg is average*. It followed, in Neil's anxious way of thinking, that 300, the whole of the stash, might be even better. Three little pills and bugger the paucity of supplies. All gone by tomorrow, but tomorrow was another day and the rest of his life could take care of itself, if only he could keep her for a few hours.

'I got a present for you,' he said, coming back from the bathroom. The wine and the food had worked; she was languorous and mellow and leaned back against him as he draped the shawl round her shoulders. Against the background of his small, nondescript room, she was lovely; her skin soft and warm, and he never wanted her to think, I could do better than this.

'I can't stay all night,' she said. 'I'll have to get back, eventually.' She lived with her parents. He liked the *eventually*. It would not take all night.

Maggie passed an hour in the most anonymous public house on the seafront, talking to old men about their dogs, drinking a glass or three of indifferent wine until she decided she could do better than that, caught the off-licence before closing time and exchanged cash for two bottles of chilled Sancerre and three packets of nuts. She hauled this booty indoors, beaming vacantly at Timothy and Peter, who both wanted to chat but backed away when they saw how the land lay. She went upstairs, inflicted a manic tidying up on her room in order to give herself some sense of control, and then sat down to think. There was the nagging memory of Uncle Joe, but that was largely irrelevant, like a fly buzzing in the corner of a room, since most of all, she wanted to savour a feeling of triumph and read his letter for the third time. *Could I please come and see you?* Not what he might have said: *Why don't you come up to town and see me?* He was suggesting that *he* make the effort to visit a scrubby little town he had always despised. Men are so blind, Francesca had said. I can't stand the way they leave and then have to come back later and tear the heart out. Look, Philip, I have a *modus operandi* here, Maggie wanted to say. I live a small life with none of your entertaining; remember how we entertained, Philip? As elaborately and generously as the proprietors of my guest house cook for guests, Philip, only they do it at a fraction of the cost, treble the effort and with a genuine desire to please rather than impress. You tried to make me into a sophisticated clone of yourself but my favourite vegetable is still frozen peas and I prefer the kind of man who can enjoy an overcooked pizza and not notice. I *let* you dictate the whole progress of our lives, so that when you decided I was superfluous, I became a spare part.

She crunched on the nuts and reached for pen and paper; the

wine scarcely pleasant. He had been a wine snob, messed and tinkered with the stuff and agonized over labels. Dear Philip, other people have better things to do and drink what they're damn well given, so they can get on with talking. Why did I let you distract me from anything that was ever really important? Why do I waste my time on lousy choices? She would write him a tremendous letter if only she could find the pen, not any of the old ballpoints that littered and clogged her bag, but the fountain pen which gave some dignity to her handwriting. Oh yes, she would let him have it in words, a verbal battering fit to shake him out of his own peerless prose and make him feel the rat he was. Then she remembered another of those poems she had memorized so easily, long before the marriage days.

> *When I loved you, I can't but allow*
> *I had many an exquisite minute;*
> *But the scorn that I feel for you now*
> *Has even more luxury in it.*
> *Thus, whether we're on or we're off,*
> *Some witchery seems to await you,*
> *To love you is pleasant enough,*
> *But Oh! tis delicious to hate you!*

The nuts were finished and she felt a vague, nauseous hunger, temporarily sated by another glass of wine. They would fret about her a little downstairs, but these locked-in evenings of hers were not without precedent, although they had been far less frequent, lately. '*Oh, tis delicious to hate you!*' she wrote again, noticing how the writing was not steady. The fountain pen was running out of ink and she had no idea of where she had put the refills. Or whether she wanted Philip to come and see her and look at her life and what she had made of it in fifteen months sitting in a closet. But the one thing she did know, even as she underlined the word, was that she did not hate him. She had never hated anyone for longer than a day; she did not have it in her; she might be absurdly hurt by the slightest hint of rejection, but she could not hate. Perhaps that meant she did not have the capacity to love men either. Of course you do, Francesca said, but only if they look at you. Recognize what you are. Anything else is insulting.

That was what she was, insulted. It was too soon for sleep; the wine was winning and by now Maggie did not want anyone to see her in this indecisively maudlin state. She washed, cursorily, in the upstairs basin, thought with a token guiltiness of all the other business of the day, brushed her hair until her scalp hurt as much as her head ached, tidied up rigorously and went to bed. Confused thoughts scuttling like rats, Angela, Harry, Henry, Harry, Neil, was Neil fishing on the beach with that dog, Henry. Fishing. Philip and how she had glibly explained the demise of that marriage. Not quite the success we hoped.

Not quite the success he had hoped. Not the answer to a girl's prayer, or even a man's. A bit thorough and brutal, if Neil remembered it right. Not as prolonged as it might have been, although he had rather lost touch with the passing of time. Marvellous to fuck but not so entirely pleasant to be fucking and wondering all the time how long it could last. The erection, the relationship, the fierceness of her embrace which had gradually turned into rather more dutiful gestures of fatigued encouragement as he went on and on, culminating in a noticeably timid curling away from him after the final groan. She kissed him in response to his smothering of grateful kisses and choked, heartfelt thanking her and telling her how wonderful she was, but it did not seem so long afterwards that she said she had to go, you know the way it is, becoming insistent about it. And when he rose, with difficulty, to dress and escort her the short distance, she had kissed him again, more hurriedly and said, what nonsense, it was only a spit away down lit streets and she would not hear of it. This was not London, it was Warbling. She was chattering a bit, slipping away and gathering her clobber with twice the speed of his dressing, and then, before he could insist, was gone. She was running away. She left behind the stolen shawl, folded over the kitchen chair. This hurried escape would have alarmed and worried him intensely, if the symptoms did not alarm him more. Neil lay on his bed, considering the implications of a foul headache and dizziness not lessened by closing his eyes. When he opened them, all that he could see appeared to be tinged with pink, giving him the impression of a mildly fluorescent evening or the colour of the sinking sun on the sea in summer. He blinked to dispel it, but the pink tinge remained and when he turned on the overhead light, the brightness of it attacked his eyes. He was trembling and his mouth was dry.

The bleeper was going on his pager. Some bugger was in the castle and he could not see.

The only priority was to catch the bird. It fluttered at the next window and the sound of its fatigue was so cruel, Henry wanted to weep. He retreated two steps, very slowly, bent down and fumbled with his shoelaces until they were undone and he could slip off his boots. He shed his jacket quietly; it was too heavy to use as a snare; the little thing would be crushed to death. His cashmere pullover, because Henry had a weakness for fine woollens, was light and fine for all its protective warmth. The ground was cold and damp, soaking his socked feet as he tiptoed forward blindly. The wall rounded to his right. He had just made out the outline of the bird when he stumbled on a loose brick, put out a hand to steady himself and swore, *shit*. The starling came back to life, disappeared in a smudge of black and began again the ghastly battering of a window further round. If he could only somehow get beyond it, he thought, and frighten it into going back to where he knew there were windows which were broken or open or free of glass, perhaps it would find its way out of its own accord. Perhaps it was better to chase it forward in any event; they might come round full circle to the larger space where it could fly with ease or settle. And then be lost for ever and even harder to catch. Or maybe this rounded passageway led nowhere but to further obscurity; maybe it petered out into a pit, a cellar, a well. Henry swallowed.

With pullover draped round his neck, he inched forward, testing the wet ground with his stockinged feet and keeping one hand on the wall. The starling became visible again; he felt as if it was looking at him and waiting. He removed the pullover, remembering to breathe quietly. Up ahead there was another sound, a *drip, drip, drip*, and from the window he passed a draught and a tantalizing sound of rain. The starling beat its wings and flew drunkenly to the next glass. It would die from fear and exhaustion. Henry's feet were icy cold; he flexed his fingers silently. The sound of rain outside would muffle the noise of his own progress, but only a fool would think that a starling had senses as unrefined as his own. Three times more, creeping forward and the bird detecting him, but each time, he told himself, he was that small bit closer. Then, beneath the merciful glow of a tiny light in the ceiling, which showed the gleam of moisture on the stone of the ledge where water dripped, he saw the starling bathing in an irresistible shallow bath of collected water in a dip hollowed by years of drips. Henry was close enough, threw his net and followed.

Gently, gently, does it. A furious struggle inside the garment. Keep still. He cupped his hands round the heaving bundle he had made and cradled it, feeling, as he began to stumble back the way he had come, the frantic beating of a tiny heart, feared the bursting of it. Quick. He needed both hands to keep the captive; his feet would have to find their own direction. He stubbed his toes and cracked his elbows, stumbling from side to side and letting the wall, curving to his left, lead him. He tripped on his own shoes, felt the material of his jacket in the puddle underfoot and did not stop. Another window, another and another, and then the blessed draught.

He stretched to push the pullover through the narrow aperture of the window slit, gently, then shook it. The opening was so narrow there was scarcely room for both his hands and the stone grazed his arms. He could feel the starling fight, thought maybe it was stuck with its claws in the wool and he would have to drag it back and crush it in the process of disentanglement, not be able to see in the dark, let it free inside this hole and have to start all over again, oh please God, no. He shook the ends of the pullover again, letting one hand go; then he felt it lift and fall as the bird flew free. He strained to look and see where it had gone, but all he could see was sky. *Don't fall, FLY*, he shouted, and told himself he could hear the sound of wings above the sound of rain and knew he was unable to hear anything of the kind. Simply his own breath *uhuh, uhuh, uhuh. Keep moving.* Henry retreated from the window and plodded on, touching the wall on his left, feeling rather than consciously noting two more windows which could have acted as escape routes, muttering to himself. They should not leave it like this, they should fix the windows and not trap birds. Someone should check, someone should *hang*, and then, all of a sudden, he was back at the foot of the slope, moving uphill to the big room where he found a patch of light against the fireplace wall and slid to a heap on the dry floor. He still had the pullover which he had trailed along behind him, pleased with himself for not letting it go, otherwise the starling might have plummeted to earth in its own net. Absentmindedly, he drew it over his head. He was shivering. The pullover felt sticky to the touch, smeared at the front with bird excrement. A lot of it; never mind. Henry wiped it down with his hands and rubbed his hands on his trousers. Now it was all over him. Never mind again if he smelt a bit, the damn bird, that silly, terrified little thing, was free and he himself was momentarily, quite bizarrely, happy.

But he was cold. He felt his feet with his filthy hands and massaged his toes. They were sticky and sore and wet with blood; the cold was doing him a favour and preventing real pain. He should go back and get his jacket and also his shoes, force his feet inside and keep them warm. The jacket would keep him warm and hide the bird shit. But on cooler contemplation of the whole idea, Henry knew there was absolutely no question of going back down the slope and into that passage. Cold be damned and everything else, the thought was so repellent it increased his tremor.

The room was no longer warm, but far above freezing and the woman was not going to come back. Nobody was going to come back. There was a bar of chocolate in his jacket pocket; there was moisture dripping into the Runs, enough to clean his hands and deal with a raging thirst, but none of that was enough to make him go back. No. There were cigarettes in his trouser pocket and a working lighter. Life was suddenly tenable; the bird was *free* and the freeing of a starling was the sole purpose of this evening in hell. That was why he had been put here. It was all as simple as that. He got to his feet, planned a route (*a root, Henry, not a rowt*) and began to walk round the rooms. Close to the door, another security light winked as he crossed the beam and tried the handle. He waved at it. Walked in wide circles and thought.

Why did she lock me in?

What had I done to deserve being locked in?

Did she know what it might do to me? No. How could she? But she must have known I would be . . . frightened.

The child knew I would be frightened and cold. Or that *someone* would be frightened and cold.

Another Henry.

Will I get gangrene?

I hope the starling can fly in the rain.

Is the desire to protect stronger than any other?

He tried to think of a silly verse, began to sing. He had never thought much of his ability to hold a tune; singing was a private occupation reserved for the bathroom, but he could always remember the words.

Was it raining when Harry went out? Who called for him and made him follow into the cold?

'Wake up, Maggie wake up. Wake, bloody *up*.'

Peter was shining a light in her face. Or so it seemed. The mobile phone bleeped.

'What the hell is wrong with you, Maggie, woman, wake *up*.'

'Wwake,' she said indistinctly. 'Stoppit. Fuck off.'

'Your phone, Maggie and—'

'Go 'way.'

'Answer it.'

'No. Wha'for ?'

'*Answer it!*'

She did, the button-pressing, fiddling-about business automatic, even from the very centre of a bad dream. Peter and Timothy could not fathom how it worked and didn't need to know. It was the only phone in the house and only when she was there; they took the shrill noise of it far more seriously than she. It seemed to whisper to them from a great distance, although she also suspected that on evenings like these, they checked on her. She spoke to the phone.

'Bugger off.'

'Francesca, I'm dying. I think I'm going to die . . . I took too much. Everything pink, head like hell and there's someone in the castle. Can't go.'

'Neil, slow down.' She was upright now and the effect was painful. Not as bad as she had known, but not nice. She saw, with a slight and irrelevant satisfaction, that she had managed to put on a nightie before she got into her bed, also to hide the bottles. She could smell soap. Cleanliness is next to godliness, and all she could feel was relief in that small thought, followed by acute irritation. She was not Francesca. At least Neil might have remembered that. Recalled that she was not that omnipotent person in whom everyone confided and whom everyone resented when she could not help; she was simply a poor substitute.

'Taken too much Viagra. Can't see. Headache. Got to get that American out. He's a doctor. Know what to do. Bring him, Maggie, bring him here . . . Ah, please. Please, Maggie, please. He'll know. I know he'll know . . . Blue pills. Pink pills to make it better. Call him, Maggie, please.'

'He's not a doctor. He's the wrong kind of doctor, he can't make people better. Call a real doctor, Neil.'

'Can't. Gonna die. Help me.' The end of the call, the contents of it reverberated around the room like ricochets.

'Someone wants Henry,' she said carelessly, as if she was his secretary, looking at Peter for inspiration. Timothy hovered in the doorway and she felt cornered into good manners. They were never less than courteous; they were, she thought briefly, the kindest people on earth.

'They can't have him.'

'Why can't they have him?'

'Because he isn't there,' Timothy said flatly. 'He's never come back. Two in the morning and he isn't back. He's lost.'

Heart pounding, she went upstairs and found Henry's room, pristine, the fire made for him leaving nothing but a faint trace of warmth. The laptop closed, the room all neatly stacked as if he lived in the cabin of a ship about to set sail, instead of the way she kept hers, like a schoolgirl, subject only to intermittent discipline. A variety of destinations crossed her mind – castle, Neil's house, Angela's flat – images of places meeting one another in imagination like vehicles crashing at crossroads and she groaned out loud. Bugger responsibility; SHE DID NOT WANT IT. From the door of his room, the two darling men hovered with expectancy, body language announcing, *say what you want us to do and do it we shall.* Maggie sighed. Her brain was full of fungus. Alcohol was a dead loss so far. So was freedom. It encouraged moss on the mind and fur in the throat and had never yet had the grace to create oblivion. Her nightie was clean; there was an awful pride in that, enough to give her authority. What a stupid, shallow, spoiled brat she had always been. She had to keep calm, let the dreadful anxiety turn itself into energy rather than curdle into paralysis.

'I'll just get dressed,' she said. 'Is it cold, out? I'm so sorry, darlings, we should none of us be awake at this hour, should we?' No notion of the hour, of course, but best to get going regardless; think of England. 'Can you remember where I put my car, Peter? And you really don't have to come if you don't want to.'

'Harry's in that castle, isn't he?'

'Not the Harry you mean, but very probably, yes. And Neil is poorly and has the key, yes. Don't know why, but yes.'

She was back downstairs and stripping off the nightie, finding a nasty sweatshirt and a jumper over the top and the trainers without laces which were nearest and the car keys which were hidden behind something, getting the order of things wrong, so she found herself puzzled by bare legs and feet with shoes and no trousers. Peeled the whole lot off and started again. Something had happened in the course of a drunken evening without her thinking about it on any conscious level at all. Somewhere among the scribbling and scrabbling, she had sorted out an outfit of trouser suit, boots and spurs, top coat et al. of the kind fit to meet a repentant ex-husband and intimidate him with a sense of style. Still a proper lawyer, see? She dragged them on, lit a cigarette and stubbed it out immediately. She just about made the ashtray and the whole business was worse than she thought. They were waiting outside the door in their motley dressing gowns, the sweetest and, ultimately, most unaggressive of men. Unless she had been a child, in which case they would have ignored the legends of ghosts and gone out with her, armed with homemade cudgels. The very thought made her even more tired. Peter and Timothy were greatly reassured by her uniform. She looked like she could deal with an army.

Raining hard. Snow melted and pelting rain, desperate place, disgusting, why ever live here . . . along the front, left to Neil's, stop. Everything deathless with silence, making her want to shout. Rapping at his door until there was a response. The door opened by him, squinting at her, all eyes and shame. The pink at the corners of his vision had faded; the headache was terrible; there was no one else to call, sort it, Franny, will you? *I am not Francesca. My cousin of that name lived in the castle and, as a cousin, I came here often and I know, as she did, how to get in. She never really relinquished her ties to it.*

She stood over Neil in his living room and reflected dispassionately that he looked worse than she felt, but he would live. 'I'm feeling better,' he muttered. 'Sorry, sorry, sorry.' The pager, connected to the castle's alarm system, blinked on the table. 'It went ages ago. I can't go in there, I can't, I can't. The ghosts . . .'

'Call the police.'

'They'll laugh. I'll lose my job . . . I can't.'

'Oh, for God's sake, give me the key. Angela dropped it back, I suppose?' He nodded. She noticed the shawl folded over the chair, took the key and went back to the car. She could never have any patience with anyone afraid of ghosts or the castle at night; it had been her occasional playground for hide-and-seek, although she never quite knew the hiding places her cousin had known. She tried to question her own conviction that Henry was in there, blundering around like a moth. *I guess I might leave out the stuff about being afraid of the dark, scared to death about being locked in.* She hurried.

She left the car by the castle gate, heard the *rat, tat, tat* of her smart heels on the wooden bridge and felt the rain on her face. The key was easy, the door heavy. There were chocolate wrappers on the floor of the shop; ghosts feasting in Neil's absence, of course, leaving litter to annoy him, of course. Or a hurried departure by Angela Hulme and Tanya. Maggie swore. She should never have sent Henry here.

She took the keys to the keep from behind the counter where they always remained, flicked the master switch for lights, walked out into the rain round the slippery stones to the inner door. If there was no one to find, she would be furious; she might be equally furious if he were there. The lights were harshly bright. There was a man in the room below, walking a slow circle, hands clasped behind his back, his feet in dirty socks and his sweater stained. He was singing. Then he seemed to notice that he could see, stopped moving and turned slowly, blinking, still singing.

'Hallo,' she said.

'*You may esteem him a child for his might, Or you may deem him a coward for his flight,*' Henry sang, and then stopped and turned and saw a woman, smartly dressed as if for a powerful meeting, pristine in matching clothes, shimmering in the spotlight, mercilessly efficient. Oh, *shit.*

It didn't help, him disliking the cold. Didn't help that he was old enough to experience vanity; I wonder when vanity begins? As soon, I suppose, as a baby can see itself in a mirror. Didn't help that his speech was affected, so that it was difficult for him to articulate clearly because it added to his frustration. Didn't help the poor darling that he loved so easily, even though he scowled like a dragon. He did that when he was concentrating to learn things, and I always found it endearing. I always had difficulty learning things without looking for the nearest distraction; I understood the effort. I had the concentration span of a sparrow until I was far older, which is why my father always held Maggie up as an example, because she learned so easily.

I think I imagined that Tanya might be to Harry what I once was to Maggie: an older cousin who loved her and would always be there, in the absence of a sibling, just as he would be there for her. I forgot how much rivalry and impatience there was. I was trying to turn us into a family, herd us into a group. I sound like a sheepdog. Of course, it was not quite like that.

FMC

CHAPTER TEN

SHE walked down the slope towards him, aware only of the crunch of her boots on dry stone. Her hair shone with rain droplets, flying away as she shook her head. Closer to him, she was aware how dirty he was; shockingly so for a meticulous man with a passion for clean clothes and personal ablutions.

'How does the rest of this verse go?' Henry asked conversationally. 'Might be one you know. It's so irritating to forget.'

'*But if she whom love doth honour,*' Maggie recited tonelessly, '*be concealed from the day . . .*'

'*Set a thousand guards upon her, Love will find out the way,*' Henry finished, beaming with satisfaction like a child triumphing in getting the right answer.

'What the hell are you doing here?' Her temper was ready to explode and her right hand itching to slap his face if only it were not so filthy.

'Oh, this and that. I'm a very conscientious tourist, I have to see everything.'

'Well, I think it's closed, Henry, and we'll go home now. Where'd you put your shoes and that jacket?'

'In the Runs, ha ha . . . down there, somewhere –' vaguely pointing.

'Would you like to go and fetch them?' The voice was now sweet and persuasive.

'Nope.' He was shaking his head apologetically. 'Nope. Can't do that. Absolutely not.'

'There aren't any ghosts,' she said. He seemed vaguely surprised at the suggestion.

'Of course not. But I'm not going.'

She clattered away out of sight, footsteps receding angrily in the downhill direction of the Runs and Henry listened, rather than watched, feeling only slightly guilty. What did he need a jacket and shoes *for*? He was doing OK as he was. A minute passed; then the half of another, and the cold crept back beneath his skin. One more verse and then he would have to go and look for her in case she was lost, like the starling. '*Some think to lose him by having him confined, And some do suppose him, (poor thing!) to be blind. But if ne'er so close you wall him, Do the best that you may; Blind Love, (if you so call him,) Will find out his way.*' Seventeenth century, he seemed to remember. Footsteps coming back, slower than they went, and there was Maggie with his jacket in one hand and his shoes in the other, holding them both away from her soft, camel coat as if they were contaminated while he still hummed the song. He could just about squeeze his feet into his shoes with a degree of pain and without any possibility of tying the laces, and he found it surprisingly difficult to get his arms into the sleeves of the jacket. 'I've been thinking . . .' he said as he hobbled after her up the slope and out of the open door, waiting for her to fiddle with keys while he breathed in the fresher, colder air and felt the rain on his face.

'Don't think, Henry, don't. You aren't good at it.' Maggie was conscious of an appalling headache forming like a stormcloud behind her eyes and she was unwilling to open her mouth, least of all for discussion. She pushed Henry into her car, drove by Neil's, posted the key through the letterbox, ground the gears twice in the short distance back to the seafront. Henry was still humming, not exactly at his best.

'What do you do for an overdose of Viagra?' she asked, to concentrate his mind and deal with another, residual worry as she watched the shiny surface of the road in the dipped headlights of her very old car.

'You wait for it to pass, I suppose. Was it raining on the day Harry got pushed into the sea?'

'Oh for God's sake, Henry, I don't know.'

The House of Enchantment was lit like a Christmas tree. It made Henry expect to see seasonal decorations in the hallway and he was slightly disappointed to find there were none. The sea on the far side of the road made soothing sounds and the rain fell. Peter and Timothy hugged him in turn and he hugged them back with enthusiastic affection, calmly grateful to be delivered back like a parcel into the domain of men and a bath full to overflowing. Soon it would be dawn. Henry lay in his own, high bed, his feet and hands stinging and throbbing, and he thought of the starling. The words of the song would not go away and what was the difference between a song and a poem? Before sleep intervened, he found himself entertaining the thought that Maggie had engineered the whole episode; or Angela and her, between them. A woman thing; teach the silly beggar to mind his own business; show him not to interfere. The thought drifted away. She would not have done that; they were poles apart, those women, and it isn't all about facts Henry, it's as much about *instincts*. Trust *them*, he admonished himself. Instincts. And there was a last irrelevancy . . . would he have spent so long on the trapped bird if it had been a fat, ugly seagull instead of a starling? Yes, of course, but it might have been harder. And sacking would have been better to contain a seagull beak, whereas the starling required the softness of a shawl.

Happy birthday to you, happy birthday to you . . . You look like an elephant. Go back to the zoo. Maggie woke to the sound of

continued rain and saw through one eye the patch of grey sky
which signalled another winter day. She closed the eye and tried
to calculate the time. Raising her head to look at the bedside
clock was effortful; about eight-thirty, at a guess. She could
sleep again, if she wanted, but the headache clawed at her skull
and the longer she lay, listening to the rain, the worse were the
reflections which hurt more than the aftermath of the wine and
the dull sense of shame attendant on it. She groaned. The suit of
clothes she had worn in the early hours of the morning hung
neatly on the wardrobe as if already inhabited and ready to
march, a last act of discipline before she had got back into bed.
She put on her thick dressing gown, a hairy thing in tartan,
chosen for warmth rather than elegance, shoved her feet into
slippers, looked out of the window down at the Wendy house in
the garden, groaned again and aimed herself towards the
kitchen.

Happy birthday to you . . . a humming again. The kitchen of a
house had always been her favourite place, along with back bed-
rooms and small gardens. Francesca had referred her to the House
of Enchantment and she had never left. The choice had plenty to
do with preoccupation and lethargy and nothing to do with the
fact that she might have been able to see her second cousin in the
garden, cavorting with Peter and Timothy on the three afternoons
a week when they minded him. She had had the opportunity, she
supposed, to know Harry better during the brief interval between
her return and his demise, but she had not taken it, a fact which
rankled now. There had been in her mind the certain thought that
if she had insisted on a child, her husband would not have left her
and she did not want to pay attention to other people's children.
Nor had she wanted to cry on the shoulder offered by Francesca,
because she had resorted to it once too often and slightly resented
the fact it was being offered again. How sad it is, she thought, that
we recoil from the people who have helped us. They know too
much. Each heavy step down to the ground floor brought a fresh
onslaught of misery, *I should have, I should have, I should have done*

this, that, the other . . . I should have noticed. I should have been con-
ciliatory to my husband instead of forcing him away; I should
have been nicer to little Harry, and now to grown-up Henry, and
I do not know what the fuck to do next, what the hell it is I've
started or even why.

'You should have some breakfast,' Timothy said. 'Bacon?'

'Ugh.'

'Toast, then. Tea.'

'Stop being *nice*, for God's sake or I might cry. You're so bloody
kind, you're a lousy example to a woman with a conscience. Toast,
please.' Toast and marmalade marked a point when life was tenable. Not necessarily pleasant, but at least ongoing.

'Henry told us he stayed after closing time in the castle and got
locked in. It might have been a mistake, he said,' Peter stated.

'How very diplomatic of him. No one has ever been incarcerated in there by mistake. And there's something else I'll have to tell
him, too. Bloody Neil got in here the other night, I don't know
when, and went through Henry's room. Took the shawl on the
bed. It's in his house. What nice friends I've got. They're all
duplicitous.'

'What about us? We're merely simple . . . what on earth did he
want?'

'Little blue Viagra pills, I think. He may have been convinced
that Henry had a supply and that's probably my fault, too.'
Timothy giggled. Senta came and laid her muzzle on Maggie's lap,
a kind, sensitive animal, born to give unconditional affection
whenever it was required, or maybe wanting some of the toast.
Cupboard love, any kind of love, would do.

'If Angela Hulme locked him in, what was she trying to say?'
Peter asked, remarkably chipper for a few hours' sleep.

'Get away from me and my child. Go home, Yank. Something
subtle like that,' Timothy ventured with a wise expression. 'And,
by the way, our little Harry has no opinions whatever, at the
moment. It was far too cold for him last night. He may drift in for
tea.' She was silent.

A competing kitchen smell began to overpower the toast and Tim bolted towards the oven. There were times, especially now, when his frenetic movements made her dizzy and wrecked the languor of the kitchen. The results of his culinary anxiety were delicious but the price was the hypermanic way he went at the preparations, swinging from sink to cooker to table, unable to go slower and gibbering en route, *oh dear, oh dear, oh dear,* as if each manoeuvre might result in starvation and disgrace. Face flushed and spectacles misted, he produced from the oven two perfect, golden sponge cakes which he upended on to a cloth and reversed on to a rack to cool, where they looked to Maggie like a pair of yellow hillocks, stolen from another landscape. The air was fragrant with sweetness; she swallowed the last mouthful of toast.

'What do you think? Strawberry jam, or blackberry filling? White icing, he loathes pink. Candles, of course.'

'*Candles?*'

'Harry's birthday,' Peter said, patiently. 'He adores a nice Victoria sponge. Will you be back for tea?'

'Oh, *bollocks,*' Maggie said.

The smell of cake seemed to permeate the whole ground floor by the time she had fled to her room and back downstairs again, pausing only to dress, wondering for an irrelevant second quite how many hours of her life she had spent choosing what to wear. Philip would hate the dressing gown. Philip would be waiting for an instant response to his letter: let him wait. Should she wear the suit which announced her as someone who had come to cut off the gas/electric/blood supply, or should she look benign? A pale face in her mirror told her that all clothes were ineffectual disguises of mood.

The rain had stopped and all such mercies seemed small. She walked to clear her head. Her car, parked against the sea, looked lonely and salty; the pier looked like something erected without planning permission for no particular purpose and even from the depths of self-recriminatory depression, she was suddenly smitten with affection for it. Story of your life, she told herself; you love useless things: high heels, husbands, redundant castles, inconvenient cousins imprisoned for life, silly little dogs and verse. She stopped to look at the sea, staring out to where a ferry smoothed its way across from left to right, going away from home or towards. The sky was breaking up into clouds and she wanted to be on that boat.

Was it raining on the day Harry died? What did it matter? Maggie sat on a bench, the better to postpone the day, rose again swiftly when she felt the damp, moved on slowly. From the entrance to the pier, she would be able to see the castle and the window of her cousin's flat and that would be the place for pausing. Angela was likely to be at home. The seafront was deserted. The right approach was to get Angela out of doors and into a quiet caff where she might be inhibited about raising her voice and, in the eyes of a few unconcerned but gossipy members of the public, pretend she had nothing to hide.

The new sculpture which stood on the pavement at the entrance of the pier was only called new on account of not having reached a certain majority. It was, by all agreed standards, modern; therefore tolerated after the original and inevitable protest died down and the shiny metal of its construction (designed to dazzle the eye in the sun) had dulled down with verdigris and the salt that stained it. The first protest had been forced into submission by the surprising fact that children loved it and concluded that the base of the thing, composed of metallic waves and fishes, was ideal for running round in circles, hitting the edge of the small boat in which the solid fisherman sat with his overlarge head, clutching his giant, fat fish and gazing at it with huge, sad eyes, locked in a tussle of love. The whole of it was too rounded for climbing, but little hands somehow desired to strike and stroke. It made a satisfying sound and was warm to the touch when the sun shone. Small children hid behind it, playing tag in defiance of the no running, no jumping restrictions which applied on the pier.

As Maggie approached the statue, admiring it for its durable surface and squat power, a head with recognizable hair poked out from behind and ducked away again. Aha. This was irritatingly unexpected and more than a little shocking. She stopped and walked forward casually, circling the statue's base until she found Tanya, leaning into the curved spine of a fish as if trying to rub her own back against it. There was a deliberate nonchalance in her pose as if, dressed in pristine clothes suitable for school and clearly during school hours, she was simply a detached part of an outdoor study group instead of a truant concealing herself. There was a dearth of ten-year-olds out on streets at this hour of a term time morning. To Maggie's eyes, Tanya was trying to make her presence appear official, which meant having the wit not to run away; she was anxious rather than defiant, which in Maggie's slight but regular acquaintance with her, was rare. Neither knew quite what to say until Maggie thought of something suitably innocuous.

'You waiting for a bus, Tanya?'

'Sort of. Only I'm early.' A swift, relieved response.

'I'll wait with you.' The child shrugged, not a confident, fuck-you, shrug, more one of resignation from a small person who was privately close to tears. They leaned in uncomfortable silence, Maggie reaching into her bag to retrieve Philip's letter, not because she seriously intended to re-read it, but simply to look as if she was attending to something else. There was nothing else to read apart from a list. The words blurred slightly, filled her with momentary fury, *we all make awful mistakes, me more than most . . .* such pathetic, self-serving ruefulness; so bloody *coy.* She glanced forward and back over the edge of the crumpled sheets towards the gravel of the beach for a full minute, then stuffed the letter back in the bag. By her side, she heard Tanya let out a long, tremulous sigh of relief; Maggie followed the child's gaze to where the flag rose above the central turret of the castle. It was raised slowly, the flag of St George, red cross on white background, fluttering without enthusiasm, then lying flatly against the pole. Unseen hands tied a rope. 'That's *good,*' Tanya muttered.

'It doesn't look very happy,' Maggie said, chattily. 'But I don't suppose that's the point of it. I never quite know what flags are supposed to do.' How silly she sounded to her own ears, gabbling for the sake of filling a void and keeping her there.

Tanya was nodding, wiping the damp sleeve of her jacket across her nose and leaving a trail, noticing it, rubbing at it with the other sleeve and looking so much happier now that she was ready to be condescending to a pig-ignorant friend of her mother's. 'It doesn't *do* anything. It only means that *somebody's* come in, Neil prob'ly, an' got inside, 'cos you have to to get at the flag. So if some silly bugger was still stuck inside, he'll be all right now, won't he?'

'He might be a bit cross,' Maggie remarked, innocuously. 'But I expect he'll get over that, people do, don't they? It was his own silly fault, really. I suppose.' The child shook her head.

'No, it wasn't. Mummy locked the door. I screamed and screamed and she wouldn't listen, and I couldn't sleep for thinking and . . .'

'You bunked out of school to let him out? Do you want a cuppa before you go back? Coke or something, on the pier? She could not say, stay with me, talk to me; she had no right. Tanya looked longingly back down the length of the *Titanic* and rubbed her hand against the nose of a sculpted fish.

'Can't,' she said finally. 'I don't like it. It's so fucking boring. I don't like the pier. I like *this*, though.' She continued to stroke the nose of the fish. 'Harry talks to it,' she added, inconsequentially. 'He tries to get into the boat, but he falls out, always falling. Gotta go.' But she was not entirely certain about whether she wanted to go, stood with her feet crossed, staring first at the flag and then, longingly, back down the length of the pier to where the caff promised warmth and something sweet. The longing glance was tinged with indecision. *Don't ever mention Harry to that child, do you hear? Don't ever do anything so cruel.* The words of a command came into Maggie's mind and she could not remember from where, or who had spoken them when: Angela, or Francesca, something in a fax, written words, spoken words, blurred into a stern command so earnest it stopped her now. All those promises she had made.

'Shall I come with you?' she asked. 'In case they've missed you at school? What'll they say?'

'I'll tell them Mummy was poorly, made me late, only I never went in, you see, only looked like I did an' I shouldn't tell fibs, should I?' Maggie bent towards her, suddenly longing to push the hair out of her blinking eyes and wipe the pert nose which twitched on the brink of a sneeze. Such a child was not suitable for keeping as a pet although she had all the soft, self-willed neediness of a kitten.

'Fibs are generally bad,' she said gravely, producing a coin. 'But you have to tell them sometimes in a good cause. You've got a rumbly tummy. Get some chocolate on the way.'

As she watched Tanya sprint across the road, it crossed her mind to wonder whether children only began to trust other adults when they began to see the fallibility of their own parents. She felt a dull thudding in the region of her heart, wished she had taken a chance and grilled the child and wished again she was on the boat, which had now disappeared. No one had asked the child about Harry; not at the time. The child was too fragile, too damaged, and on a practical level, no information she gave could be reliable; the best thing to do was to encourage her to forget.

There was no answer from Angela's flat. She went back to the comfort of the statue and watched her cousin's neighbours come and go. Harry *talks* to the statue meant Harry *had talked* to the statue; children confused tenses as well as identities, or at least she remembered having done exactly that. Maybe Tanya meant that *she* liked to talk to the statue and maybe it only meant that it was the mute companionship of the solid man in the boat which had drawn Harry out of doors on a cold day when it might have been raining. She looked at the length of the pier and saw what Henry had meant. No little boy would cross a road and run so far, unless he was running away.

There were always excuses for not working. The state of the room, the height of the chair, the need for a cigarette, food, company and a preference for fishing. 'Dear Mrs Dodder,' Edward wrote, crossed that out and wrote 'Hodder': 'I am only writing this letter because I am disinclined to do anything else. I do not care about the proposed changes to your will necessitated by your nephew failing to send a Christmas card. Regrettable of course, but hardly worth cancelling his bequest. Your last will and testament has sixteen codicils already . . . suggest you wait and see if he acknowledges your birthday . . .' He might also drop a line to the nephew, but such an approach would be interventionist. Mrs Hodder had marked every item of her considerable porcelain collection with a piece of Elastoplast on the base bearing the name of a legatee; on good days, she dusted it and on bad days, changed the labels. When he himself was old and decrepit, he would do nothing but fish, topple into a river if he found himself counting the spoons. So difficult to prioritize the affairs of others. Lawyers were theoretically objective, treating clients equally from the distance of their own, mysterious qualifications, but that only meant pretending that he did not dislike the majority apart from the few of whom he was fond.

In the midst of the morning's work displacement activity by reverie, Edward removed his gaze from the ceiling cracks and found Henry sitting on the opposite side of the desk as if he belonged. He was wearing the same jacket but it was shrunk and the texture and colour had changed into something vaguely reptilian. It made him occupy the chair as if he was a person in a straitjacket unable to hold his arms to his own sides. Either it had shrunk or the man had grown. He looked pathetically grubby and out of place in a jacket like that, but he had obviously wielded either authority or stealth to get past that phalanx of bosoms downstairs and in one moment of wry observation, Henry Evans was elevated in Edward's estimation into the ranks of clients he liked rather than tolerated. He leaned across the desk, arm extended for a handshake, as if he had been expecting him to call. Henry's attempt to reciprocate was awkward enough to send flying a pile of correspondence which both of them ignored. There were no apologies or awkward attempts to pick it up and Edward approved of all economies of effort. Both settled back into their chairs and regarded one another frankly.

'Do you ever think,' Henry asked, 'that you might have missed your vocation?'

'Frequently, yes. But I've very little idea of what it might have been, so it doesn't cause me much distress. One always assumed that a vocation would obviate boredom, but it doesn't follow, does it?'

'No, it doesn't. Scientists are bored; so are millionaires, I guess . . .'

'Carpenters must be bored. Policemen must be bored. Can't be a thinking man alive who doesn't imagine he could be doing better or different. I shall go to my grave mourning the fact that I haven't had enough fun. Or caught enough fish. What can I do for you?'

'Cup of coffee would be nice.'

Edward went to the door and bellowed down the stairs, '*COFFEE! TWO!*' 'It might work,' he said, resuming his chair and the endless search for a cigarette. 'The women here don't consider it beneath their dignity to make coffee. Perhaps you would have preferred tea?'

'No. Thank you. I just wanted to run through a few facts with you.'

'I thought you might,' Edward said, immediately understanding the subject. 'All we can ever rely on, facts.'

'I was beginning to prefer instincts.'

'Bugger instincts. They're almost as bad as principles. As soon as I hear somebody say, it's a matter of principle, I want to scream. Likewise when they say, I *feel* this is right, or I've got a gut *instinct* about that person or this. At the end of the day, it's rarely anything to do with guts, only money, which you don't keep in your gut unless you're very odd indeed.'

The coffee arrived. Ineffectual coasters were produced to guard the wrecked desktop and a plump woman floated away in a waft of splendid perfume. Henry struggled out of his jacket.

Leaning forward to pick up a mug would otherwise have been impossible. 'Which is why,' Edward continued, 'I can't detect any alternative explanation for the untimely death of Harry Chisholm other than the one given. No one else had any motive for killing him, especially not a financial motive. If there was a cousin and an inheritance I could see it, but there isn't. There's desperation; there's pity for a life which is not going to unfold well, there's a woman at her wits' end having a moment of madness with a child who is being naughty and there's no other motive at all. An *instinctive* killing. Nagged at me for a long time before you came along. Nags me every day. My own bloody instinct, telling me she was far too controlled a woman to lose it like that. Or to have let that child out of her sight.' A plume of cigarette smoke curled towards the yellow ceiling. Henry lit one too. Smoking was infectious.

'What I see as inherently unlikely,' Henry said, 'is this child who hated the cold going out on his own. Was it raining, do you know? I can't find anyone who can tell me if it was raining. Seems important to me: less reason than ever for him to go out, more reason for him to slip. And the woman downstairs can't remember that he ever did go out without his mother unless someone came to take him. I know it wasn't raining when he was found, it says so in the case papers.' The coffee was intensely good. Fuelled by coffee like this, Henry could understand how Edward survived a day in this uncomfortable room. He would probably float from task to task in his own, peculiar haze.

'Good Lord, man, the weather changes every five minutes here or haven't you noticed? Nobody could possibly remember. And suppose he was *driven* out? A screaming row about nothing or something, an order, GET OUT – something of the kind happens in my house once a week. The mother being dictatorial, cruel even. You see, Mr Evans, you may have to accept that your own blundering investigations, if such you call them, may reveal Francesca Chisholm in a worse light than ever. I hope you've thought of that. By the way, what happened to your jacket?'

'I don't think it's even mine,' Henry said. 'I was on my way to buy another. And a hat. All those thrift shops . . .'

'Thrift? Oh I see. I get it. Second hand.' The slightly dreamy look of an enthusiast came over Edward's face and it occurred to Henry to guess the source of his ill-fitting clothes. He could see Edward throwing out the whole wardrobe at the end of each month and starting again and the thought of doing such a thing was appealing.

'And it crossed my mind,' Henry went on relentlessly, 'that all kinds of junk end up in thrift shops' – he did not add, *such as you wear* – 'and if I hunted around, I might find Francesca's things. She threw out her clothes as well as his and where did they go? They had to go somewhere. This isn't the kind of place where people throw things away.'

'Good point, but I doubt there'd be any of it left by now. Were there any other facts you wanted to mention? And while we're on the subject, I think our client has faxed us from prison. I faxed her, she faxed Maggie. She's allowed to do that. Only to her lawyers. Old lawyers don't die, you know, they simply lose their appeal.'

'Does she write it herself? What does she say?' He wanted to see her handwriting. Edward scuttled beneath the desk to emerge the other side among the pile of spilled correspondence, clutching the shiny paper of a fax in one hand and a cigarette in the other. 'What does it say?' Henry repeated.

Edward adjusted his glasses, squinted at crumpled paper. *Henry? Who's Henry?* he read, his mouth forming the words which he failed to speak as he scrunched the thing into a ball and thrust it into his pocket. 'Says nothing,' he sighed theatrically. 'The fucking fax machine only works on Fridays.' He skipped round the desk and slumped back into his chair which swivelled with a mind of its own and spun him round so that his back was to Henry and he faced the fish. Henry could see tufts of his black hair above the chairback and see the curl of smoke. 'There's something very odd going on with Uncle Joe,' he announced. 'There seem to be two of him. I think it might be in everyone's interest if you went to see one of them.'

Edward was far more articulate when not facing an audience. Henry could empathize with that. 'Uncle Joe?' he queried.

'Disgraced Uncle Joe. Whom Francesca visited regularly. She refused to take notice of tarnished reputations. Angela Hulme took over visiting a few months back and I wonder why? Sits and talks for hours to someone, I'm told, but whoever it is, it ain't a Chisholm. It's a man who picks up strangers, so you'll do very well. Do your shopping first. I would.'

There was just about enough in this High Street to keep a small-ish mind happy. A true city sophisticate might think otherwise, but Bond Street was a long way off, in another country entirely and it was another person than the one Maggie now recognized in herself who had agonized over which neutral shade of carpet for which room in a branch of John Lewis big enough to cover the whole of this row. There were exquisitely furnished houses in Warbling and, occasionally, well dressed people who did not do their buying here, and it was when they replaced their finery that the rest had the benefit. The richer of Warbling (the larger houses behind the town and out of the wind; the buildings with lawns, away from the warren of narrow streets of mixed fortunes adjacent to the seafront) dutifully recycled clothes, artefacts, pots and pans, linens, redundant toys, but mostly clothes, into the charity shops.

There was a time of her life when she would not have been seen dead inside a charity shop and Maggie regarded her present pleasure in their very existence as an indicator of how much she had changed: she loved them without a thought and so did everyone else. It was almost mandatory to explore them on a weekly basis; it was risk-free shopping; it was a common denominator for the eldery retired in Harris tweed jostling politely with impecunious young mothers with babes in arms, each with a different avenue to explore and nobody minded the fact that windows would be rehung with dead Aunt Ethel's velvet curtains, or that Jimmy went to school in the cast-off clothes of someone two forms higher. The same garments were unrecognizable on a different body; they changed with a new owner. Reborn, rejuvenated, given a lease of life, Peter said. The shops were an acceptable aspect of change, decay and death, but there was another thing about the clothes. Displayed on hangers, crushed together like a crowd trying to get out of a door, it was impossible to visualize who might have worn them last. There were uniformly coiffed, grey-haired ladies who wore the stock and counted out change with great precision, sharing the excitement of bargains. Maggie had a distinct preference for one shop out of the five; Timothy pre-ferred Oxfam for the towels and sheets, while she favoured Age Concern for varied clothing and the manager's frivolous inability to turn away any kind of hat.

There were better things to do; she knew it, but she could not do what she had set out to do – find Angela – and she did not want to digest her encounter with Tanya; she did not want to do very much at all. It was a state of non-specific indecision, halfway to misery and useless introspection, so she pressed her nose to the window of the shop. Dear God, there was a swimsuit in there, draped artfully over a plastic plant and topped with a deerstalker, dreams of winter and summer combined. Someone would buy it to encourage the weather to change, and if it didn't fit, it didn't matter. Seasons did not dictate stock; winter coats were next to summer cottons, woolly scarves along with beads and boots mark-ing time with sandals on the floor. Maggie loved an organized mess. New hats, right at the back there, hats left over from forgot-ten weddings and christenings and never kept for funerals, all the more interesting for being dented. She needed a hat like she needed a hole in the head. She needed prayers, not a hat, but Henry needed a hat and as long as somebody needed a hat, there was reason to look.

Think of the devil and he arrives; never was the saying truer than in a small town. Pausing for a minute, she caught Henry's reflection in the glass, standing beside her looking through the window in perplexity, as if her thinking of him had conjured his presence. He had noticed the dirt on his leather jacket and was trying to rub it off. She touched his arm; the material felt rough and ruined and his arms were held stiffly. He smiled his infectious, forgiving smile and she found herself smiling in return. Oh dear, what had she done to him.

'Were you waiting for me?'

'Nope, but I'm glad you're here. I've never been inside a thrift shop. Don't know the code.'

'Henry, you haven't lived. There is no code.'

There was a surge of warmth and a draught of smells. From the makeshift changing room at the back there came a bellow of laughter before a woman emerged in a skirt which touched her ankles and gaped round the middle. Henry could see how this was a place where looking ridiculous and being too fat was a cause for celebration and perhaps in this town, the beautiful people were few and far between. He eased himself out of the jacket which saturation or something had wrecked to the extent that it had changed in colour as well as in size and made him feel fatter than anyone. His eye was drawn to the deerstalker; he reached for it and put it on his head. It was oversized for a large man and the brim descended to his nose to land on the bridge of his glasses, so that he had to tilt his head back in order to see. A very silly person was visible in the cheval glass, looking like a retard newly released from an institution which could have kept him in, while next to him, made a foot higher by the addition of a large black hat with an excrescence of veil and a broken feather, Maggie peered at them both with her head at a similar angle. The black hat was like a piece of broad stovepiping, the net which exploded from the top a desiccated bird's nest. The feather had once been turquoise. They looked at their own images seriously and nodded in unison. The hats wobbled. Slowly, Maggie removed her hat with a flourish and handed it to him. He took off the deerstalker and handed it to her. Each donned the other hat. Sizes were deceptive. She wore his hat halfway down her face with the peak turned to the side, giving her the profile of a duck, while the stovepipe sat on his crown like a saucer on top of a cup.

'I'll take two,' Henry said.

'No sillier than the hat you lost,' Maggie said.

He handed her a scarlet beret which made her look like a tired streetwalker in a 1950s French film, while the blue Breton cap she handed him gave him the look of an idiot savant. The balaclava he tried next was so difficult he knew he was as honour bound to buy it as never to wear it. Released from temporary blindness, he saw Maggie, wearing a tartan cap, leaning against the counter and shaking silently while immediately behind her the manager was in the act of selling Henry's leather jacket. He watched without protest as it was carried out of the door by a man several sizes smaller than himself and wondered why he had ever liked it, and there was a moment as the door closed when he seriously wondered if it was his coat at all.

'How did you know I lost a hat, Maggie?' he asked over his shoulder as, now well into the swing of things, he looked at a crowded rail of unattractive and musty-smelling woollens. There was a way of behaving in here which would not be useful in other shops. Here, you could treat the clothes as if they were already yours and nobody gave a damn. 'You told me,' she said airily, and he tried to remember if he had.

He found a jacket: brown, serviceable and cleanly nondescript, seven dollars and big enough for that sum to be able to shrink with impunity. She had bought nothing and said that was not the point. To the side of the lady counting change and yelling comments into the tiny changing area beyond, there was a wodge of scarves spilling from a basket. He sorted through them, feeling the harsh texture of synthetic fabrics, and then his fingers encountered something softer. Pulling at it, he saw the edge of a cream, embroidered shawl. He felt the texture between his fingers, thrust it back and then pulled it out again. It was old and yellowed, but still soft. Henry held it against the light and saw the holes and a label stating £5. No wonder it had not moved: £5 was a lot in a thrift shop. He seemed to remember he had spent much more than that, even in India, twenty years ago. He fancied it smelt of heat, spices and dust. Maggie had stopped laughing and looked at him with concern. Tears stung his eyes. 'Nobody should be thrown out,' he said. 'Nor their belongings either.'

'Would you want them all to die with you, Henry?'

'No. I hate waste.'

'Time we talked properly, Henry. No messing.'

'Time you stopped fobbing me off.'

'Yes.'

The jacket felt inexpensive rather than cheap and he felt it gave him anonymity. Now that his shoes were broken in and his hair unstyled he could meld into this street by the simple expedient of wearing someone else's clothes. Maybe he would begin to think and talk in the same roundabout way, never quite getting to the point, like they did. People who looked like Edward seemed to command respect; people who looked like him certainly did not. No one would know him now. Out in the street, the sunlight blinded him. It ricocheted off the wet ground and straight into his eyes. He stuffed the balaclava into his pocket and resolved to get rid of it soon, lifted his face to the light and sniffed in sheer pleasure at the sensation of relative warmth. Maggie pulled at his arm and he resisted the irritated urge to shrug her off, not because he didn't like her close, for all her cryptic commentary, but really, she should stop leading him round. He wasn't a dog.

'This way,' she said, urgently.

'Which way?' And he must stop asking questions. She pulled, he resisted, bumped into a person made featureless by the reflected light. 'Sorry,' he said, automatically.

'Angela,' Maggie said formally. 'How nice. I was just coming to see you.'

The figure of Angela Hulme recoiled, shopping bags rustling angrily.

'Oh, really? Don't bother. And don't bring him.' She leaned forward, thrusting her face into Maggie's, close enough to exchange breath, speaking through clenched teeth, loud enough for everyone to hear. 'Do you know what he was doing on

Sunday? He was putting his dirty hands up my little girl's jumper, that's what he was doing. He won't leave her alone. He wants locking up. So keep him away or I'm getting him arrested. Are you listening to me?'

Henry saw himself captured in a brief reflection, in the plate glass window of the betting shop on the other side of the road, where a posse of men were visible only because their noses were planted against the glass. He looked like a shifty specimen himself and all he got was the impression of a dozen sets of cold eyes. The urge to make a face and stick out his tongue was quick in passing. The population moving through the bottleneck at the junction of two streets parted like a wave against a breakwater. This time, Henry allowed himself to be guided away. He did not feel quite so anonymous any more.

Inside these walls, dress becomes important. 'Taking care' with appearance is encouraged and we have our own clothes. Taking care of washing and clothes is tantamount to taking care of self, not letting go entirely, although the thought is tempting. There's a sharp division in the reactions to compliments, so that if I were to say to my friend in the kitchen, 'You look nice', the response could be pleasure, hostile suspicion or a denial of looking nice at all, accompanied by the explanation that the dress, skirt, whatever are really pieces of shit. This may mirror the generally low self-esteem: I'm not a shrink; I don't know, but I still think a compliment is worth the risk of a slap in the face.

There's a hairdressing salon, too, as part of the educational programme; there are some fine hairstyles. It looks like a regular salon, bit old-fashioned, with the difference that all scissors and implements, numbered and coded, go back into a safe, triple locked against the wall, at the end of the day. Just like the knives in the kitchen, displayed beneath bulletproof Perspex to show how the regime is only a distant relative to normal life after all, although the odd reactions to compliments are probably the same when I think of it. If ever I told Maggie she looked nice in the days of her metropolitan chic, she'd always tell me what a bargain it was. Tanya loves clothes in her own fastidious and possessive way, they had huge importance for her, because she'd once been dressed in rags, I suppose. Harry was too messy to notice.

There, I was going to write a page without mentioning either of them, but since there will never be a day when I do not think of them, trying to evade it on paper is futile. I was trying to resist telling the story, but it has been gnawing at me, the fact that no one knows the truth, no one who is ever going to tell it, I hope, and while I thought I wouldn't mind that, I do. Each night I write a little of this, either resisting or avoiding the urge to write a literal description of what happened . . . and at first I didn't do it in case someone found it. Now I know it would make precious little difference if they did; it would be my fantasy, but it grows and grows, this cancerous need to confess.

It was the old rule in murder that the victim had to die within a year and a day of the crime in order for a charge to be made.

This perpetrator has only to relive the facts on her own anniversary.

A strange, garbled message from Edward . . . I do not want anyone to pry . . . I cannot have them adding up two and two to make five . . . and yet . . . and yet, I wish they would.

There; I have survived his birthday and neither kissed nor told. I hope it will last the week.

FMC

CHAPTER ELEVEN

'THE awful thing about loss of reputation,' Henry said, 'is the way it makes you feel a stranger to yourself. Like this can't be you with this dirty mark stuck to your forehead.'

'A shouting match on a street corner hardly involves a loss of reputation, Henry,' she said sharply. 'Especially if you didn't have one to lose.'

'Well a minor form of it, then. I certainly felt disgraced. Even you let go of me for a minute.'

Maggie was silent, acknowledging the fact. 'I didn't *mean* to let go of you. I was going to hit her. She's neurotic. Everyone knows that.' Henry shook his head.

'Nobody knows that I'm a guy who fights shy of kids,' he said. 'This kind of stuff sticks like shit on a shoe.'

'It's a *convenient* accusation,' Maggie said, furiously. 'It justifies her in locking you in the castle and it makes sure you don't go near her again. It panders to the idea of the paedophile as bogeyman; it justifies her calling the cops and making up anything she wants.'

'She wouldn't want to make her daughter tell lies.'

'She wouldn't have to. It wouldn't have to go that far. She could get you brought in for questioning, stuck in a cell for an hour or two and—'

'No, *NO*.'

'. . . And then withdraw the accusation. The object would be achieved, wouldn't it? An hour of that and you and your claustrophobia would be gone.'

Henry let that pass. They sat in the pier caff. Henry had watched her walk straight through the door with the unerring sense of direction of someone who came here often and always sat in the same place, away from the counter and the cosier area of the place. She would always sit in the spartan summer room, with bare Formica tables and big metal windows showing nothing but sea. The tide was high, lapping at the fishing platforms, echoing through the slats. Facing to the front, it felt like being in the prow of a ship, watching other ships and the endless theatre of the sky. With the sun casting arrows into the waves, he could believe the water was warm, welcoming, harmless. There was a large brown pot of tea between them, so strong it reminded him of the bitter tea of Ceylon. He wanted to say as much, but resisted it. It was for the English to discuss irrelevancies and set people tests.

She had torn an empty sugar packet into several pieces, put her hands in her lap out of sight when she saw him watching.

'I don't think you're right about what people think of Mrs Hulme,' he said. '*They* don't think she's neurotic; *you* do. They think she does great, with a beautifully turned out child, she doesn't complain. And they'd be right, too, wouldn't they? She does a terrific job with that kid. The kid's clever and brave and bright. I had a kid like that, I'd be protective, too. She's going to be a star, that kid.'

'You wouldn't go round accusing others of imagined violations.'

'I don't know what I'd do. I don't know who I'd love or hate or want to kill. I think I might do almost anything to protect, wouldn't you? Especially if I *chose* that child, had her on trust and knew what she'd suffered already.'

'You're very forgiving, Henry. She locked you in the damned castle. And Tanya wanted to rescue you.'

'I'm not forgiving at all about that. Or about her making up reasons for it. But I can't feel mad about how anyone behaves when they feel under threat. They're like that starling I found in the Runs, all mad and silly.'

'And you got it out, did you?' He nodded. She looked at him, judging him, deciding on something. Go on, he urged her silently; be reckless, be honest.

'Look, I don't know about the Francesca you knew once, but let me tell you about the one I met after the police took her in. She was colder than ice. She wouldn't let me look after her or interrupt the questioning, even when she went on saying one damning thing after another. She wasn't naive; she was trying to give them no alternative to a murder charge. They would have let her off with less, probably. To charge murder you must prove the *intention* to do serious harm. She gave them the proof. "*When I went to look for him, I saw he had slipped through the boards and he was stuck. I considered what to do and thought this was the ideal opportunity to finish it all. I knew exactly what I was doing and I knew in these temperatures he wouldn't last long . . . the suffering would be minimal . . . it was quite deliberate . . .*" And do you know, listening to her, I believed her at the time. There was regret, but only of the most intellectual kind, I mean regret *that it had to be done.*'

'I read it,' Henry said tersely. 'I read the whole of it. The bit where she said where she was when she decided it was inevitable. When they were on that beach up the coast, in the summer before. The beach where they go from the nursing homes because you can get wheelchairs down, where she saw the cerebral palsy sufferers who go there in the vacation, thirty-year-olds looking like old men, with their parents or nurses, still wiping bottoms and dribbles and carrying those skinny, twisted limbs into the sea. Some of them blind. How people would be kind and help, once, and then remember not to come back to the same place the next day. How she would be an old woman with an old child, picking up pebbles with one hand. She would rather be in prison, she said. *I might still have a mind,* she said.'

'You memorized it well.'

'Somebody had to. When you learn it like a text, you can see the whole fucking thing is full of holes. Completely acceptable as a thesis for a cause of death because it has its own logic and she was so convincing. Could be a true thesis, could be one entirely rehearsed. She was good at learning things by heart. Daddy taught her. But that boy didn't go out by himself. That's the weakness.'

She stared into the remnants of the rust-coloured tea, her hands still in her lap. She felt as if she were being interrogated, complicit with Francesca and ready to defend her, sick of questions and yet resigned. This was, after all, what she had wanted.

'Why wouldn't he?'

'Francesca *stopped* other people asking about the details of how Harry behaved by first giving a comprehensive account of what happened which effectively stopped everyone looking further and secondly, lying about the prognosis. No one questioned that either.'

'*I* did. But only later.'

He nodded approval. 'So you would know it might not have been anything like as bad as she painted it. He didn't have cerebral palsy in the worst form, he had hemiplegia and a normal intelligence. He might not have turned into a cripple and I'll bet she was believing he wouldn't. But there was no evidence that he *often* ran out on the pier, no evidence of behaviour patterns. Tim and Peter could have helped, but no one asked them either. Angela pretended not to know, but of course she knew. It was all gone, along with her clothes and the books and all the evidence of whatever therapy she used with him. But I know that he hated the cold. The bad limbs feel the cold more, swell, sometimes; they made him less mobile, more embarrassed. I keep asking about the damn rain. Rain's cold. Granny says the door stood open most of the time, everyone welcome, but he never went out further than the door. So what persuaded him on a cold day? To go out without his jacket?'

'Did he?'

'Sure. No one found a jacket. A jacket might have stopped him slipping too far through the boards . . . stopped the grazes, maybe. His clothes kept him afloat for long enough . . . you don't go straight down. A jacket adds weight. I should know.'

'It was sunny,' she said. 'Like today. And no one found your hat, either.'

He placed his hands flat on the top of the table, daring her to present her own. She stared at the square tips of his practical fingers and he gazed beyond her artificially tinted head towards the vastness of the sea.

'So where were you on that morning, Mrs Lawyer? Taking the air while other folks got ready to take their kids to school? You're crazy about this pier at dawn and you might have been crazy about your cousin, too. I didn't tell you about the damned hat; you watched it go. You eavesdrop; you watch. It's what you do. You filter and distort facts. When you've got time left over from carrying around that damn load of self-pity you put on your damn back. What's a bit of hard fact going to do for you? Make your fake blonde hair fall out?'

She rose to her feet to give the heels of her shoes better purchase on the floor and gave him a resounding slap with the palm of her hand. It left a red mark on his cheek, a ringing in his ears and the echo of nervous laughter from the counter. Then she turned away from him and brushed the wind tangles out of her hair with her fingers as if to announce this was not a proper argument and she had better things to do, merely a tiff. She looked like a furious princess sitting with the pauper and him being insolent, too. Sat back and crossed one leg elegantly across the other.

Looking beneath the table with his head still crooked from the blow, Henry could see that one foot in a Cuban-heeled shoe was describing an irregular circle, as if her toes hurt. Not as much as his face. Totally unbidden, a pair of hands removed the teapot and replaced it with another in the interests of peace. Maggie nodded thanks; he remained still. She tucked one hand into the mass of her hair and leaned on her elbow, confidentially.

'You do *not* kick a woman with a hangover, Henry. It simply isn't cricket. Were you saying something?'

'Oh no, not at all. Just wondering what you would do to prove to me that you weren't a scheming liar with some hidden agenda. And a sad old conscience as big as an ice floe. Breaks the surface from time to time.'

'I don't have to prove anything to you. And I don't really do lies. I don't know how. Evasions, maybe. My motives are entirely pure, Henry. It's the end result might be a bit sullied.' She had picked up her bag and shrugged on the coat. He followed her out of the caff. The two men at the counter were suddenly busy, not looking in their direction. She ran down the steps on to the fishing platform with the intact boards and again he followed. He had never been so far, only looked at it. Down below, with the caff resting on girders above their heads, they were in a different, shaded world. From a distance, the platforms looked as if they were built on afterthoughts, flying additions to give ballast to the end of the pier, with nothing beneath the building, but from here there was one continuous arena, guarded by waist-height railings, high enough to avoid any accidental falling, low enough to balance a rod. At one side, he noticed a purposeless set of barnacled steps going down into the sea. The height of the tide obscured most of them; they seemed disused. The area beneath the caff felt like a vast, open-sided shelter.

'Before everyone became so safety conscious,' Maggie said, ever the tourist guide, 'when people came here just to see the damn pier, they ran boat trips from here, or the other side.' The undulating water lapped at the steps and the platform boards with calm curiosity. From the darkness of the shade, the sea ahead appeared luminous with sunlight, while inside and beneath, it made sucking sounds. He was following her again, to the near edge of the platform with the broken boards. 'I tell you what, Henry,' Maggie was saying, chattily, 'you don't trust me one teeny, weeny bit, so what about a nice medieval test? Either I'm a scheming liar and a bit of a witch or I'm not. Bloody well decide to trust me or I'll jump in.'

'Oh, for Chrissakes . . . what would that prove?'

'That I mean what I say.'

He shook his head, prepared to laugh at her, grinning contemptuously until she threw him her coat and kicked off her shoes. She wore tight-fitting pants and a sweater and the laughter died as she placed one neat foot on the bottom rung of the railings, swung herself over and hung on to the other side, looking down at the water. The drop was about the same as her own height; she seemed to be considering it, holding on to the rail and looking down, judging the distance, wiggling her toes. Then she let go with arms outstretched and a banshee yell and dropped. He scarcely heard a splash; the water slurped and echoed, like an animal with appetite. Henry let the coat fall and ran to the railings.

She hit the water on her back, star shaped, sank briefly and reappeared. He could feel the current and almost touch the swell. She was treading water furiously, shook her head to get the hair out of her eyes and then, as his eyes adjusted to the sun on the sea, she rose on the cusp of the swell and was swept beneath the pier. Henry felt a groan tear itself out of his chest: he peered down, heard the sucking sound of the mountainous water gurgling among the buttresses beneath, imagined the *crump* of a body driven against concrete. Which way would the current go? Would it take her out to sea, in to land? Would it merely sweep her beneath the lethal superstructure of this thing? Down here in this cavern, they were entirely out of view; no one from the caff would notice, yet, or was the constant shifting of the ocean a noise sufficient to deaden any other sound? Lifebelts? *Where?* Rescuers? *Where?* Jesus God, why did they all want to *die?* Paralysis gripped and he did nothing, then at last began to shout and run in the direction of where she had vanished, dropping her coat, ripping at the buttons of his secondhand jacket with stiff, clumsy fingers. He saw a lifebelt and grabbed it; it wouldn't budge. And then, like some ghost, that damned black dog appeared and barked at him. Stood in front of him and barked. He followed it to the steps and tripped on his way, his yelling echoing back into the cavern, whipped away by the greater sound. The steps – he would go down the day trippers' steps and get into the water; anything better than nothing; the shoes would weigh him down: fuck the shoes.

He ran, climbed over the locked gate at the head of the steps, stumbled down, feet crunching on shells. He could see the steps continuing below the clear water, an invitation into another world and another life below, the steps all crooked and wavy, distorted and oddly inviting if it were not for the cold. Stunning cold on his skin, the afterthought of a scientist: *how long could one survive this? Four minutes? One? Two?* His waist was lapped with ice; the weight of water shoved at his chest. Don't drown, not you; I couldn't bear it. And there was Maggie, hauling herself up by the same railing he touched, gasping for breath. He grabbed at the other arm and hauled. They both fell backwards on the steps, barnacles sharp on his back, relinquished hold of one another and scrambled back up. She was shaking and flicking water from her fingers; he could not decide whether she was helping his progress or he hers until they both stood upright on the platform, breathing heavily. When she smiled a lopsided smile, his fury was uncontrollable. He grasped her hair in both hands and shook her until she rattled. A momentary lapse; he would have yelled instead but his voice was all gone. His hands fell to his side and he saw the water streaming from his clothes.

'You crazy lunatic . . . You . . . you . . .'

'Come on, Henry, before someone calls a fucking lifeguard. Come *on.*'

Back to where they were, collecting coats, putting them on; she forcing feet into shoes, both of them striding back down the *Titanic* length as if it were perfectly normal to do it in a dripping trail of seawater. Two fishermen, the only ones, stared. Maggie grinned at them; they winked, acknowledging some kind of joke, and Henry felt perfectly hysterical. The mark on his forehead was now a gigantic turd. They passed through the nondescript portals of the entrance and the notice *sea temperature today is . . .* and he shuddered. Her car was parked next to the hotel, bravely bearing a parking ticket. Inside it, heater full blast, he felt as if he had come out of the bottom of a pond. The only remotely gratifying thing was her hand trembling violently as she lit a cigarette.

'Do you believe me now?'

'I don't know what the fuck I'm supposed to believe!' he yelled. 'Except you being mad as a snake. What kind of fucking trick was that?'

'Language, Henry, you're becoming quite Anglo-Saxon.'

She was smoothing her dripping hair with her free hand, making a face in the rearview mirror. She dropped the cigarette out of the window and started the car. He leaned over, twisted the key back so the engine stopped. She should stay still; no driving yet. She did not protest, spoke through chattering teeth and uncontrollable shivering.

'It was a *trick* you learned as a child in order to scare your parents to death and make them take notice of you, if you had them. Let the current take you from one side to the other. I did it Christmas Day when I was twelve. Last chance.'

'You *bitch.*'

'If only I was,' she said. 'Life would be so much easier.'

There was this insane cheerful thought at the back of her mind which cleared it beautifully and made everything as bright as the sun. No way would Philip ever have attempted to get into the water and find her; he disliked getting wet. It was always the thought that counted.

They sat in his room. She admired the tidiness of it, the carefully stacked papers, the book of poetry, the laptop, the room of the soon to be off, journeying man. Henry preferred the penitent look of her, with the metallic curls scraped back; she was a certain kind of animal which looks better when sleek, wet and unadorned.

Outside, a row of seagulls lined the edge of the waves, waiting for the revelations of the tide.

'Look, I'm sincerely sorry about this, Henry. When I was asked to represent Francesca, and it *was* her choice, I certainly believed she was guilty. She made me believe it. Which might have been why she asked for me, because I always believed her, was always slightly in thrall to her superior wisdom, she was always more powerful than me. If she said a thing, it was the truth. Will of iron. She was so calm, it was repellent. And the calm could have meant she was resigned to the truth, no room for self-pity, *any* pity, or it could have meant a ridiculous level of self-control. Either was consistent with the way she was. We always talk about her in the past tense, as if she was dead, don't we? May as well be. She won't talk to me. I broke my promise.'

'She wasn't in a position to exact promises. I never can understand how she manages to manipulate from afar.'

'You give away your car, your video, your valuables, you can ask for things in return, can't you? On one level, anyway, although the promise she exacted from me had nothing to do with that. I promised on my solemn, ten-year oath – we exchanged blood, you know, down in the moat of the castle, and a little blood goes a long way – anyway I promised I'd never look into it. That I'd do her the honour of never questioning what she'd done. Accept it as all for the best, she said. If she ever heard that Edward or I were making further enquiries, and she would hear, somehow, then she'd sack us and make a statement saying we were deluded. She wanted her flat sold and the money given to Angela, that was all. Otherwise, forget about it. I promised.'

'And?'

'I had to take it literally. Not difficult at first, otherwise distracted, you see, by the relative disappointments of my own life. Then it just creeps up, the nonsense of the promise as well as everything else. Some of the things you've thought of, some I have. But *I* couldn't open the can of worms, *I* promised I wouldn't. Somebody else had to do it. A stranger and a *determined* stranger at that. Some completely objective searcher after truth. Walking into Edward's office, you were manna from heaven. We just had to tease you along a bit.'

'A sting,' Henry said.

'You don't come with a bundle of preconceptions and you can look at the place with a cold eye. That's an advantage. You don't know the people involved.'

'You lived here and you don't either.'

She paused. 'True.'

'Are we doing what she wants? That's the main thing.'

'I've no idea. We could turn away. God knows, I've wanted to.'

He stood by the window and watched the seagulls. They looked like sturdy, disinterested guardians of the shore, incapable of squabbling or even flying, waddling round, awaiting orders and he no longer felt the same.

'I don't know if I'm trying to prove guilt or innocence,' Maggie said.

'I want that boy's death to have a purpose,' Henry answered. 'I can't think of another way to justify it.' He looked with distaste at the jacket flung on the bed. 'So I'm going on my fucking errand. With my fucking jacket.'

'Where? Can I come, too?'

'Nope. I'm going to see an Uncle Joe and I don't want you wrecking things, because . . .'

'I'm not objective,' she finished, flatly. He grasped the arms of the chair in which she sat, leaned into it and kissed her lightly on the cheek. She flinched and then smiled sadly. ''Course you aren't objective,' Henry said. 'You're a lawyer. And you might get cold.'

It was a grey hinterland into which the taxi with creaking springs took him round the back of the town where big houses diminished into small and the grey fields began. Never too cold or too hot, Francesca had told him; she was wrong about the first and he had no means of testing the second. He did not think he would wait to see the spring or feel the legendary heat of a summer; he could

not imagine a day when that cold ocean would welcome a swim-
mer without the water feeling like a grave. The flat land gave way
to fields of undistinguished crops and three miles beyond the
town, his taxi took him through the Fergusons plant. The sight of
the factory shocked him; it was a reminder of another world. It
rose out of the mist like a strange mirage, all chrome and steel,
spreading out across the emptiness. The buildings shone with
acres of glass buttressed by gleaming metal: the lights of a hundred offices and laboratories illuminated the gloom of the
afternoon and the vast carpark housed hundreds of new cars.
This was his own territory; this was where he would work, if he
stayed, in a place constructed out of anything but brick. Henry
asked the driver to slow down. They crawled, creaking, beneath
the bridge which spanned the road in an arch of steel, connecting
one wing of millennium industry with another, and through the
glass of the walls Henry could see a rising escalator on one side,
thronged with people. The edifice radiated cleanliness, efficiency,
prosperity; the contrast between it and the town he had left
behind was breathtaking. It looked like a spaceship recently
landed on alien terrain and Henry reminded himself that this was
where he rightly belonged: in buildings like this half of his adult
life had been spent. Perfecting scientific processes to improve the
lives of the twenty-first century. Prō-cesses, not prah-cesses, he
told himself, and you don't put flowers in a *vaice*, you put them in
a *vahz*. Grasshopper mind, Henry, he told himself as they left
Fergusons behind. And the natives imagined that all Fergusons
did was make Viagra. The fucking English might as well be going
round covered in fucking woad; they were blinkered and prejudiced; they did everything they could to keep themselves
confined.

It felt like a long time since ever he had ridden an escalator or
even seen a building bigger than a castle. Or seen one committed
to the future, and the sight of these made him grimace with home-
sickness. There would be no smoking and no dogs allowed inside
Fergusons. Henry had a faint sense of panic at the thought of

returning to normal life. It suddenly seemed impossible to imagine himself going back to a structured existence which had nothing to do with the past, or secrets, or idiotic promises made by himself or anyone else: he had a yearning for a world of bright, clinical lights, no shadows, no dark corners, no suspect motives, nothing but the driving imperative of work which had bored and dismayed him and now seemed infinitely attractive.

Everything in that little town, so old, so pessimistic compared to this. People content to remain in a tiny world. They were not even interested in prosperity. Look at Maggie: bright enough for a brilliant career, content to junk it; Edward, an attorney who failed to make money; Francesca who let her own, unambitious life eat her alive because she could not or would not move . . . didn't she want to get on? They all avoided their duty to be *happy*. It was the sea that mesmerized them all into collective stupidity. *Under floods that are deepest, Which Neptune obey, Over rocks that are steepest, Love will find out the way.* Get out of here.

The car crawled uphill, gears grinding on a steep gradient, and the ocean appeared below at a turn in the road. Henry saw the jagged outline of a white chalk cliff meeting the shining water, found himself smiling. The guttural sound of his humming alarmed the driver, who shifted uncomfortably in his seat and revved the engine.

Henry had been happy that his own father had never had to leave his own house in order to die. Died with a view of the walnut tree in his precious back yard, without any of the upheaval involved in a removal to a place like the one the taxi finally reached on the headland. Dad always did have a good sense of timing and he would have liked the view. The ideal place if you liked to watch from the windows either the stormclouds on the horizon or the golfers on the greens behind, but it seemed to Henry far too remote for its purpose of housing the old. It had an air of faintly distinguished decrepitude, like the occupants, but the isolation of it made him obscurely angry. Put the elderly on a headland, away from sight, as if they were lepers of a kind. The interior reassured him slightly. It was warm and green with plants, like a comfortable hotel. The woman in the office seemed kind.

There must be some confusion, she said. No one had visited Joseph Chisholm in months. He lay sleeping in a pleasant room at the back, overlooking the golf course, waking to moments of increasingly rare animation when there was football on the television. Still able to goose the younger female staff occasionally but deteriorating like a piece of old stone. The man who received the Sunday visitor was that one, over there, the one with the white hair and ruddy skin, holding the newspaper. He had taken possession of Joseph's favourite place as soon as Joseph had taken to his bed. He loved company, that one. Sat and watched the comings and goings as if he was watching a play. Henry took the seat alongside. The old man had a smile of great sweetness. His speckled hands folded the newspaper with neat certainty and he looked at it, as if pleased with the achievement.

'I think,' he said, 'that I only have a small part in this play. I knew you'd come. Or someone like you. *She* won't come any more, will she? She *won't.*'

'I don't know who you mean.'

'You liar, of course you do. My beautiful Angela . . . her beautiful daughter. *Those* two. You've stopped them.'

Henry patted the mottled hand. It had the feel of warm, dry paper. He knew the feeling of it. 'Tell me why,' he suggested. The old man sighed. 'Oh, it's obvious, isn't it? *She* might realize that my name is George, not Joe. *She* might realize that one old man is distinguishable from another. But I couldn't resist, you see. In she came with that gorgeous child and said, Are you Uncle Joe, I've been sent to see you. I knew she'd be wasted on miserable old Chisholm, so of course I said, yes, who else would I be? It doesn't matter who you are at my age.' He sighed and the smile twinkled back across a distinctive, ruddy face, with devastating effect. 'I was once handsome, you know. Like all Chisholms are. I used to eavesdrop when the last one came. I'd look at the way he listened. They were good at that. Handsome or mad, usually both. And all I had to do after that was occupy the same seat and listen myself. Which has been a positive pleasure.'

'Why shouldn't it continue? What made you think it would stop?'

The face of the old man blurred into that of Henry's father, weatherbeaten from fishing, and the greenery behind blurred into the yard. The walnut tree, the lines of the face becoming beautiful, and he was going to ask him about Francesca until he remembered that this man had never met Francesca and might know nothing.

'I'll come and see you if she doesn't,' he said, rashly.

'*Shall* you? How absolutely lovely.' He began to fold the news-paper, slowly, sadly. 'I'd prefer Angela, I must admit, and that talkative child. She talked and talked and then Angela didn't bring her back. They talked as much as one another actually.' He crossed his legs and his arms. 'She shouldn't have done it, you know; it was frightfully bad . . . that poor child . . .'

'Why do you think she won't come back?' Henry wanted to shout it.

'Because she told me too much,' the old man said, simply. 'Far too much. I knew there would come a point when she would realize that.' He smiled again, blithely confident of Henry's understanding, then the smile faded into a frown. 'Oh dear, you young people are so *slow*.' He leaned forward. Henry could smell mint on his breath, admired the closeness of his shave and the careful combing of his hair. A man who had not lost an element of vanity and was always expecting a visitor. 'You see, I never really knew what she was describing, or any of the people she was talking about, so I just agreed with everything she said. Agreeing, placating, an echo, really. I didn't want to talk: I just wanted the joy of listening to her. And once it's obvious that you're spellbound by a person *dying* to talk and you really won't be *able* to repeat it because you're too old and dumb, well you're a whatsit, aren't you?'

'A receptacle,' Henry said.

'That's the word. Fancy a Yank knowing a word like that. She'll bring us some tea if you wave.'

Henry had a yearning for a double espresso from Starbucks, the sort of coffee that made a man sweat. 'And you can smoke out here,' the old man added. 'That's why Chisholm sat here. Probably what's killing him now too.'

'Well I guess a cigarette helps conversation,' Henry said, producing a packet in case this was a hint. The offering was looked upon with disapproval; Henry put it away. He had misunderstood. The only oil the conversation required was the weak tea which he loathed; he should have brought a gift. They looked downhill over a peerless view, enhanced by the glass of Fergusons laboratories, or ruined by it, depending on your point of view.

'I'm eighty-seven, you know,' the old man said with a touch of defensive pride. 'Lost my wife to a Yank at the end of the war. You had the money, you see. Now what was I saying?' Henry cleared his throat in an attempt to modify his accent when next he spoke. 'And I suppose you work at that place,' he gestured towards the barnacle on the view. 'Where they make all them happy pills that can't keep me walking or daft old Chisholm alive.'

'You were saying that you were a receptacle and Angela told you too much,' Henry whispered helpfully, speaking through pursed lips to make his voice sound rather more BBC.

'Speak up, will you? Yes. Far too much, but it does make a change from someone sitting there and watching the clock, wishing they could *go*. A bit like you. Talk, talk, talk, about this and that, such a storyteller she should go on the wireless. Not much of it true, I shouldn't think. People like making up things to make their lives more interesting. Never enough drama in daily life, I found. You need a newspaper for that. That's where things happen. Not that I believe them entirely either. Mad axeman strikes again, that sort of thing. Not here he doesn't. It's more like fog remains on coastline for third day running.'

Henry smiled. He was beginning to see how visiting this old man was less than a chore. He himself could feel an anxious enjoyment.

'What kind of stories did she tell? Murder, rape and mayhem? Burglary, robbery? Happens in the best of places.'

'Well, I wish it happened here. Not in Warbling it doesn't. Absolute nonsense. The way that girl of hers talked in the beginning, well, of course I didn't believe it. She learned how to fantasize from her mother, I suppose. Very entertaining. *Matilda told such dreadful lies . . .*'

'*It made one gasp and stretch one's eyes,*' Henry murmured.

'. . . about someone I was supposed to know pushing a *child* off the pier, as if anyone would. I just said, how dreadful and let her go on while her mother went to the lavatory. Then she had to go and sort out the car, water in the brakes or something on the way up this damn hill. And anyway, telling me all this and getting me to pull faces made poor Tanya upset. I managed to shush her before her mother got back, get her to talk about school. I didn't really approve, you know.'

'Approve?'

The old man lowered his voice and leaned forward. 'She could describe it in such detail, you see. How the child was pushed by a dog on the pier. Her mother shouldn't have told her such stories, even though she's an angry woman. Very. They need a dog. Mind, I wasn't going to say anything. None of my business and she might have stopped coming to see me. Angela's forgotten about it. Other worries. Now she's got a whatsit, you know, one of those buggers who goes after kids, a . . .'

'Paedophile,' Henry supplied through gritted teeth.

'One of them, running round the town. I ask you. I told her to get a dog!' He laughed uproariously at his own suggestion. The teacups rattled as he slapped the table. 'Bite his balls off! Lock him up!' Henry winced. Then the old man became sombre. 'I might have caused offence,' he said sadly. 'Is that why she won't come any more?'

'No, I'm sure it isn't that. And I'm sure she'll come back. Why shouldn't she?' Henry rose from his armchair. He needed to think; the warmth was oppressive and the door was closed; he could feel the beginnings of the familiar agitation and he was ashamed of it. 'And so shall I,' he added, wondering at the wisdom of what might be a lie. The old man grabbed at his sleeve; he shook his hand, feeling the surprising strength of the bones. His own hand seemed enormous by comparison.

'Those things she told me . . . None of them were true, were they?'

'No,' Henry said. 'Of course not. Remember Matilda? None of them.'

The old man winked, a slow, deliberate wink. 'You haven't heard the half of it. So you'll have to come back, won't you? Bring some of that Viagra with you. We could do with it.'

He stood on the headland and watched as the fog rolled in. Down below, before the mist covered it in blanket, the Fergusons buildings caught the light and then faded into an insignificant part of the white landscape. Without being able to see the details he could make out the shape and thought he knew where everything was. When the fog rolled back, a slightly different picture would emerge, but he would still know what was there. And he had been looking at all the wrong books.

The taxi moved off with evident relief and a horrible grinding of gears. He had the impression that the vehicle could find its own way back to the flatlands, to speed home on automatic pilot for the sake of a real fire in a warm garage. He wanted to weep. The driver grumbled under his breath because of the open window which made them both shiver.

He got out in front of the House of Enchantment and paid what seemed a small sum. Almost a third world sum. He thought that might have been why he always went back to the East for his travelling; the cheapness and the idea that it might have been a deciding factor did not exactly cheer him up. So undemandingly demanding, the English. They had an aversion to making money.

He crossed the road and sat on the steps which led from pavement to shingle beach. The cold seeped into his *ass, arse, bottom, behind, bum, an English person doesn't have an ass, not even to go to work on.* His spine, then. The cold was calming and chilling; he liked it.

Then the dog with the warm muzzle inserted a fat, moist nose into the crook of his elbow as he held it tight against his side in the awful jacket. He felt the interference of a snout, burrowing away in there. *Snout: an informant; a muzzle.* He had looked it up. He moved his arm to contain the shoulders of the animal, loosely, exerting no pressure, no suggestion that it could not go whenever it wanted to go. The big black dog sat beside him, allowing the touch of his arm, both of them staring straight ahead.

'You've got some secrets, I bet,' Henry said.

I was always proud of my ability to keep a secret. The obligation to keep a confidence was one I learned early and it was one of the earliest surprises to discover that not everyone else did the same. It was exactly the same with promises. I would be the one waiting at the bus stop because I had promised, but no one else turned up, because there were promises which are not really supposed to be kept, just as there are secrets which are meant to be told. The instruction 'don't tell' might mean 'do tell', but only selectively, with the right interpretation. It might also mean what it says. To save a minefield of confusion, I've abided by my original principle of keeping quiet as the proverbial grave and denying the knowledge I've received rather than break the seal. The irony of this high-mindedness is that it turns the keeper of the secret into a liar while the teller of it goes on to share the burden with other close and confidential friends, all seventy-five of them. The one thing I've learned is never to confide anything vital about myself unless the person told is quite unable to repeat or understand. Confessing to a brick wall, in other words, someone who can't be moved or distressed, simply to get it off one's chest and rehearse out loud what to do.

Which is why I took the coward's way out and told Uncle Joe, the day after. He was deaf, after all, and mimicked the act of listening with every sign of enjoyment. (Such dissemblers, the Chisholms.) I could decode what he said, but few others could. And he understood, poor soul, what it was like to face loss of reputation and disgrace. He might have forgiven me.

I told him how the door was open; I hated closed doors. It was far too early and wet and Harry was fractious. Tanya appeared in new clothes, a jacket of shiny stuff she loved and wanted to show off. Harry clung to her; he always did. I encouraged them go out together, God help me, only on to the pier where I could see them, and not for long. She wanted to go; Harry wanted her to stay inside with him, but the lure of doing anything with Tanya was too great to resist. They went. The peace was marvellous. I don't know how long after that I realized I'd sent him out of doors without a jacket and I started to go down the stairs with it. Quite some time, I think. I crossed the road. She was huddled by that statue, trying to get inside it. Hysterical. Her sleeve was torn.

There was a black dog running off the pier. Harry hated dogs; they knocked him over.

That dog . . . It reminded me of how she had been when she first came to us and I tried to capture her on camera. A scared, vulnerable savage, with nothing to call her own and no ability to trust. Rudderless as a boat in a storm; she was nothing but a promise. Angela, somewhere, Neil's fishing stuff, he often left it . . .

I can't go on with this. None of us ever really tell the truth. It might be better to be deaf and dumb, like Uncle Joe.

FMC

CHAPTER TWELVE

'I wish you'd turned up sooner,' Henry said to the dog. 'Your eyes and ears for a start. Love the coat.' The dog shuffled. Henry stroked the rough hair of its flank and tickled its chest. There was adequate flesh on the bones, contoured muscle on the legs and the animal, though still, was poised for flight. 'Don't let me hold you back,' Henry told it, removing his arm. The dog remained, turned a large head to sniff his face and then, satisfied, leaned against him and resumed contemplation of the sea. The water sounded suspiciously sullen beneath the mist, plotting something.

Gradually, as the cold at Henry's back became acute enough to be almost painful, the dog seemed to hear a signal, shook itself and trotted away to the right. It had the gait he had noticed before, unhurried, even paced, like a distance runner with a long way to go and no doubt of the destination. Someone cared for the dog and someone had taught it to cross a road. An educated hobo with a place to sleep, so they had something in common, Henry thought, except that the dog, close to, was a handsome beast which left a fine coating of hairs on his jacket. Inside the house, catching sight of himself in a mirror in the hall, Henry wondered how he had become quite so sartorially challenged in such a relatively short space of time.

The dim lighting of the hallway gas lamps irritated him, although they did him the honour of blurring his reflection. Gas lamps, in this day and age, for Godsakes, as if the house was not merely a unit for living but a piece of theatre. Which it was, he realized, looking at the details he had scarcely noticed before. The hall and the first stairwell were decorated with oriental hangings and above these, flags. The mirror was framed with ornate gilding and looked valuable until careful examination revealed the chips of gold paint. There was a reason for retaining the dim light of the gaslamps with their delicate sconces and flickering glow. Henry could hear the murmuring of the radio from the kitchen; the rest of the place was comfortably silent.

He looked into the dining room, where the walls were covered with a variety of pictures, the windows draped with heavy, faded velvet and the mantelshelf covered with framed photographs set between two tall candlesticks which were moved to the centre of the table at mealtimes. The table itself was covered with a heavy linen cloth; Henry felt the surface with his fingertips, the mended patches which were invisible to the eye when the table was laid with its magnificence of mismatched plates and cutlery, the items individually charming but never forming a set. The carpet, like the runner on the stairs, was threadbare and rich in colours. Mess up the artful arrangement and all it would be was secondhand junk.

The sitting room, currently empty of human life, followed the same pattern. There were gleaming fire tongs and old armchairs with hand-stitched covers to obscure the frayed ends of the arms, rugs lying upon other rugs, a small table polished to such a shine he had failed to observe its mended leg. Henry looked at the photographs, framed, it seemed, in driftwood, and saw the black and white images of two lithe young men dressed for swimming, standing against a backdrop of waves, laughing. There were no recent photos. Cameras cost money; Henry counted up what he

had paid for his lodging and was embarrassed by his late realiza-
tion of the stringent budget which must govern their lives. No
phone, no wasted expenditure, no new possession of any kind,
except of course the video in the kitchen, looking odd in there, like
a garden spade in a bedroom.

He guessed the source of the video. Francesca had given her car
to Angela, her books to the granny who had never wanted them,
anything else useful in her apartment to various others. Did she
use her gifts as blackmail? Was there a price for receiving them,
such as Angela going to see Uncle Joe and Peter and Tim guarding some votive flame for her dead son? Henry noted the décor of
his own room with new approval. The ornateness of the ground
and first floor fell away into sheer simplicity by the time he reached
the second landing. Bare walls and striped wooden floors of sweet,
yellow pine, the runner on the stairs muffling his footsteps, the old
silk coverlets on his high bed the only colour in the room apart
from the turquoise seat of a comfortable chair. A room for Van
Gogh to paint in celebration of a minimalism which was not stark,
but comforting. Peter was there, fussing over the fire, coaxing the
kindling to light and embrace a log from the basket of wood he had
hauled upstairs. A small bucket held the ash cleared out of the
black iron grate. The missing shawl was neatly folded over the
bedstead. Peter grinned at him, not quite comfortable with being
seen on his knees, genuflecting to his own labours.

'It is the *cheapest* form of heating, you know,' he said defensively.
'Especially if you go out and find it. We've got plenty of time for
that. I think having *time* to make and mend is better than having
money, don't you?'

'Why did Francesca give you her video?' Henry asked, taking
off his jacket and slinging it across the room. How nice to have a
garment he could treat with contempt: he had an unaccountable
desire to throw the contents of his suitcase, vitamins and minerals
included, out of the window. Peter looked surprised.

'Do you know, I was never quite sure why she did. It simply
arrived with all her tapes. She must have known we'd never use it

much, apart from looking at the one with darling Harry, 'cos we didn't even have a telly before. We've no time for it, it's so *unstimulating*. I can't see the point in sitting down gawping at a film unless there's someone in it you know.'

The flames lit the logs. Peter looked on with satisfaction, as if the fire was his own invention and his mastery of it a triumph.

'There are other tapes?'

'Yes, of course. Cartoons, Walt Disney. Home videos and kids' stuff. I must admit, I *love The Jungle Book . . .*'

'Can I see them?'

'Of course, you only have to ask. I'll bring it up here, shall I? Do us a favour, though. Keep Maggie off the booze tonight. Otherwise she'll get depressed and think about going back to her husband.'

'I didn't know she still had one.' Henry adjusted the log with the toe of his shoe and watched sparks fly.

'She doesn't. But she may be able to get one returned from the cleaners if she wants.'

Henry was furious with all these ambiguities. The log crackled, as if laughing. He wondered how much extra money he should leave them when he left, only he didn't want to go. He wondered about the etiquette of relative poverty, remembered the same puzzle from other travelling days. He was feeling lightheaded.

'Do you know where she is?'

Peter looked at his watch. 'The pubs are open. She could be there.'

'Well I doubt I'll keep her off the hooch,' Henry said. 'It's my turn for that.'

He would go back to the old man on the headland with a bottle of whisky. Just like they did in the old and new films, where all you had to do was pour alcohol down the throats of reluctant spies and out came *vino veritas*. Fat chance. It would not work with Maggie either, any more than it would with the damn dog. But he was still a tourist, obliged to experiment, and perversely, he needed a noisier place than this for analysing his thoughts.

Henry had never been much of a drinker. He could hear his father say, what a pity, it did a man's career as much good as harm and loosened up the soul, while Henry himself thought it merely depressed it. Freedom from addictions up until now had not managed to save him from embarrassments, nor from the contemptuous eyes of contemporaries when he fell over his own feet. There were times, he thought to himself, when he may as well have been drunk on all the occasions when he was tongue-tied and sober. You prudish guy, he reflected as he donned the ghastly jacket and hit the road; prudish about drugs, trying the stuff once or twice and hating the way it made the company talk in mono-syllables. He hated loss of control, but the hell with it; if control was going to be lost it may as well taste nice. He would do the famous English pub crawl, go native.

The first beer in the first pub made him shudder. He sipped at the foamy scum of a clear, warm soup and wanted to gag. The pub was called the Smugglers but showed no sign of serving the fine wines available on the other side of the Channel, smuggled or not. They liked slop. They actually preferred this and did not seem to give a shit what they ate or drank away from home: just look at the menu on that blackboard. LIVER AND ONIONS, IRISH STEW. When he went home, he would take that notice as an abiding memory and laugh about it, but then a native from here would find HASH BROWNS equally unappealing. The greatest cultural divide known to Western man was not one of nationality, he decided; it was simply the food and drink and the difference between those who lived in cities and those who lived away from them.

He sipped his half-pint to aid his own reflections, wondering if Uncle Joe ever got to a pub and whether it was wimpish to order a half-measure when the other men had pints. Forgetting his specs made him slightly myopic and dizzy, but no one else was looking at anything much, except at him. They were staring at him. Not consistently, he had to admit and not many of them either, because at this early point in the evening there were not so many to meet his gaze and let their own slip away into the surface of their pints or to the far point on the opposite wall. They were the sort of glances exchanged with a dead haddock in the fishmonger's. Conversation was lacking. A man came in and said 'Lo and then took his pint glass and went off to sit nursing it in a corner. There was an interval Henry marked before the customer moved or spoke and only then to present the same glass on the counter with another 'Lo, answered with a nod and a refill. There was the small clink of money. Isn't this fun, Henry thought. Are they always like this or is it me? The mist outside seemed comparatively attractive. He left his drink on the table and departed, pretending he was suddenly in a hurry.

Which he was, but not out of need. He did not like the idea of going into one pub after another simply looking for Maggie: it made him feel like a father trying to round up a wayward child or, even worse, some jealous boyfriend. He had to admit the thought of a returning husband piqued him for some indefinable reason, probably because it was one more thing she hadn't explained to him and it irked him. All these subtexts. Henry considered his own life an open book from which anyone could read and he found it difficult to see why everyone else kept their pages stuck together. In the second pub, this time sipping wine and taking refuge behind a newspaper, he came to the conclusion that the monosyllabic conversation between patrons was simply their natural, limited discourse; they just didn't go in for back-slappings and big greetings. In the third pub, he changed his mind. There was a woman behind the bar who responded to his polite request for a drink with a stony stare and then told him to fuck off in a quiet, but definite command which made him think better of asking why. He went. So much for an evening of riotous inebriation. Outside, he found himself looking for the dog. Henry could feel the dirty mark of disgrace on his forehead and remember the shrill accusations in the street. The fish and chips he ate sitting on a bench facing the statue at the entrance of the pier were solidly delicious, the more so for being served with spontaneous friendliness. There were only a dozen more pubs to go, increasingly crowded as the evening drew into night, and the prospect was distinctly unpalatable. Henry put the greasy paper into a garbage can like a good citizen and went back to the place he called home.

He was becoming separated from anything he could think of as home. His empty house in the environs of Boston seemed utterly remote and the splendid modernism of the Fergusons plant where he might resume his career was equally alien. In the house, there was a bridge game in the room Peter called the parlour and up on his own floor Henry found the TV, video and a stack of tapes.

'Two can play,' Maggie said evenly. '*You* can fling mud in the street against a nice and harmless man, how *dare* you? *I* can take a stand on the same corner and say how I found your daughter playing truant from school, sadly neglected by her mother.'

'You bitch.'

'Now there's another accusation I keep denying without it making much difference, I wonder why?' Maggie said airily. 'And after I've bought you a nice bottle of wine, too. Oh come off it and stop playing hard to get. I'm not a nasty witch any more than you are. Otherwise Francesca wouldn't have loved us. She wasn't exactly discriminating about the people she loved – look at her bloody husband – but she did have some judgement. Just drink it.'

Angela's hand strayed towards the glass Maggie had poured and set down on her kitchen table. She looked at it longingly and knew the drinking of it compromised her. She had tried to shut the door in Maggie's face, but Maggie was stronger. The child was asleep and a shouting match would wake her. Trapped. She wrapped her fingers around the bowl of the glass to warm the red wine within and stop Maggie noticing that her hand was unsteady.

'Just tell me why you locked Henry Evans in the castle overnight and disturbed my sleep, will you? That'll do for starters.'

'Neil should have . . . It was a mistake.'

'No, it wasn't. Tanya knows it wasn't. Don't give me that crap.

What was it you didn't want him to know? What's wrong with answering his nosy questions? What harm can it do?' Angela took hold of the glass and swallowed half the contents. *Good: drink the rest, will you,* Maggie urged silently. *It makes fools of us all.*

'He brings back the guilt, that's what he does,' Angela said, in a rush. 'He's made Tanya remember what she ought to forget. It's not bloody *fair.*'

'Why should you feel guilty?'

'Are you mad or just stupid?' Angela yelled and then remembered, stopped, went at the wine again and took one of Maggie's cigarettes. She examined it between work-worn fingers and then put it back in the packet. 'Of course I feel guilty. I never liked Harry . . . there was something about him I couldn't like and I thought I was someone who loved all kids. Well, I'm not. I love my own, that's all. I didn't want to share her. I didn't want her held back by a kid like Harry. He was so ugly. He needed such a lot. I'm sorry, I detested him, which is enough to make anyone feel guilty, isn't it?'

Maggie resisted the cigarette. The atmosphere inside here was conspicuously smoke free, a good example to children. She wanted to rush around and open windows, let in a bit of healthy mist to neutralize all the cleanliness.

'I don't think you can do much about native dislike, can you? You either like someone or not, children included,' Maggie said. 'What you feel doesn't matter nearly as much as how you behave. You weren't mean to him, were you? Didn't hit him or anything?'

There was a palpable hesitation. 'No . . . I . . . No, of course not.'

'Did anyone? Was there anyone he was afraid of?'

'*NO!* He wasn't afraid of anyone. No one gave him any reason to be, everyone treated him with kid gloves, even when he screamed. He was only afraid of dogs. That was the one time when Neil hit him.'

'*Neil?*' The glass was empty. Maggie refilled it quickly, spilling some down the side.

'Neil has rages. You don't think I'd have chucked him out just because of the sex, do you, with Tanya to consider? I couldn't have him throwing things around. And he always wanted to come back . . . well, he did then. He tried to be more of a father then, keep in my good books, win us round. He bought us this dog, see. Typical, silly Neil, but he knew I'd been thinking about it. Only when he brought it round, this puppy, Harry was here. He was often here, just as often as Tanya was round at Francesca's.' Maggie dabbed at the spilt wine on the table with a tissue and watched the tissue turn pink. Harry was always knocking things over, Peter said, a habit not confined to children, but Harry was always afraid of losing his balance.

'. . . Such a sweet puppy, but Harry took one look at it and screamed and screamed. He backed into a corner and wouldn't come out. I told him not to be so silly, but nothing worked. I dunno why,' she mused, 'but I reckon Neil sort of thought that the puppy was his last chance, thought we'd be thrilled, but I told him we couldn't have it, not with Harry reacting like that and Harry being a bit of a fixture. I told him he'd have to take it away, whatever he'd spent on it. That's when he picked up Harry, shook him a bit and gave him a clout. I think he hated Harry for being in the way, nothing personal, that was all and that was the only time.'

'The dog it was that died,' Maggie murmured. 'Whatever happened to it?'

'Neil sort of shares it with Granny round the corner; she feeds it. It keeps on getting out. He never could keep anything, Neil.' She was calmer now. And is that all you wanted to hide? Maggie wondered.

'Anyway, that was when I told Francesca we shouldn't be so dependent on one another. Separate out a bit. Better for the kids. Why shouldn't Tanya have a dog? But I don't suppose it helped, me saying that. She might have thought I was telling her we didn't want her at all, which wasn't true. Might have pushed her further over the edge, so of course I feel bloody guilty. She wasn't useless, she was bloody brilliant and I don't know what we'd have done without her.'

Maggie wished she had something to chew. She shredded the tissue and knew the action was irritating.

'I'm surprised you let Neil look after Tanya if he has these rages.'

'I haven't a choice, have I? I've got to organize our lives, work where I can. And he's never been a danger to Tanya, never. He loves her. Everyone does.' The voice rose in defensive pride

'Of course they do. What happened that morning?' Maggie asked gently. Angela shrugged.

'Nothing happened. Like I said, Francesca said she'd take Tanya to school for me while I waited in for the electric. I told her not to bother, I'd get Neil to do it. But then he was late and Tanya had a temperature so neither of us went anywhere. Then *she* came, looking for Harry. She was out of her mind. I don't think she could take in what she'd done.'

Maggie could not pinpoint why this had the sound of a rehearsed speech and she struggled to remember where she had heard it before. Mrs Hulme's statement, made to the police, word for word, no deviations, no hesitations.

'So perhaps,' Angela said with cold confidence and some of her aggression returning, 'you can tell all that to your stupid American and stop him bothering me. Why should I answer a *pervert's* questions?'

They stood at the door, Maggie uncomfortable, wrongfooted, wary, and it seemed trite to say goodbye when so little had been achieved. Somewhere in there, there had been a momentary spark of mutual tolerance, sympathy even, understanding of how Francesca had admired her, all fading into Angela's fixed, farewell smile. Angela, anxious but triumphant, the key to the mystery, telling her there was no mystery at all.

What should she do now? Go home and report faithfully to Henry? Listen to whatever he had to say about Uncle Joe, but only with the same lack of curiosity she had always had about that missing relative she had never been invited to know. The lightship was out to sea, winking at her blearily through the mist and the seafront looked as if it was beginning on a series of slow preparations for sleep. She was weary; she could feel the itchy nose and blocked throat which heralded a cold; what a fool to jump into the water like that, serve her right. She lit a cigarette. She should have written to Philip, and how pleasant it would be to be able to put her thoughts in a logical order of priority, stop them bumping into one another like a crowd at a football match scrabbling for a view.

Such a view, the sea and nothing else. The gates to the pier were locked and that took her by surprise: she had forgotten they were ever locked. It made her want to rattle the bars and demand entry. She stared through the iron gates at the empty concrete road and decided no one had the right to close the pier, not even to stop people coming out of the pubs and jumping off the end.

Neil: the rages of impotence, why not? Neil could have killed Harry in mistake for a ghost. Frustrations of love and lust turning into violence: maybe he had cause to fear his ghosts. The thought chilled her. He had a tendency to theft which she had never suspected either, and he was there, wasn't he, round the corner when someone pushed Harry into the sea . . . That's what he was, that child, an object of love and an object of hate. I wonder if he knew. And then there was Angela, exerting the divine right of motherhood which allowed everything and made her perfectly capable of killing the opposition. And then there was Francesca, the homicidal parent about to be abandoned by her closest allies and all her ambitions for a family unit destroyed. The obvious culprit, underlined. I should never have started this.

There was a fisherman on the beach with a fire. He turned to retrieve something from a satchel. She looked at him twice, hesitated, moved on hurriedly. There was a light from the top floor of the House of Enchantment. The attic in occupation could never be anonymous; the light shone out like a beacon at the highest point in the row. Henry's room had once been given to her until she rejected it in favour of her own, nicely enclosed little room with a limited view on the world. It gave a lift to her spirits to know that Henry sat up there with his quiet patience and his laptop and his tidy, innocent mind. She was always diminishing Henry when she described him, she realized. *Nice, harmless, tidy.* She was making him out to be smaller than she knew he was, as if she was trying to contain him and make him safe. As she went upstairs, Maggie was trying to work out what it was about Henry which made him both appealing and abrasive to others. She was perfectly aware of what made him appealing to her, but that was nobody's business. Perhaps it was his consistency, his clear set of moral values which stood out like the light from the window; perhaps it was his normality. Being *normal* was something she had always found desirable; it would be a barrier, a bedrock; it would mean being a person who went on obeying the Ten Commandments as if they made perfect sense. *Thou shalt not covet thy neighbour's wife, thou shalt not steal, thou shalt not kill, thou shalt not neglect to wash the car and thou shalt not pity thyself.* He was so free of that.

There was nothing she had found out this evening which she had not, strictly speaking, known before, nothing which was not included in the statements she knew by heart, and therefore little enough, apart from Neil, to report to nice, normal Henry. Music played softly from inside his room; he had a tiny CD player she envied. The door was open a crack. She knocked and pushed it wider.

Henry had his back to her, facing the silent TV screen. He sat crosslegged on the floor in front of it, clutching the control monitor, staring fixedly at the images which moved in front of his eyes. A homemade video, jerky camera, an amateur record of a family outing. She stepped into the room, stood unnoticed behind him and joined in the watching. There was a bright summer scene, blue skies and green grass with a red ball by a deckchair. From the right of the scene, a little girl moved into focus to climb into the deckchair with a doll. She stared at the camera, challenging it, swimsuit slipping from her shoulder, legs splayed, all of her sprawled aggressively, eyes squinting. The camera moved closer, catching the texture of her pale skin and stick-thin arms: the child smiled, a sudden vision of laughter and welcome, but there was something about the scrutiny she did not like. As the camera came closer to her face, her expression contorted with startling ferocity. Then she spat; it looked as if a gob of phlegm hit the lens. The child covered her eyes. The camera moved away abruptly, abandoned on the ground hurriedly. The film went on for a few seconds, showing grass and sky and a pair of bare feet. Then it stopped and resumed, showing the child as she slept in the same deckchair, curled into it with her little buttocks exposed in the too big swimsuit and the small hand of the doll stuck into her mouth like a dummy. Her hair was covered by a white sunhat. The rest of the doll was strewn in pieces round the chair. The camera lingered lovingly on her limbs. There were the marks of faint scars on her thighs.

Henry sent the film fast forward. There was the same, unmistakable girl child, equally half naked, balancing on the shingle at the edge of the sea, those thin arms extended and one foot exploring the feel of the water. Frightened, stepping back from the sensation, unable to move without trying again, hesitant, anxious, then kicking at the water to punish it. The camera turned away from her before she turned towards it, panned to a view of the pier reflected in a sea as calm as a quiet pond. That seemed to capture Henry's interest for a second; then he went back to the swimsuit girl and her skinny thighs in the deckchair and froze the frame. Maggie for the first time recognized an infant Tanya, smaller and more ferocious, ready to spit. She drew closer to Henry's back, fascinated and repelled.

Pervert. Sitting alone in an empty room, studying images of a half-clad infant, lingering on her skin. She watched as he flicked forward through the frames, featuring others, unknown grown-ups, scenery, a birthday party, until he found Tanya again. She was the star player, usually captured from behind with her vivid hair identifying her. He went back to the scene by the sea. Angela must be right, then, Maggie thought in a rush. Normal Henry Evans was abnormally interested in images of little girls, *yeuggh.* She was close enough to touch his shoulder and did not want to touch. He had crossed his arms across his chest and rocked back and forth. She felt she might as well have discovered him masturbating, took a step back.

'Oh dear,' he sighed. 'Oh dear, oh dear, oh *shit.*'

The voice bought her back into the room. She watched him scratch his head, turn his face away and then rub at the tears in his eyes with his fist. He was suddenly childish and entirely normal, someone locked into the wrong TV channel and wanting the programme to end.

'What the fuck are you up to, Henry?' Her voice was loud but did not seem to disturb him any more than her presence, as if he had known she was there all along. He straightened his legs, leaned back on his arms and stretched his toes. There was a draught from the window. His left cheek was pink from facing the fire and his hair was tousled. His trousers were crumpled and she noticed his socks were different colours. 'Would you like a drink?' he asked, nodding in the direction of a bottle of sherry and two glasses on the bedside table. 'It's not bad stuff for a cold night. Better than beer, but then anything's better than beer. And I was supposed to keep you off the hooch, but I didn't feel like setting an example.'

There was not a trace of guilt on his face, nothing of the shifty expression of a man caught in the midst of private sexual fantasies. Maggie tried to retrieve her suspicion, her righteous revulsion and the fleeting belief that he was here with some other, appalling agenda he could not confess; that he had come to find a child like Tanya . . . but he was simply the Henry she admired with the American twang and the traces of tears beneath his eyes, getting to his feet awkwardly, stiff from sitting too long. Maggie took his place on the floor while he poured sherry. Sherry reminded her of vicars and the way her own parents had entertained, cocktails, lunchtime and evening drinks, old-fashioned even then, before the universal devotion to wine. She had forgotten the soothing texture of sherry, a drink to calm and comfort rather than inebriate.

'A nice little tipple,' she said.

'A what?'

'Nothing. Never mind.' She wanted to soothe him. He looked fevered; his face puckered and he sneezed, then blew into a handkerchief with an unselfconscious trumpeting sound. All these actions restored him. He put another log on the fire and came and sat beside her with his back resting against the bed.

'Are these all Francesca's tapes?' Maggie waved her hand in the direction of the spilled pile surrounding the TV.

'I suppose so. She never appears on any of them so I presume it was her with the camera. Or someone with a camera who never included her on the tapes because they knew she hated that. Someone who wanted to capture the kids in all their moods, make a record of progress, something she could look at when they were grown and flown, remember what they were like.' She proffered the cigarettes. 'That child, Tanya, she was scarred, you know. Someone hurt her very badly.'

'I told you that.'

'Yes but I didn't quite believe it until I saw it. Cigarette burns, I think, it puts me off smoking. And I don't think I know much about love. I don't think anyone who hasn't had kids knows about that kind of love. You know fuck all. You know about the breakable kind you can put down and pick up, make a little sacrifice for, but not that much. Turn it in for another model.'

She realized he was really rather drunk. Or ill. Controlled drunk and flicking through the videos, looking for a glimpse of Francesca who was not there. Still with a rough command of words, wavering rather than drowning. She felt entirely excluded, watched as his eyes began to close and then snapped open.

'I don't suppose Tanya's *her* daughter, is she?'

No. Definitely not. A daughter of a kind, but a real daughter, no.'

'Ah, shame. That might have explained it. I don't understand love like that,' Henry repeated. 'I really don't. It makes all other kinds seem . . . incomplete, corrupt.'

'I beg your pardon?' she said crossly. 'What about liking?'

'*For if the darkness and corruption leave, A vestige of the thoughts that once I had . . .*' Henry intoned, dreamily. 'C'mon, what's the next line?'

'How the hell should I know?'

'How the hell? *Better by far you should forget and smile, Than that you should remember and be sad.* Just as well she doesn't remember. Poor thing.'

'Who's a poor thing, Henry?' He waved, expansively, his back sliding down slowly towards the floor.

'All of us. All of us poor things. So stupid not to have worked it out. It's perfectly obvious. Dunno what I do know, though. Why do you pretend you don't know the last line?'

She watched silently as he hauled himself to his feet and then, uncertain of the next task, sat down abruptly on the bed. Got up again and walked towards the fire, leaned against the mantelpiece in a parody of nonchalance. She could see him as an archaic academic in a study, holding forth over the port on the finer points of Chaucer. He was not made for the real world. Then he squatted by the fire and warmed his hands against the flickering blaze.

'I saw Angela,' she said, briefly. 'She puts Neil in the arena too. He hit Harry, didn't like him. It was all about a dog. He *hit* him.'

She watched, tense with caution. There was a strange temptation in fire; like water, it lulled one to destruction and promised no harm. His hands went closer to the flames and he stretched his long fingers like a pianist preparing to play, then dipped two fingers into the half-full glass of pale sherry and flicked drops of it into the fire. The flames sputtered in response. His hands went back to clutch the glass at a crazy angle. 'Don't put your hands in the fire,' Henry said. 'My dad told me that, but I did it anyway. A dog, huh? They couldn't have kept a dog.' His eyes glittered: she wanted to mollify him, prepare him for the headache he would have in the morning, clouded with poisonous sherry and thick with snivelling cold, and yet at the same time she suspected it was all a bit of an act.

'Did I tell you about Neil? He broke in here, looking for Viagra. It was him took your shawl, I got it back . . . I put it on the bed. Neil could have been on the pier, fishing on the morning Harry went down, you know . . .'

'He's not a fucking ship!' Henry roared. 'He wasn't launched off the jetty with a bottle of fucking champagne, he was pushed under. And I read that statement, I can *read*. Could your fucking

Neil have done that, do you think? And why should he think I keep Viagra?' He scratched his nose. Anything rather than him putting those long fingers towards the fire. She shifted, guiltily. She wanted him to stop everything, even reciting poetry like a maudlin bore, the way she herself did sometimes, although her tastes seemed to have become cruder lately, her memory for verse selective. *Oh love, will you not linger, like a sticky little finger, With your digit on the fidgit, are you true?* she recalled to herself.

'I haven't the faintest idea,' she answered crisply. 'You can ask him if you like.' *If you stir your cock in custard, It will never cut the mustard, Oh my darling is this person really you?* Now where had that one come from? Out of an empty wine bottle, like a genie, something she had composed for Philip.

'Ask Neil?' he repeated stupidly his eyes suddenly sober and full of hope. '*Neil?* That fella? If only. Where is he? Gotta talk to him. If *only* it was him.'

'He's outside on the beach. Fishing. Got his dog with him. The black one.'

'Oh shit. If only.'

His eyes closed and he put down the glass carefully, got up again and walked towards the bed where he lay down on the silk covers staring at the ceiling with his hand supporting his head. He was not a healthy colour.

'Yes, I need to talk to him. But not now, obviously. Might ruin my reputation.' He laughed. 'Sorry about this. Upset. Dunno what to do. Need to think again. Poor things. Talk in the morning.'

She stacked the video tapes, saw the description of contents noted on the outside in Francesca's neat hand, picked up the glasses and the bottle, turned out the central light, moved the fireguard and went to close the window. Henry spoke out of the corner of his mouth.

'Maggie, don't go back to that husband. Look what he made you. Took away the poetry. And *don't* close the window, please don't.'

CHAPTER THIRTEEN

AFTER she had gone, Henry waited. He stared at the ceiling and saw the cracks he had never noticed before, either, tried to conjure up Francesca's face as he had last seen it, on the bus which drove her away, twenty years before.

It was light that distorted faces, gave them a different texture. If he were to see her now, in the same light as then, he would know her for sure, but he had never seen her under the grey skies which had influenced her flawless complexion. He could not really remember the face or what it was about it which had convinced him of the goodness within. Sitting on the train, coming into Warbling, he had tried to recall it and tried, painstakingly to reconstruct what it might look like now. What he could remember was a series of dissociated details, such as a prominent eyebrow, so much darker than the colour of her hair, the tanned cheekbones, the lack of jewellery, her profile against the sun, how she put out a hand with bitten nails to wave away the camera he had carried through a continent. The way she coiled her long, fair hair against the back of her neck and how soft it felt when he touched it. He remembered the happiness she had brought to making love. *When did I start wanting you, Henry? Was I five, or six, or seven?* How typical of a man that he could recall the details of her slender body far better than he could remember her face. And the feeling of heat and sheer belonging; the acceptance that she was the centre of his universe as he was of hers and always would be. How little he had mattered in the scheme of things, how naive and selfish and insecure to resent other loyalties. He was not the love of her life; he was merely one of them. Francesca had a cast iron set of priorities, like his own father. 'Dad,' Henry sighed. 'What would you do?' His forehead was sticky with perspiration.

He got off the bed and tiptoed out of the door and down to the next landing. Staring down to the ground floor, he could see the shawl on the newel post, Maggie's signal that she had gone for a late night bath, and there was the distant rumble of the plumbing. He went back to his room, picked up his shoes and rummaged in his case for the lightweight rainproof cape he had packed somewhere so carefully he had forgotten its existence. It crinkled as he went downstairs. He carried his shoes until he reached the outside door.

So much easier to act drunk when distress made him feel it. He could feel the booze at the back of his throat like a metallic taste with the sherry as the last note, a single glass of the bottle which had lasted all week. He didn't like it much. The lightheadedness persisted, the sweat froze. The cold dispelled the last vestiges of the earlier wine and beer. Between here and the castle, on the beach by himself; that was where she said Neil was. Neil was the last hope. He was not going to talk voluntarily, none of them were now. He would have to be taken by surprise. Henry broke into a jog.

The mist was damp. He pulled the hood of the cape round his face. There was nothing intimidating about the dark unless it was enclosed. He could have heard himself from a mile away. It was weeks since he had jogged or done anything sensible like that and he felt his legs creak in protest and his breath telling him to stop. His shoes were all wrong. He could see the light of the fire on the beach ahead and the shadow of a black umbrella. He slowed down. If he crossed on to the beach now, the noise of his footsteps would waken the dead and he would be slow. Henry stayed close to the inland side of the road, huddling against the houses until he was past the campfire. Not a fire, he noticed; a burning Camping Gaz lantern sufficient to illuminate and warm the hands. Two forms huddled around it. If he jumped down the steps at the nearest point, Neil would have no time to move. Henry would walk towards him slowly, like a fellow fisherman with a query about his luck, ask him how he was doing.

The sound of his feet landing on the shingle seemed unnaturally loud. The drop was further than it seemed and Henry felt as if he had crashed to earth. The two forms by the umbrella moved as he approached, broke apart and doubled in size. The breeze made Henry's cape flap and crinkle noisily as he strode towards them, ready to say hi, as if this almost midnight encounter was natural. He waved and the cape waved with him. Then the gaslight was held aloft, illuminating his galloping form as he moved closer like a great moth with large, nylon wings. There was a gasp; the lamp crashed to earth; the dog barked and Neil staggered. Henry had a brief glimpse of a grimacing mouth and then the other man began to run, sidestepping him, better used to moving on shingle, more familiar with the contours of the beach. Reaching the edge he clambered up the steps Henry had not seen, the dog at his heels. 'Come back!' Henry shouted, but the words came out like a whisper.

He followed, memorizing the steps of the man, reaching the sidewalk and seeing him make off in the direction of the castle and the pier. He was suddenly furious, as if the man had slapped him for no reason or pushed him to one side. *I only want to talk to you, why won't you talk to me?* Nobody wanted to talk to him; he was sick of it, began to jog again, pacing himself, fuelled with sullen determination. Neil ran unsteadily, his unathletic build encumbered by enough extra weight to slow him down. The dog pranced around him silently as if it was a game: Henry could see them in the streetlights, their disparate heights making them look like an odd, comic team. Then the dog got in the way of Neil's feet and he stumbled, correcting himself before he hit the ground, losing all rhythm to his running and moving slower and slower. The dog seemed to try and impede him and Neil seemed to forget where he was and the direction he wanted to go. He looked over his shoulder and as he did so, the dog stopped. It stood still for a second, a growl sounding in its chest, its body braced. Then it launched itself forward and tore back towards Henry. It grew in size in the approach, turning into a big black wolf.

He stood stock still for a moment of terror, keeping his eyes on the man rather than the animal, waiting for the man to give an order, convinced that the dog would leap for his throat, knock him to the ground and tear at him. He clenched his fists beneath the cape, but the dog did nothing but slew to a skidding halt and stop by his side, panting. Still with his eyes on the man, Henry could see the despairing slump of his shoulders, as if he was saying, you traitor, you damned traitor, leaving me now. Henry began to move again, striding until they stood level, the dog between them. When he was close enough, Henry saw that the other man was trembling. Fear in his case, downright anger in Henry's own.

'What'ya do that for?' he demanded. They were level with one of the archaic bus shelters which littered the front at random intervals. They were like solid concrete bunkers facing the sea. Neil moved inside the shelter with a groan and sat down; Henry followed. It was a bleak enough place to avoid the world. 'I thought you were a fucking ghost,' Neil said. 'Flapping about like that. Fucking Valkyrie with no hair and a tail.' He began to laugh, a harsh, breathless sound which was more like a wheeze and singularly lacking in humour.

Henry pushed back the hood of the cape. The bunker was icy cold, he was burning up with heat and not disposed to be apologetic. Far too irritated for that.

'What ghost?'

'Oh ghosts who live in there –' he pointed to where the castle walls loomed in the near distance. 'Those ghosts.'

'Crap,' Henry said. 'You were running away from me.' Neil nodded as the trembling began to cease. 'I might have done that too, if I'd known,' he conceded, 'but I was really just running. I always knew they'd get out one of these days.'

'Nights,' Henry corrected, breathing heavily.

'Yes, I meant nights. Of course. Anyway when the dog left me I could see there was no point. They'd got me at last.' He laughed again. 'I should be grateful it's only you.'

Neil shuffled on the bench seat, withdrawing into a corner, not wanting to be close and patently embarrassed as awareness of Henry's identity hit home. *Only you.* He looked utterly miserable.

'I suppose I owe you an apology,' he said resentfully. 'Several, really. Should have been in a fit state to let you out of the castle, but I wasn't. Shouldn't have got into your room, but I did. I'm bloody sorry about that.' Henry shrugged. Apologies disarmed him, he was as ready to accept them as make them, whatever the circumstances. He nodded.

'You couldn't have found much,' he said. 'Vitamins are all I carry and if you want Viagra, why it's easy. You can order it on the net, like everyone else does.' Neil began to laugh again, nervous hysteria, tinged with relief. 'I *can*? Oh Christ, why didn't I think of that? Jesus Christ.' Then he sobered, sighed gustily. 'Might be better if I stuck to fishing. At least I know what I'm doing.'

'Catch much?' Henry asked, chattily.

'No, that isn't the point.'

He would never understand the English. Fished without wanting to catch fish.

'I owe you,' Neil said. 'You could have reported me to the police. I'd have left fingerprints all over. You could have complained about being locked in . . . Maggie could have shopped me for ignoring the alarm. I owe you.' Henry raised his hand to stop the babbling. He wasn't going to say there was small chance of fingerprints because of the way Peter and Tim scoured and dusted, nor would he say it would not have occurred to him to go anywhere near the police in case it was himself who would be put into a cell.

'You owe me sweet nothing. A few facts'd be nice.'

'Facts?' Neil said scornfully. 'I don't deal in facts. Only history.'

'This is history. All I ever did want to ask you was do you think Francesca killed her boy?' The words came out badly; he was making a hash of this. 'I mean, were things really as bad as that? You knew them all and your wife won't talk to me.'

Neil began to shake again. The bus shelter saved them from the breeze which shooed away the mist. He seemed to have a resurgence of the fear which had made him run and he looked at Henry as if he was the fang-toothed spirit of his nightmares. 'Don't,' he said. 'Please don't. It isn't fair.'

'It's perfectly fair. You weren't ever asked for a statement, were you? No need by the time they got round to you. They had all the answers. She'd given them. Just tell me what you think, that's all. I'm not going to tell anyone else, I just want to know.' Henry crossed his fingers to save himself from the curse of telling a lie. There was a silence, punctuated by the background sound of the sea and the sigh of the dog as it settled itself with its head on Henry's knee. At another moment, he would have felt absurdly comforted by this gesture of allegiance, but for now he was pleased with the animal for conspiring with him to isolate its owner. Or what passed for an owner. He might even have admired Neil Hulme for being a dedicated fisherman except for the fact that this dog, which was clearly his, wandered around by itself all day and that was cruel. The silence continued and the shaking increased. It seemed to communicate itself to the walls.

'OK, OK,' Henry said, leaning down to stroke the dog's ears. Silky soft, not such a bad owner after all, not so much cruel as negligent. 'Just take me through the morning it happened. You went round to get Tanya to take her to school . . . so there you were . . .'

'Did she say that? The bitch, the bloody bitch . . . why did she have to mention me? That's about all the use I am. A bloody alibi . . . the bitch.'

'No, not really. It means she's an alibi for you, too. In case anyone should reckon you were on that damn pier, fishing away, catching dozens, thinking away when along comes this irritating little kid who kicks over the bait and snags the line and pisses you off just when you have the hangover from hell and a bad night with a woman and life's a bitch and your temper's gone, man, really gone.' Henry exaggerated his drawl and his alien vowel sounds, making himself the caricature American. 'You fisher*meyen*, tetchy critters. Kind of man, sitting out there *all aloan*, when every other son of a bitch is tucked up with his sweetie . . .'

The response was not quite what he had predicted. If he had ever predicted at all about what he was playing by ear, he might have expected to be punched in the nose, which would not have bothered him much, especially as he was aping the role of a second-rate sheriff in a B movie. Henry did not expect the sigh of relief and the slow expulsion of nervous, spontaneous laughter so free of artifice that his heart sank. Neil was not the answer; Neil was not going to give him an alternative explanation to the one he thought he already knew.

'Oh is *that* it? Fine. I'll own up, then. Killed the little fucker, never liked him anyway. February's a bad time of year. I don't care, I don't care. I'll swing for that. I *thought* that what you were going to say was . . . was . . . was . . . Oh Jesus.'

He dived into his pocket for a ready-made spliff, fished in the other for a lighter and sucked greedily. Henry could not avoid the curiosity of his prudish self which wondered why the saliva-coated stub handed to him in bizarre courtesy should present such a challenge. He took and sucked tentatively, remembering a code of conduct abandoned long since. Pass it back. Hide the distaste of its lousy texture and pretend gratitude. Neil had stopped shaking. If this was all it took to keep out the cold and shove emotion into a corner, he might try it. Another long, shuddering sigh erupted from him as he sat back against the unwelcoming shelter of the concrete. A shadow of moss grew above the corner he occupied. Henry looked at the featureless ceiling, grey, yellow, patched with black, as worn and speckled as his own conscience.

'I *thought* you were going to say it was obvious. That *she* did it. Angela. She fucking loathed him, poor little brute. She had time to do it, 'cos I was late, see? *Very* late, s'far as I knew. And there was no one there, no one at all. They'd already gone. Lights on, no one at home, like the *Marie Celeste*, but doors locked. Then I looked at the time, and thought, Christ, I am late. Serve 'em right. They don't wait for me, they just use me, they don't even want my dog. But I'd lost the dog already.' He went into reverie. 'That's right. I'd given her to Granny to look after for a day or two. I'm always giving her to Granny for a day or two and she's always getting out, daft bitch. Anyways, on *that* morning . . . Christ, I was glad when Franny admitted it was her did for the kid, 'cos I thought it was Angela.'

'Angela shoving Harry through the broken boards?'

Neil looked at his feet. 'Yeah.' He nodded in rueful agreement with himself. 'Yeah, she could do that. Got a temper like nobody's business, you might have noticed. When she loses it, she really loses it.'

'There was a fisherman on the pier,' Henry began. The single inhalation down his throat made him dizzy and slow and when the spliff came his way, he handed it back after a token pretence to draw on it.

'No there wasn't,' Neil said with sudden precision. 'There was a brolly and a box of bait, I remember that, how could I forget it? You'd think I was fucking rich the way I keep leaving stuff. I'm always fucking leaving it. Awh, bugger it. I've got to go back.' He rose and then sat down again, abruptly. Huddled back into his corner and resumed his morose stare at the ceiling. 'That's why I was late. Went fishing early, forgot the time, the way you do, because it was good. You don't look at the time when you're waiting on a fish. Then Granny let the dog out. It was wandering round. I shooed it away and went home with my rod. Nobody really wants that dog, never did. I was going to come back for my brolly and the bait and the spliffs later on, but after what happened, I never did. I wasn't going to say they were mine, was I, no more than anyone else. Saying there were *signs* of a fisherman doesn't mean to say there *was* one. I was long gone. You didn't really think it could be me drowned that kid? I was cleaning fish. Give us a break. All I'm good at is catching fish. So I better go back for my rod.' He turned belligerently to the dog, which remained with its muzzle on Henry's knee, eyes closed as if afraid to hear anything to its own discredit. 'Are you coming or not?' Neil demanded. Henry could feel the weight of the dog's heavy head and its damp jaw staining his tan trousers. The constant stroking of its ears made it a big, soft sloth.

'Where do you take her?'

'Home with me if it's too late to knock on Gran's door. Don't worry. She's fed and bedded. She roams but she's always got somewhere to go.'

The sound of his boots striking the concrete floor made the dog spring into life. Henry felt the thrashing of its tail against his legs as it stood and Neil patted its back with rough indifference. It would never be sure of him. 'Always looking for something, aren't you?' Neil demanded of the dog without unkindness. 'So take me back to where I left my fucking rod. And while you're at it, tell him . . . oh fuck it, don't tell him anything.' He stretched his arms above his head. 'Tell him I couldn't hurt anyone I don't care about. Like you. I might not be very nice to you, doggie, can't even give you a name, but I only the hurt the ones I love.'

The dog stood indecisively between them, large head regarding them in turn.

'I cuffed Harry once,' Neil admitted gruffly, suddenly more expansive now he was on the move. 'But that was all it was and I wasn't too sorry either. He had a scream set your teeth on edge, you'd do anything to stop it. But I haven't got the bottle to do more. Unlike my wife.' He fingered his jawbone as if remembering a blow, nodding with rueful wonder, a slight smile altering his features. 'Never passionate enough, me. Not like those two, Fran and Angela. Pair of furies.' He looked down at the dog. 'C'mon, girl.'

'Go on,' Henry said softly.

They began to walk back in the way they had come. The dog would go with Neil; that much was established. It would find his rod on the beach in the absence of light and be rewarded for usefulness. 'Everyone stopped laughing when Harry died,' Neil said, pointing at the dog. 'I thought Tan would want the dog after all, but they didn't. Neither of them would let me in the house for months. Tan stopped talking and stayed off school. They spent the summer on the beach, away from everyone. It was only in the autumn it all went back to normal. As normal as it ever is. Christmas came round again, wasn't bad. Then you came along, you berk.' It was said without recrimination, simply a sad fact. He stopped and put his hands on his hips, facing Henry under the dark eaves of the hotel. 'Making a mess 'cos you were so sure Francesca couldn't be a killer. But how can you know? How can anyone ever know?'

Henry shook his head in agreement, suddenly anxious to explain himself, for his own benefit at least.

'I began with the belief she had to be innocent,' he said, earnestly. 'I began with a belief in her *virtue*. But that isn't why I went on. I went on because the facts didn't fit . . . it's galling when facts don't add up. Offends me.' They continued walking, a little faster in response to the cold. The dog's paws clicked softly.

'Well now you've got them to add up, perhaps you'll be going home soon.'

Henry stopped, arrested and grief-stricken by the very thought. The dog stopped with him, careful of the presence of them both, waiting for a sign of aggression. 'Yes,' Henry said slowly. 'Yes, I probably will.' The light of his room shone out in the distance. The sky was ominously clear. Peter had told him that clear skies were an announcement of forthcoming storms and if he could see the shores of northern France from his window, the omens were bad. Better to run from a storm than face it. He turned to Neil. 'I'll get you the Viagra,' he said. 'Least I can do.'

'For what?' Neil's voice was full of shocked surprise. Henry shrugged.

'For settling something. Making me face up to truth.'

They did not shake hands. It was not a deal; it was two men walking away from one another, one of them possessed of an animal which the second one craved. Only the dog looked back.

As Henry drew nearer, he could see there was a head sticking out of the top window of the House of Enchantment. The head retreated hurriedly. There was so little which could be done in a town this size without anyone noticing. Except kill a child, throw stones, break hearts. The head retreated as he drew level and waved at it. The window remained open. Henry felt churlish about being observed, just as he had felt foolish about being rescued. He wanted to spite her and not go in, go off wandering simply in order to make someone worry. Like he had done once or twice as a child, like all children did. Except Harry, who would probably rather sit indoors than go out in the cold when it was raining. He was too small and frail for the luxury of runaway gestures. Pity the child and what he might have been. Francesca would have made him better.

Henry sat, his legs suddenly weak. He seemed destined to sit on the wall outside the house across the narrow road from the big front door. Watching the sea and wondering for how long he would watch. When he would go home, by what means, what he would do when he got there, to whom he should write, e-mail, fax his next intentions. Whatever they were.

> *She bewitched me*
> *With such a sweet and genial charm,*
> *I knew not when I wounded was,*
> *And when I found it hugged the harm.*

Who wrote that? Francesca would know. He sat still from sheer weariness and an aversion to climbing all the stairs which would lead either to a night of disturbed dreams or to Maggie, standing guard like a protective housekeeper, scolding him for going out. Let her wait; she was not his guardian, and yet there was a faint pleasure in the knowledge that someone was concerned about him; it was a novel sensation to know that someone might register his comings and goings and a long time since such a thing had happened. He had begun to enjoy coming back to a house which was inhabited and he was sure he was becoming immune to the cold. Nothing seemed to touch him. He took out a cigarette and smoked contemplatively.

Ten minutes? Fifteen? Two cigarettes and his fingers numb. Amazing the difference in the time it took for a person to smoke a cigarette. Some took two minutes, others seemed to make the thing last half an hour. Amazing how time eclipsed. How long you could sit still in a state of indecisive shock, grief for an unknown child, admiration for sacrifice and work out you were feeling too ill to move, like someone falling over in the snow and finding it was a nice, warm place to be, comfortable to sleep. He could stay here all night, looking at the sea, waiting for the frost to form. He could sort everything into clinical order, label his con-clusions and put them into bottles. He could smoke another cigarette if he could work out where he had put them. He felt something hit him in the back with a light thump. Then another small object whizzed over his head and crashed on the sidewalk beside him. He bent to see what it was and saw a smashed brown bottle and a litter of pills of a familiar size, the colour difficult to distinguish. A plastic canister followed, about the size of a camera film, but heavier. It was shiny and he knew by the shape of it as he bent to retrieve it what it was. Henry found it was difficult to turn his head up towards the window; he seemed to have frozen to the spot; he put his hand to his face and found his fingers were numb. Squinting towards the light he saw another missile and realized what she was doing. Chucking out his supply of vitamins and stuff. Perhaps she had shouted too, but he had not noticed that. He tried to pick up one of the ginseng pills but his fingers could not grasp it. Henry got to his feet slowly and gestured surrender. Realized she was right; he could scarcely move. Serious cold; everything slowing to a halt and his vision of the house on the other side of the road slightly blurred. He thought of the boy who could not grasp with his right hand.

There was a crackle of thunder.

Maggie was behind the door when he reached it; she closed it softly behind him and began to push him up the stairs. His hands were ghostly white. The stairs were endless 'People die of pneumonia, Henry,' was all she said, calmly enough but with a catch of anxiety he may have mistaken. His teeth were chattering; there was nothing he could do to prevent it.

Beneath the silk coverlet, the warmth began to come back slowly and then he was raging hot and his chest was on fire. She went away and was a long time coming back with water and a kind of pill which, when he swallowed it, had the bitter taste of aspirin. Her absence and the fluctuations of temperature alarmed him; all that wanting to be alone and now he did not want to be alone at all. 'Don't go,' he said to her. 'Please don't go.'

'No, of course I shan't go. I should never have gone in the first place.' The glow of the fire turned her into a mere silhouette, a sweet smelling creature in a mannish dressing gown.

'Where *did* she put her letters and diaries?' he asked petulantly, his eyes closing with the effort of keeping them open.

'In the Wendy house. But they don't help, honestly they don't.'

'Oh.'

He found he was squeezing her hand tightly, relaxed his grip. He could grip; he could count her fingers; he could learn to fish. He tried one more time to conjure up an accurate picture of Francesca's face and begged her forgiveness.

Where's Henry? I asked her. I referred to him as Henry on formal occasions. I pushed him, she said. I pushed him under. He's a wanker, Harry is, he wouldn't leave me alone. The dog came on the pier and he started to yell; he pushed me first, he did. He's a baby, he's such a baby. WHERE? I was screaming. I thought we could have been heard on the moon, but it rained and the sea was crashing. Show me WHERE. No, no and no. I dragged her along the pier, past where the fisherman had been. We started running. Got to the end where she showed me the barrier she'd climbed and he stood whingeing behind. She said she was trying to get away from him; he couldn't run anything like as fast. She wanted to hopscotch over the broken boards and trespass, of course she did; it was the sort of thing I'd taught her to do. He was timid, crying for company when the dog appeared. And then he would have got over the barrier out of sheer terror. He ran at me, she said, he pushed me and he slipped. It was only a dog, it was MY dog what I couldn't have 'cos of Harry. Then he slipped into the crack and got stuck. I laughed at him and he screamed. So I went to pull him out. He looked silly. He grabbed at me and bit my jacket, my lovely new jacket. He tore it with his teeth and I pushed him off with my feet. Fucking big tear. Where do you want to go? I shouted at him. You going to swim or wait for that dog? You bite like a dog! So I shoved him down with my feet. I lost it, I just . . . Did you hit his head? Yes. Did he go through the first time you used your feet? No, but I heard when he hit the girder thing down there. I heard a thump. I thought he'd just come up the steps the other side. But he never. The dog kept barking, didn't it? You pushed him really hard, didn't you? YES YES, his jumper was up by his neck, he wouldn't go . . . How long since? She was always good with time, knew how long things took. Well, she said, I waited for him to come up, an' the dog made funny noises, an' I walked back, again an' again. Fifteen minutes?

I wanted to kill her there and then. I knew it was too late to save him. He could swim a little bit, but no one can swim against that current. I tore off my coat to jump in after him, but she clung to me, reminding me there was no point. It was bitter. Survival time is about five minutes for a grown man in February and he was hurt. I know this sea; it was my playground, my friend, my enemy. I made her tell me again, blow by blow as I walked her back, just in case. The dog sat at the end and howled. I knew he was dead. And knew what I held by the scruff of her beautiful neck was a child with no conception of what she had done. No one appeared; no one at all until we saw Angela at the door. And I made Tanya tell it, all over again.

So I knew what to say when they asked me. I knew how each injury had been caused. I knew they would find him soon. The sea always yields up the dead. I knew they would question family first. Murder is done by those who purport to love one another. If they got as far as Tanya, it would be too late. If they took her away from her mother, everything that had been gained would be lost. She would be ostracized and institutionalized; she would become another lost child. She could become one of the faceless girls in my prison.

And Harry would still be dead.

I still miss the sea most of all. It saves me from remembering that I have no one to love any more. No child to love. And I did love them both, with all my heart.

I knew he would not believe me, but the chaplain says catharsis is good for the soul.

There, the anniversary of my arrival has passed.

Everything has a purpose, and I have achieved mine. My only achievement was to be believed when I lied.

FMC

CHAPTER FOURTEEN

AFTER the rain, the temperature rose. The office was warm.

'No one will believe him,' Edward said. 'Is he all right in the head?'

'Not exactly. Nobody with a temperature that high can ever be described as all right, but he's better. He talks less than he did. No more deliriums.'

Cigarette smoke spiralled up into the air. Maggie seemed to have lost weight in a matter of four days. The small gold studs in her ears were her most vibrant features. Edward wondered at the fact that she had remembered the earrings as well as the brushing of her hair.

'I've been worried to death. I thought we might have killed him.'

'*You* might have. Mine was the small part. All I did was confirm things with the bogus Uncle Joe.'

'Yes. *I* might have killed him. Me. Margaret F. Chisholm. Me.' She gazed at the fish and its lifeless profile. Edward's fingers, free of his black half-gloves, beat a mild tattoo on the desk. He coughed to clear his throat of the last cigarette before lighting another.

Cigarettes had been forbidden from Henry's sickroom, but elsewhere Maggie smoked as if survival depended upon it.

'An old-fashioned chill equals pneumonia. He's a heavy man to move. He loves being nursed and a clear conscience aids recovery. It reminds me of how much I like looking after a man and how much I hate those macho types who won't succumb to weakness.'

'I didn't think you were a natural nurse, but you are, aren't you?' Edward paused. 'You must mean Philip. He came here for directions.'

'So what about him? He arrived without warning. I was too busy with Henry and his highly articulate nightmares. Philip took one look at the boys and the House of Enchantment and finally at *me*. He's even blinder than most, oh dear, oh dear.' She laughed, softly. 'We took a look at one another. He's so distinguished. He wore a suit. He was *born* in a suit.'

'So was I,' Edward said, shooting his cuffs, holding his arms steady the better to observe the unequal lengths of his dark sleeves.

'Not that kind of suit, not even a cousin to *that* kind of suit. Philip would die of embarrassment. Still,' she added carelessly, examining the coffee mug for cracks, 'Henry appreciated the flowers.'

Edward stood looking out of the window into the bustle of the High Street. From where he stood, he could watch the traffic in and out of the greengrocer's and hazard guesses about what they carried away in their bags. The grocer had five different kinds of potato, his wife had told him. There was the sonorous clanging of the church clock striking midday, a reminder of work undone and yet to do. He was relieved and depressed; truth was better than fiction, but not always as cheerful; it felt like the interval between one headache and the next. The storms had licked everything clean; the hotel had been flooded again in a minor way. The owner wanted to sell it. They were at the beginning of the season for storms. Fishing would be out of the question. He wanted to be outside to take advantage of the temporary blessing of the sun.

'Did you really have no idea?' Edward asked, casting the

question over his shoulder. She shook her head. Even her hair seemed to have shrunk a little.

'No, but I should have done. Should have been able to work it out the way Henry did because it fitted so well with what Francesca's really like. It accords perfectly with what she would have done. She would have taken the blame and taken it soon enough to stop Tanya being questioned because Tanya would crack. Henry has a huge imagination or perhaps he really did know her better than any of us. On a different level. He told me the story as he saw it in every detail, as if he'd been there. It all makes sense. Angela so defensive and protective, keeping Tanya apart . . .'

'. . . Francesca hiding medical books with someone who would never read them and videos with someone who would never watch them to see how often she filmed Tanya. With love and curiosity. No one should see what Tanya could be like. No one could see what Harry was like. How much, how little she changed. How fucking sad. Does Henry *know* what he told you?'

'Yes, he knows. He's repeated it all when sober, if you see what I mean. But if he hadn't been so ill, I doubt he would have said a word. He would have kept it locked up and said, I can't talk now. And neither, I suppose, can we.'

'Not without permission, no. I faxed the prison. We should get a reply saying whether she wants to see him, oh, any time now. Let's go for a walk before it rains again.'

'Not the pier, not today.'

'No. The other place. The back way.'

He was too well known for the High Street. On a day when the sun shone in late February and the populace was out on errands they might otherwise have ignored, it would take Edward half an hour to survive the greetings and the chatterings and the sheer duty in acknowledging the length and breadth of his acquaintance. Francesca had once told him it was the same for her: she could not walk down here without meeting a parent of a child, or a child, or latterly an ex-schoolchild, hoped it would be so until she saw the

ex-pupils walking here with their own children, but she sometimes wanted to do her shopping in the dark, to make it shorter.
He tried to remember what he had written to her, what sort of a
code he had used, so that she would get the meaning and no one
else, then remembered he had given up trying to be clever, had
given up some time ago since words of more than one syllable
were rarely understood.

Dear F.

A detective called Dr Henry Evans (mentioned before)
has unearthed the truth about T; not only the pros and the
cons, but also the whys. He awaits further instructions and so
do I. Do you wish to meet him? Can be arranged if so. A confidential fellow who will doubtless disappear on request; no
profit motive. As discreet as myself. Regret to inform you
that Uncle Joseph Chisholm has died.

Deepest sympathies and understanding.

'I don't understand,' he burst out. 'She could phone, she's
allowed to phone. If she was worried, she could always phone. She
doesn't.'

'She'd say too much. She can't talk now. She never could, don't
you see? Henry sees. Henry sees it all.'

'I don't. Why are there so many kids about? Oh, sod it. Half-
term. They tread on the daffodils.'

They were approaching the castle from the back of it, where the
bridge over the dry moat met the road and where there was the
sign saying when it was open and when it was shut. Such a squat
beast, this castle. Sitting there like a great, solid mushroom.
Almost beautiful in this light, he said, if you liked every permuta-
tion of grey. Look at it, Edward said; a grim place, like a prison. A
Victorian prison might have been made on similar lines, with the
slight difference that it would be designed to keep them in rather
than keep them out. A small amendment. The interior could be as
spartan as one pleased to ensure the rigours of the soul. Doubtless

Francesca's prison had a few more creature comforts, he thought sourly, such as TV and reliable hot water and heat, as if that would make all the difference. Probably, in her own way, with her own upbringing, she was used to confinement. He told this to himself to make himself feel better.

'Miserable place,' he said. 'Look at it. I don't know why anyone bothers.'

'There's no choice about it. You can't destroy it and it's quite incapable of falling down.'

They had moved from the road on to the seaward side where the swathe of grass separated the environs of the castle sunk into its own vast well, so that they walked the perimeter railings erected to protect the unwary. Dark inside at sea level and darker still beneath sea level in the Runs. Edward was looking out for the daffodils traditionally planted on this stretch of green. They tended to bud during storms and he never knew why. Any sensible thing would stay beneath earth until it was over and the spring as certain a thing as it ever was. Not very certain. He could see the green shoots, with only a single yellow bud in sight.

'How can you dislike it, Edward? It's your heritage. Look.' Maggie dragged him across the green to lean against the rails and look down into the moat. There were pools of water and crops of winter crocus, brilliant blue and yellow even in the shadow. Cotoneaster and hebe, privet and rhododendrons, nothing that minded shade. 'You can grow anything here,' she informed him, 'it's a nursery garden.' She was leading him from the precipice back to the bench against the beach where the sound of the sea soothed and no one would pause for long because of the wind, which worried the backs of legs and made the pennant flutter. 'Please don't be a cynic, Edward, don't. It was wonderful to be here, I promise you it was. We stood at *that* window. You had to stand to see out, you got used to it. *That* one.' She was pointing towards the middle keep, where a silly wooden turret protruded above the rest. It was like the tuft of a nest sticking out of a tree.

'What a cold place to live. Who stood?'

'Oh, me, Francesca, my aunt and uncle. After my parents died.'

She wanted to tell him something else, but he sprang to his feet. Pointing, still with his gloves on, quivering with worry and rage. 'Will you look at that? Will you just look at that? Jesus fucking Christ, they should be shot, look at that. Who let her, ohmyfuckingGod, oh jesusbloodychrist, *GET DOWN!*' He bellowed with his hands cupped round his mouth and his cheeks distended like a trumpet player. '*GET DOWN!*'.

There was a figure dancing round the walls. The balancing act looked like the dance of a butterfly in a patch of sun which caught the vivid auburn of the hair swept back by the breeze into a huge halo. She stepped to her own tune, nimbly moving from brick to brick around the curved and inward-sloping walls of the nearest inner keep, arms outstretched with the elegance of a ballerina, oblivious to the height and the slope and the remnants of frost. She tested herself and went a little faster, tried a skip. Slipped and landed with her long skinny legs each side of her body, supported on her hands. Raised the body by the hands in one effortless movement, extended her arms again and ventured on. She turned her progress into an elegant goosestep, each leg swung forward in a high kick, extending the opposite arm to touch the opposite toe. Then sat on the last sunny part of the wall, examining the abyss below without any sign of fear, delved into the pocket of her windcheater for something to chew. Lay down on the sloping wall and looked at the sky, crossed her legs like a miniature sunbather, sprang up in a single moment, continued the act, snapping her fingers to some indiscernible beat, body vibrating with it.

'That's Tanya.'

'Ah. I see what she meant, oh Christ. Take me away. I can't stand it. She'll fall, she'll bloody fall.'

'No, she won't,' Maggie said, pulling him away. 'Not if you leave her alone. She'll thrive if she's left alone.'

★

Edward's room had reached a stuffy temperature which was almost intolerable. The building was emptied for lunch. Prominent on the mess of the desk was the fax.

Dear Edward and Maggie,

So that's why you haven't been to see me, Maggie. You've been breaking promises all over the place and much as I love you for it, why can't you just ACCEPT? Accept that of all the people involved on the morning 'in question' I was, without doubt, the only one who knew what I was doing. I'm over the worst; I can stand it, if only because the alternative would really break my heart. What's left of it. Don't do ANY- THING. I DO NOT WANT TO APPEAL. Not until she's far older, anyway. Can't you ever see the virtue of doing NOTHING?

Henry Evans? Of course I don't want to see him. What are you up to? Bring some daffodils, just so I can look at them. Get a garden and tell me about it. Get a bloody LIFE and tell me about that.

These ARE my formal instructions.

Tell Henry Evans to go home.

I love you very much, Maggie Chisholm. You're better than a sister. I've given you a lot of duff advice in my time, but this is for real.

Edward, go fishing.

FMC

Maggie looked at the fax and wondered what it had cost to write. All Chisholms had a talent for the stiff upper lip. *If this is what you've got, get on with it.* She found that she was crying, copious, effortless tears.

Henry combed his hair and tried to select from his jumbled suit- case an item of clothing which was not ruined either by adventure or the enthusiastic cleaning attempts of Tim, who was willing but less able than Peter. He had never really replaced the original hat, might not be in this weakened state if he had done so. You lose half your body heat from your head, someone had told him once and now was the time he believed it. There had been a kind of pleasure, latterly, in lying up here, listening to the storms, forgetting for a while where he was other than at the wheel of a big, safe ship, ploughing through the sea towards a headland and not, as he had been in the other kinds of dreams, sinking beneath the waves, weighted with sadness and wishing he had learned how to fish.

He went downstairs in a motley array of clothing, ready to compete with his hosts for the prize for inept dressing, not caring. He had told Fergusons to put the job on hold and he could not bring himself to care about that either. In this land of the relatively poor, he was still relatively rich. He could feel the touch of Maggie's hand on his fevered brow and hear himself talking more than he had ever talked. And no amount of talking would tell him what to do. Knowledge did not point him in any direction.

'You see,' he said to Peter in the kitchen, watching him pour the tea from the teapot which looked as if it was too heavy to lift, 'it's in the nature of us Americans to believe that things can be fixed. Nothing broke that can't be fixed. No illness can't be cured. No tragedy can't be turned round into a happy ending. No mess can't be negotiated into success. I'm stuck with it. Positivism. The secret of our success. Compromise is a no-no.'

'How completely unnatural. It's *all* compromise, isn't it? And what's the point of striving all the time? What you can't accept is the fact that life's full of mystery and you aren't *supposed* to know all the answers. *Acceptance* is the key. There's no hardship at all in going along with a whole lot of broken things. You have to *accept* fate, just like you have to accept a hefty measure of ignorance. Go with the flow, Henry. You can't actually *change* anything.'

Henry followed him into the garden, where Timothy was tidying up. There was the reassuring sound of a broom swishing on the paving stones with an even rhythm, gathering together broken twigs and scattered leaves. The door to the Wendy house was open and the inside was empty when Henry looked, except for two folders of assorted papers and an old leather writing case.

'I wanted to make a fire,' Tim said. 'Get rid of it all.'

'All what?'

'Harry's things. He's gone, you see. I think he's gone somewhere with his mother. I told him we didn't mind, but I don't think he'll be back. We'll leave the Wendy house, just in case. Might keep an ostrich in it.'

'Why do you think he's gone?' Henry asked with a massive lump in his throat. Timothy shook his head, warningly. '*You* might know, but we don't. Don't want to. That isn't for us to know. But something's been settled. He's stopped flitting around. I think he's finally understood that it wasn't all a waste. He was looking for a purpose, you see. I don't know what it is, I don't want to know, but he's found it. I think he finally understood that he was . . . loved.'

'Don't burn the letters and things, will you?'

'Should we not?'

'No. Keep them. And the videos. She'll want them, some day.'

'She?'

'She. Someone.'

The Wendy house was sparkling clean from the hosing down of rain followed by ministrations with detergent. The plastic colours were weatherworn and faded out of their original garishness; Henry could see it as the cake icing house, shrouded with shrubs as it was and perfectly comfortable in these surroundings. Perhaps it was true that things grow into their own places. Senta prowled around it disdainfully, sniffing and oddly subdued. She sniffed Henry's ankles with a greater show of animation.

'She misses him,' Peter said. 'They kept each other company when we were busy, you see. It's always been like that. We're a bit too old for her, really, that's the problem, aren't we, Senta? Can't keep up with you, can we?'

Henry wondered about the other person he had been a mere two weeks ago, who might have bridled at this archness and gagged at the sentimentality of talking to animals and ghosts, hating it all the more for never doubting its appalling sincerity. He put his arm round Peter's meaty shoulders.

'What's *old*, old man? Middle age is man's greatest dignity, his *pièce de résistance*, the age of wisdom and just about enough vigour to go round. I got an idea. Don't turn me down. Can't waste the damn Wendy house if Harry doesn't come back. What say you to another dog? There's a beauty...'

'A black beauty,' Timothy said, dreamily. 'Wanders round by itself all day and finds somewhere to go at night. I *long* for it, can you get her? I never know where she goes. Oh yes. Now how did I know you were going to suggest that?'

'You must be psychic,' Henry said glibly, but his heart was beating to a strange tune, *kerthump, kerthump, kerthump* and he felt slightly giddy so that the words came out rather careless. 'I think I can get her,' he said. 'Or get Maggie to get her. Got something to trade.'

'Fetch,' Tim yelled and flung the broom in the air.

Henry drew a deep breath. 'You know the first night I got here? How did you know I was coming along? Psychic again?' Peter had the grace to look shifty and looked down at his shoes; brogues as violent a brown as brogues were ever made, polished to a piano varnish finish the better to offset the canary yellow socks. Some people did better out of thrift shops than others. He stood with his hands clasped behind his back, gazing at the shoes so hard that Henry thought he would overbalance and tensed himself to catch him.

'Maggie has to check the hotel register every day. Make sure they do it right. Must have seen your name, I suppose. Told them to send you along. Told us.'

Somehow, it did not surprise him. He was rather relieved to find an instance of cooperative cunning rather than anything weirdly telepathic, although if the explanation had been obscure enough to feature some message from either God or the Devil, he would not have been surprised either. Henry was beyond surprise and into anticlimax.

He knew where the dog was, he had seen it from his window. He saw everything from his window as if he were filming each scene. He could always get as far as the window and watch the people without the people watching him. Watch the dog and know where it sheltered; he knew that it came as far as this door every day, imagined he knew where it was now, grabbing a halfway sunny spot on the shingle for as long as it lasted.

'Excuse me,' he said.

The sunlight made him giddy, he didn't know why, it was a pretty pallid sort of sunlight only made brilliant by the sea with the dark clouds backing up on the horizon again, ready to spit and blow and snarl and bite and fight. *The thunder God went for a ride,* he recited and couldn't remember the next line. He crossed the road and whistled. My only talent, he thought to himself. I can whistle for the dog I never owned. I can whistle for the wind and be heard on any other planet and by any other species than my own. The dog gambolled off the beach and sniffed his ankles. I would die to be able to run like you, Henry told it. And once we're inside, behave, right? It's me who'll square everything after, like the price of a decade of food. And something for Granny and tablets for Neil.

The dog wanted to come upstairs. He said no and heard it greeted in the kitchen with wails of delight. The stairs seemed longer and longer; halfway up, he heard a door slam and did not look back. He did not want to talk to her just now. The only way that Maggie had ever seen him was when he was pathetic and she was in control. Whenever he looked like shit, she looked like a birthday party; whenever he felt like shit, she was there at the rescue and whenever he thought shit, she had thought it first. And such a user, such a manipulator. How could a woman like that have a cousin like that, but all the same . . .

All the same . . .

All the same . . . He felt weak at the top floor, checked the view from the window again, just to make sure he could not see the dog on the beach. A copy of a fax was on the bed, pristine black and white and almost warm. Henry read it, once, twice, three times, absorbed the message, leave me alone, *leave me alone, LEAVE ME*

ALONE, until he thought he had understood. Well, what had he expected? Gratitude? For what? From whom? It wasn't as good as it was before he'd got here and learned to swear, and it wasn't good now, but at least someone knew a lot more truth than they knew before, and godamnit, they didn't want to know it and they wouldn't have been bothered if they didn't know it and there was nothing he could do. Could do, fucking should do, *FUCK NOTHING*, he yelled at the wall.

Cool Ms Chisholm. You can go now, Henry, and let us resume our lives. She does not want to see you. What you do next is entirely up to you. Thanks a lot. He sorted money into piles. The early days of archaic Warbling taught him that cash mattered more than anything. He counted madly: food for the dog, benefit for Granny, Viagra he would send, no cash needed, biggest stash ever for P and T, Edward had refused payment. He touched the shawl which was grubbier now, because Maggie had wrapped it around his throat when his temperature was way high and he shrieked at her not to close the window. He put it in an envelope and scrawled her name on it. She would know what he meant; she would never ask for anything more. He checked his watch. These were the hours for cooking.

His suitcase was extraordinarily light. No potions, no minerals, no whatsits, a few antibiotics in his washbag and the seagulls outside friskier than ever from what they had picked up. Seagulls freaked out by vitamins and ginseng: he tried to cheer himself with that idea, checked his watch again. Trains went on the hour. The sky was slate and the wind ominous. If he went now, quietly, he would have to wait, but if he did not move, another kind of madness would descend. The horror of doing, being nothing.

No hat. It was mild for the time of year, gathering energy for another storm, going to be horrible soon. *Horrible*: he toyed with the word on the way to the station, going the back way. It was an unfamiliar description and he tried to think what he might say instead. *Awesome, terrific, incredible, nasty.* Not nice. The station was deserted apart from three kids with one bicycle between them. The smallest one sat, kicking the wheels as if it was an enemy instead of transport. He waited for a sense of relief. Checked on his fingers for the things done and left undone. Waited.

CHAPTER FIFTEEN

THERE were starlings under the eaves of the station canopy, putting out clarion calls, shrieking for mother. He walked to the edge of the platform and trod along a yellow line explained by a notice which said, DO NOT CROSS. He looked at the plants which withered in the aisle between eastbound and west. The train failed to arrive. He was way too early and the next city train was going to be late because of the weather. The sky turned from slate to black and even the birds fell silent as the wind began to rattle. Henry checked the breast pocket on his jacket, one last time, as if it would be the last time and he would not do it again and again. Back in the twenty-first century which Warbling had managed to suspend, he could feel himself slipping into the benign neurosis of everyday concerns, and the need for everyday documents.

A woman appeared in charge of the kid who was kicking the bike, and cuffed him. Henry leapt to his feet, about to intervene and then sat down again as she followed it up with no more than a scolding and a crushed packet of crisps taken from her bag. He moved to the far end of the platform and sat on a metal bench out of the wind, adjusting his scarf and his gloves and feeling his feet warm in his boots. He might look like a tramp, but he was well insulated.

Should have said goodbye, but why did anyone need goodbyes? Because it closed the chapter. He found himself imagining what the reaction of the two men would be when they found he had gone, told himself they would not be quite reconciled by the over-generous payment, that was not the point with the English he had met. Money in quantity was not important; they were weird like that. And what about *her*? Would she shrug her shoulders and say to herself that was exactly how she expected him to behave? What was it she had needed from him anyway? She needed what he had achieved, without breaking any of her ridiculous promises to her cousin. She did not need *him*. If that woman needed anything, she was not going to say. He stared at the trees on the far side of the platform, pinned behind the high railings and shaking in the wind. The waves on the seafront would be high; he had liked it when the waves were high enough to throw shingle into the road.

A train pulled in opposite, a slow-moving bullet of light. Probably the only train on the track, going all the way to the end of the line before coming back for the patient few on this platform. They should be throwing things at it in protest. He was never going to smoke again and only ever eat nutritious food.

If he saw Maggie from the outside, as if he was a stranger, what would he see? Someone who had moved heaven and earth to find out the truth about the cousin she loved like a sister. Someone who went on serving the interests of that same person, doing her bidding, remaining faithful to her, inhibited by ridiculous promises to a self-confessed murderess, as if that made no difference to love or loyalty. Perhaps it didn't. Perhaps it made you suspend judgement entirely. If you *loved* someone, you didn't leave them whatever they had done. Any more than Angela would abandon her daughter, or Peter would abandon Tim. You would do *anything*. You would lie, for a start; you would trade on affection and sentiment. You might even blackmail people with their own decency. You would put yourself on the back burner, wipe yourself out.

There was an unfamiliar lump in one of the pockets of the jacket and it dug into his thigh as he sat on the metal bench. Henry investigated and found a bar of chocolate and a tube of extra strong mints, examined them carefully. Now who had put those there? Someone who knew that he was inclined to forget about sustenance and needed to take a little something for his blood sugar in his weakened state? Don't you be going out without something to eat, she had scolded him only yesterday in that maternal way she had developed with the patient. He could not blame her for himself becoming ill, but in a way, he had. It was not her fault that he had ignored the impact of cold and shock and incurred the almost inevitable sickness, but it was she who had started it all. He was trying to make himself angry, but the presence of a bar of chocolate was preventing it.

He could not fault her care of him in the last few days and the way she had responded to his words. She had made sure that he did not feel ashamed to be so helpless; she let him keep his dignity. She had been peculiarly sensitive in her presence and her absences. He would miss her, of course he would miss her; he had always missed her.

You don't just leave people, Henry, that's what you always do. Once it gets messy or complicated, or hurtful, off you go. His father's voice; Francesca's voice, both saying the same thing in markedly different accents. No, he argued with himself, that isn't what I do, not any more. I *didn't* do that, this time, I didn't. And no one *begged* me to stay; it's clear they don't *want* me. Francesca doesn't want me; *she* doesn't want me. *How do you know? You never asked.* Maybe she *would* have told you if you'd waited to be asked. You aren't the only one who needs reassurance to get beyond their own reserve; you aren't the only one who shies away from confrontation like some frightened thoroughbred at a fence. Francesca does that, too. Whatever her name is.

She took me for a fool, he told himself. So, you're going to leave her to her grieving, let her cope with the frustration of doing nothing, just because of that, are you? She still has all that mess on her plate. You bum. You've spent half your life carrying round bits and pieces of unfinished emotional business, frightened of being exposed. Who are you to criticize? Fear or ridicule weighs heavier than vitamins or water or clothes. C'mon. There are times when you just can't let people get away with their privacy. Even if they want it.

Henry asked the man in the ticket office to keep his bag. I have to go back for something. You'll miss the train, the man said. OK, so I'll miss the train; there are other trains in and out of here. There are trains you should never even try to catch, Henry said. There are buses which should never leave on time. He walked out of the station.

The wind caught at his hair and seemed to lift it away from his scalp. He kept his hands in his pockets and pushed his way through the parking lot. No rain, yet, simply the godforsaken wind which pushed him downhill past the shops that were shutting and placing barriers to guard against weather rather than vandals. There was a lull in the dip by the crossing where he seemed to enter another climatic zone, and then the road rose again towards the sea. The weather was a better enemy than most, he thought. It was at least entirely even-handed, impersonal and indifferent and you did not have to waste time reasoning with it. The streets were clearing rapidly, everyone scurrying indoors, bringing the afternoon to a premature end. They all knew what to do. No one argued with English weather; they simply evaded it. Unless they were Maggie Chisholm, who liked to hide in the back of the house but also liked to be outside in a storm.

Henry stood in the doorway opposite the hotel and considered his direction. Without baggage and rain, the wind was exhilarating and the sea was in a state of glorious rage. He crossed the road to the entrance to the pier and stood in the inadequate shelter of the fisherman statue, touching the cold metal with affection. The pier was her favourite place, she had said and even with its terrible associations, it had become his. Especially now, with the waves so high they lapped at the walkway, sucked at the structure and sent up spumes of spray. The whole structure vibrated and hummed with the sound of the sea. He wondered why some prudent town official did not close the gates, but no one had. It felt more dangerous than it was and if the whole thing was going to fall down, today was not the day. Out on the horizon, the bigger boats rode unperturbed. If the wind blew him sideways, all he had to do was sit down. Sit down and *think*, but he was done with thinking. He walked the length of the *Titanic* steadily enough, keeping his eyes fixed on the darkened windows of the caff at the end. He could see a figure, holding on to the railings at the end with her back to the shore.

Tuttttt, he would say. *Look at me*, he would say. If you sit out here, he would say, you get cold and sick, and I can't let you do that, can I? *You* wouldn't let me do that, would you? You look after me when I'm sick. You did it twenty years ago and you've done it again this last week and I'm telling you, I'm sick of it. It's my turn. Do you hear me? That's what he would say if he could yell the words. I'm sick of it, Francesca.

There was her yellow hair which would be soaked with spray. He could see her now, clearly, and Henry could have howled with relief. Not too late. This time he had turned back in time. As he approached, she moved to sit on the bench by the caff door, relatively sheltered by the overhang in the place where he had slept after his late breakfast on the first day, a century ago, and woken to feel someone was watching him. She was entirely oblivious to his presence. Henry had the sharp and appalling remembrance of that face on the ramshackle Indian bus, two decades sooner. The shawl round her neck and pressed against her face, her skin pink and inflamed with weeping. Not at her best, not then, or when she should have said, *please don't leave me; I need you*, instead of saying, *you must do what you think best*, Henry. Did not plead, any more than he had offered. What a pair of fools. He remembered himself, beginning to run, bashing his fist against the dirty rear window of the bus, yelling, *Wait for me. I'm not just another passenger, I'm ME.*

I came back. And in the same uncoordinated way he had begun to run then, he started, clumsily, to run now.

She turned and noticed his awkward progress, gave a tremulous smile. Then she went back to what she was there for, crying. Sobbing into a handkerchief sodden with tears or spray, he could not tell which. He stopped, halted by the jolt of recognition. A crying face took on the contours of a childish face and assumed its own, unmistakable distinction. It was the same face which had wept against the window of that bus. Weeping like that, she was instantly recognizable and he wondered why he had ever doubted it, how he could ever have been fooled by her height, the heeled shoes, the polish, the little bits of jewellery, the distracting effects of years, all conspiring to confuse, as if a person were no more than the sum of all their visible details. He had known; he had ignored, but then he was a literal man who tended to believe what he was told. He was the scientist who believed in the evidence of his own eyes and first-hand reports from reliable sources. He let instinct take second place, and sitting next to her now, alongside the roar of the sea, he tried to recall when it was he had guessed her identity and if the precise moment of his guessing and concealing really mattered. He was there; she was there, and nothing else was important. She was the one. Francesca. Maggie. Francesca. They had blurred, but they were quite distinct.

'Shh,' he said. 'Shhhh, now. I don't know the half of it, do I?'

She went on crying. If she made any sound in the process, the sea drowned it.

'It doesn't matter,' he said, putting his arm round her shoulders. 'You shouldn't think it matters at all. I just don't know what to call you, I really don't. It's embarrassing. Can't call you Fran. You hated your name to be shortened. I'm surprised you ever consented to *Maggie*. I like Margaret better, but I'd never get used to it now. Couldn't stand another variation, so you're Maggie, OK? You still bite your nails, don't you? I never thought you'd dye your hair. You didn't seem the type then for tinted hair, but who knows? And you were going to be a teacher.'

She carried on crying, not bothering to stem the flow. He pulled her a little closer, fished in his pocket for a handkerchief, found the chocolate and proffered it instead. She smiled a bit at that, shook her head. They sat as they were. Even the bone of her shoulder was familiar. She could not stop her compulsive weeping. Henry told himself that for once he was the one in control, but he doubted his ability to manage the tremor in his voice. They must look like a couple of eccentric tramps, and who gave a shit. 'Francesca Margaret Chisholm is in prison,' Henry said, matter of factly, 'and Margaret F. for Francesca Chisholm practises law. Why did you call yourself Francesca all those years ago when you went to India? What's in a name? Come on, Maggie. Tell me, please.'

She heaved herself upright. Blew her nose until it shone red and attempted to put the handkerchief back in her pocket. It fluttered to the ground and the wind took it towards France.

'Because it's a much nicer name than Maggie,' she said gruffly. 'I *hated* being called Maggie. And Francesca was a much more glamorous person to be. Glamorous and kind. That's why I went travelling in the first place. So I could be someone else. I wished I had lived in the castle. It was my second home. I wished her parents were my dead parents and I was as nice as her. And although her father wasn't *my* father, he was as good as . . . and he loved me as if I was . . . oh shit. I should be crying for Harry. I *am* crying for Harry. I'm crying for every bloody thing.' He nodded, close to tears himself. No one would know it was not the spray.

'And I'm not Francesca,' she muttered. 'I'm whatever I've got left. Some bloody muddle.'

'You're the one who remembered poetry,' he said. 'The crazy one who looked after me and made me feel . . . whole. The one who laughed with me and never at me. That's you. The fact you like to play charades doesn't alter that. I know who you are. I just don't know why you felt you had to go on playing charades. Couldn't you trust me?'

The rain began, thundering on the concrete. She cried a little more and wiped her face with the sleeve of her coat. '*Trust* you?' she shouted over the storm. 'I did trust you. But not with everything and not with that. You would have despised me.' She sniffed. 'How pathetic to have borrowed the identity of somcone else, even at eighteen. Self-aggrandizement. Why should you help poor, deluded Maggie Chisholm who travelled under false colours? But I thought . . . I thought . . . you might be curious enough to enquire into Francesca because you carried a torch for her. You never carried a torch for Maggie. Not for me.'

'A *torch*?' He remembered where he was. Remembered the history he had read, about wartime sailors, putting up misleading flags in order to get close to the enemy. *False colours.* 'They weren't false colours,' Henry said. 'You just added in a stripe or two. Altered the shading. I'm colour blind anyway. I *knew* you.' His voice also rose to a shout. It was a mad way to conduct a conversation. 'I *know* you now and I'm telling you, there aren't so many surprises. You're the kind one. But you *used* me. Never mind *false colours.* You hooked me like a fish and reeled me in.' The weeping continued.

'Yes, I did. I'm sorry. There was no one else.'

'It was extremely calculating.'

'Yes,' she yelled.

'You're cunning and dishonest.'

'*YES! All right,* yes.'

He pulled her hair gently and laid her head against his shoulder. Gradually the crying ceased. The storm lulled into a temporary calm, as if taking a breath.

'I'm sorry I left you that first time,' Henry said. 'Shouldn't have done it. Never forgot it. I guess we're quits. Do you think we could start all over again?'

She looked up in tearstained surprise, her face puffy and pale, the nose red.

'Don't be ridiculous. Why?'

'Got a cigarette?'

'Somewhere, yes.' A packet emerged from her handbag. He

watched her pale white hands, no longer hiding bitten nails, Maggie turning her head into the shelter of the dreadful jacket he pulled across them both to forestall the wind and rain long enough to light one smoke and another one from the first for him. 'These are bad for you, Henry,' she said, earnestly, handing him his. 'I told you twenty years ago, don't copy my bad habits. And anyway, why?'

One inhalation and the cigarette tasting of salt. Never again. The rain drenched his hand. He felt utterly, bewilderingly certain and as obstinate as the weather.

'Because I've always loved you. I do mean *you*. That's a long, long time. And I want the whole thing. Dog, garden, care of your cousin. That sort of stuff.'

'You're out of your mind. I am *not* Francesca.'

'I don't want Francesca. I want you. And I'm just about done with turning back.'

A huge wave crashed into the pier at the end nearest the gate. Someone by the entrance, flanked by the profile of a dog, waved at them anxiously, shouting, voice lost in the boom. The wave broke into a plume of foam, washing the floor with a vicious *shsshhh*, slinking away. Another followed. The surface before them flooded and bubbled rapidly. The waves hit again, irregular in their onslaught, murderously precise. The tide could go higher. Henry dished the wet cigarette.

'Well, kind Margaret, we either stay here all night, or run for it. What do you say?'

She buttoned his jacket first, then her own coat, looking sideways down the length of the pier, judging the distance. She shuffled her heeled boots like a soldier on parade, testing the circulation in her feet and took his hand.

'Run,' she said. '*Now.*'